The Devil's Chalice

D.K. WILSON

The Devil's Chalice

M
MadeGlobal Publishing

For more information on
MadeGlobal Publishing, visit our website:
www.madeglobal.com

'You shall enquire whether you know of any that use charms, sorcery, enchantments, witchcraft, soothsaying, or any like craft, invented by the Devil.' - Archbishop Cranmer's charge to diocesan bishops, 1549

Two of the prisoners in the Tower of London in 1549 were described in these words: 'Robert Allen for calking [making astrological calculations] and prophesying ... William West, gent. Intended to poison Lord De La Warr'.

Prologue

THE MAN WITH no name was taken in a covered wagon. It was dusk before the wagon arrived at its destination - the destination with no name. The flaps were unlaced. The man stretched as the wagoner helped him down. It had been a long journey.

Looking round, he was confronted by a massive stone wall, decayed and blotched with creeping ivy. Mounds of weed-robed rubble lay everywhere. From one, a horned devil glared stonily. A damp mist filtered through the elms bordering the track. The man shivered.

'This way.' His guide steered him along the wall to a heavy oak door – substantial yet seeming too small for the massive masonry in which it was set. Within seconds of the wagoner's heavy knock the door opened inwards. A whispered conversation and then the man was ushered inside.

The first thing he noticed was the smell – acrid, smoky, yet mingled with an aromatic fragrance he could not identify. The chamber was small and seemed even smaller because of the cluttered objects strewn and piled everywhere. The only light came from two candles set on iron pricket sticks standing on a trestle table in the centre of the room. The flames were reflected in bottles, jars and a large glass alembic which had pride of place among the scattered tools, books, papers and potted plants cramming the oaken surface.

As the door closed behind him the man peered into the surrounding gloom. To this moment, he had felt no anxiety about his self-imposed mission. Now his heart raced with sudden panic. This alien space clamped him like a carpenter's hand-vice. He started as something brushed against his leg. Glancing down, he saw a hooded crow hopping across the floor, trailing a silver chain. He stood motionless, left hand on his sword pommel, ears straining for any sound. None came save the sputtering of the cheap candles. What creatures might lurk in those tomb-dark corners or the blackened rafters above? Had he, perhaps, been lured into a trap? Was this scholar, supposedly skilled in arcane studies, in reality a cut-throat with a novel way of luring victims into this choking hellhole?

'Hello,' he called and the word sounded like a croak.

'Have you brought the money?' The voice came from behind him. The man spun round.

The magus was standing by the door, his features partially obscured by the man's own shadow thrown by the candles. The man could make out a thin face; below it an unkempt dark beard; above it a square cap such as clergy wore. All else was only a faint outline The long, black robe merged with the shadows as though its wearer had appeared from the darkness and might melt back into it at any moment.

'Have you brought the money?' The repetition was calm, emotionless.

'Er … yes …' The visitor fumbled in his purse and held out gold coins.

'Take the money to the table.'

The man turned – and let out a strangled cry. There on the other side of the table stood the magus. Not a breath before he had been by the door. There had been no movement in the room – or so his senses told him, and yet …'

'Come, man, the money. We have not all night!'

Trembling the man advanced and let fall his fee upon the table.

'Good. There is your potion.' The magus pointed with a short wand to a phial of violet liquid.

The man stared at it. 'You're sure it will work?'

'It worked for the Bishop of Trier and the Elector of Brunswick. Why should it lose its potency for a mere English gentleman.'

'Oh, I … I did not mean to suggest …'

'But you must employ it properly. The potion must be administered when the moon is in cancer. That will be three and four days hence. Be sure that the elixir is served in a silver chalice and swallowed at one draught. Once administered you must say the Lord's Prayer and the Creed three times daily for seven days.'

'I see … your … yes … Thank you.' The man reached for the phial.

Swiftly, the magus covered it with his left hand. 'One more thing is needful to conclude our business.' He pressed the sharp point of his wand against the flesh between the man's thumb and forefinger. A swift jab drew blood.

The man yelped and held the wound to his lips. 'What in the name …?'

'A simple precaution.' The magus held out a clean kerchief. 'Wipe your hand with this.'

The man made no move to comply. 'There is trickery here. Poison on the cloth or some such devilry.'

The magus smiled. 'Devilry? No 'tis to avoid devilry that I need this safeguard. Wipe your hand. You will come to no harm.'

Cautiously the man dabbed the cut. The magus took the stained kerchief. 'Now I have your blood. I will know from it the moment you tell anyone of this meeting or in any way betray me.'

'Why should I do any such thing?'

'There are many who are enemies of the ancient ways. Someone might try to reach me through you. I have to protect myself in every way possible. If you should be persuaded to reveal to anyone what has passed between us today … Well, let me just say that I would not want to send spirits to set a permanent lock upon your tongue.'

He held out the phial. 'Now, you will be anxious to return to London. I wish you safe journey.'

The man pouched his potion and turned towards the door, which was once more open. On the threshold, he thought of one question he had forgotten to ask. When he looked round there was no sign of the magus.

Chapter I

'I FEAR 'TIS urgent.'

I looked at the address on the letter: 'Master Thomas Treviot at the Sign of the Swan in Goldsmiths' Row, London.'

'Messages from his grace usually are urgent, particularly when they are written in his own hand,' I said, as I broke the familiar seal.

'He values your discreet and efficient services very highly. He remembers very clearly ...'

'I sometimes wish the archbishop's memory was rather less clear.'

Ralph Morice laughed. 'Even after five years or more he is scarce likely to forget a man who saved his life.'

'And nearly lost his own in the process,' I muttered.*

It was high summer 1549 and we were seated in the first-floor parlour over the premises of my family business at the cathedral end of Cheapside. My guest, Ralph Morice, secretary to the Archbishop of Canterbury. A lean figure in a cleric's gown, he looked younger than his fifty or so years. Despite his deeply creased brow, his eyes were bright and a smile was seldom absent from his lips. I read the few lines written in Cranmer's somewhat florid hand.

---

* See *The Traitor's Mark*

4

Master Treviot, my hearty commendations. This is to
request you to accompany Master Secretary Morice to
Lambeth Palace where I will acquaint you of an urgent
commission in need to be undertaken with that sound
judgement and closeness with which our Blessed Lord
has well endowed you.

T. Cantuar

'So, Ralph.' I looked across the table at my visitor. 'What is
this about?'

'I'll explain as we go. The barge is at Blackfriars' Stairs.'

'Must we leave immediately? I have several ...'

'His grace is away straight after dinner to attend on the king at
Hampton Court. We must not delay him.'

As soon as I had left instructions with my assistant, Bart Miller,
we began our brisk walk down to the river. We strode around the east
end of the cathedral to avoid the noise and the clouds of dust which
filled the air on the building's north side.

''Tis taking a long time to pull down the cloister,'
Morice remarked.

'Aye, long work and very unpopular. The Duke of Somerset, the
Lord Protector cares not what people think. He must have his fine
new palace, no matter where the stone comes from.'

Morice stepped aside to avoid a ball being kicked around by a
group of boys. He sighed. 'Aye, his grace did his best to persuade him
but Somerset now listens to no one.'

'He is patterning himself on the old king,' I suggested.

'I fear you are right but the Good Duke, as some people call him,
is no Henry. He is only young King Edward's uncle, permitted to rule
by the royal council. He cannot afford to continue on his reckless way
making enemies.'

'I trust this has nothing to do with my summons by
the archbishop.'

Morice uttered his high-pitched, rather girlish laugh. 'Oh,
certainly not.' He paused. 'Well, not really.'

The hesitation brought me to a sudden standstill. 'Not *really*?
Just what does that mean? If 'tis a matter of high politics, much as I
respect his grace ...'

'No, no, no! Nothing like that.' Morice linked his arm through mine and we resumed our walk. 'His grace simply wants you to have a talk with someone.'

'With whom?'

'He is called William West.'

'Not a name I recognise.'

'Nor should you. He is a man of no importance – not really.'

'And just where do I find this man who is not really of any importance and who is not really connected with politics?'

Morice quickened his step as we turned into Carter Lane. 'In the Tower.'

◊

Twenty minutes later we arrived at Lambeth Palace. During our brief crossing of the Thames, I had elicited no further information from Morice other than: 'His grace will explain everything'. In the Archbishop of Canterbury's audience chamber, I took one of the chairs at a long table running down the centre of the room. Morice had passed into the private quarters beyond and I was left to my own thoughts. It was not altogether unusual to be commanded to Cranmer's presence. Since the business with the painter Holbein back in '43 the archbishop had called a few times on my services during the last years of the old king. Usually, he sought information about mercantile affairs. It was important for the royal council to gauge the mood of the City regarding current policies and Cranmer, like the other members of that body, had his sources of information. Of course, the relationship worked in both directions. Even though our church had been purged of ornaments and costly furnishings since the new regime of Protector Somerset had taken over, it was still a major patron and Treviots had certainly benefited from the patronage of the Primate of All England. However, I hoped that whatever errand I was being sent on this time would not take long. I was keen to get away from the heat and stench of high-summer London and spend some time at my house in Kent. Servants came and went.

Every time a door opened I looked up hopefully but it must have been an ample half-hour before Morice re-appeared to take me into the archbishop's parlour.

◊

'Welcome, Thomas. I trust you are well.' Cranmer held out his hand for me to kiss the ring.

I had not seen the archbishop at close quarters since a feast the Goldsmiths' Company had given in his honour a year or so before. I noticed that his beard had become long and wispy but that his eyes still had that penetrating, enquiring stare I knew of old.

'Very well, I thank God.'

'Good, good, and your growing family?'

'My wife's first child did not long survive but we have a new little daughter who gives us much pleasure.'

'That is good news. You must allow me to make the little one a small gift.' He nodded to Morice who opened a casket on a side table and from it handed me a gold half-crown of the new minting.

'Now, to business.' Cranmer waved aside my profuse thanks. He seated himself in a window embrasure and motioned me to a heavily carved backstool.

'You appreciate, I am sure, how blessed we are in our young sovereign.'

'Indeed. All men speak well of King Edward.'

Cranmer's beard fluttered like a flag as he nodded vigorously. 'Wise beyond his years, a keen student and devout.'

I made no response, wondering where these affirmations of loyalty were leading.

'Yet he is young.'

'Some three months short of his twelfth birthday by my reckoning, Your Grace.'

'Even so. As a father, you will know how important the next few years are. Your own son is near his majesty's age, is he not?'

'Raphael will be fourteen in the autumn and is just away to the university.'

'Excellent. I doubt not he will be a great credit to you.'

I thought of Raffy, my eldest, an excitable, unstable, bubbling cauldron of resentments. 'I hope so, Your Grace. But I think this is little to the point regarding the small service you wish me to perform.'

Cranmer smiled. 'Ah, there speaks my merchant – business above all, like the tale of the mercer and the elephant.'

'Your Grace?'

'You know not the old story? 'Tis said that when the first elephant arrived in England as a gift for King Henry III, a bishop, and a mercer were admiring the beast. The bishop went into ecstasies about the wondrous works of God. "Does this great creature not fill you with awe?" he asked his friend. "Only one thing amazes me more," the mercer replied, "and that is what it will cost to feed him". Well, then, as you say, "to the point". As his majesty's godfather, I have a responsibility to him and to the country to safeguard his well-being until he reaches his majority.'

I sensed anxiety in the archbishop's tone. 'Is his majesty's health …'

'The king is excellent well!' Cranmer responded sharply. 'If you hear anything to the contrary give it no credence. Better yet, report to me anyone spreading false rumours. These are difficult times, Thomas, uncertain times. There is scarcely a shire in England where the peace is not disturbed by agitators stirring the common people and preachers who urge galloping change. If only his late majesty could have been spared a few years longer, until Edward …' He left the uncompleted sentence with a sigh.

After a long moment's silence, I said, 'Master Morice mentioned someone called William West. Is he one of the troublemakers you speak of?'

Cranmer shook his head and again the beard danced. 'Poor West? No, he is a victim rather than an instigator of discord – at least, so I believe. It is on that score that I need your opinion. He stands accused of a heinous crime yet refuses to speak a word in his own defence. You must talk with him and report to me on how you see the truth of the matter.'

'Why me, Your Grace?'

'Because I respect your judgement and because anyone interesting himself in Master West's fate will not connect you with me. He is allowed some visitors and you will pose as just a friend come to offer succour and comfort.'

'What crime is laid to this man's charge?'

'Attempted murder.' The archbishop stood up. 'I must say no more at this stage. I would not colour your judgement in advance. Bring me your honest opinion and God grant you wisdom.' The interview was over.

As Morice walked with me to the privy stairs I challenged him. 'There is more to this than his grace has told me, is there not? I feel as though I have been introduced to a new song and only been given the refrain.'

'No, Thomas, 'tis really a simple affair. We wish to be assured that West is innocent of the charge laid again him.'

'And what exactly *is* the charge? What crime am I supposed to be probing? It would be useful to know.' I tried – not very hard – to keep the sarcasm out of my voice.

The secretary shook his head and grimaced. 'Thomas, you must not press me to go beyond what his grace has already told you. This is merely a matter of attempted murder. No one has died and, for sure, the whole story is a patchwork of lies and perjured evidence. By my troth, there is no more to the business than that. Now, we must hurry. The boatmen are waiting.'

My response was to come to an abrupt halt. 'I would fain continue in his grace's favour but unless you tell me the whole story you can go back in there and tell him that, on this occasion, Master Treviot is unable to oblige him.'

'Thomas, I have my orders.' Morice gave a long sigh. 'By Jesu, I know that stubborn frown. The facts are few and simply stated. West is the nephew and heir of Baron De La Warr who has no children of his own.'

'Old De La Warr?'

'Aye, old is the point. Long years are keeping Master West from entering his inheritance. The baron claims that his nephew has resorted to poison and black magic to speed up that happy day. He has had West arrested and means to try him by parliamentary attainder. There, Thomas, now you know all.'

I shook my head. 'You must do better than that, Ralph. Why should the archbishop take an interest in West's fate one way or the other?'

'His grace is concerned for justice. As you know, attainder means a simple vote in both houses and the accused has no way to defend himself. His grace feels he must do what he can to save an innocent man from the gallows. Now are you satisfied?'

'Almost. Can you swear to me on your honour, that this West is of no more importance than that? Or is he, perhaps, a special protégé of the archbishop; an agent who must be protected?'

The question obviously discomfited Morice. 'The man has friends at court,' he muttered. 'They, naturally, wish to do what they can to help him. There is nothing more to it than that.'

'Nothing political?'

'No, Thomas. You must not build castles on sand.' He stared across the water at Whitehall Palace. 'Anyway, even if there were some substance in your suspicions you could not come to any harm by carrying out this simple commission. Have a talk with West. Make up your own mind about the man's honesty. Present your report, in person, to his grace at Hampton. Then go back to your thriving business and your lovely wife and family. What harm is there in that?'

Before I could reply, Morice hurried on. 'Here are some details about William West, his family, and close friends.' He handed me a couple of sheets of paper, neatly folded. 'From these notes, you will be able to make up a story to explain your visit. That and a few coins will satisfy the head jailer and gain you admittance. Let me know when you are coming to Hampton and we will dine together. For now, God's speed.' He turned and walked briskly back towards the gatehouse.

I read the notes more than once as I sat beneath the barge's silken canopy. By the time we reached Blackfriars Stairs I was still uneasy about my mission. But when I reached home all thought of William West and his troubles were driven from my mind by a crisis of my own.

Chapter 2

A DIE WAS WAITING by the stable-yard gate, anxiously looking up and down the street. She had obviously been crying.

'At last, Thomas! At last! Oh, Lord be praised!' She almost threw herself into my arms.

I held my wife close, my hand stroking her dark hair. 'Sweeting, whatever is the matter?'

'Oh, Thomas, Thomas, 'tis Raffy!' Fear surged through her body into mine.

'Raffy? He's here? Sick?'

'No, still in Cambridge … I think. Master Segden is here. In the kitchen. He's arrived not a half-hour since, hungry and saddle-weary. I've given him food. Come through quickly. Oh, Thomas, what's to be done?'

I strode through the workshop and into the rear quarters, with Adie in my wake. Robert Segden sat slumped across the kitchen table, a half-empty bowl of potage beside his sprawl of long, blond hair. Robert was the young scholar I had hired as tutor to my son, Raphael – always known as 'Raffy'. Segden was somewhat a dreamer who lived in the world of books but he was conscientious and – what mattered almost as much – Raffy liked him. I had last seen him some four months earlier when the two of them had set off for Cambridge. A university education had not been my idea and Raffy was far from being a book-loving student but the boy was eager to be away from home and, after the endless arguments between us, I had not been altogether sorry to see him go.

There were two reasons for our estrangement. One was Adie. Raffy had never been able to accept his stepmother, though, God's my witness, she had tried hard enough to win him over. The other reason was the arrival in our household of Carl and Henry Holbein whom I had adopted after their father's death.* Instead of welcoming them as new playmates, Raffy chose to look on them as rivals. In truth, he had some reason. They were bright, intelligent lads who took a genuine interest in the goldsmith's craft, something to which Raffy had always been indifferent. In one of our many arguments, when he was about twelve, his anger boiled over. 'I'm not going to spend my life as a mere tradesman! Take Carl for your apprentice. He'll be better at it than me!' In that he was right. The elder Holbein boy, scarcely a year younger than Raffy, had stepped easily into my son's cast off shoes, while Raffy went to university to embark on a career path that, he confidently assumed, would lead him to fame and fortune as a lawyer or a soldier or a courtier. Now it seemed that that plan had quickly met some obstacle.

I gently tapped Segden's shoulder. He shook his head, rubbed his eyes and struggled to his feet.

'Master Treviot, I am right glad to see you, though the news I bring ...'

'What of Raffy?' I demanded. 'My wife tells me he is not taken ill.'

'He is well, Sir ... but ... I beg you will not think it my fault that he is in trouble.'

'Sit down and tell me calmly what has happened.' I drew up a stool opposite as Segden began his tale.

He rubbed a hand over his beard which was little more than stubble. 'I think you will own, Sir, that young Master Raphael is somewhat self-willed.'

'He is as witless as a cony and as stubborn as a leech. We both know that. I hoped that wiser heads and scholarly discipline might tame him.'

---

*   See *The Traitor's Mark*

Segden sighed. 'He began well enough. I made sure he attended lectures and disputations. In tavern arguments with new friends, he showed a quick mind.'

'That is good. He should have his opinions tested by companions of his own age.'

''Tis true, Sir ... but ... Oh, I should have seen the dangerous ideas he was developing.'

'Dangerous? Why say you, "dangerous"?'

'Well political. There have been really bad disturbances of late in Cambridgeshire and neighbouring counties. The protests grow daily more numerous and more violent.' The young man drew a hand across his dust and sweat-streaked brow.

'But this is happening everywhere – small farmers complaining against landlords enclosing common land for their own pasture...'

'That is only the part of it, Master. There are places where the rebels seek nothing less than making rich men poor and poor men rich. I have seen estate stewards and even a town mayor locked in the stocks to be pelted by the rabble. Venture from London and with every league you may feel the common anger rising. Nothing else is talked of in alehouses but the grievances of the people. As you pass along you may find such bills as this thrust into your hand.' Segden drew a crudely printed scrap of paper from his purse and laid it on the table.

I quickly scanned the few uneven lines.

> In the name of our Gracious prince King Edward the Sixt
> We will have Down with
> Closing of Bridle ways
> Fencing off Commons
> Evicting honest Tenants
> bribing of Lawyers
> turning Arable to pasture
> New boundary Walls
> rich men's Pleasure Grounds
> So say we
> the Commonwealth Men

Segden stared mournfully at the artless manifesto. '*O navis referent in mare te novi fluctus*.'*

'What?' My patience was wearing thin. 'You still have not explained how any of this has to do with my son.'

He looked up, pale and trembling with exhaustion. 'I'm sorry, Master Treviot. 'Tis a line from a poem by Horace in which he deplores the collapse of the Roman state. I was teaching it to Raphael, trying to make him see how easily nations decay when law and order break down.'

'Why was he in need of such a lesson?'

'Because he has taken up the rebels' cause. The students, not unnaturally, have been arguing among themselves about the rights and wrongs of the rioting. Master Raphael came down on the side of the poor farmers. A few days ago the trouble spread to Barnwell, just outside Cambridge. The rioters broke down hedges and fired barns, some belonging to the colleges. Raphael and a group of other hotheads decided to show their support by joining in the fight.'

'Beef-brained whipsters!'

''Twas quickly settled. The mayor and the vice-chancellor raised a body of university servants and dispersed the trouble makers.'

'I hope they learned their lesson – especially Raffy.'

Segden shook his head, his face a picture of misery. 'All's not yet told. Master Raphael was among those arrested and made to watch the ringleaders hanged, before being thrown into the town jail.'

'God grant that cools his hot head!'

'This is the news I set out to bring this morning. Then, just as I was leaving, word came that Raphael and some of his friends had broken out of the prison and fled the town.'

'Where have they gone?'

'No one knows. I spoke with some of the less foolhardy students. They said that Master Raphael and his followers spoke of joining the main rebel army.'

'Army?'

'Yes. The latest news is of groups from all over the region – perhaps thousands in total – all converging on England's second city.'

'Norwich?'

'Aye. 'Tis said they mean to take it by storm and hold it to ransom till all their demands are met.'

---

*   'Your sides stripped bare of oars, shattered masts and groaning yards'

I struggled to grasp the full meaning of what Segden was saying. My son a criminous vagabond! An empty-headed scapegrace wandering the country playing at treason.

'Norwich is miles from Cambridge. Do we have no idea where the runaways may be?'

''Twill be hard to track them. Oh, Master Treviot, I'm so sorry. I should have …'

'I am more to blame than you, Robert. But this is not the time for regrets. We must work out what's to be done.'

Adie, sitting beside me, said, 'We must try to get a message to him.'

''Tis more than a message he'll have from me,' I muttered. I shared her concern but was also angry at being made to feel anxiety. 'We must be practical.' I pushed emotion aside. 'Our first aim is to find him. Robert, you must go back to Cambridge and pick up the trail from there. I'll send three of my men with you. If you need to hire more, spare no expense. Pray God you come upon these runagates before they reach Norwich. With fast horses, you should be able to overtake them. As soon as you've any news send word back with one of the others. I'll come straight away. For now, nothing's to be served by more chattering. We need action.'

I hurried into the stable yard and gave instructions to Walt, my ostler. 'You should reach Cambridge by tomorrow noon,' I said.

He scratched the grey stubble covering his head and glanced up at the sun, glaring from a cloudless sky. 'I'll not want to push the horses too hard in this weather, Master.'

I nodded. 'You're right of course but make the best time you can.' I drew coins from my purse. 'This will serve for your lodging.'

Minutes later, Adie and I were sitting in the window embrasure of our chamber watching the little group of horsemen clatter away towards Newgate. It was pleasantly cool indoors away from the heat beamed down from the July sun and trapped in the city's cramped lanes and alleys.

'What's to be done with him, my Dearling? What's to be done?' I put an arm round her and held her close.

She took my hand in both of hers. 'Most boys of his age go through a trouble stage like this. Raffy will come through it. You'll see. Now, tell me about your visit to Lambeth. What did the archbishop want?'

'The archbishop? This business has put him clean from my mind. What did he want? He wanted me to go to the king's great prison to talk to a murderer.'

'Murderer!' Adie's eyes opened wide.

Her look of horrified surprise brought a smile to my lips – which may have been what my clever wife intended. 'Well, perhaps not a murderer. That is what I'm supposed to discover. Anyway, I shall have to decline. This business of Raffy is too important. Anon I shall write to his grace and begged to be excused.'

'You have not told me who this villain is.'

'His name is William West.' I gave Adie an account of my meeting with Cranmer. 'And that is all I know,' I concluded. 'I liked not the sound of it and am glad now to have an excuse to take no part in it.'

Adie was silent for some moments. Then she stared straight into my eyes, her brow creased in concentration. 'Perhaps you should not be too hasty, my dear. If you do his grace's bidding it will help to take your mind off poor Raffy.'

I opened my mouth to protest but she continued. 'And might this not be the answer to your question?'

'What question?'

'The one you asked not ten minutes ago, "What is to be done with Raffy?"'

'Sweeting, I do not see …'

She held a finger to my lips. 'Raffy has these grand dreams of becoming a courtier, a landed gentleman, someone of real importance.'

'The boy has no idea what he wants. All that concerns him is not to inherit the family business.'

'And when he gets an idea in his head, nothing this side of heaven will drive it out. Raffy is as stubborn as his father.'

'I suppose there's some truth in what you say.'

'So, why not give him what he wants or what he thinks he wants?'

'This is woman's logic,' I muttered. ''Tis too deep for me.'

'What I mean is this.' Adie's enthusiasm grew as she developed her idea. 'If you do this service for the archbishop he will be grateful, will he not?'

'He is always generous in his appreciation but what …'

'Then that will be a good time to seek a favour. Ask him to take Raffy into his household … have him trained as one of his gentlemen.'

I sighed. 'Ah, my dear, you know not how these things work. His grace receives such requests daily.'

'And grants some of them.'

'Well, yes.'

'And why should he not be good lord to you? For sure you will have earned it.'

My wife's ability for sudden changes of mood was something I could not share. 'If Raffy does not meet his death in an East Anglian ditch, or at the end of a rope and if he manages to escape this escapade without covering himself in shame, then there might be some merit in your idea. For the moment, my only concern is to find Raffy and bring him safe home.'

Adie rested her head on my shoulder. 'Oh, my dear, I long for that, too, with all my heart. But until we have news from Master Segden all we can do to help him is pray for his safe return and make plans to keep him out of trouble in the future.'

'I suppose there may be sense in what you say, but ...'

'Then that is settled. You will talk with Master West. Robert will find Raffy and you will present our errant boy to his grace.' She jumped up. 'Good will come out of this evil. You'll see. Now I must go feed little Meg.'

For several minutes I sat alone, considering the crisis from every angle only to conclude that Adie's proposal was the only alternative to mournful brooding. There would be no news of Raffy for a couple of days at the very least and concentrating on the archbishop's problem might take my mind off my own. The first thing I decided to do was talk matters over with the man I regarded as the wisest in London.

For a dozen years or more I had counted Ned Longbourne among my closest friends. The old man had been many years a monk but since the disappearance of the monasteries he had maintained himself as a herbalist and a mender of broken bones. He had no ambitions to be called 'surgeon' or 'apothecary'. 'The body's its own healer,' he told those who sought his help. 'God has graciously given me some understanding of herbs and flowers that may help it to mend itself – as long as they are applied sensibly and prayerfully.' It was but recently that he had been unable to find remedies for his own aching bones and had reluctantly allowed others to take care of him. Bart Miller, my business assistant, and his wife, Lizzie, had made room for him and it was to their house in Milk Street that I made my way the next morning.

Lizzie greeted me at the door with her usual warmth. I never knew a more straight-up-and-down woman than Lizzie Miller. She was her own person and spoke her mind without wrapping her words in polite half-truths. She had no time for convention which was why, though in her thirties, she still wore her dark hair loose with only a band across the front to keep it free of her face.

'Thomas, we are honoured, though I would wager a sovereign if I had one, that 'tis Ned you come a-visiting.'

'How is he?'

'Well enough for a man of his years. Lord be praised his mind is still sharp. You find him playing schoolmaster this morning. He is taking Jack through his Latin. I never thought any child of mine would be a scholar but,' she lowered her voice as we walked through into the kitchen, 'Ned has a way of making learning fun.'

Her words received instant confirmation. Ned and Lizzie's six-year-old boy were sat at the table with their heads bent over a hornbook – and giggling.

Lizzie crossed to the inner door. 'Come along, Jack. Master Treviot has come to see Ned. I'm just going to fetch Annie. Then we are going to market.'

The boy pulled a face. 'I want to stay with the men. I'm a man.'

'Yes, indeed,' my old friend said. 'You are a man. And men look after women. Would you have your mother and sister venture into Cheapside market without your protection?'

The boy looked up with a frown unsure whether he was being mocked. But Ned met his enquiring gaze with a completely straight face. Jack jumped down from the stool and strode across the room.

'Lizzie does well by her three bearns,' Ned remarked as I took my seat opposite him.

'Three? By my count, there is just Jack and his elder sister.'

Ned laughed. 'Would you not agree that Bart is sometimes the biggest child of them all?'

It was good to see the old man in such high spirits. He had aged much in recent years and I noticed that some movements of hand and arm made him wince. After we had briefly disposed of greetings I related the events of the previous day.

When I had finished, Ned said wistfully. 'Poor Raffy. Not an easy childhood. He was too long without a mother. By the time he was provided with one it was too late for him to adjust.'

'What more can I do for him. Jesu knows, I've tried all I can think of.'

'I like Adie's idea. You know I abhor our archbishop's religion. This latest wave of violence against holy images in so many churches … Yet, he is a good man. I am sure he runs his own household with firmness and fairness. A fresh, disciplined environment … Yes, I can see that might be what Raffy needs.'

'So you think I should take on his grace's commission because of the faint hope that he will show his gratitude by finding a place for my son?'

Ned tapped his nose with a long forefinger, something he often did when he was deep in thought. 'There is more to this business than you have been told. 'Tis about politics, as you have rightly guessed. The outcome is obviously of great importance to Cranmer and, I dare say, to Cranmer's friends on the council. You know the rumours. They are everywhere. Men say the king's uncle cannot long survive. This trouble in Norfolk is but the latest proof of discontent. The duke has already sent troops to Devon to deal with the unrest there. How long before we see Yorkshire in arms? Or the borderlands? Or even your own beloved Kent? Also, there's many in parliament and the court who would delight to see the Protector plucked down. In the midst of all this, I doubt whether our archbishop would have Master West secretly interrogated just to see that justice is done to a defenceless prisoner of little account.'

'True, true, without a doubt. I wrung all I could from Ralph Morice but there is much more to be squeezed. All this is very good reason for me not to be involved.'

'Hmm!' Again the nose tap. 'There is another thing that concerns me more.'

'What is that?'

'Poison. Unless Master West is a private herbalist he must have bought the evil substance from somewhere.'

'Unless the accusation is completely false.'

'True. We may be dealing with a wholly slanderous accusation. What do you know about West's uncle?'

'Old Baron De La Warr is well into his seventies … perhaps older. A remarkable long-liver.'

'I can see why that might be frustrating for his heir.'

'Yes but there must be more at stake. His lordship is one of the biggest landowners in Sussex. He spends most of his time in the country and avoids coming to the parliament house. He is no friend of the new order and some say that he bides his time, ready to encourage the spread of rebellion in the South-east.'

'Ned frowned. 'If De La Warr is of the old faith – the true faith, as I think it – it is hard to see why he would support these "Commonwealth Men" as they call themselves. They are cheek by jowl with the preachers of novelties and the sacrilegious mobs who go around our churches, smashing and burning with the approval of Somerset and the government.'

'We live in confused and confusing times.'

'Aye, Thomas, you never said a truer word. That is why the black arts are flourishing. The land is a-swarm with fortune-tellers, necromancers, alchemists, dabblers in cabbalistic magic, astrologers, peddlers of poisons and love potions and spells for conjuring spirits and stories for turning lead into gold.'

'Charlatans preying on the simple-minded.'

'Some certainly. But there are those who do consort with demons and could let loose the hounds of hell upon the earth.'

'You believe so?'

'I know so. When I was in the monastery …' He scowled and shook his head. 'But now is not the time for reminiscence. If there is an evil here we must confront it in the name of God.'

'We?'

'Thomas, should there be truth in this poison story, you will not fathom it unaided – and you could be walking into danger.'

'Surely not …'

'Of a certainty. If this West is in league with demonic forces or made captive by them, you will be up against you know not what. I have some experience in these matters.'

It was clear that Ned was not to be deflected from what he considered to be his Christian duty. So it was that I agreed to his accompanying me to the Tower. Thus, the following morning, we travelled together to the royal palace and prison, and an encounter that would change our lives much more than we could ever have imagined.

Chapter 3

'OVER THERE WITH the others behind the barrier.' A captain
in part armour motioned us to an area of Tower Green marked
by hurdles.

Ned and I ambled our horses across to where a growing crowd
of people - who, like us, had business in the fortress - were having to
wait. The reason was obvious. A procession of wagons loaded with
piles of armour, iron-bound chests, and stands of pikes was rattling
across the causeway over the moat and making its way northwards
close to the city wall. When we turned our gaze towards the river we
could see the wharf lined with cannon and heavy equipment waiting
to be loaded onto ships.

As we approached a group of mounted men on the edge of the
crowd, I recognised a fellow member of the Goldsmiths' Company.
'What's afoot, Brother?' I asked.

Simon Dannery, a large man with flaccid features, drew a
sleeve across his glistening brow. 'Trouble somewhere obviously but
'tis no use trying to get anything from these fellows.' He indicated
the soldiers controlling the traffic. 'They either know nothing or
say nothing.'

A young man in a feathered cap and riding a dapple-grey joined
the conversation. 'Some say these are reinforcements bound for the
Channel ports against a French landing.'

'Nay, that cannot be,' Dannery replied. 'If there was a foreign threat, we'd have had a general muster. 'Tis like to be one of these peasant rabbles that needs to be brought to order. I hear things are really bad in Norfolk.'

'Norfolk!' The word startled me. Was the disturbance there bad enough to warrant all this ordnance? 'What know you of Norfolk?' I asked.

'My wife's family is from Thetford. For several weeks, they have been sending warnings to the council about mobs wandering the countryside unchecked, but Lord Somerset does nothing.' Dannery scowled. 'If he had acted promptly – strung up a few upstart rabble-rousers – there would have been no need for all this.' He waved a hand at the passing cavalcade.

I was about to press the speaker for more details but Ned intervened. ''Tis a sad time when common folk feel they must take the law into their own hands to protect their way of life.'

The mild comment clearly irritated Dannery. 'Waste not your sympathy on such vermin! Today they pull down hedges. Next week they will be pulling down rich men's houses and destroying all decent order.'

Neither Ned nor I responded and, changing his tone, Dannery favoured me with a wide smile. 'What brings you here today, Brother Treviot – business at the royal mint?'

'No, I have a private matter to attend to.' I did not intend the reply as a snub but the man had irritated me and the words came out more sharply than I had intended.

'Private?' Dannery raised an eyebrow, clearly wanting me to elaborate.

I said nothing and moments later the last wagon rumbled past and we were allowed to proceed across the causeway.

One advantage of the delay was that the porters at the bulwark gate, having a surge of visitors to deal with, spent less time than usual checking everyone. A harassed warder glanced at the warrant Ralph Morice had given me, referred to his prisoner list, muttered 'Martin Tower number three' and waved us through.

We moved to the tethering place. As I was dismounting I happened to glance back towards the gateway. I saw Dannery talking earnestly with the porter and pointing at me. I smiled to myself. The man had a reputation in the Company as a busybody. It was gratifying to give him something to puzzle over. The Martin Tower was on the far side of the inner bailey and the keeper, when we knocked, was in no hurry to come to the door. When the man – a sloven with a greasy overall covering his tunic – did appear he looked suspiciously at the bag I was carrying.

'Food and wine for our cousin,' I explained.

'Let's see,' he demanded and eyed greedily the capon, bread, and wine that I had brought. 'I'll look after that for him' he said.

'I think not,' I replied, clutching the handles firmly.

'Them's my orders,' he countered.

To avoid further argument I produced a groat from my purse and that had the desired effect. 'First floor,' the jailer muttered, standing to one side.

The door of West's lodging stood open, a sign that he was among those prisoners allowed to take exercise in the area between the inner and outer walls. However, the man we had come to see was in residence, seated at a small table beside the narrow window and reading a book by the morning sunlight.

He looked up in alarm. 'Who are you? What do you want? I can tell you no more than I already have.'

My first impression of the person I had been sent to see was of a man around thirty but one whose slender frame and gaunt features made him look older and fragile. His face was fringed with straggling hair, which indicated that his beard had seen no barber since his incarceration. His pale grey eyes glimmered faintly within their deep sockets. I was shocked by his appearance. Never had I seen anyone so devoid of hope, so broken, so 'lost'. The question that filled my mind was, 'How can we help this poor fellow?'

'Master West, pray do not distress yourself.' I advanced into the room, followed by Ned, who closed the door behind us. 'My name is Thomas Treviot and this is Ned Longbourne. We come, in friendship as emissaries from his grace of Canterbury.'

West sprang to his feet, knocking over the stool, and stepped back a couple of paces. 'The archbishop! Then 'tis true he has begun a purge of necromancers and the like.'

'I have heard something to that effect,' I replied as calmly as I could. 'In these uncertain times, fortune-tellers and false seers are flourishing. His grace is, naturally, concerned.

'Go back to him and say that I have nothing to add to what I have told the Lord Chancellor's tormentors.'

The man, deeply terrified, collapsed in a corner. Nor was it to be wondered at. If he had been interrogated by Lord Chancellor Rich in person recently he would know that his case was one in which the government took a serious interest.

Ned tried to calm the prisoner. 'Master West, I swear by our precious Saviour, our Lady and all the saints that we have no connection with anyone who has been ill-treating you.'

'Then you are sent by my uncle.'

'It has never been our pleasure to meet his lordship,' I said. 'We are truly here at the bidding of the archbishop, who wishes you nothing but good.'

West let out a low groan and leant back against the wall. 'I know not who to believe. No one can help me. I am as good as dead, either way.'

Looking round, I realised that Ned was not troubling himself with reflections about the prisoner. He was an image of busy activity. He went across to the table, removed the scrip that he carried over his shoulder for gathering herbs and from it extracted a medley of items. First, he covered his head with a black skullcap. He spread out some small pieces of paper bearing black printed characters. When he had arranged these in a circle he placed in the centre a candle in a small stick and proceeded to light it with the aid of a tinderbox. Beside it, he placed a sharpened pen and a small stoneware flask sealed with a wooden stopper.

West followed these preparations in absorbed silence.

'Now, Master West,' Ned spoke prosaically without looking up. 'What you need to understand is that there are two kinds of magic – black and white. The white is far stronger because it calls on the power of God himself and not on any inferior demons. The spell you are under – and which I am about to remove – is a black one. Can you name the magus who placed it on you?'

'No! No! I dare not!' West was gripped with a violent trembling and pressed his back against the wall, as though willing it to absorb him.

'Yes, I suspected as much.' Ned's businesslike tone did not change. 'You have been placed under a blood curse. No matter.

We can free you from that if you do exactly as I say. <u>Exactly</u>! Do you understand?'

West nodded. He appeared to be mesmerised by this performance, as, I must confess, was I.

'Good.' Ned uncorked the flash. 'This is holy water from the River Jordan in which Our Lord was baptised.' He placed a small square of paper beside it and handed West the quill. 'Dip this in the sacred water and write the name of the magus. You will be safe, for neither I nor any other mortal eye can read it. You will then make the incantation I give you while I burn the paper and place the ashes within the magic circle. Is that clear?'

West muttered something but stepped forward and took the pen. With a shaking hand, he wrote something which, of course, was illegible and gave the paper to Ned.

'Very good,' the 'white magician' pronounced solemnly. 'The incantation is three paternosters, proclaimed boldly facing east, towards Jerusalem. Please turn to the window.'

While the prisoner did as he was bidden, Ned muttered some strange, foreign-sounding words and held the paper to the flame. It was consumed in an instant and its ashes dropped to the table.

When West turned back to face us Ned smiled at him. 'There, now you are free. The demons have no more power over you. How do you feel?'

For a moment, West seemed dazed. Then he stepped forward and grasped Ned's hand. 'Thank you! Oh, thank you, thank you.'

Ned shook his hand. 'The thanks are due to God, not to me. He has lifted the weight from your soul. What we must do now is lift the threat of prosecution. This magus must be found and interrogated to make him reveal the truth. We will do our best to track him down but you must tell us all you know.' He hurried on as an anxious frown crossed Ward's face. 'Except, of course, you must still not reveal the name of the magus. There is power in the name and I cannot guarantee your safety if you reveal it. Now, please tell us all you can.'

We drew up stools to the table and for the next half-hour the man who had been terrified to speak poured out his story in a torrent of words. His tale was simple but bizarre. Several years previously his childless uncle, Lord De La Warr, had nominated him as his heir and welcomed him into his household to learn about the management of his wide estates. The two men were on good terms. 'We were not of one mind about religion. He is very set in the old ways. But I do not think he bore me a grudge for that,' West explained. 'People say I want to see my uncle dead. That is a lie,' he protested. 'The old man is often ill but I never wished him other than recovery from his ailments.' One of De La Warr's painful afflictions, the narrator explained, was kidney stones and he was forever seeking remedies. At length, he heard of an alchemist who boasted of a cure for this complaint and accordingly he sent his nephew to go and buy the potion. The stipulated arrangements were bizarre and, to my mind, West's willingness to comply with them indicated that he was a dutiful nephew prepared to do all in his power to help a demanding and eccentric relation. He was instructed to ride to Saffron Walden in Essex and there stay at the sign of the Sun until he was contacted.

'Did this arrangement not seem strange to you?' I enquired.

'My uncle insisted that we could only obtain the medicine if we followed rules of strict secrecy.'

'A common practice among practitioners of the black arts,' Ned said.

West nodded. Yes, and highway rogues. I made sure I was accompanied by two well-armed servants.'

He went on to explain how he had spent the night at the Sun Inn. The following afternoon, a young boy had led him out to the stable yard where a covered wagon was standing. The wagoner – probably the lad's father – had thoroughly laced up the canvas once his three passengers were aboard. The ensuing journey had seemed endless. West and his companions had grown increasingly anxious as the grey, moist daylight, seen through chinks in the covering, dwindled towards evening. When, at last, the journey ended the travellers found themselves in front of what West guessed was one of the abbeys deserted and defaced in King Henry's time.

West began to tremble and stumble over words as he described the gloomy chamber to which he was admitted. He had, he said, been particularly alarmed by a squawking crow on a silver chain that hopped about amidst the clutter of magical equipment.

'That was the necromancer's familiar,' Ned explained.

As to the magus himself West could give no clear description. The one thing that had made the strongest and most terrifying impression was that the man could fly. In the blink of an eyelid, he had travelled from one end of the room to the other. 'You can imagine, Sirs, how eager I was to be quit of that place. Fortunately, our business was quickly concluded and I was returned to Saffron Walden.'

'Not before you had been placed under the blood curse,' Ned suggested.

West nodded. 'Yes, before I knew what was happening my hand was scratched and …'

'The magus told you he would know if you ever betrayed him.' Ned finished the sentence. 'These evil sorcerers are not very original. They all work from the same spellbooks. Tell us what happened when you returned to Sussex.'

West bent forward over the table, head in hands. 'This is what I shall never understand. My uncle was very pleased when I brought him his medicine. I explained the instructions the magus had given me about how the potion was to be drunk. He was very specific about the time it should be taken and the goblet to be used. All this we followed precisely. I watched my uncle drink all the medicine. It smelled ill and, according to my uncle, it tasted worse but he drained the cup and suffered no obvious ill effects. Then, two days later, the local constable burst into my chamber with a brace of armed tithingmen, saying I was under arrest for attempted murder.'

'How came you to be lodged here, in the king's prison?' I asked.

West shook his head wearily. 'That, too, I cannot understand. I was brought straight here and not to our local jail. I was not charged before the magistrate. My uncle means to have me tried by parliament, without any chance to state my own case.'

'And here you have been examined by the Lord Chancellor?'

'Aye, and by his predecessor, Lord Southampton.' He drew back his sleeves to reveal vivid bruising round his wrists. 'They strung me up to make me confess. But what should I confess? Only that I have obediently and in Christian charity satisfied an old man's whim. Then they wanted me to name others I knew to be involved in witchcraft but, as God is my judge, I have no dealings with such. I find my friends among scholars and men of good conscience who love and revere God's word. For that, I will pay with my life.'

'That you will not,' I declared with all the conviction I could muster. I assured West that he had friends in high places, friends determined to establish the truth. How convinced he was I know not but I think he was a little less dejected when we left.

27

'The man you need to find – this evil magus – calls himself Parafaustus.'

Ned and I were returning along Tower Street and just passing All Hallows Church.

I looked at him in surprise. 'How can you possibly know that? West refused to speak his name.'

Ned laughed. 'Oh, Thomas, surely you were not fooled by my simple charlatan's tricks.'

'What tricks? With my own eyes, I saw our friend write the name in holy water …'

'Water that has never been farther east than the Great Conduit in Cheap.'

'Do you mean that all that magical ritual was a sorry jest?'

'I assure you, Thomas, I was never in more earnest. I dabble not in magic – black or white – but I had to make West believe that I have real powers. I must confess, it was easier than I thought. That poor man is so desperate to escape from his enchantment that he was ready to be fooled by even my theatrical nonsense.'

'I still don't see how you can know the name of this magician. You burned the paper it was written on.'

'Only after holding it before the candle flame until the secret writing was revealed.'

'Secret writing?'

'My little flask contained a strong solution of lemon juice – colourless normally, but brown when heated. The name was quite clear. Parafaustus, indeed! You know what that means? "Better than Faust". The man actually takes pride in comparing himself to the hell-hound villain who did a deal with the devil.'

I laughed. 'Your "theatrical nonsense" was very convincing.'

'In knew we would gain nothing by ordinary questioning. That was confirmed as soon as we met poor Master West. You recall that he said, "I am as good as dead, either way". He was facing a choice. If he refused to say where he had obtained the potion the law would take its course. But if he told his interrogators what they wanted to know, he was equally doomed. That could only mean that his silence had been secured by means of a curse. I know how these people work.'

'He was certainly terrified by this … Parafaustus. What did you make of his account of his meeting?'

'Pah!' Ned snorted his contempt. 'Elaborate trickery! Think what state of mind West must have been in by the time he reached the magus's lair. Then he was shown into a dark chamber with a chained crow fluttering about and impressive alchemical equipment viewed in dim candlelight.'

'But what of the magus flying through the air?'

Ned chuckled. 'Aye, a nice trick that but very simple to manage. The rogue had a double – someone dressed to look like himself. The deceit would be easy in the gloom. So the magus could appear to change places.'

We rode some way in silence. I reflected on what West had told us in the light of Ned's explanation. And I became suddenly angry. Why, I asked myself, would someone go to such lengths to frighten West … to frighten him to death? What devilish plot lay behind it?

Ned might have been reading my thoughts. 'This evil must be stopped,' he said. 'Tell Cranmer what we have discovered so that he can have his men scour the Suffolk countryside …'

There was sudden flapping of dark wings. A crow that had been gorging on the entrails of a dead rat started upwards almost under our horses' hooves. Ned's mount reared. The old man was unseated. With a cry, he fell heavily to the ground. I made haste to calm my mare, then jumped from the saddle. My old friend lay motionless on the rutted ground. Blood was already oozing from his head.

Chapter 4

'NED! NED!' I knelt beside him and called his name. There was no response – not even the flicker of an eyelid.

I bent close and listened for breathing but could hear nothing over the sounds of the street.

Fearing the worst, I put my face close to his. To my relief, there came a slight rasping sound. The eyes remained closed, though, and the old man made no movement.

A small crowd was gathering and it was all I could do to keep a space around the recumbent form. 'Someone fetch a physician!' I demanded.

'There's a barber-surgeon down St Mary Hill,' someone responded.

'Bring him,' I said, 'and, in God's name, be quick!'

'Best get him inside. My house is close by.' The speaker was a large woman, a fishmonger's wife by the smell of her.

'Very well. Lead the way. And, you three, give me a hand.' I pointed to a group of apprentices who were looking on. Under my direction, they lifted Ned's limp body while I supported his blood-soaked head.

We carried him the few yards to the fishwife's house where we laid him on the table she had cleared to accommodate him. Straightway she brought water and cloths in a bowl and gently bathed his head.

'A bad cut.' She indicated a three-inch welt at the back of the skull which still leaked blood.

'Ned! Ned!' I called, patting his hands and desperately trying to call forth a response. There was none.

Nor was there before the barber, a gaunt fellow with a crimson-streaked apron over his clothes, arrived several minutes later. 'Everyone out!' he ordered. 'Give me space for the patient.'

'I shall stay,' I said. 'This man is my dear friend. See you tend him well till I can fetch a physician to him.'

The man scowled, his professional rivalry obvious, but he nodded and turned his attention to Ned.

I must confess that he did his work with careful, gentle skill, first staunching the blood, then applying a sickly smelling salve, before binding the patient's head. 'That is all I can do,' he said at last and added hurriedly. 'It is all anyone can do. If the old fellow wakes, he may mend. If not …' He shrugged.

I thanked him and paid him, then had time to express my appreciation to our hostess and her neighbours.

'What's to do now, Sir.' The woman asked anxiously. 'The old fellow cannot stay here.'

'No, of course not,' I agreed. 'I'll away to my house and return with a horse litter.' With a last glance at Ned, I set off.

◊

It was a couple of hours later that my stricken friend lay in a good bed in Goldsmiths' Row with our family physician, Henry Drudgeon, re-examining his wound.

'The skull is bruised but not, I think broken,' he pronounced.

'Then, the wound is not … mortal?' I asked

'Come and steady him while I bind him afresh,' Drudgeon ordered.

Gently I eased Ned into a sitting position.

The doctor plied fresh bandage. 'The answer to your question is "No", not of itself but what the blow has done inside his head is past knowing. If he does not wake within a day it may be necessary to trepan.'

'Trepan?' Adie was at my side holding Ned's hand and stroking it.

'Make a hole to release harmful vapours,' the physician muttered, calmly, distractedly.

Adie shuddered. 'How awful! Poor Ned!'

'Mmm … sounds worse than it is.' Dudgeon tied the final knot.

At that moment, the door opened and Lizzie slipped in 'I've just heard,' she said softly, joining us at the bedside. 'How is he?'

'We know not,' Adie replied, putting an arm round her friend to draw her closer. 'The doctor it talking of a tr.. tr…'

'Trepan,' Drudgeon said, as we gently lowered Ned's head to the pillow. 'Pray you that that is not necessary; that the old man wakes soon. Someone must attend here all the time, watching for any change. If there is the slightest movement, or sound, send for me.'

I looked at him frankly, intently. 'And if …'

'That, too. Send for me.'

As Adie escorted Drudgeon from the chamber, Lizzie said, 'Go, take some rest. You, too, Thomas. You have much to fret over, what with Raffy and all. I will stay here a while.'

It was a relief to take her advice and I retired to my chamber with Adie. We sat together in the window seat and for a long time neither of us spoke.

It was Adie who broke the silence. 'Tell me all about your visit to the Tower. Who is this mysterious Master West? What were you able to discover about him?'

'I? It was Ned who did the discovering.' I explained how the prisoner had been tricked into giving us the information we wanted.

Adie smiled. 'Dear Ned. He is so clever. Oh, I do hope and pray …' She quickly changed the subject. 'So, now you have much to tell the archbishop. He will be pleased.'

'Perhaps. But you are right. I must set everything down in a letter while all is fresh in my mind.'

'No, Dearest.' Sunlight picked out gold strands in her dark hair as she shook her head. 'Best you go in person. His grace will want to ask you questions.'

I put an arm around her shoulder and drew her close. 'You are still wanting me to make an impression, for Raffy's sake.'

Adie pouted. 'It is surely just that favours should be returned. And after what has happened to poor Ned … well, this favour has been hard-earned.'

'But I must be here, for Ned's sake.'

Adie laid a finger on my lips. 'Lizzie and I shall be his carers and I will have some of the servants share the watching.'

'Well, perhaps it would be as well. I will go to Hampton in the morning ... if there is no word of Raffy.' I stood up. 'And now I must go down to the workshop.'

She reached up and clasped my arm 'You will take care when you go to the archbishop ... *extra* care?'

'*Extra* care? What mean you?'

'Well, after what happened to Ned ... the crow that caused his fall.'

'What has that to do with my visit to the archbishop?'

'Well, you know ... the crow.' She stared at me with an impatient frown.

'What of the crow?'

'Did not Master West say this magician kept a crow as his familiar.'

I laughed. 'Oh, you think this Parafaustus will set his crow on me to do me a mischief?'

Adie pouted. 'Thomas, you must not mock me. We should be careful of things we do not understand. There are powers ...'

'Powers! This fellow is a charlatan, a trickster. Ned has explained his counterfeit magic. He can do me no harm.'

She gazed mournfully out of the window. 'It worries me when you sound so sure. You remember Mother Caundle?'

'She they call the Witch of Shoreditch?'

'What happened to the parish priest when he crossed her?'

'A foolish gossips' tale. I recall not the details.'

'She kept a dog as her familiar – an ugly brute. One day a carved dog fell from the church and struck her enemy dead.' She crossed herself. 'All I ask is that you take extra care until this sorcerer is locked up. Promise me.' She stared at me imploringly.

'Well, I promise that I will keep a careful watch for crows and stone dogs. And now I must attend to my business.'

◊

The next day, a Monday, I made an early start. The royal court was always crowded with suitors and others having business with courtiers and household officers. I hoped to be among the first seeking audience with the archbishop.

Early light was just invading the shadows of Creed Lane as my gelding picked his way with precise care among the servants milling around the conduit and the vendors holding out their trays of pies and cakes to early travellers. I cleared the throng and urged the bay into a trot. But twenty yards on the way was part blocked again, this time by a heavy cart. There were three men in the vehicle and, as I approached one of them pointed at me. He and his companions jumped down. Before I grasped what was happening one of them seized the bridle. I reached down for the poniard I carry in the saddle holster. A strong hand closed over my wrist. On my left another attacker tried to wrestle my foot from the stirrup. As I lashed out with my fists, the horse was dragged to the right into a narrow alley. In this dark space, all three villains set about pulling and pushing me from the saddle. I fought back fiercely. I struck one of them a blow across the throat that made him yelp and fall back. But my legs were losing their grip and I felt myself sliding sideways.

Suddenly, I heard a shout. 'Master Treviot!' The fellow gripping my right arm leg go. He fell backwards, clutching his head. I regained my balance. I was aware of a fight going on all around me. It was all I could do to calm the horse. Then I saw my assailants running away up the alley.

'All safe now, Master.' Carl Holbein was peering up with a wide grin on his face.

I recognised two of my other young workers, both brandishing staves.

'What are you doing here?' I gasped.

'Mistress Treviot bade us follow you. She was afeared you might meet trouble. She was obviously right. By your leave shall we come along?'

I realised I was shaking. 'Perhaps it would be as well.'

My three rescuers accompanied me to the waterside, jogging behind the horse. I left the bay in the stable yard at the Half Moon Inn, hired a wherry at the staithings and had myself and my companions rowed upstream to Hampton.

'Who were those villains, Master?' It was Dickon, a swarthy, freckled redhead who asked the question.

'Mulish cutpurses,' I suggested casually.

Carl disagreed. 'No. Not enough fight in 'em for regular thieves.' He spoke with all the authority of his thirteen years.

'Who do you think they were?' I asked.

It was Harry Standish, at seventeen the eldest member of the trio, who ventured an opinion. 'Mistress Treviot warned us to be on the watch for evil spirits.'

Carl laughed. 'Nothing much of the spirits about them. I've raw knuckles to prove it.'

'Did you see the one who went off hobbling up the street? I caught him a good blow on the shin,' Dickon boasted.

I left the young men to their victorious reminiscences and pondered to myself Carl's question, 'Who were those villains?'

When we reached the palace stairs at Hampton Court I showed Cranmer's pass to the guard, left the others in the outer court and went in search of the archbishop's quarters. I had not long to wait in Cranmer's first-floor outer chamber before Ralph Morice appeared and ushered me into his own office.

'Thomas, it's good to see you so soon. Have you been to the Tower already? Have you talked with West?' The secretary indicated an armed chair beside the empty fireplace and seated himself opposite.

'Yes, I spent an hour or more with Master West yesterday.'

'Good, good! Excellent news! What did you discover? Tell me everything.' Morice's tone betrayed more than eagerness. It was close to anxiety.

I gave my reply briefly and dispassionately. 'The man you are looking for calls himself Parafaustus.'

Morice stared for a moment, wide-eyed and open-mouthed. 'Parafaustus!' he exclaimed at last. 'But this is marvellous. Parafaustus! We had long suspected ... but could not prove ... You are sure you have the name right. West was not deceiving you?'

I explained how Ned had tricked West into revealing the name of the magus. 'And now, perhaps, you will tell me what it is you have involved me in. On the way here this morning, I was set upon by a group of murderous ruffians. I cannot believe that was not connected with your business.'

Morice was scarcely listening. 'Parafaustus! This is good news indeed. We must report straightway to his grace.' Without another word he jumped up and went through an inner door.

He was back almost immediately. 'Come! Come!' He beckoned me from the doorway.

Within the chamber Cranmer advanced to greet me, hands outstretched. 'Master Treviot, I knew you would not fail us. You have done surpassing well. Better than you can know.'

'I am happy that your Grace is pleased. May I now be told just why this information is so important?'

He appeared to consider the question, keeping his hold of my hands. 'Yes, I think, perhaps … Ralph.' He turned to his secretary, 'could you ask Sir William to join us?'

As Morice left, Cranmer explained, 'Sir William Paget is secretary to the council and a close confidant of the Protector. The two have been closeted together for many hours since Sir William's return yesterday from a diplomatic mission abroad. He will have the very latest news.'

The man who entered with Morice a few minutes later was a bustling figure in his mid-forties dressed all in cautious grey and carrying a sheaf of papers. Anxious, questioning eyes probed mine as we shook hands.

Having made the introductions, Cranmer seated us all around a table. 'William, thanks to Master Treviot we have taken an important step forward. As you know, I asked him to meet William West. I know you were doubtful about calling on the aid of an outsider but I felt that that poor man in the Tower just might be more open with someone less politically involved. As you will hear, it has all turned out very well. Thomas, please tell us about your meeting with West. Spare no detail. Even the smallest piece of information will help us to build up a picture of this strange affair.'

My small audience listened in silence as I described the visit to the Tower. Then the questions began.

'How did West describe his relationship with his uncle?' Cranmer wanted to know.

'He believed himself to be on good terms with the old man.' I replied. 'They took different views on religion but West insists that their disagreements were not bitter.'

Morice nodded. 'That is borne out by what we know. West is a convinced member of the reformed faith, much influenced by his friendship with Sir John Cheke, his majesty's tutor. Lord De La Warr cannot be shaken from the Roman heresy but I doubt he would die to defend the pope.'

Paget stroked his forked beard. 'Did West say that his uncle asked him, in person, to fetch a potion from Parafaustus? The instruction was not relayed through a third party?'

'He was very clear on that point,' I replied. 'Someone else must have persuaded the old man to have dealings with this charlatan – someone who not only wanted to murder the baron but who also planned to have West sent to the gallows for a crime he did not commit. As the lawyers say, "Cui bono" – who benefits from the death of the old man and his chosen heir?'

Cranmer gave a wistful smile. 'If we were to go down that road, Thomas, we would find it very long and winding. Baron De La Warr is the eldest of no less than nine brothers and half-brothers born to his father by three wives – and, of course, there are sisters and half-sisters, too.'

Morice added, 'The only way to get at the truth quickly is via the poison-monger. If we can locate the villainous dabbler in spells and potions we can make him reveal the name of his customer. For some time, we have had our suspicions about Parafaustus but he is very elusive and we had no evidence against him. Thanks to you, Thomas, we should be able to lay our hands on him.'

'Just who is this mountebank magus?' I asked.

The three men exchanged glances. Cranmer nodded. It was Paget who spoke.

'His real name is Robert Allen, a lying, cheating, papistical rogue. In the place he hails from some call him 'the god of Norfolk' but, there is more about him of Satan than of our Saviour.'

Cranmer added, 'He casts horoscopes and has prophesied the death of our young king.'

'Surely, that is treason' I said. 'Why has he not been arrested?'

'Because he has all the guile of the arch-fiend,' Morice growled. 'Few people know where he lives and those who do know are terrified into silence by his curses and spells.'

The archbishop nodded. 'And I fear he has the support of some of the backward-looking clergy. Those who hate to see the church purified spare not to protect this devil's spawn and use him to spread disaffection among the people. It is a paradox that the rebels who call themselves the Commonwealth Men and are all for reform in church and state are egged on by priests who would undo those very reforms.'

'This is one reason why the situation in Norfolk is so grave – and complicated. There have been disturbances elsewhere. The Protector prefers to deal with them by agreeing to hear complaints and offering full pardons to all troublemakers who disperse. This policy works in some places, though, as I have often pointed out to his lordship, we must take care not to appear weak. Leniency, I fear, will not serve in Norfolk. Men are gathering from all over the shire and beyond. They have made a camp on the heath outside Norwich.'

My thoughts went immediately to Raffy and his young companions. 'How many are gathered there?'

Paget shrugged. 'No two reports tell the same story. Some speak of three thousand; some five thousand; some as many as ten. All we can be certain of is that we are not dealing with a rabble, a mob. We are confronted by an army.'

'Aye,' Morice added, 'and a disciplined army at that. They have a captain. Not an ill-tutored ploughman or alehouse orator. His name is Robert Kett, a local landowner. It is said he leads with brutal efficiency – He sends out raiding parties to commandeer cattle and grain to feed the growing horde. He holds a court where prisoners are put on trial and sentenced … some to death.'

Cranmer breathed a deep sigh. 'It is tragic. I pray – we all pray – for wise counsels to prevail but I fear that it will come to fierce fighting, Englishmen against Englishmen. Troops have already been sent from London to restore order. Many of Kett's deluded followers are sure to die at the hands of their own countrymen as their camp is dispersed.'

'No! No!' Involuntarily, I held up a hand as though to ward off the violent images.

'Thomas, what is it? Are you unwell?' Cranmer leaned forward across the table.

'Pardon me, Your Grace. 'Tis just that … well … I fear my son – only a boy the first time away from home … I believe he is on his way to join the rebels!'

The others stared at me without speaking.

The silence was broken by a tap at the door. A servant in royal livery entered. 'Forgive me, Your Grace, there is a messenger arrived who must speak urgently with Sir William.'

When Paget had left the room the archbishop asked, 'Your son, Raphael, involved in this uprising? How can that be?'

I explained the situation Raffy had got himself into and found myself making excuses for him. 'Of course, he does not understand this conflict. At his age issues of right and wrong, justice and injustice seem very simple. Wise counsel looks like weakness. Everything can be solved by headstrong action. And now 'tis leading him into the middle of a war. I must go and find him without delay. Some of my men are already seeking him. I must take some more. I must scour every village and farmstead between Cambridge and Norwich. Whatever is needful …'

Cranmer held up a hand. 'Thomas, you have our sympathy and we will certainly aid you with your quest in any way we can. It should not be difficult for your own servants to catch up with the runaways. There is only one good road from Cambridge to Norwich, much of it across fenland and marsh. Yet there are other ways than pursuit to apprehend Raphael and his companions.' He stood up. 'If you will be good enough to wait a few minutes Master Morice and I will confer about how best we may go about finding your son.'

The two men withdrew to the secretary's room. I crossed the chamber to a window and found myself overlooking the palace's small chapel court. I gave no thought to the scene before me. Too many anxieties were tumbling around in my head. Then I realised that I was looking down at my young king. Edward was walking slowly around the enclosed space or it would be truer to say that he was being walked by the man at his side who had a hand on his shoulder. It was not difficult to recognise the Duke of Somerset, head bent slightly forward and talking earnestly to his nephew, while three attendants, boys of the king's own age, followed a few paces behind. Edward gave every impression of listening respectfully to his uncle's words. There was no doubting where the real power lay but how long would it be, I wondered, before Edward threw off Somerset's tutelage and asserted his royal will? It did not seem so long ago that Raffy had been content to be guided by his father. How quickly children changed, I thought. At that moment a figure appeared from a doorway opposite, bustled up to the Protector and his charge and made obeisance. It was William Paget. Somerset drew him aside and allowed the king – with unconcealed relief – to join his young companions. I heard voices behind me and turned as the archbishop and his secretary re-entered the room.

As we resumed our seats Cranmer said, 'Matters are not so grave as you fear, Thomas – at least, I hope not. I will have letters under royal council seal sent to the sheriffs and justices in Cambridgeshire and Norfolk. They will be ordered to apprehend and hold in custody any university scholars found within their jurisdiction. This will be a more effective way of netting your son and his misguided companions before they reach Norwich.'

'Your Grace is too kind – kinder than I deserve.'

'Nonsense, if we can run to earth this pestilential necromancer who calls himself Parafaustus you will have more than earned any favours it is in my power to bestow. He is an important strand in a web covering much of England.'

'For what purpose, Your Grace?'

'To make the nation ungovernable and thus to bring down the Protector and his government. The centre of this web is not far from where we sit. So you see how vital it is that we can bring in Master Robert Allen for questioning. Please go over again in detail what William West told you about the magician's lair.'

I repeated all I could remember of West's account of his journey from Saffron Walden to his rendezvous with Parafaustus.

Morice unrolled a large sheet of parchment on the table. 'I think we can assume that Allen is making use of some abandoned abbey building. This is a sketch map that was made when the religious houses were being dissolved. It shows all the monastic sites.' He folded the chart so that the eastern parts of England were shown. Saffron Walden is not marked,' he said, 'but 'tis about here.' He laid down a silver penny to mark the place. 'There are three usable roads running from the town.'

'Have we any idea which direction the wagon was travelling?' Cranmer asked.

'West did not say and probably did not know,' I said, 'but I imagine he was being taken farther away from London.'

'He cannot have gone more than twenty miles in the afternoon,' Morice suggested, drawing an imaginary half-circle to the north and east of his marker.

I made a quick reckoning. 'That gives us about fifteen possible locations.'

'We can narrow that down somewhat,' Morice said. 'Langston Nunnery has been converted into a house by Sir George Avery. Cragwell Priory is now used as the parish church. Flangton Abbey ...'

At that moment, the door burst open and Sir William Paget strode in. 'Norwich has been captured by the rebels,' he announced. 'The city is being held to ransom.'

Chapter 5

THE NEWS WAS received in shocked silence. The three of us stared at Paget in disbelief.

'The whole city?' Cranmer asked. 'This is a confirmed report?'

Sir William nodded. 'Doubtless some details remain confused but the main facts are clear. Bartholomew Butler arrived in a lather straight from Norwich, not an hour since.'

'Butler?' Cranmer's face wore a puzzled frown.

'York Herald,' Paget explained. 'sent by the Protector to *negotiate*' – he sneered at the word – 'with the traitors. He says that he confronted the rebel leaders and offered a pardon if they and their men dispersed. Some were eager to trust the royal clemency. Then, this Kett fellow shouted the herald down. "'Tis all a trick," he called out. "We have done no wrong, so need no pardon. The Protector knows our cause is just." He thrust a paper into Butler's hands. I have it here.'

He held up a close-written sheet. 'It lists the rebels' *demands*. Twenty-nine of them, if you please! Shall I read them?'

Without staying for an answer, he recited, '"No manorial lords shall pasture their animals on common land. Land prices are to be fixed at their value in the first year of Henry VII's reign."' He looked up. 'That is sixty-four years ago!'

He resumed. '"No priests shall be suffered to buy land." Kett's peasant parliament would have an end of church patronage: "All parish priests to be appointed by the people and to preach only such things as please them." They will shackle our wool industry by limiting the size of flocks any landowner may graze. They want free fishing in all rivers. And much more of the same.'

He tossed the paper onto the table. 'Thus, would they level all, overthrow traditional rights and customs. What need we of parliament, Council or king when simple men of little substance and less learning shall make all our laws?'

'But what is this news of Kett's men taking control of the city?' Cranmer asked. 'Surely the corporation and the reinforcements sent from London ...'

''Tis true enough,' Paget insisted. 'Straight on Butler's heels comes another messenger from the Mayor of Norwich begging for more military aid. The rebels have ransacked castles and towns in the region for weapons. They brought cannon to bear upon the walls and made breaches. A force of several hundred broke into the city, took possession of the armoury and ran through the streets wielding swords and bows. This is no peasant rabble armed only with staves and pruning-hooks.'

The archbishop sighed. 'This means we shall have to send more troops to restore order. That in its turn means more bloodshed, more innocent but misguided men slaughtered, more women and children made widows and orphans.'

There was both mournfulness and indignation in Paget's voice as he responded. 'The duke is calling a council meeting for tomorrow to agree on the sending of a large military force to retake Norwich. There is no alternative. The decision is forced upon him. If we do not regain the city quickly other Ketts will appear all over the land. Chaos!' He shook his head. 'If only he had listened to me. But nowadays he trusts no one and suspects everyone. Do you know he even uses Henry Stanley of the privy chamber to spy on anyone who exchanges so much as a word with his majesty? Have I not always said that if we maintain order we can consider further reforms from a position of strength. We dare not allow concessions to be forced from us.'

In this debate of high politics, it was almost as though the councillors had forgotten my presence. 'Your Grace,' I said, 'you and

your colleagues have important matters to discuss. By your leave …'
I stood up.

With a rare sign of impatience Cranmer gestured me to remain seated. 'William, before your return, we were considering how to apprehend Robert Allen. Putting a stop to his activities is just as important as regaining control of Norwich – perhaps more so. If we send our best general, the Earl of Warwick, with sufficient force there can be no doubt of military success. But if Allen continues to spread his poisonous prophecies we are like to find ourselves having to defend other towns and cities. We must run him to earth and discover who are his paymasters and supporters here at court. Kett and his ilk are blemishes on the apple's skin. We need to seek out the worms in the core.'

Paget nodded. 'Agreed. What plan have you devised?'

Morice pointed to the map before him. 'Thanks to Master Treviot we now know that Allen has made his base in one of the deserted monasteries in Essex or Suffolk. There can be a very few suitable for his purposes – buildings deserted and far from places of habitation.' He pointed to two sites. 'These are the most likely, though just possibly we should add the old Austin priory of Tinsham to the list. We must make haste to investigate them.'

Paget asked. 'Can we interview West again to help narrow the search?'

'I think not,' I suggested. 'That might arouse suspicion. I suspect my visit to the Tower may have already alerted Allen's associates.' I described that morning's attack.

Paget and Cranmer exchanged glances. Paget said, 'It would be reassuring to be able to regard that as a coincidence but, unfortunately, it fits into a pattern we have come to recognise. Whenever we have come close to unmasking the principals in this business some "accident" has occurred. Informants have disappeared or been silenced.'

'Do you not have your suspicions regarding possible ringleaders?' I asked.

'Oh yes.' Paget's laugh was cynical. 'Unfortunately, the list of suspects is a long one. There are those who dislike the reformed religion. There are those who dislike the Protector. And there are those who dislike both. But this is not to the point. What are we to do? Of a certainty, we must act with speed and guile.'

It was Morice who outlined a course of action. 'I believe I see a way which may help us all. Because of the crisis, there is much traffic between the court and Norwich. One more armed group supposedly riding into Norfolk would not attract much attention. I could lead this party, suitably disguised in part armour as one of his grace's guards. Once well clear of London, we could turn aside to investigate these sites and, God willing, flush out this traitorous necromancer. Now, Master Treviot here also has good reason to go to Norwich in search of his son. Suppose he, too, were to join us – again as a counterfeit soldier. His presence would be valuable since only he has a description of the place we seek. If we lay our hands on Allen we would then split our forces; I to return with the prisoner to London and others to escort Master Treviot to Norwich.'

Cranmer looked doubtful. 'Our adversaries seem to be one step ahead all the time. Apparently they knew that Thomas was on his way here to report to us today about his meeting with West.'

Morice nodded. 'That is certainly possible Your Grace, but they may not know what Thomas discovered from West. Indeed, I rather think that whoever set the ruffians on Thomas did so in the hope of finding out whether or not he had learned anything damaging to their plans. But I agree we must not assume that. We must act swiftly and secretly.'

I listened bemused as the others discussed the details of the projected expedition. However, I was content to allow myself to be caught up in their plans. I could not sit at home doing nothing while Raffy was in danger, so the opportunity to reach Norwich quickly under armed escort was not one I could miss.

As I was rowed downriver around noon with my young rescuers I gave strict instructions to them to say nothing about the attack earlier in the day. On no account were they to mention anything that might alarm Adie. The story we concocted was that I had spotted my followers and invited them to accompany me. However, when we reached Goldsmiths' Row I discovered that my wife had news that, temporarily, at least, had banished from her mind her anxiety about my safety. As soon as I entered the shop she left a customer studying our pattern book and hurried to greet me.

'Wonderful news, Thomas: Ned has woken.'

'That is a great relief. How is the old man?'

'Shaken, and agitated because he cannot remember what happened to him but he is sitting up and has taken some broth.'

'Excellent. I'll go to him straightway.'

'He has been asking for you but you must not tire him out. The doctor insists that he needs rest.'

'Rest' was not a word that I readily associated with my old friend. It certainly did not describe the scene that confronted me when I entered his chamber. Ned, propped erect by pillows was speaking slowly to Lizzie who sat beside the bed with a silverpoint rod and prepared parchment writing down what the patient was saying.

The scribe looked up with relief. 'Here, Thomas, you can finish this. I am too slow at my letters.'

Ned shook his head and the movement made him grimace. 'No need, Lizzie, you are doing excellent well and sanicle was the last ingredient.'

'What are you doing?' I asked. 'Has this become a schoolroom?'

'More like an apothecary's shop,' Lizzie responded. 'This hasty-witted manikin trusts not in physicians but must dose himself. He must needs have me order this concoction from the Flemish apothecary in Candlewick Street.'

'He is the best in London – perhaps in Europe,' Ned muttered. 'Though any novice should know that a balm of self-heal, sanicle and oil of roses is a sovereign cure for skull wounds and headaches.'

Lizzie stood up. 'I leave you with this peevish fellow.' She tossed her loose hair. 'I must away to do his highness's bidding.'

As the door closed behind her I sat on the vacant stool and looked closely at the man in the bed. His face was almost paper-white and carried a moist sheen The eyes, usually sparkling, had a duller glow than usual.

'I'm relieved that you are here,' Ned said. 'I have something important to tell you.'

'What is that?'

He screwed up his eyes and replied through gritted teeth, 'I cannot remember!'

'You must not fret yourself,' I said gently. 'You will recall it in time.'

He ignored the comment. 'I know we went to the Tower. I know we spent time with one of the prisoners. I know some of the things he said. And I know something was not right. Oh! What was it?' His fists on the coverlet clenched in frustration.

'My dear friend, you …'

Ned glared at me. 'If you tell me not to worry, I swear on my immortal soul that I will leave this bed and walk all the way to the Tower to talk with this man again.'

I laid a hand on one of his. 'If that be the case I must humour you. What would you have me do?'

'Tell me everything that passed between the prisoner and ourselves … everything we talked about … everything he said.'

'Very well, but,' I wagged a finger at him, 'if I see you getting too tired I will leave you to rest and, if necessary, I will have you strapped down.' That, at last, brought a smile to the old man's face.

As best as I could, I gave an account yet again of our interview with William West. Ned listened, eyes closed, nodding slightly from time to time. When I had finished he gave a long sigh. 'No, it will not come. Now, Thomas have you reported all this to the archbishop?'

'Yes, I have been with him all morning.'

'Tell me about it.'

He was not to be denied, so I described what had happened at Hampton Court.

This time, Ned responded with brief comments during the narration: 'Ah.' 'I see.' 'Can that be so?' When I had finished he made a gesture of annoyance. 'So many loose ends. Difficult to see how they connect. But of course, they must.' He smiled. 'Thank you, Thomas. That has been useful … given my addled brain something to get to grips with.' He closed his eyes. 'But now I think I will take your advice and rest.'

I rose and went to the door. As my hand was on the latch there came a croak from the bed. 'Torture! It has to do with torture, Thomas. Think on that.'

I had dinner served in our chamber so that Adie and I could talk privately. She, of course, wanted to know about my meeting with the archbishop and I had to prepare her for my imminent departure. I was careful to say nothing about Robert Allen. I did not want to re-ignite our argument about black magic. Instead, I presented a slightly coloured account of the decision to travel to Norwich.

47

'You were right about his grace's appreciation of my services,' I said. 'And he indicated that he would like to meet Raffy. He is providing me with an armed escort in order to go in search of the boy.'

She stared gloomily across the table. 'This is all so terrible and confusing. I know not what to think. Sometimes I am angry with the rebels – and with Raffy for getting involved with them. And then I feel sorry for what the common folk are suffering and I feel a little proud of your son for wanting to help them. Oh, Thomas, why is everything in this mess?'

'I think because so much has changed in such a short time. The new religion has come in and people know not what to believe. Most are content to accept the Protector's plain church with all its paintings and statues and the like removed as "superstitious". But others feel a great sense of loss.'

'You know about the trouble at St Mary Woolnoth last Sunday?'

'I heard some people in the shop talking about it. What exactly happened?'

'The bishop sent along one of his men to preach the sermon. As soon as he went into the pulpit the parish priest ordered all the bells to be rung and the choir to sing. What with all the yowling and clanging people say 'twas worse than a hundred Bedlams. 'Twould be funny if 'twas not so sad.'

'Aye, but sadder is the confusion in the countryside. When all the monks and nuns were cast out their estates and houses, they were taken over by a horde of new landlords who knew little and cared less about the old customs. They only want their pastures and arable to be as profitable as possible.'

'So you do agree with Raffy, then. He says all right-thinking people must stand up for those whose livelihoods are threatened.'

'I fully understand his indignation at the cruelty and injustice of the new men but to take drastic action ... well, 'tis rather like your tale of the preacher and the priest. The only outcome is chaos. By the way, what happened to the priest at St. Mary's Woolnoth?'

'He is in the bishop's prison and like to stay there for a long time. Oh, Thomas, I pray that you can get Raffy out of all this. I shall not rest easy until you are both returned safely.'

'We shall, Dearling, you will see. Now that we have the help of the archbishop's men it will not take long to find Raffy.'

◊

The city still slept when I set out the following morning well before dawn for my rendezvous with Ralph Morice and the members of the archbishop's guard. We had decided that if I was being closely watched it would be several hours before my absence from Goldsmiths' Row would be noticed. That, we hoped, would give us a good start in our quest for Parafaustus. I rode at a fast trot along Cheapside, Lombard Street, and Fish Street. As I approached the bridge I saw that my escort was already there – twenty or so mounted men gathered under the gate arch.

Ralph urged his horse forward and greeted me. 'Well met, Thomas.'

'I hope I have not kept you long waiting.'

'No, but we must get under way quickly. The sooner we start the better and the men will be glad to be on the move. It has been a cold, clear night.'

'And another hot day to follow, I'll wager. We should cover as many miles as we can before the sun is high.'

A trooper rode forward carrying a bundle wrapped in a riding cloak.

'Your disguise,' Morice said.

With expert help I exchanged my own outer garments for breastplate and helmet, tabard and cloak bearing the archbishop's insignia. Then we set off, clattering through the quiet streets and leaving the city via Bishopgate. Not wanting to tire the horses, we travelled at a steady trot and did not rest until we had put several miles behind us. Only when we reached Bishop's Stortford did we stop to break our fast.

It was as we sat on a bench outside the alehouse close by the hospital that I questioned Morice about something that had been puzzling me – Ned's reference to 'torture'.

'Is it true that the Lord Chancellor carried out West's interrogation in person?'

'Yes. I believe Baron Rich went to the Tower two or three times.'

'And employed torture?'

'Yes, he was accompanied by his predecessor, Thomas Wriothesley, now Earl of Southampton. He is an expert in what is politely called "persuasion".'

'Oh, aye, he is notorious for cruelty and persecution.'

'Indeed. If anyone could make West talk it would be Wriothesley and Rich.'

'And yet they failed.'

'Yes, which indicated either that West knew nothing or that he was far too frightened to tell what he did know. We were all baffled. You, Thomas, were our last hope of getting at the truth. But why all these questions?'

'Because I cannot understand why a case of attempted murder – and it is only *attempted*; Lord De La Warr is still alive and well – why it is so important to the council as to require personal investigation by the senior law officer of the realm?'

'Poison and sorcery in high places are serious matters. It needs only a few creatures like Allen to create mayhem. We have to do all we can to stop them. All magistrates have been alerted to keep watch for magicians and his grace has charged the diocesan bishop to be vigilant. And now we must be on the road again.'

He made to rise but I laid a hand on his arm. 'No, Ralph, the time for putting me off with half-answers is past. I am too far into this business. Why is this West affair so important to the archbishop? In God's name, give me a plain answer. Have I not done enough to earn your trust?'

Morice sighed and nodded. ''Tis justly said, Thomas. You do merit a fuller explanation though I swear on my sacred oath it was as much for your own safety as for any "political" reason that we did not confide in you completely.' He lowered his voice though there was no one close enough to hear our conversation. 'In very truth there is little I can add to what you already know or have guessed.' He stood up. Come, let us walk a few paces along the road. My legs are stiff from our long ride.'

We moved away from the group of troopers sitting on the grass finishing their cheese and ale.

'When blessed King Henry died,' Morice began, 'he entrusted the realm to a council of regency until his son should come of age. The members of the council agreed that, for the sake of good government, real power should be vested in one person.'

'The Duke of Somerset.'

'Yes. It was always understood that the Protector would act in consort with his colleagues.'

'But, in fact, he has become increasingly dictatorial. This everyone knows.'

'What everyone does not realise is the dilemma this creates for the other members of the council. Should they challenge the duke's policies, even threaten to overthrow them, or bear things patiently until his majesty comes of age?'

'I suspect his grace is of the latter persuasion.'

'Indeed, as is Paget, the Earl of Warwick, the Lord Chancellor and some half of the council. Others would like to unseat the Protector and call on Princess Mary to be regent. We know that she receives envoys from Emperor Charles at her retreat in Norfolk. If she were installed in power with the backing of an imperial army...'

'The changes in religion of the last fifteen years would be reversed. England would once more be under the pope's authority.'

'Exactly.'

'Now I see why the archbishop is so worried. His would be the first head to roll. But what has all this to do with ...'

'Lord De La Warr and his nephew? I wish I knew the answer to that question. Perhaps by the end of today, we shall know. When we heard that West had been arrested by order of parliament and was to be tried by attainder we were shocked and puzzled.'

'Because De La Warr could have disinherited West and had him tried in the king's courts.'

'Exactly. But a hearing in open court before a jury could be inconvenient to West's enemies – whoever they are. He would be free to speak in his own defence and, after the trial, the matter would be over. The accused would be a free man or a dead man. Attainder ensures West's silence and also means that he can be held indefinitely and subject to increasing pressure.'

'Ah, now I begin to see more clearly. West told me he was urged to name names; to accuse others involved in necromancy and conspiracy.'

'Yes and the objective must be to undermine the Protector.'

'How, exactly?'

''Tis quite simple – Guilt by association; an old political trick. West is of no importance but he has many friends at court – men like Sir John Cheke, his majesty's tutor. If Somerset's enemies could build up an atmosphere of fear and suspicion, they could suggest that the king is surrounded by undesirable companions and have them removed. Every royal servant dismissed from the privy chamber and the council could then be replaced by someone of the opposite party.'

'How devious.'

'Devious and destructive. John Chrysostom, one of the early fathers of the church, described calumny as worse than cannibalism. A savage may feast on his enemy's body; a slander monger devours his reputation.'

We turned to walk back to our companions.

'You referred to West's enemies "whoever they are",' I said. 'You must have some idea.'

'Nothing we can act on. That is why today's expedition is vital,' Morice said. 'In my opinion, West knows nothing of the plot which threatens to destroy him but Allen does. He can tell us who is behind it. All we need is a name. Pray God we find him.'

Through the early afternoon, we rode northwards. Leaving Saffron Walden behind us we went in search of our first location. We had identified three possible sites for Allen's lair and I felt increasingly nervous as the day wore on. I knew that Morice and the archbishop were relying on me to identify the place, but West had only given me scant details of it. Would I recognise it if I saw it?

The first, Tinsham Priory, presented no problem. When we arrived we discovered a scene of great activity. Twenty or so men were attacking the conventual buildings with picks and hammers and loading stone onto wagons. The workmen stopped and stared with obvious anxiety at the troopers.

'What is happening here?' Morice called to the man who seemed to be in charge of the demolition.

The countryman stepped forward and inclined his head respectfully. 'Taking stone for road repairs. We have Sir John's permission. The road up Hambley Hill is impassable most winters.'

'No one lives here, then?' Morice enquired.

'Here?' The man laughed. 'Why no, not since them idle monks packed their bags, ten years since.'

'Then we will leave you to your labour,' Morice replied. 'It is good to see this stone put to such excellent use.' He gave the signal for us to ride on.

Our next stop proved equally fruitless. Trittisham Abbey stood adjacent to its village and sheep grazed amid the doorless, window-bereft buildings. This certainly did not tally with West's description of a place far from human habitation.

The light was beginning to fade as were my spirits when we approached the once impressive Benedictine house of Thraxley. A rough wooden barrier had been set up where the doors of the gatehouse had once hung. Three of Cranmer's men had little difficulty in pulling it to one side so that we could all pass through in single file. Once within the grounds, I held up a hand to motion everyone to a halt.

Before us lay a long-weed-strewn drive lined with elms. At the end, we could see a formidable grey wall.

'I think this may be the place,' I said quietly.

Chapter 6

WE DISMOUNTED, TETHERED our horses and walked cautiously down the drive, keeping in the shadow cast by the lowering sun. With each step towards the windowless curtain wall which lay ahead, I felt a mounting sensation of something which went beyond curiosity or excitement about what we might discover within this long-abandoned place. Here monks had been wont to offer their repeated cycles of pious prayer. And here a dabbler in demonology had taken possession of their sacred cloister. My feelings were undoubtedly affected by the atmosphere pervading the old abbey at that tenebrous hour. The day's sultry heat lingered. There was not the slightest sound of a bird or earth-bound creature. The sky above staged a silent, lurid conflict between black westering clouds presaging storm and wispy mares-tails yellowed by the declining sun. At the end of the avenue the drive turned left to flank the wall, while, to the right, the creeping vegetation had reached the building.

'This way?' Morice pointed along the drive.

I stared up at the bare stone hoping for some clue. Then, looking to the right I noticed some clumps of fallen masonry and recalled that West had mentioned something of the sort. I took a few paces in that direction and saw a low postern door.

I pointed it out to Morice. 'That must be where West went in.'

'It looks very solid,' he replied. 'It may be that there is an easier entrance.'

He went over and spoke to the guard captain. After a brief exchange, two groups of men were dispatched, one in each direction, to circuit the wall. The rest of us settled to wait.

Morice gazed up through the overhanging branches. 'We must get in before the light fades. Perhaps we should try that door. It may, perchance, be unlocked.' He spoke to the guard captain. 'send someone to try the handle, very quietly.'

We watched as a sergeant and four troopers, all with drawn swords, approached the postern. The leader stretched a hand towards the large iron ring. The next instant he leapt back with a cry of alarm. He pointed at something on the ground. Then, all five men, shouting and calling, ran back to where we stood.

'Stop this caterwauling!' The captain glared angrily at his men.

He was met with a gibbering response.

'We dare not!'

''Tis the evil eye!'

'There's a curse on anyone entering.'

'Aye, a curse! Evil eye!'

'Evil eye! Evil eye!'

'In God's name, keep your voices down.' The captain drew his sword. 'The next man to say "evil eye" will feel the wrong end of this. Now, you, Carter, tell me quietly what all this is about.'

The sergeant responded with a quavering voice. ''Tis true, Sir. There's no going that way. Someone has left a warning. You may see for yourself. But for sweet Jesu's sake, go not too close.'

'That will I,' the captain responded. 'I'll not have men under my command behaving like gibbering cowards. Wait here – and not a word from any of you. Belike we have already alerted whoever is inside.'

He stepped forward. Morice and I went with him. As we drew near to the postern the captain pointed with his sword to something on the ground. Before the door, there was a circle of white-painted stones. In the centre was something we could not make out until we were close.

'Ah, I see.' Morice nodded gravely. 'Very clever. 'Tis certainly enough to warn off most simple-minded folks.'

On a piece of wood, some twelve inches square, someone had painted, in garish red and black, an open, staring eye. I must confess my heart missed a beat as I stared at the menacing image.

Not so Ralph Morice, personal secretary to the senior bishop of the English church. 'There is one way with this devilish nonsense.' He kicked at the stones, scattering them among the weeds and ferns. Then he bent down, picked up the sinister talisman and flung it away among the trees. 'Now,' he said, rubbing his hands on his cloak. 'let us see if we can discover what secrets this devilry was meant to protect.' He grasped the iron ring and turned it. He set his shoulder to the oak and pushed.

I watched and thought he had made no impression on the barrier.

But Morice leaned against it again. 'There is some movement,' he muttered. 'Come, lend me your weight.'

The captain and I joined him. Straining with all our force, we managed to open the door an inch or two.

'There must be something stacked against it,' the captain suggested. 'What we need is a battering ram.' He waved to his men, who came forward with little obvious enthusiasm. 'See what you can find to have this door down,' he ordered.

As they spread out to search the undergrowth their companions who had been sent to explore the site returned. They reported that the main gate and two other entrances were securely locked and that the wall was still intact.

'And no sign of anyone about?' Morice asked anxiously.

All the troopers replied that they had not seen anything that would suggest the abbey was inhabited.

'Nevertheless, we must be on our guard. If Allen is here we must not let him slip through our fingers. Captain, may we have a couple of men sent to each door to keep watch?'

The order was given and a few minutes later the foragers returned with a moss-covered length of tree trunk some ten feet long.

The captain divided his men into teams. 'A groat for the first one inside,' he called out.

The men fell to their task with a will, the prospect of gain overcoming their fear of magic. Each blow with the ram made the door shudder and the opening did widen. But, though each team, in turn, threw in all their effort, it was several minutes before, with a resounding crash, whatever had been holding the door fell inwards and a swarthy trooper with a red beard gave a triumphant shout and leapt through the opening into the darkness beyond.

'Find another door!' Morice shouted.

Moments of confusion and oath-shouting followed as the invaders blundered about, bumping into each other and into furniture but at last pale light entered the room as an internal door was thrown open.

'Spread out! Thorough search of all buildings!' the captain ordered.

His men dispersed into the abbey's courtyard. Morice and I stood in the doorway and watched them.

'It seems we have missed our quarry,' Morice observed gloomily.

'I think not. Look!' I pointed to the hearth. In the gloom, we could just make out wisps of smoke rising from a pile of ash.

'By all the saints!' Morice cried. 'Burning evidence! He cannot be far. I will go and take the others. Stay and see if you can discover anything useful.

I found candles on a table and even located a lantern. With the aid of this light, I explored the room. The alchemist's debris was strewn over the table and the floor, much of it smashed by the tramping feet of our troops. There were jars and books and distilling apparatus and pestles and mortars and implements whose use I could only guess at. I turned my attention, first of all to the fireplace. There was a scattering of papers, some partly burnt, which had escaped the flames. I rescued all I could and set them on the table. On the first that came to hand I read out the following instruction: "When you go forth to play at the cards and dice let the Ascendant be in a sign moveable, such as ♈ or ♋ or ♎ or ♑.* And let the lord of the Ascendant be well disposed in a good place and let the 7 house be feeble and impotent … "Pah, what yammering nonsense is this?' I muttered.

'Nonsense that the credulous will pay good coin for,' Morice replied reappearing at my side. He carefully turned over the charred leaves. 'Much of this I have seen before. Here is a spell for finding buried treasure and the plan for a magic circle used to summon aerial spirits. But what have we here? He peered closely at a printed sheet, the title page of a pamphlet: "A True Prophecy whereby it shall be known when His Majesty Edward VI shall suffer Death revealed to Master Magus Parafaustus". This will be …'

---

*   Zodiac signs for Aries, Cancer, Libra or Capricorn

At that moment, a tall trooper appeared breathless at the door. 'Come quick, Masters,' he panted. 'We have seen him!'

We followed him around the outer perimeter of the abbey to a door on the far side, which stood wide open.

'Where is he?' I demanded.

'He made for the wood yonder,' the young man replied, indicating a line of trees beyond some fifty yards of open ground. 'Ben Turner went after him.'

'Find the captain!' Morice shouted as we set off in pursuit of our quarry. 'I want everyone to search the woods. And hurry. There is little daylight left.'

We ran as fast as we could across a space where ferns, nettles and briars clutched at our legs. Once among the trees, where the undergrowth was more sparse, we paused, listening for any sounds. Hearing nothing, we called out, 'Ben, where are you?' An answering cry came from somewhere ahead and to the left. We set off in that direction shouting repeatedly until we found the guardsman. He lay sprawled at the bottom of a steep incline and was struggling to get to his feet.

'Sorry, Masters. I lost him. Didn't mark that dip in the ground. 'Tis getting too dark to see anything much.'

We helped the man to an oak stump and seated him there.

'Which way did Allen go?' Morice asked.

Trooper Turner pointed to the left.

'Very well, Master Treviot and I will follow. Do keep calling out to attract the others. Have them follow us.'

Immediately we resumed the chase. The chances of success were slim. Progress was slow in the half light and the threatened storm now burst upon us. Heavy rain bent the foliage above and fell upon us. I sensed that we were running almost parallel to the west wall of the monastery and this was confirmed when we came upon a break that had been cut through the woods. Looking along it to the left we could see the abbey wall.

'Which way?' Morice stopped to regain his breath. 'God's blood, we must not lose him now!'

'I will fetch our horses,' I said. 'We can ride along this open way and cover the ground more quickly.'

I raced away along the break, found my way to the drive by which we had entered and ran to the gatehouse. A shock awaited me.

The horses were not where we had tethered them. They were ambling freely about the drive and the neighbouring fields. It was immediately clear what must have happened. Allen had escaped and, to hamper our pursuit, had untied the horses, probably taking one for his own flight.

I gathered up the reins of the first four animals I could find, mounted one and, leading the others, hurried back to where I had left Morice. I found him sheltering under a thick-boughed oak. Several of the troopers had joined him.

'Curse the cunning devil's spawn!' he cried when I explained the situation. 'Now we are helpless till morning, by which time he might be anywhere.'

There was, indeed, nothing to be done but gather the rest of our wandering mounts (As I suspected, Allen had stolen one of them for his getaway) and then make ourselves comfortable for the night. We chose the abbey refectory for our lodging. It was a long, barrel-vaulted hall with three fireplaces and the men soon had collected branches blazing in each of them. They dried their sodden cloaks and gathered round in groups to talk and sleep. Meanwhile, Morice and I returned to Allen's chamber and collected up all the books and papers the magus had not been able to burn.

'I must return with them to the archbishop. There may yet be some scraps of information which will link Allen to his paymasters,' Morice said.

I found some string and tied the loose sheets into a bundle for Morice to pack in a saddlebag. 'After all this effort 'tis a pity he 'scaped us.'

'Well, we have flushed him out. When his grace alerts the local magistrates I doubt not he will be run to earth.'

'Perhaps he is making for Norwich in hope to find protection among the rebels,' I suggested.

'If so, he will have jumped from the cauldron to the fire. When the Earl of Warwick arrives with his little army there will be great slaughter of any who fail to surrender.'

'It is certain that the earl will command this force?'

'Who else? He is by far our best general.'

'Hmm!'

Morice looked up sharply from buckling the saddlebag. 'What does "Hmm" mean?'

'Just that there are some in the City who wonder if Warwick is no longer in favour. It is noted that he spends much time in the country and is rarely at court.'

'Then I hope, Thomas, that you will use your influence to stamp on such rumours. The Protector understands well the size of the problem in Norfolk and what must needs be done to solve it.'

I did not pursue the subject though I might have pointed out that many in our civic community of merchants and lawyers were often more accurately informed of affairs at court than Morice might care to acknowledge.

I returned to the refectory and found a place near one of the fires. Folding my cloak to make a pillow I laid down thankfully. It had been a long and exhausting day. Before I drifted into sleep I could not help hearing the conversation of three young members of the archbishop's guard, lying nearby They were discussing our vanished quarry.

One: 'What think you of this sorcerer?'

Two: 'That I would like to make him feel the flat of my sword – the horse-thief.'

One: 'But what of his conjuring of evil spirits?'

Two: 'Mystical nonsense to impress old women and love-sick wenches wanting potions to get their men into bed.'

Three: 'Nonsense, say you? You jumped out of your skin when you saw that evil eye.'

(Laughter)

Two: ''Twas just the surprise of the thing. I've no belief in evil spirits.'

Three: 'Best not let his grace hear you say that. He'll show you that the Bible is full of Satans and demons and such.'

Two: 'Oh, and I suppose he'll tell me there's fairies and goblins and foliots and Robin Goodfellows in the Bible and I must believe in them, too.'

One: 'Them's different. The likes of them cause murrain in cattle and kill babies in the womb. That is why we need our white witches and our cunning men.'

Two: 'Well, I'll not believe such country clodpoles' tales.'

One: 'So how do *you* explain all the evil in the world?'

I know not whether they resolved their argument, which was still running when I slipped thankfully into sleep.

The next morning Morice returned southwards with most of the archbishop's men while I set off for Norwich, by way of Thetford with an escort of five troopers. I was soon glad of their protection. In several of the villages, we were met with sullen stares. In Attleborough, a woman shouted from an upstairs window. 'Guards for the rich men against the commons! Devil take you all!' In Windham, there was a barrier across the road and a group of burly countrymen demanded, 'Money for the champions of the poor in Norwich'. My companions would have drawn their swords and forced a way through but I stopped them and tossed some coins into the cap being held out. Such incidents were alarming but what was worse was the traffic. Beyond Windham, we covered scarcely a mile without overtaking at least one group of men and women heading towards the city. It was like the Exodus of the Jews from Egypt – only in reverse. The dust-begrimed travellers, some on foot, some in wagons might have been pilgrims heading for a holy shrine. I wanted to shout a warning – 'Stop, you will be killed if you join the rebels in Norwich'. Had I done so it is likely that I and my companions would have been the ones facing a violent death.

Amid all this chaos and the threat of certain imminent disaster my only real concern was for my son. Where was Raffy? Was he somewhere in this dreary cavalcade of bedraggled humanity? Had he already reached the rebel encampment? Was he even now among the recruits of Robert Kett's doomed army. Intently I studied the faces of everyone we passed. Whenever I saw groups of very young men and boys I called out, 'Are you from Cambridge?' or 'Have you come across any university students?' The only responses were shaken heads or uncomprehending stares.

As we drew near to Norwich towards the end of the day I had to face up to the fact that I had no idea what I would do when I reached it. I had been so absorbed with seeking Raffy that I had made no plans for myself. It would be very ill-advised of me to enter the city. Yet, if I did not do so, how could I continue my quest? I decided that my most prudent course would be to find someone with local knowledge who might be able to advise me and whom I could safely approach for information. Having enquired at an inn who were the most substantial landowners in the area, I was directed to Ketteringham Hall, home of Sir Anthony Heveningham.

Turning aside from the highway we followed a narrow lane which led directly to a squat gatehouse whose solid portal was firmly shut. We rang the bell hanging beside it and in response the side door opened just wide enough to allow the keeper to peer out.

'We are from the archbishop,' I said, 'and would be grateful if Sir Anthony could give us a little of his time.'

Wordlessly the door closed. We waited. We let our horses nibble the grass along the track's edge. And we waited.

'Nervous of strangers,' one of my companions suggested. 'No wonder with all that's going on hereabouts.'

'Perhaps the gentry of Norfolk are just not very hospitable,' I said.

I gathered up the reins and turned my mount's head away from the house.

At that moment, with a rattling of chains and bolts, the gates opened. I have seldom seen a more bizarre figure than the man who stood in the gap. He was about fifty, straggle-bearded and crowned with an unkempt frenzy of grey hair. He wore no doublet and his shirt lay open to the waist. But what was most alarming that he was brandishing an arquebus and the match was smouldering.

He advanced a couple of paces. 'I'll have no heretics here!' he yelled.

At that moment, he stumbled. The gun went off with an enormous bang. Fortunately, it was pointing skywards and no harm was done but it scared the horses. Two reared and the others skittered around. By the time I had calmed my mare and turned my attention back to the man I assumed to be the master of Ketteringham Hall other figures had appeared in the gateway. A lady in a pink kirtle had one hand on Sir Anthony's shoulder while gently easing the gun from his grasp with the other. She handed it to one of the two servants standing beside her.

I saluted her. 'I am sorry if we have caused such distress.'

She smiled wearily. 'Please forgive my husband. He is unwell. The recent troubles ...'

'I quite understand,' I said. 'Life must be very difficult for you at the moment. I, too am much affected by the rebellion. It is that that brings me from London.'

'Then you must come in. If we can be of any service we will.'

Servants directed us to the stable yard and then to the kitchen where our hostess ordered a simple meal to be set before us. When we had eaten, the lady, who introduced herself as Mary Heveningham, led me to the sparsely furnished great hall. The house was of the old style and most activities, I judged, were carried out in this large space whose bare stones reached up to an unusually intricate hammer beam roof. Despite the summer heat, chill draughts moved through the hall and a pile of logs blazed and crackled in the large fireplace. I guessed that Sir Anthony and his family were not able to live in the style enjoyed by their forebears.

As though reading my thoughts, Mary Heveningham explained. 'I fear we are not accustomed to entertaining guests. Not here. Our main house is some miles away. We have come here to escape the trouble – because of my condition.' She patted her stomach which was just beginning to swell.

We were seated before the fire, within the glow of torches which flamed in wall sconces above.

I was puzzled. 'You come *here* to escape these disturbances?'

She laughed. 'Yes, that must seem strange. We have very little land here and do not farm it. In Suffolk, we keep several hundred sheep. That makes us a target for the hedge-breakers. Though our neighbours here suffer much from Master Kett's rabble we are not pestered – not yet. Oh, Master Treviot, this chaos reaches ever wider. When will it stop?' Her brow creased in an anxious frown.

Lady Mary was, I thought, in her mid-thirties, pale of complexion, though her features were strong. She was obviously carrying heavy burdens.

'I think we may safely say that Kett will very soon be either dead or in irons. I trust you will be left in peace to have your child and tend your husband. What ails him?'

She sighed. 'I know not. Neither, it seems, do any of the many physicians we have paid to answer that question. No potions work. I try to keep him in his chamber with his books. They, at least, provide him with some solace. He is of a melancholy humour but also given to sudden bouts of rage. The doctors say that is an unusual combination. Today, for example, it was the word "archbishop" that threw him into a frenzy. Anthony likes not the new religion. When he heard that you and your men wore Cranmer's livery ... well, you saw his reaction. The only cure the medical men can counsel is rest. He sleeps much and is always the better for it – until the next attack. But enough of our problems. What brings you here and how may we help you?'

I explained how I had come in search of my son who had absconded from Cambridge with other empty-headed youngsters. When I mentioned the name of Raffy's tutor Lady Heveningham looked up with wide eyes.

'Robert Segden, did you say?'

'Yes.'

'Well, now, there's a strange thing.'

Chapter 7

'DO YOU KNOW Robert?' I asked.

'If he is Robert, the son of John and Susannah Segden of Peasanhall, yes, we do know him.'

'I think he must be the same person. He certainly comes from Suffolk.'

'We have not seen him for some years since he left to study at Cambridge. He was always bookish – a quiet, shy boy, as I recall.'

'Are you still in contact with his parents?'

'Yes, indeed. We count them among our friends. Oh!' She gasped as a new thought struck her. 'I wonder if they know he has become involved with the rebels. We must write to tell them.'

'I would not want you to alarm them unnecessarily. I have no idea where Robert is now. I know he will be trying to deflect my son and his companions from joining Kett's host in Norwich.' A sudden hopeful possibility entered my mind and I hastened to grasp it. 'I wonder if he might have turned them aside from the Norwich road – taken them to visit his parents. They would have been tired and hungry after trudging from Cambridge.'

'We can certainly enquire. I will send a message.'

'That would be a great kindness. Yet I am loth to await a reply. The Earl of Warwick is already on his way here with an army of hardened soldiers.'

At that, Mary Heveningham looked up with wide eyes. 'The great Warwick is coming? The general who captured Boulogne and quelled the Scots? Oh, the Lord be praised! We shall see an end of this turmoil.'

'There will, I fear, be terrible bloodshed when he arrives and I need to find my son before then.'

'Yes, of course, but you should not venture into the city unless you really believe he might be there. Let me make enquiry of our friends. Peasenhall is only forty miles away. If I dispatch a messenger at first light we should have a reply 'ere nightfall or the next day at the latest. Meanwhile you and your escort are welcome to stay here. I fear we can offer scant hospitality but …'

'I would not put you to that trouble. I fear Sir Anthony will not want the archbishop's men beneath his roof.'

Lady Heveningham insisted that she would pacify her husband but I had no wish to take unfair advantage of her hospitality. At last, we agreed on a compromise: I would stay at Ketteringham in the hope of receiving news of Raffy but Cranmer's men would return to London the following day.

I could not wait in idleness and spent the morrow in more anxious searching in the neighbourhood. I scanned the groups of people heading, it seemed, in ever greater numbers for the city. I enquired in inns and alehouses. I called on the local magistrate. No one had news of a group of Cambridge students – or if they had they were unwilling to share it. In the evening, I returned to Ketteringham Hall hoping that Lady Mary's friends had replied to her letter and not daring to hope that they might have something to report about Raffy. No such letter had been received that day. Nor the next.

By Friday 29 July I could wait no longer. Having spent four nights and three wasted days at Ketteringham I had to resume my journey to Norwich. It was while I was fastening my saddlebag that a lathered horse cantered into the stable yard and the boy I recognised as Mary Heveningham's messenger jumped from the saddle. I followed him into the kitchen and saw him deliver a letter to his mistress. She beckoned me into the hall and I sat watching impatiently while she read. One reason for the delay in Susannah Segden's response was immediately apparent. The epistle covered three sheets of paper and must have taken some time to compose. As I watched Mary Heveningham's response it was evident that the news was not good. At last, she handed the letter to me without comment. This is what I read:

> To my good friend Lady Mary Heveningham greeting.
> I was pleased to learn how you and my lord, your
> husband fare in these greatly troubled times. Here every
> day brings news of fresh disasters ...

There followed several lines describing outrages suffered by the Segdens and their neighbours. I scanned them quickly until my eyes fell upon the name 'Robert'.

> Whereas you are pleased to enquire about our elder son
> Robert what I can tell you is that he too has suffered the
> impudence and cruelty of the rabble. He is not here nor
> yet in Cambridge where he is employed as tutor to the
> son of a London merchant. He has been travelling with
> a group of students and we had word from him not four
> days since at Windham*. He and his charges were staying
> at the Green Dragon inn when one of his friends fell
> sick. Obliged to extend their stay and to pay for potions
> from an apothecary they soon emptied their purses.
> Robert sent to us for money. Husband John set out
> straightway to go to their relief. He is just returned and
> tells of knavery and thievery you would scarce believe.
> There was no sick friend. The young men were being
> kept prisoner until they might find money for their
> release. The money was for the monster Kett who now
> as we are told keeps court at Norwich ...

The letter rambled on but there was nothing more of interest to me. Its content was both encouraging and frustrating. It told me that Segden had found Raffy and his friends but not why he had failed to make them change their plans or what the group was doing now.

I handed the letter back to Lady Heveningham. 'Your friend writes nothing of what has become of Robert and his companions. Are they still held in Windham? Have Kett's leeches sucked all they

*   Wymondham

can from their hostages and let them go? Have they seen sense and returned to Cambridge?'

She shook her head. 'Who can say? God grant your son and his friends now see what manner of men these rogues are. Windham is not a good place to be. 'Tis Kett's town where all this turmoil started. The people there are ardent for their local hero.'

'Aye, I was stopped there and money demanded. 'Tis a bear pit of rebellion and now I must go back there in hope to find Raffy or pick up his trail.'

I said my goodbyes and thanks, then hurried out to the stable yard. Within the hour, I had handed my mare to the groom at the sign of the Green Dragon. I went into the inn and found myself a seat at a corner table, aware as I crossed the room that several eyes were scrutinising this stranger closely. Though it was early in the day the hostelry was half full with men, all of whom seemed to be engaged in earnest conversation. It was not fanciful to detect at atmosphere about the place – zealous, determined, conspiratorial – and hostile towards any who did not share its commitment to change society. I ordered ale and sipped it slowly, trying to decide how I could go about my enquiries. If I asked questions of these people I would undoubtedly arouse their suspicion. I did not care to imagine where that might lead.

At that moment, someone passing my table dropped his platter of food. As he crouched down to gather up his bread and cheese he whispered, 'Master Treviot, meet me in the abbey churchyard.' Then he moved on to sit at another table with his back to me.

I continued slowly sipping my ale and puzzling who this man was who knew my name. He seemed familiar but I had caught only a brief glance and he had deliberately – or so it seemed – kept his face away from me. Whoever he was, he presumably had news for me and that I could not ignore. I brushed aside the thought that I might be heading into a trap, emptied my tankard and casually sauntered out into the street. I headed in the direction of the church whose tower was clearly visible above the roofs. The abbey grounds were extensive and presented a prospect of decay. Piles of stone indicated where the monks' living quarters had once stood. The eastern end of the church which had been reserved for the Benedictines was, itself, partly demolished, leaving only the nave for the worship of the parishioners. It was not difficult to understand why there should be so much bitterness and resentment simmering in the town. The economic impact of the dissolution of the monastery must have been immense. This important religious centre had, as long as anyone could remember, brought visitors and wealth into Windham as well as providing jobs for local people. The ruins which surrounded me as I walked towards the church must provide, I reflected, a daily goad to the inhabitants, prompting their rejection of any changes being imposed by local grandees.

For several minutes I wandered alone amid the desolation, looking for my anonymous contact. At last, a figure appeared on the edge of a small grove standing close to what was left of the old curtain wall. The man waved, then disappeared among the trees. I moved cautiously in that direction, one hand on the knife at my belt. I entered the copse and before my eyes accustomed themselves to the shade I heard my name again.

'Master Treviot! Saints be praised, it is you, Master.'

'Matt!' Now I recognised one of the stable hands I had sent with Robert Segden and Walt, the ostler, to find Raffy.

Overwhelmed with relief, I embraced him warmly, which must have embarrassed him, for he stood, awkward and silent, for several seconds.

'Come, man,' I urged. 'Tell me everything. Are the others all here with you? How is my son? Are you all safe?'

Still he hesitated. 'Well, Master, so much has happened I know not where to start.'

'Start at the beginning; that were best.'

'Aye.' Matt brushed a lock of dark hair away from his sharp features. 'Well, then, we set off, as you said, for Cambridge with Master Segden. There was no sign of young Master Treviot there and we discovered that he had left two days before with the Preacher and a few others.'

'The Preacher?'

'Yes, Master, 'tis a name given to one of the elder students. He has quite a following because of his … er …'

'Preaching?'

'Yes, Master. He's very clever with words. The others seem to be under a sort of spell.'

'And this Preacher was taking other students to Norwich to join the rebels?'

'Yes, told them that they were going to start what he called the New Commonwealth.'

'So you followed them on the Norwich road?'

'Aye. They had more than a two-day start on us but we rode hard and caught up with them on the road 'tween Thetford and Attleborough.'

'When was that?'

Matt counted on his fingers. 'Two, three, four – yes, four days since. Saturday evening. Right footsore they were.'

'And you told Raphael that you were come to take him home?'

'Yes. Master Segden argued with him … but … well, Master, sorry I am to say this: Master Raphael would not listen. He even turned deaf ears to Walt and, as you know, Master, he is right fond of Walt. But he only pays attention to the Preacher. We could not halt them, so we travelled with them at their walking pace – arguing fiercely all the way. At one point the Preacher and Master Segden came to blows. After that, there was a plot to steal our horses.'

'What? They were going to leave you on the road and ride away with your horses – my horses?'

'Yes, Master, but Walt was too clever for them. He made sure to keep the bits and bridles with him all the time when we were not riding.'

'How did you fare for food and lodging?'

'We slept in barns or under hedges and Walt used the money you gave him for a simple dinner every day. Walt had the idea that as everyone got more tired and hungry it would be easier to persuade them to give up. It began to work. The students fell to complaining and quarrelling. As we got nearer Windham Walt and Master Segden made a plan. Walt would say the money was all gone and Master Segden would suggest that we went to his father's house not far away to rest and get more supplies. All this we put in a letter and sent Dickon to bring it to you. I did not think you could have received it and got here so quick, Master.'

'I was already from home by then. So, what happened next?'

'The plan was working well till we got here. The Preacher was losing his power over the others. But the Windham folk are fiery for Kett and rebellion. The Preacher told some of the locals that Master Segden and Walt and me were traitors to their cause. They set on us – about six of 'em – and beat us up and locked us in the cellar of the inn. Then they made Master Segden write to his father for money. They said they wouldn't let us go for two pounds.' Master Segden's father did come and he did pay the ransom. Right angry he was at that, I can tell you.'

'And with cause. So, when did these robbers let you go?'

'Yesterday afternoon.'

'And the others all went on to Norwich?

Matt nodded. 'We had already agreed our plan. Master Segden and Walt said that you had given them charge of Master Raphael and they would not abandon him.'

'That was brave.'

'Aye, Master, but I'd have gone, too. Only we agreed I was to slip away as soon as I could and wait here in hope that you would come this way.'

I clapped the young man on the shoulder. 'I scarce deserve such loyal servants. They are riding now into real danger. There will be slaughter in Norwich 'ere many days are past.'

'Aye, the gossip is that the Marquis of Northampton is on his way with a mighty army.'

''Tis true, but the Earl of Warwick is in command.'

Matt shrugged. 'That is not what men say. 'Tis bruited abroad that Warwick loves not the Protector and will not come.'

'Idle gossip from people who know not how things are managed at court. For sure the marquis is no soldier.'

'Well, Master, whoever comes I hope he will know what faces him. 'Tis said that Kett has a force of twenty thousand or more at his camp on the heath outside the city.'

'Then we must lose no more time. Ride back to Goldsmiths' Row as fast as you can...'

'Nay, Master, I must come with you.'

'Not so, Matt. There is little to be served by you also facing danger. Mistress Treviot will now, I am sure, be frantic with worry. Your best service is to set her mind at rest. Tell her only that I and Master Raphael are both safe and will be returning shortly. Say nothing about the Preacher and the ransom and suchlike. Tell her that all stories of battles between king's men and rebels are nothing but gossip. Is that clear?'

Matt frowned. 'Quite clear, Master, but ...'

---

*   This equates to approximately £500 in modern currency.

'No "buts", Matt. You have done excellent well these last days. See you do my bidding now. All will turn out well, you will see.'

I know not whether my words convinced Matt. They certainly did not reflect any optimism I felt as I resumed my eastward journey.

◊

Norwich had a surprising appearance of normality. As I approached St Stephen's Gate I expected to be challenged by guards posted by the rebel leader. In fact, as I soon discovered, Kett's encampment lay beyond the city's northern wall on Mousehold Heath and he kept all his followers there. That is not to say that he was not in control. Having taken Norwich once and afterwards broken down some of the walls, he could take it again at any time. Everyone knew this but, just to make the message clear, he held the mayor and other civic leaders hostage at Mousehold. All this I learned soon after my arrival at the Maid's Head Inn where I easily found lodging – few travellers were coming into a city where they might at any time be attacked or robbed.

Anxious to learn as much as I could, I joined three prominent local men at their dinner table that afternoon. There was a young priest, John Norsby, Jacques Rievaux, a printer whose accent betrayed his Huguenot origins, and Nicholas Orme, a stout wool merchant whose ringed fingers and finely-broidered doublet blazoned his wealth. Their attitudes to the crisis varied but what they all shared was fear.

'What news have you of the royal army,' Orme asked me. 'Will they be here tomorrow, do you think?' Glints of reflected sunlight flashed from the jewels on his fingers as he nervously drummed the table. 'The sooner these devils are put to the sword, the better.'

'Pray God, rather that the king's general comes with promises of pardon to persuade the rebels to disperse,' Norsby said. 'We should not wish for pitched battles in our streets.'

'That seems to be how tumults have been calmed elsewhere,' I said. 'In several places rioters have been dispersed by words, rather than blades.'

The Frenchman shook his head. 'This Kett is cast from a different mould. I have spoke with him. He believes he is not traitor. He and his men have no need of pardon.'

I recalled Sir William Paget's reservations about the Protector's policy. 'You mean Kett thinks of himself as some kind of government agent?'

Rivaux nodded. 'He says he does what the king – or the Good Duke – desires. He guards the people against the wicked landowners.'

'And who guards us against the wicked commons?' Orme responded. 'We are like to have our homes broken into at any time and our shops looted.'

'Do not think the soldiers of the king will be any better behaved,' Rivaux warned. 'Most of them are mercenaries – Italian, French, Saxon. Foreigners fight only for what they can pillage. Their officers cannot control them. I know it. I have seen such things in my own country ... Well, it would appal you to hear what I have seen.'

I tried to bring the conversation round to what interested me – the conditions in the rebels' camp. 'How much control does Kett have of his followers?'

'He is strict,' the priest observed. 'He has to be. He must keep up the appearance of a champion of justice and good order. He dares not allow his people to become an unruly mob. He has given us assurances that there will be no looting in Norwich.'

Orme gave a snort of a laugh. 'Fine sounding words! They smell like an empty wine firkin and are about as much use. While he makes these promises he sends out raiding parties to steal kine and sheep and grain.'

The only 'plan' I had formed for detaching Raffy from the Mousehold rebels involved dealing directly with their leader. I pressed the printer for information. 'Monsieur Rivaux, you have met this Robert Kett. Is he a reasonable man? From what I hear, he is no ranting fanatic.'

'No, he is quite *aimable* ... agreeable. Anyone may approach him. There is a big oak tree on the heath and he sit beneath it on a grand chair, like a king on a ... throne. He receives petitions and issues orders.'

'King Robert!' Orme scoffed. 'Ruler of wastrels, rogues, and vagabonds – and he no more than a yeoman. Seated on a throne, indeed! God grant I live to see him raised even higher – swinging from a gallows!'

After dinner, I went straight to one of the city markets seeking one of the stalls that offered cast-off clothing. In order to venture safely onto Mousehold Heath, I would have to change my appearance. My cambric shirt and Spanish leather jerkin would certainly have attracted attention. I found an old patched smock and a woollen cap from which some of the threads were hanging loose. Back in my small single chamber at the inn I tried on these clothes and satisfied myself that, thus dressed, I would be as inconspicuous as possible. I was now ready for the last stage of my quest.

And yet I hesitated. For five days I had been in a hurry, eager to catch up with my son. Now anxiety held me back. Was it fear of entering the hostile environment of Kett's camp? Certainly I was apprehensive about that. But it was my encounter with Raffy that worried me more. How would I be able to persuade him or force him to return with me to London? Here, in the midst of a host fighting for justice, he must be feeling elated, excited, thrilled in a way that he had never felt before. He would resent any attempt to drag him back to the humdrum life of Goldsmiths' Row. I delayed my departure for Mousehold Heath until the morrow,. I told myself that this would give me more time to locate Raffy and decide how best to achieve my objective. How easily we deceive ourselves with reason!

I headed north through Norwich's narrow streets, crossed the River Wensom and walked to Pockthorpe Gate. As I left the city I noticed a gap of some twenty yards in the wall which gave every appearance of having been breached recently. Two of the city's cannons were pointed towards it from within. I wondered how effective they would be against a determined charge.

The ground rose gently to the open heathland and it was not until I had covered a hundred yards that the rebel encampment came fully into view. Not until that moment did I fully appreciate the fear that had driven many citizens to flee their homes and now haunted those who remained. Clusters of people filled the landscape as far as I could see. Many were gathered around open fires and columns of smoke rose in the still air like the pillars of some vast, roofless abbey. There were a variety of rude shelters – dead branches overlaid with cowhide, simple windbreaks of stakes and woollen cloth, a few military tents of conical shapes but from the scattering of rugs I judged that most of Kett's followers slept beneath the stars.

The reports I had heard about the size of this peasant army had not been exaggerated. Mousehold Heath was temporary home to thousands of men. There were also some women and even a few children, who ran to and fro among the 'islands' of habitation which seemed to be afloat on a sea of bracken and furze. As I wandered, unhindered, through the camp I realised that the first impression I had gained of an unorganised assembly was wrong. The general of this army had his lieutenants who could be seen moving purposely from group to group. They wore coloured armbands proclaiming their authority and appeared to be checking lists and issuing instructions. Some of the men were being directed to an area at the far side of the field. When I reached it I saw groups practising archery and pike drill.

I turned to make my way back towards the town. In my mind, I had divided the camp into two halves – east and west. This was the only way I could attempt an organised, single-handed search of the whole area. I concentrated first on the western sector and set off down the slope with purposeful tread, looking to the right and left in hope of sighting a familiar face. I had quickly discovered that the best way to deter inquisitive glances was to give the appearance that I was engaged on important business and knew exactly where I was going.

The task I had set myself was large and it grew in size as the morning wore on. The groups divided as their members finished their morning meal and went about their various tasks. My spirits sank lower as the sun rose higher. How would I ever find my son among these thousands of moving people?'Twere best to remove that ring, Master. There's many here who would cut your throat for it.'

I spun round to find Walt standing behind me.

I grasped his hand. 'Walt, 'tis good to see you! How fare you? And Raffy – how is he? I fear 'tis a heavy burden I have laid on you – heavier than ever I imagined.'

The old man's weather-beaten face creased in a smile. ''Twas no hardship, Master. The boy had to be kept out of harm's way. I was happy to look after him.'

'So, where is he now?'

'Down at what they call the speaking place. 'Tis where Kett and his preachers speak to the people to keep their spirits up. Come,

Master, I will take you there. Master Raphael wanted to hear the magician everyone is talking about.'

'Magician?'

'Aye – a mad fellow but dangerous, I think. Calls himself "Prior Fustus" or some such.'

I stopped in my tracks. 'Do you mean Parafaustus.'

'Aye, Master, that is the name – Parafaustus.'

Chapter 8

THERE WERE, I guessed about a hundred and fifty or two hundred people sitting on the ground in a semi-circle around a small knoll on which the speaker stood. Walt pointed out Raffy close to the front and to one side. I worked my way round the edge of the crowd so that I was behind my son and also so I could get as close to the performer as possible. Then I sat down and studied him intently.

So this was Robert Allen who called himself Parafaustus. This was the man Cranmer and his colleagues were anxious to lay hands on – a stirrer of sedition a spreader of treason, a dabbler in black arts, a peddler of poison and – if the archbishop's suspicions were justified – a tool in the hands of powerful political figures. It was frustrating that the man I had been sent to find and capture now stood before me and I was powerless to arrest him. The only thing I could do was fix his face firmly in my mind so that, if ever I encountered him again, I would recognise him instantly.

Allen was a small man. His spare frame was enveloped in an ankle-length black gown onto which various bright zodiac symbols had been sewn. A cluster of chains hung around his neck to which were fixed a variety of what I supposed were amulets – strange objects of wood, metal, and bone. He wore a black, clerical-type cap over dark hair which cascaded to his shoulders. Allen's complexion was sallow. Thick brows overshadowed his eyes, an effect he had enhanced by the application of soot, or some such, to his lids. Slightly hollowed cheeks flanked a thin mouth. His chin was beardless. He carried a long staff, which he sometimes waved and, at other times, drew imaginary signs on the ground before him. His voice was harsh and strong.

'Tomorrow, my brothers, tomorrow he comes – the agent of Beelzebub, the enemy of true English people. Tomorrow he shall meet his doom. How may I prophesy this? Because I am the great Parafaustus, master of more astronomical knowledge than all the teachers of Oxford and Cambridge and Paris and Padua. I have conjured Arrimanes.'

Here the speaker paused, raising his staff heavenwards. 'And what has this spirit of war revealed?'

Allen glanced around his congregation. For several silent moments. 'Victory!'

He brandished the staff and a chorus of cheers rose from the audience. 'Yes, my friends, with the moon in Leo bold actions will be rewarded. We will defeat the oppressors of the people.' (Cheers)

'England will be once more a land where the common weal of the people is restored.'

(More cheers)

Allen held up a hand and his obedient disciples fell silent. In a subdued, sepulchral tone, he continued. 'But there must be a cost. Blood will be shed. Some here may, perchance, be slain.' Again the speaker resorted to a dramatic pause. 'Now, who here would know that he will survive the coming battle?'

I could not see a man whose arm was not raised.

The black-robed magus thrust a hand into the scrip hanging from a strap across his shoulder. He pulled out a sheaf of papers. 'Here I have a spell. Oh, a most powerful spell. A protection spell. A spell that summons the aerial spirits to stand guard over the wearer. Take this spell. Keep it close to your heart. Say twelve *paternosters* at the going down of today's sun and twelve *aves* at his rising on the morrow and you will live to sing the songs of victory. This powerful spell is yours for a mere farthing. The tiniest coin for the greatest prize – your life. Who will take one?'

The audience rose as one man and moved forward.

Walt and I moved away a short distance.

'Now I must seek out Raffy,' I said.

The old man shook his head. 'Think not to talk any sense into him after that display. His noddle will be full of all this magic nonsense. I know him well.'

I sighed. 'Aye, better than his father, I think.'

'Do not flail yourself, Master. You have many things to think of. My care is only for the horses and the wagons. Master Raphael has always loved to be about the animals – and a right good horseman he is, too. And to me, the lad has sometimes seemed like the son I never ... But no more of that!'

'I have always been grateful for your interest in the boy. I am sure you have been trying to knock this rebellious nonsense out of him these last days. If you have failed, I doubt I will succeed. But I have come all this way. Perhaps he will realise how concerned I am for him.'

'Master Raphael has the makings of a fine man. He needs only to come through this headstrong stage.'

At that moment, a strident trumpet call rang out.

''Tis Master Kett calling a general muster,' Walt explained. 'I must go. We have to form up in our companies. You were best be off, Master. You are like to be recognised as not one of our number.'

'But Raffy...'

'Leave him to Master Segden and me for one more day. Where are you staying?'

'At the Maid's Head.'

'Then we will bring him there tomorrow evening.– whether he wants to come or not.'

I walked back into the city with a crowd of troubling images jostling in my head and making little sense of any of them.

The next day, Sunday 31 July, Norwich was buzzing with expectation. The relief force was known to be nearing the city. From mid-morning people lined the walls to watch, many carrying flags to wave at their deliverers. Others, however, rode or walked out to the riverbank and the northern wall to observe the reaction of the rebels. The question on everyone's lips was, 'What will Kett do now?' Would he send his men back into the city to repel the king's army? Would he march them around to the southern approach to bar the way? Around the tables of the Maid's Head Inn, amateur strategists put forward their opinions on the military situation.

'Kett will attack before Northampton's men have time to form battle order.' It had by now become well known that the Marquis of Northampton was the general in charge of the royal contingent.

'If Kett is wise he will come out under a flag of truce to seek terms.'

'Why would he do that? His host outnumbers the king's men ten to one.'

'I say Northampton will bombard the rebel camp with his artillery.'

''Twere better that than fighting in the streets.'

'If I were Northampton I would put a ring of troops round Mousehold. Blockade the devils. Hem them in. Starve them into submission.'

'That would force them to seize the city again.'

'The first rule of strategy is to retain the initiative. 'Tis no good for rival generals to watch each other to see who moves first.'

Yet that is precisely what happened. The relief force, some fifteen hundred mounted men, mostly Italian mercenaries, came to a halt outside the city. I had a good vantage point on the south wall and watched a delegation of senior citizens ride out and confer with the king's general. Then Northampton led the way into Norwich, through St Stephen's gate, to the beat of a drum and the proud fluttering of flags. The 'liberators' of Norwich set up their camp in the Market Square while their captains were feasted in the nearby Guildhall.

And Kett? He did nothing. The watchmen on the city walls reported no belligerent activity in the rebels' camp. Norwich held its breath, awaiting a response from the rebels which never came.

But I had other concerns. I waited with mounting impatience, for Walt to make contact. It was only as darkness began to encroach on the streets and lamps were being lit that the faithful head groom came to my chamber. He had Robert Segden with him.

The young tutor was full of apologies. 'Master Treviot, I am so sorry it has come to this. I pray you believe that I have tried to turn Master Raphael from this dangerous course, but …'

'You are not to blame, Robert,' I said. 'Raffy is a hasty-witted loggerhead. I doubt not this is all a great adventure for him. But where is he? You said you would bring him with you? Has he come to some harm amid that cutthroat rabble?'

Walt eased himself uneasily onto a stool. Until that moment, I think I had not realised that he had grown old in my service. He had always been in my life, highly valued by my father and promoted to the headship of the outdoor staff long before I took over the business. 'Master Rafael is well and in high spirits. He is looking forward to the battle.'

'Battle!'

'Aye, Master Treviot,' Robert explained. ''Tis what we are come to tell you. Kett has announced his plan to regain control of Norwich. He means to attack before dawn. I fear the marquis has played into his hands.'

'Indeed,' Walt agreed. 'Had he kept outside the city his mounted force would have had the advantage. Within the walls, they must needs dismount and fight, hand-to-hand with men who know all the streets and alleys.'

'They will meet arrows fired from windows and rooftops. They will be ambushed at every corner.'

I was appalled by the images Robert conjured. 'This is terrible! We must warn the general straight away.'

My two visitors exchanged glances.

It was Walt who spoke. 'There is a danger in that, Master?'

'How so? It is, for sure, the only way to avoid danger.'

Walt ran a hand over his grey-stubbled head. 'We have discussed this long, Master. If the marquis is alerted he will, for sure, withdraw his men from the city.'

'Of course. 'Tis why …'

'Do you not see, Master Treviot.' Anguish creased Robert's young face, 'Kett will, thereby, know he is betrayed.'

'And he will soon know who has betrayed him. He has a short way with those who displease him. He sits in judgement under a great oak on the heath and condemns to hanging any who break his own laws.'

'But why should he suspect you?'

'I fear we are suspect already.' Robert explained. ''Tis known by many that Walt and I are here at your behest to draw Master Rafael away. We are watched. Now, we have managed to slip away while all in the camp are going early to their makeshift beds to be well-rested for the fray. We must return quickly.'

I struggled to grasp the implication of what I was being told. 'So, if I pass on this information, you both face a hanging?'

'Aye,' Walt said, 'and mayhap Master Rafael, too. What better way to punish you than to kill your son?'

'But if I do nothing there will be butchery in these streets 'ere morning and my son is like to be among the slain or marked a traitor in the final reckoning.'

'Final reckoning?' Robert looked puzzled.

'Oh, aye. Think you the Protector will leave Norwich in the hands of traitors? This rebellion can only have one ending. Then there will be hangings aplenty.'

I went to the window and stared across the open space of Tombland, now occupied by groups of soldiers whose bonfires lit up the stonework of the massive cathedral gateway. I wondered what the citizens were thinking in their locked and shuttered homes. Did they feel safe now that professional troops had been sent to protect them? Were they reassured by the lack of activity in the rebels' camp? If they knew what I now knew …

I turned to face the others. 'It seems I am a doomed gambler faced with two cards. Whichever I turn 'twill prove to be the ace of spades – the death card.'

'Nay, Master Treviot we have a plan. 'Tis, I grant, a slender one, but all we can devise.' Robert looked at me imploringly. 'There is risk but if you approve it, it may save Master Raphael – and all of us.'

'Go on.'

'The attack will take place at several points around the city. Our company has been charged with the easternmost assault. We are to storm Bishop Bridge, break down the gate with gunpowder and make for the centre. Only the good Lord knows how long it will take us to do our job – or even if we shall succeed. But if we do, every man will be his own captain. Some will be looking for foreign troops to kill. Others, I think, will be breaking into houses and shops to steal all they can. Kett has forbidden looting but that will not stop them. There will be chaos.' Robert shook his head. 'Bloody chaos!'

Walt nodded. 'Aye but 'twill give us our chance to bring Master Raphael here. What say you, Master? Do you approve our plan?' He stood up.

It was a moment for instant decision. No time for gravely weighing arguments or nicely calculating consequences. 'As you say, you must return quickly. I would not add to your risk by delaying you.' I stared at my two servants, moved by their loyalty and shamed by the danger I had, unwittingly, plunged them into. The choice they were presenting was terrible. Since that night, I have never known whether the decision I made was the right one. What I do know is that, as I looked into their enquiring eyes, there was only one answer I could make. 'Go,' I said, 'do what you have to do.'

That night I made no attempt to sleep. More than one of my candles burnt down and was replaced as I lay, fully clothed, ears straining for the first whisper of the coming storm. Yet, alert as I was, the sudden thudding of distant cannon fire alarmed me. The cathedral clock had scarce stopped chiming midnight. Too early, surely, for the planned rebel attack described by Walt and Robert. I went to the window and threw it open. In the square below the soldiers were scrambling around in some confusion. One leapt to his unsaddled horse and cantered off in the direction of Bishopgate. Others dispersed in small groups and left Tombland in different directions, buckling on swords and jamming on helmets as they went.

The sound of gunfire ceased as abruptly as it had begun. The silence that followed seemed equally menacing. It was as though the city was fearfully holding its breath. But all remained quiet and, after a few minutes, I closed the window and returned to my bed.

At one o'clock the cannon roared again. Again I looked into the street. Again I saw the soldiers, who had returned to the comfort of their fires, jump up to patrol the streets.

An hour later the sequence of events was repeated. When the guns sounded again at three o'clock it was clear that Kett had set up a menacing ritual, designed to unnerve the city's defenders and remind them that he could strike at any time of his choosing. At last, unsettled by inaction, I wrapped my riding cloak around me, took up a closed lantern and ventured into the streets.

There were many other people abroad, soldiers and civilians. The citizens wandered aimlessly or stood at corners in anxious groups but even the troopers seemed to lack purpose as they searched the city by the light of flaring torches, their task hampered by mist seeping up from the river. My steps were irresistibly drawn to the eastbound street leading to Bishop Bridge. I had to see if there was any sign of the promised attack.

Before I was halfway to the bridge the nocturnal silence was shattered into confused splinters of sound – trumpet calls, cannon fire, shouts, and screams. I stood still, trying to locate the source of the uproar. Noises were coming from different directions and mingling in the air above to fall like a wave on the city. The four-pronged attack had begun. All I could do now was return to the inn to hope and pray for the safe arrival of Raffy and his companions.

I had not gone more than a few paces when a small group of men, women and children burst from a side street. One of them ran into me and sent me sprawling. The lantern flew from my hand. I heard rather than saw what I supposed to be a panic-stricken family, fleeing from some unseen terror. A child screamed, 'Mammy! Mammy! Where are you?' a man called, 'This way! Hurry! Hurry!' Then, with a clatter of running footsteps, they were gone.

I stood up in the misty darkness and knew that I was lost. There could be no gain in feeling for my now-extinguished lamp. I could only walk along the dimly visible street, ignorant of my direction and hoping to meet someone who could point me towards the city centre. After a few minutes, I saw a feeble light and discovered that it came from a chink in the shutter of a window. I found the house door and hammered on it. There were noises within but no one came to answer. I knocked three times before realising how foolish I was to expect anyone to open the door to an unknown visitor on a night such as this.

Walking on, with the tumult drawing ever nearer, I reached a wall and was obliged to turn either right or left. I chose to go to the right. Suddenly, I was aware of running feet behind me. I stepped into a gap between two houses as a body of soldiers – perhaps twenty in number – came rushing past, their arms and equipment jangling.

'Where are we?' I called out.

The response was a curt order. 'Stay indoors! The rebels are at Pockthorpe Gate! If we cannot hold them they'll be here in short time.'

Prudence dictated that I should head in the opposite direction but I had a strange compulsion to see for myself what was happening. I strode after the soldiers. Within a hundred yards I reached the point where the buildings became sparse and gave way to an expanse of open ground. Now the frenzy of battle dinned in my ears. I began to distinguish lights and movement ahead. I could smell smoke. Then I almost stumbled over a pile of rubble. I made out the ruin of what had, perhaps, been a cottage or animal shed but was now a mound of bricks and smouldering timber. I scrambled up it in the hope of a better view.

At that moment, there was a thunderous explosion. I stared in the direction of the sound. Scarcely a mile ahead a plume of flame rose in the air. It was followed by raucous cheers. And after that, I heard the steady beating of a drum, the rumbling of a flowing human tide and saw a score or more of brandished torches advancing down the road.

I hurried down from my vantage point and ran away from the following tide. Whenever I came across anyone I called out, 'Stay inside! Lock your doors! The rebels are coming!' But few people heeded the warning and, the nearer I was to the city centre the more clogged the streets became with horses, wagons, and confused people.

As I was passing one of the churches I felt the grip of a strong hand on my arm. 'You, come and help!' I turned and found myself facing one of Northampton's young captains, his face grimed with blood and dirt.

'This way!' He half-steered, half-pulled me to where an open wagon stood by the church door. Inside three wounded soldiers lay side-by-side.

'We'll have this one first,' the captain ordered.

The officer and I carried the stricken man into the church's candlelit interior and laid him down in the centre aisle beside another wounded man who was already being tended by a priest and two women. We returned to bring in the other casualties.

The captain removed his helmet and drew a gauntleted hand over his brow. 'Spare nothing in treating these men.' He glared at the cleric. 'Remember they fought to save you. We will return shortly with more patients for you. Come along.' The last words were directed at me. His tone allowed of no contradiction. But, then, how could I protest? If I had shared my knowledge of the attack the outcome might have been very different. We mounted the wagon and the captain took up the reins.

'How heavy are your casualties?' I asked.

'Very,' he muttered. 'Hemmed in by all these buildings we stand no chance. There are too many of the devils. They gush down every street like water from a damaged conduit.'

'Have the rebels broken through everywhere?'

'Worst in the North and East. We still control St Stephen's Gate. We need it to complete our retreat.'

'Retreat?'

'Aye, what else should we do?' There was bitterness in his voice. ''Twas folly to make camp in the city. In open ground, we are more than a match for this horde of undisciplined savages. Perhaps now my Lord of Northampton will see how disastrous his tactics are. If we withdraw with the men we have left we can regroup.'

'That is why you are rescuing your wounded men.'

'No!' He bellowed his reply. 'I am rescuing them because they are *my* men! I'll not leave them to be mutilated by Kett's blood-crazed felons.'

By now dawn light was spreading over the city. The noise of fighting had subsided but the evidence of the battle was all around us and plain to see. Fires were burning all over the city. We had to steer our way around debris that had once been houses. Distraught men were picking their way through the ruins. Women were crying and calling the names of their loved ones.

'Where are we headed?' I asked after a long silence.

'Bishop Bridge. The fighting has been very hot there. Last I heard some of our fellows were still penned up in an alehouse. If any have survived we will bring them out.'

'That sounds dangerous.'

He shrugged. 'There is a sword in the corner behind you. Its previous owner will have no further need of it – poor sod.'

I reached into the rear of the wagon and pulled out a trooper's heavy swept-hilt rapier. 'I fear I am no swordsman.'

''Tis easy enough.' His eyes remained fixed on the road. 'There's a handle end to hold it by and a pointed end to stick into traitors.'

Scarcely had he spoken when a group of half a dozen rebels sauntered into view. They spread out across the street to bar our progress.

'Where do you think you're going?' The speaker was a tall fellow wearing a fur-trimmed robe, obviously looted from some wealthy merchant's house.

'To collect wounded comrades,' the captain snarled. 'In the king's name, stand aside.'

'In the king's name?' the other mocked. 'Do you hear that, brothers? This rich man's lackey says he speaks for the king. We know what to do with his sort.' He took a pace forward, his friends dutifully following his example. The advancing ruffians were armed with staves and knives. Three of them had bows strung across their shoulders, restricting their movements.

The captain struggled to draw his sword but was hampered by having to hold the reins. I had to act. There was no time to think. I brought the flat of the rapier down heavily across the horse's flank. With a frightened squeal, he reared. One flashing hoof caught the tall man square across the forehead. The others leapt aside, falling over each other as they did so. I jumped down, wildly waving the sword. I know not what I intended to do. Rage took over. Days of fear, anxiety and bitterness converged and surged through me, right down to the rapier's point. I thrust and slashed. Felt my weapon penetrating flesh.

When the seizure of hatred passed, I stood panting and watching two of our attackers running up the street as fast as their legs would carry them.

'Bravely done, Master.' The captain stood beside me, calming the skittering horse. He laughed. 'You can have a commission in my troop any day.'

I made no reply. Suddenly I was like a motionless statue – except that I was trembling violently and staring down at a body which still had my sword wedged in its chest.

The captain took the weapon from me, pulled it out of the dead rebel and wiped it on his boot. 'The first time is always a shock.' He smiled a grim smile. 'Pity is, it gets easier. But come, we've a job to finish.'

Then we continued through the desolation and ruination left behind as the battle moved on and found the alehouse that had obviously been a scene of heavy fighting. It stood close to the bridge gate whose charred wood still hung at an angle from its hinges. Flames had engulfed the whole building and were still blazing in the upper storey. Molten lead fell in droplets from the roof. The alehouse had not been seared by fire but it bore many scars. Arrows bristled from its door and shutters. A dead attacker lay across the sill of one uncovered window. The captain pulled the body aside and called out. There was a feeble response from within and, after a brief conversation, the door was unbolted. Inside, we found two able-bodied troopers and four others suffering from various injuries. We packed them all into the wagon and made our return journey through the ruined streets.

Back at the church-cum-hospital, I left the soldiers.

'Thank you, Master. You are a brave man.' The captain gripped my hand firmly as we said goodbye. As I found my way back to my inn, it occurred to me that I had not discovered the young man's name.

There was an atmosphere of strange calm at the Maid's Head. The fighting had not reached this part of the city which was still held by Northampton's men. Someone muttered to me that his lordship was actually within and taking breakfast. I went up to my chamber. Beside the closed door, Robert Segden was slumped again the wall.

I shook him. 'Robert, wake up, man! Tell me what is happening. Where is Raffy!' I put my hand to the latch.

'A moment, Master,' Robert cried.

But I could not wait for his explanation. I opened the door, stepped inside. And came to a sudden, horrified halt. Before me lay the body of a man, his head in a pool of blood that had issued from his slashed throat.

Chapter 9

MY INSTANT REACTION was 'Raffy!' But in the next
moment, I realised that the dead man in my chamber was not
my son.

'Master, please go no farther in. I must explain.' Robert stood
behind me in the doorway.

I turned. 'That you must,' I said.

The young man was trembling violently. His horrifying account
came out in halting fragments. 'We came here ... as arranged ...'

'*We?*' I interrupted. 'Where is Raffy? Where is Walt?'

Robert shuffled forward a pace and closed the door behind him.
The room was now only dimly lit by light glinting through gaps
in the shutters. 'Please, Master, let me tell it my way ... You must
understand how things happened. We came here and surprised we
were not to find you ... We waited ... Master Raphael, well, he was
impatient ... wanted to know what we were doing here – We had to
hold him ... stop him going back to where the fighting was ... Then
the door opened ... Oh, Master, we thought 'twas you ...'

'But 'twas this fellow?' I pointed to the body.

Robert nodded. 'We feared we might ha' been followed and we
had ... This is one of our group from Cambridge.'

'The one they call the Preacher, perchance?'

'Aye, Master. He rushed in waving a sword … called us traitors … said Master Raphael must go back with him straightway. Walt said, "No!" and stood between them … Oh, Master, 'twas terrible, terrible.' Robert knuckled tears from his cheeks.

'Sit down,' I said. 'Tell me slowly.'

Robert sank onto a stool and I sat on the edge of the bed. The dead rebel lay between us, flies already congregating on his gaping wound.

The tutor took a deep breath. 'Well, the Preacher had his sword and Walt one of his knives. You know, Master, how sharp he kept them. The fight was … very brief. Preacher lunged. Walt stepped back. Behind him Master Raphael fell against the wall, banging his head. Preacher came on again. At the same moment, Walt swung his knife and made that gash. Preacher staggered back and fell … there.'

'And Walt?'

'He … he …' Robert struggled to get the words out between heavy sobs. 'He sank to his knees … There was blood on his chest … He fell on top of Master Raphael.'

'Was he very badly wounded?'

'I went to him straightway … Called his name … No reply … just lay there, eyes open … I listened for a breath … but 'twas no use …'

'Walt? Dead?' I was aghast.

Robert nodded. 'There was nothing I could do for him. I ran out. I could think of nothing but to find you, Master. I was affeared something terrible might have befallen you, too … At last, I came back here to wait. Oh, right glad I am to see you, Master … Would I were the bearer of better tidings.'

'So you let Raffy run away again?'

Robert sprang to his feet. 'No, Master. I looked to Master Raphael 'ere I left. The blow to his head … He was stunned, benumbed. But he was breathing. I judged it would be some time before he woke. I made sure he was well when I returned … Then I waited for you outside, praying you had come to no mischief.'

'Then, where is he?' I almost shouted.

Robert took three paces across the room and pointed to the far corner. I followed and gasped at what I saw by the dim light. There was a wide gap beside the bed. Raffy lay against the wall, head lolled forward. Across his legs lay the body of Walt, my old and faithful servant.

I knelt down, calling as I did so, 'Open the shutters! Give us light!'

I felt my son's forehead. It was warm and moist with sweat. He was breathing heavily and when I shook him gently, he moaned.

Robert stood behind me. 'I am right sorry it comes to this, Master Treviot. What's to do?'

What indeed?

'First, make some space,' I ordered. 'Move that thing out of the way.' I pointed to the dead Preacher.

As Robert dragged the body and laid it by the fireplace, I gently lifted Walt's shoulders, removing the weight from Raffy's legs. The young man blinked his eyes open. He muttered something incomprehensible, tried to stand up and fell back against the wall.

'Steady, steady, Son.' I put an arm around him and helped him to his feet.

I got him to a sitting position on the edge of the bed. He put a hand to his head and groaned.

'That hurts,' he muttered. 'What happened?' He rubbed a hand across his eyes. 'Who are you? Can't see properly.'

'Just lie down,' I said. 'You need rest. You had a bad blow to your head.'

He sat there blinking, seeming not to hear. Then he looked down.

'Walt? Is that Walt?' He dropped to his knees beside the body. 'Walt, what is it? Are you hurt?'

He reached out a hand, drew it back and stared horrified at his bloodstained fingers. He looked up at me. 'What is wrong with Walt?'

'Lie down and rest. In a while, I will tell you...'

'No! We must help Walt.' He put his hands under the old man's shoulder and tried to make him sit up. He stared up at me, his face distorted with bewilderment and grief. 'He looks ... dead! He is not dead, is he? Walt cannot be dead.'

Robert came over and together we managed to get Raffy to lie down on the bed.

'No, no, no!' He lay there moaning and moving his head from side to side. 'No, no! Not Walt!' Mercifully, after a minute or to he slipped into sleep.

'We must clear up here before he wakes,' I said. 'Get rid of these bloody rushes. I will try to find somewhere to move the bodies.'

I went in search of the proprietor and found him fussing outside the door of the inn's great parlour, in which the Marquis of Northampton and his captains were breakfasting and discussing their plans.

'Murder!' He uttered the word in a shocked whisper, glancing around anxiously to see whether anyone else had heard him.

'Aye, murder,' I replied in a low voice. 'One of several done this night.'

'But not in my inn. Get the bodies out of here quickly.'

The innkeeper had the air of a self-important little man, proud of his position in his little kingdom and accustomed to being obeyed without question.

'Certainly,' I said, raising my voice. 'Shall I bring the bodies straight through here?'

'Not so loud!' he hissed. He took hold of my arm and steered me to a quiet corner. 'Mary and all the saints! I have problems enough already. God knows my business is ruined with all this trouble. It will take years to recover. I want no scandal to make things worse.'

'Nor need there be any. The killer has already paid the price. I seek no further retribution. I only need help to convey my servant's body away, so that I can return with it to London for decent burial.'

'And what of the other one?'

'That should present no problem. If I were in your position I would hide him till nightfall, then take him to some narrow back alley. One more dead rebel will scarce be remarked.'

He shuffled uneasily from one foot to the other. I could almost see the wheels in his mind turning.

'Very well,' he said at last. 'I will come in person and show you where to put your … baggage.'

'One more thing,' I said. 'I need a carpenter who can quickly fashion me a rough coffin.'

The innkeeper raised his eyes heavenwards. 'And I suppose you will want a priest and someone to ring the passing bell.'

I ignored the sarcasm. 'No, just a stout elm box. Then we can have this unpleasant business over quickly and quietly.'

We agreed that I would return to my chamber and wait for him there while he made the necessary arrangements. I was about to climb the stairs when the parlour door opened and Northampton's officers emerged. Among them was the captain in whose company I had spent a couple of hours earlier.

When he saw me he came over and extended his hand. 'Thank you again for your help. By the way, my name is John Cantrill.'

'Treviot,' I responded. 'Thomas Treviot of London.'

'Not a native, then. What brings you to this hellhole?'

'That is too long a story to bore you with but glad I am to be leaving. I hope all goes well here, now the fighting is over.'

'*If* the fighting is over.' The captain's voice once again took on a bitter tone.

'You seem to have checked the rebels' advance,' I said.

'Aye, and now Kett is asking for truce talks.'

'Well, then?'

'Tactics,' Cantrill muttered. 'Mere tactics. I am sure his aim is to keep us sitting here doing nothing while he regroups for a fresh attack. Unfortunately, his lordship takes a different view. He actually trusts this dissembling traitor to keep his word. He wants to be seen as the "saviour of Norwich" – the general who held out against the rebels and foiled their plans.'

'What would you do?'

'Play the devil's spawn at his own game. Use the time to withdraw all our troops and surround the city. If he wants a fight, let him come to us. If not, let him starve.'

'And the citizens?'

'Aye, 'twould be hard on them, I grant – though not for long. The Protector will have to send more troops to finish the job – under a *real* general. But I shan't be here to see it.'

'You're leaving?'

'Yes, evacuating some of our wounded to London for proper treatment.'

'When do you set out?'

'As soon as I can finish loading the wagons.'

An idea occurred to me. 'Might you have room for a coffin? I've a dead servant to take back to the capital and deliver to his family.'

The officer looked at me quizzically yet asked no questions. ''Tis irregular but if ever a civilian deserved a favour his name is Thomas Treviot. How soon can you be ready? I hope to leave within the hour.'

I grasped his hand. 'You're a good man, John Cantrill. I am truly grateful. I will be ready.'

Back in my chamber much had changed. The innkeeper was already there and he and Robert had moved the Preacher's body to a corner, covering it with a cloth. The bloodstained rushes had been swept into a pile on the hearth and were beginning to burn. I went over to the bed where Raffy was still sleeping.

'We will have to wake him,' I said to Robert 'but not before we have moved Walt.' I turned to the innkeeper. 'Have you sent for the carpenter?'

'He will be here directly,' the little man replied.

Minutes later, a burly, aproned figure appeared in the doorway. 'I was told someone here wanted a coffin,' he declared in a booming voice.

It was that voice that woke Raffy. He groaned and stirred as I looked down at him. His eyelids flickered several times, then remained open, staring at me.

'Father? Why are you …' He struggled into a sitting position. 'I thought something terrible had happened.'

I reached out a hand to his shoulder. 'Lie still, Son. We are going home shortly. Till then get some more rest.'

I was too late. Raffy looked down at the body beside the bed. 'Walt!' he gasped. 'It is true.' Straightway he was on his knees beside his old friend. 'Oh, Walt, Walt, Walt, what have I done?'

I went round the bed and tried to draw Raffy to his feet. 'Come along,' I said. 'We are going to take Walt home.'

Raffy refused to move. He looked up at me, tears running freely down his face. 'This is my fault … all my fault!'

'No, no, Son. Bad things have happened but no one is blaming you. Come, now, there is much to do. Time for tears later.'

Slowly Raffy stood up. I beckoned to Robert. 'Take him outside. He needs fresh air. And see if you can get him to swallow some aquavita.'

Raffy was still sobbing as the tutor led him out. I busied myself with the hurried arrangements that had to be made.

The carpenter dispassionately appraised Walt's body. 'I think I have something. 'Tis rough-hewn, yet 'twill shift to your purpose, Master.'

'Then fetch it with all haste,' I ordered.

'Aye,' the innkeeper added, 'and if anyone questions you, say it is for an old lady that's died all of a sudden.'

Anxious minutes passed as I waited for the man to return but eventually he came with his apprentice bearing a box of elm planks. I paid the innkeeper an exaggerated price for one of his buckram sheets, in which we wrapped the body before placing it in the coffin. Between us all, we carried it down to the yard, where Cantrill with his train of three wagons and a dozen mounted men were waiting. Robert fetched our horses and, as soon as we had climbed into our saddles the captain gave the order to move. The southern part of the city we passed through bore few battle scars though St Stephen's Gate and the adjacent walls had obviously been battered by artillery fire. Never was I more glad to leave any place than I was to quit Norwich.

Travelling at the speed of the wagons meant that our progress was slow but I welcomed that. It meant that Raffy and I spent more time together than we had in years. For an hour or more he had little to say. He sat listlessly in the saddle, staring straight-ahead, locked in his own thoughts. I knew what was in his mind but left him to discover the words and the need to express them.

At last, he spoke, without a sideways glance. 'Had I not gone off with the Preacher, Walt would still be alive.'

I matched his tone. 'Had I not sent Walt to find you, he would still be alive. We both have much to regret.'

'He was such a good man.'

'The very best. I knew him and loved him since I was your age.'

After a long silence, Raffy spoke again. 'What the Preacher said to us in Cambridge seemed so ... right.'

'I expect in many ways it was. All the upheavals of recent years have led to much suffering for the common people. They have had change forced upon them.'

'Then should we not come to their aid?'

'Without a doubt. The problem is working out how we can help. You've seen what happens when they try to meet force with force.'

'Horrible! Horrible!' He sighed. 'They were like wild animals.'

'Aye, I witnessed things last night that I hope never to see again.'

Raffy scowled. 'Dogs like that are not worth saving!'

'That is not true, Son. They are flesh-and-blood men like us, driven to extremes by their suffering. I am proud of you for standing beside them.'

He stared at me, puzzled. 'Proud? Do you mean that, Father?'

'Aye. It tells me you have a warm heart. The pity is, 'tis linked to an overheated head.'

For the first time, Raffy's lips bent in a slight smile. It faded quickly. 'Yet I cannot forgive them for Walt. The Preacher killed him and would have killed me.'

'Well, I praise God for sparing you and I will never cease to be grateful to Walt for protecting you.'

He sighed again. 'Life is very complicated.'

'Aye, and I regret to have to tell you it becomes more so as the years pass.'

'When does it stop?'

'I will let you know the answer to that question as soon as I find it,' I said.

Cantrill kept the little column moving as fast as it could, wanting to get his injured men to the capital as soon as possible. At Thetford, he led his men into the shade of the woodland to make their overnight camp. I rode into the town with Raffy and Robert to find lodging at an inn. We had scarcely arrived when there was a commotion in the street outside. Going to our upper-storey window we saw a fast-riding procession of troops. They were heading south, travelling three-abreast and forcing everyone else out of their path.

'Who are these?' Robert asked.

'Unless I much mistake me,' I replied bitterly, 'these are the liberators of Norwich.'

So, indeed, they proved to be. Gossip in the inn confirmed the following morning when we rejoined the wagon train, told a miserable story. As Captain Cantrill had surmised, the rebels had swept back into the city, catching Northampton and his men unawares. Before the fury of Kett's motley army, the government's mercenaries had turned and fled. According to one Thetford eye witness, no-one had ridden faster through the town than the Marquis of Northampton.

My immediate reaction was to send Robert Segden on ahead with a message for Adie. I knew what exaggerated stories would be passing mouth-to-mouth along Cheapside as soon as news arrived of Northampton's rout so I sent to reassure my wife that Raffy and I were safe and would soon be home.

'You were right about Kett's tactics,' I said to Cantrill. We were riding at the front of the column. Raffy was at the rear with some of the soldiers.

'It was obvious.' He sneered. 'Or it should have been obvious to a general with any experience.'

'Who do you think should have been given command?'

'If the Duke of Somerset had come in person the rabble would have dispersed with not a blade being drawn. Kett insists that he is upholding the principles of the government. If he had defied the Protector to his face he would have been seen as the traitor he is. However, from what I hear, Somerset dares not leave the court because he has many enemies there. Well, he surely must come now. After his victory in Norwich, there is nothing to stop Kett marching to London. He may even be on the road behind us, picking up more recruits in every village.'

Raffy had now drawn up alongside us and was listening to the conversation. 'The only man who can save us is the Earl of Warwick,' he declared authoritatively.

Cantrill glanced a smile in my direction. 'And how have you reached that decision, young man?'

''Tis what the soldiers are saying,' Raffy admitted. 'I've been talking to some who served under him in Scotland and France.'

The captain nodded. 'A fair judgement. I was with his lordship at the siege of Boulogne. It was no easy battle but ...'

'Tell me about it,' Raffy urged eagerly.

For the next few miles, we were regaled with tales of military exploits. I was glad that Raffy was finding in such second-hand adventures something to take his mind off recent events.

However, as we used up the miles between Norwich and London I had to quiz him further about his experiences on Mousehold Heath. I would have to report to Cranmer on my return and I knew he would demand of me every detail that I could provide about the lamentable events of the last few days.

'What is your opinion of Parafaustus?' I asked Raffy that afternoon as we jogged along a narrow lane between Barkway and Hare Street.

'Why do you ask?' He replied cautiously. 'Did you meet him on Mousehold?'

'I caught a glimpse of him; nothing more,' I said. 'Some of the simple people there seemed to hold him in high regard. I just wonder what your more mature judgement tells you about the man.'

'He certainly does have power over people. He distributed written prophecies in the camp and he held meetings for those who could not read. He can stir people better than any preacher I have ever heard.'

'What sort of things does he say?'

'That all the planets and astral spirits (whatever they are) are on the side of the common people. That they will be victorious over their oppressors. That the present king will not live long. That there will be a new ruler who will restore everyone's ancient rights and bring back the old religion.'

'He must be a very useful ally for Kett.'

'Oh, aye. He can turn kittens into roaring lions.'

'And did he persuade you?'

Raffy looked at me sharply. 'Why all this interest in a magician, Father?'

'There are those in the royal council who think that Parafaustus is a real danger. I'm interested to know what impression he made on an intelligent young man like you.'

He frowned and paused for several moments before replying.

'I like not people who try to impress me with long and mysterious words I cannot understand. I know nothing of alchemy and suchlike and I do not want to know.' He paused. 'On the other hand, this magician makes up potions that seem to cure folk of their ills and that must be good.'

'Did you ever hear of him making poisons for people?'

'No. He sold spells which he claimed would make bad people sicken and, perhaps, die but I never saw him hawking poisons. That would surely be against the law.'

'Certainly. He could hang for that.'

'And you would like to see him hang, I think.' Suddenly he laughed. 'I know why this fellow worries you, Father. He claims to have the philosopher's stone which would turn tin into gold. If that was true, he could put Treviots out of business, could he not?'

'Aye,' I joined in the laughter, 'and make gold as cheap as tin and all the coin in the realm worthless.'

◊

When Raffy and I reached home the following afternoon we were welcomed like victorious heroes returning from some successful campaign. Adie and all the women made a great fuss of Raffy, and Carl and Henry wanted to hear all about his 'adventure'. The mood, of course, changed when I told them about Walt. I had instructed Robert to say nothing about his death and the news came as a shock to the whole household.

Attending to the funeral was my first responsibility. Walt's wife had died some years before but his two married daughters still lived in London and I sent word to them that very day and arranged for the simple service to take place in the little church of St Matthew in South Street on 5 August at my charge.

But I could not forget my duty to report to the archbishop. Having made enquiry and discovered that Cranmer was still with the court at Hampton I decided to go there straight after the funeral. I would be able to tell him that I had seen Parafaustus in Norwich and that I hoped he might still be there. There was also one more thing I could do to help track down the elusive magus.

I took eleven-year-old Henry Holbein to the parlour and sat him at the table with sheets of the ash-coated paper we used for jewellery designs and a silverpoint pencil. The bright-eyed lad had inherited a good measure of his father's talent. He could with remarkable accuracy draw anything from a pet nightingale to a church façade. Like the great Hans Holbein, he had a special skill in copying faces and was often to be found making impromptu portraits of servants and friends. But he had never done what I was about to ask of him.

'Now, Henry.' I explained, 'we are going to play a little game. I am going to describe someone to you and I want you to try to draw this person from my description. Do you think you can do that?'

He grinned, pushing back a lock of reddish hair from his forehead. 'Sounds fun.' Eagerly he grabbed up the pointed metal stick and held it poised over a sheet of paper.

'The man I am thinking of is about forty and his face is somewhat thin.' I stood behind the young artist while he drew an outline. 'Even thinner,' I said, and watched Henry's second attempt. 'The man's most striking features are his eyes. They are very dark and his eyebrows are thick … Yes, that is quite good. Can you make them stare more? Now, the nose is long and narrow … The lips …'

So we worked on and, after about half an hour, Henry had produced a remarkable likeness of Robert Allen, alias Parafaustus. Thus equipped, I did, at least, have something to show for what had, otherwise, been a barren twelve days since my last meeting with the archbishop.

After the funeral, we returned to the house where Adie presided over dinner for our guests. As soon as I reasonably could I left the table to gather together everything I needed for my journey upriver. I was not the only one to leave the room. Ned trod the staircase behind me and followed me into my chamber. He had made an almost complete recovery from his accident. His face had lost its usual ruddy complexion but, apart from that, he seemed to be his usual lively self.

As I was removing my blue livery gown, Ned said, 'There is something I should tell you before your meeting with Cranmer. I have not mentioned it before because you have been very busy since your return.'

'Ned, I am truly sorry that other matters have crowded in on me. I am afraid I have neglected you. I am so relieved to see you looking well. We must sit down this evening over a glass of canary wine ...'

'What I have to say will not take a moment but, I am sure it is important. Do you recall that I said there was something odd about what West told us of his imprisonment and torture?'

'Yes, you seemed agitated because you could not remember exactly what it was.'

Ned tapped his forehead. 'Well, fortunately, my old brain has not quite given up. I *have* remembered what it was. And 'tis very alarming.'

Chapter 10

A S I WAS rowed up the Thames I was thinking hard about
what Ned had suggested. Warned by my last experience when
making the journey, I was accompanied by a 'bodyguard' of three of
my sturdiest servants. They spent much of the time pointing out the
mansions on the north bank and arguing about which of our great
nobles and ecclesiastics lived where. But my old friend's analysis of
the political situation and William West's unwitting part in it filled
my mind. The big question facing me was whether I should mention
it to the archbishop. Would that help him in his dealings with his
opponents among England's most powerful men? Ned's theory was
only that – a theory, although the more I thought about it, the more
convincing I found it. It appeared to answer all the questions that
had baffled me since my meeting with West, which now seemed so
long ago. Yet, I could not prove my suspicions and to bring them
out in the open could only alert Robert Allen's patrons. That would,
undoubtedly, prove dangerous to me and, perhaps, to those I loved.
If West's misfortunes were but one aspect of a major conspiracy it
was clear that those behind it were ruthless men who would stop at
absolutely nothing to achieve their ends. I had still found no answer
to my question when the boatman nuzzled his craft up to the privy
stairs at Hampton.

'Welcome, Thomas. Did you find your son? I hope you have some good tidings.' I had never seen Morice more dejected than when he greeted me in his office. 'All here is at six and seven. First, we let Allen slip through our fingers and now we have my lord of Northampton's fiasco at Norwich. Our enemies are set cock on hoop and spreading the tale that the Protector cannot long survive.'

'Well,' I said, seating myself on a box chair and accepting a cup of Rhenish, 'I may be able to apply some salve to the wound. I know where Allen is, or was until recently.'

As I gave an account of events in Norwich, the secretary listened attentively, occasionally interrupting with questions. I concluded by producing my portrait of the magus.

'This is good, Thomas, very good.' He allowed himself a light smile. 'We will have John Day, the printer, make copies. His grace will be relieved that we have something positive to report. He has been at a council meeting all morning.'

'Deciding what to do about Norwich?'

'Aye. We cannot allow Kett and his rabble to make it the capital of a rival kingdom.' Morice muttered bitterly.

'Some people think that Somerset should go there in person to challenge Kett.'

'That he will not …'

The door opened wide and Cranmer strode in briskly, his gown billowing around his ankles. He seated himself in the window embrasure and took a long draft of the wine Morice poured for him. I made my obeisance and he greeted me with a tired smile.

'How did the meeting go?' Morice asked.

Cranmer shook his head. 'More divided than ever. The Earl of Southampton is the Duke's most loyal and outspoken supporter. He and I try to hold the council together in support of the Protector but with Lord Warwick away and now Northampton in deep disgrace …' He sighed. 'To lose a whole city to untrained ploughmen and vagabonds …'

'As to that,' Morice said, 'Master Treviot has been in Norwich these last days and gives a vivid picture of what passed there.'

I repeated my tale for the archbishop's benefit and showed him the drawing of Robert Allen.

'Your Grace, I thought we might have our friend John Day print this and circulate it,' Morice said.

Cranmer nodded. 'This Parafaustus as he calls himself is a vital link to those who would bring down the government. If we can lay our hands on him we may be able to thwart their plans.'

'May I suggest caution, Your Grace?' I said. 'I have had longer to consider how we might best use this image. Perhaps it would be better to be circumspect? Allen's paymasters do not know we have the means to identify him. If we declare our hand they may hurry the magus into hiding. Indeed, they might cause him to disappear *permanently* if he has outlived his usefulness to them.'

'What do you suggest?' Morice asked.

'Make copies available only to those you trust. Set them to a secret search. If Allen is still in Norwich he might be discovered quickly. If not, well, at least your people will know who they are looking for.'

'We must think carefully on this,' Cranmer said.

'What has been decided about Norwich?' Morice asked.

Cranmer held out his cup for more Rhenish. 'We are to despatch the Earl of Warwick there with a larger force.'

'Ah!' Morice exclaimed. 'None too soon!'

'It will take time to organise.' Cranmer observed. 'Thomas, do you think that Kett will seize the initiative to march his army south?'

It was a question I had been pondering myself. 'He is certainly decisive – decisive and devious, Your Grace. He tricked the marquis by offering a truce. On the other hand, he seems to be the prisoner of his own idealism.'

'Idealism?' Morice protested. 'Are you suggesting this bloodstained villain is a man of principle?'

'Oh, indeed. He is very insistent that he is not a traitor; that he and the Protector are as one in their concern for the common people. If he were to bring an army to the gates of London he could no longer make that claim.'

'Interesting.' Cranmer gazed thoughtfully out of the window for some moments. 'You appraise the situation very well, Thomas. I am sure Lord Warwick would value your judgement of Master Kett.'

I protested. 'I have not met the man personally. Any opinion I have formed ...'

'Is like to be a sound one,' the archbishop said. 'I have always been impressed by your cool-headed assessment of men and events. I would that some of my conciliar colleagues were as perceptive.'

Morice smiled. 'Well, Your Grace, Master Treviot is a merchant – and a goldsmith at that. Every day he deals with people who approach him for loans or try to sell him their family jewels. If he were not skilled at appraising his customers he would long since have faced ruin.'

'True enough, Ralph.' Cranmer nodded. Now, his lordship is in the country at the moment but as soon as he arrives, I will introduce you to him.'

Later, as I was on my way back downriver, I wondered whether I had been right to make no mention of Ned's theory. In fact, the opportunity had not occurred. That meant that I would have to test it for myself. Before we reached Blackfriars' Stairs I had formed a plan.

The atmosphere at supper that evening was very light-hearted. We had all emerged from a time of anxiety and sadness and were eager to turn our backs on it. Adie had ordered some of our family favourites to be brought to the table and our trenchers were soon arranged with roast capon with an ale sauce, venison pasties, and peppered cows' tongues. Only Ned, who still observed the old non-meat day rules, restricted himself to smoked herring, accompanied by a herb dressing of his own devising. Everyone wanted to hear about my meeting with the archbishop and I gave a careful-censored account of our conversation.

Raffy pounced on my reference to the Earl of Warwick. 'You are going to meet him! Wonderful! Can you take me with you?' He grimaced at the ripple of laughter which greeted his outburst. 'Well I do want to see him and this will probably be my only chance.'

'Why are you so eager to see Warwick?' Adie asked.

'Because he is the greatest Englishman alive. Everyone says so.'

'Everyone?' I said. 'You mean some of the soldiers you met recently.'

'And who better? They served under him. They know how he leads men and inspires them. He is the best general we have.'

'I think the Lord Protector might question that,' Ned observed.

'Somerset? Pah!' Raffy warmed to his subject. 'He is a second-rate general. He was only given military command because he was related to the old king. Warwick is a born soldier who has proved himself in battle.'

'Well,' I said, 'if I am summoned to meet him – and that is not assured – I will be certain to tell him how much you admire him.'

Raffy looked at me quizzically, not sure whether I was mocking him. I hurried on. 'Please God, his lordship arrives soon to end this wretched business in Norwich. It has gone on too long and the people there are in great fear and distress.'

After the others had left, Ned and I lingered at the table.

'Have you thought any more about the torturing of poor William West?' he asked.

'I have, indeed. If you are right – and I incline to believe that you are – the question is, what do we do about it?' I explained why I had said nothing of our suspicions to Cranmer. 'We must keep them to ourselves until we have proof,' I said.

'But I fear that time is not on our side.'

'Why say you so?'

'If you go over the events in order time and again, as I have, you will realise that Master Allen may be in danger and that we must find him before his paymasters decide that he has become a liability.'

I leaned across the table. 'Can you explain that in detail?'

Ned's brow wrinkled in concentration. 'We know that we are dealing with a plot to remove the Protector and his friends from power and we know that Robert Allen is an important tool in the hands of the plotters – so important that our visit to the Tower drove them to have you attacked.'

'Aye, that also tells us that the conspirators have several agents – and I have my own ideas about that.'

'When you appeared in Norwich,' Ned continued, 'my guess is that they assumed you have been sent by the archbishop in pursuit of Allen. They know that the magician's lair has been ransacked. That must be really alarming for them.'

'Yes. They will be afraid that Cranmer's men discovered incriminating evidence. Sadly, that was not the case. Morice told me today that the search of Thraxley Abbey had brought to light nothing useful.'

'Even so, they will be very anxious. Now, anxious men often act hastily, without careful forethought. What do you think they are likely to do about Allen?'

'Move him to a safe hiding place, I suppose.'

'Ah!' Ned sighed and shook his head. 'Think you that they will stop at that? You know the old saying, "He who sups with the devil should use a long spoon". I would shed no tear to learn that their knavish necromancer had reaped the just reward for all his Godless wiles and deceits but 'twould make it much harder for anyone to reach the bottom of this conspirator's well.'

I thought carefully about Ned's words. 'What you say makes sense but if the plot-masters mean to have Allen killed why have they not already done so?'

New stroked his nose with a long forefinger. 'From what you tell me, that might be difficult in Norwich where this bogus magician is virtually worshipped by a horde of devoted followers.'

'Well, let us hope that Cranmer's men can track him down quickly. His grace will have men on the road to Norwich as soon as young Henry's portrait of Allen comes from Day's press.'

'Were I Master Allen,' Ned mused, 'I'd not know who I would fear more, my patrons or my patrons' enemies.'

I yawned and stretched. 'It has been a trying day and I am ready for my bed.' I stood up.

Ned stared up at me, his right hand raised. 'One more word, my dear friend. Allen and poor West are not the only men at risk. I pray you, do not lower your guard for an instant. I sense things moving very swiftly to a conclusion. The commons are everywhere in agitation and rumours from the court tell of men positioning themselves for a change of regime. The pot boils to the point of overflowing and when that happens innocent people will be among the scalded.'

Later, as I drifted into sleep, it was with Ned's warning echoing in my head. He was not the only one haunted by a feeling of impending doom. Wherever one went in the City – in the shops, the inns, the marketplaces, the churches, one was aware of anxious faces, of groups of people engaged in worried conversation. There was apprehension in the very air, a sense that the fire beneath Ned's cauldron was burning too fiercely.

The atmosphere was certainly tense in Goldsmiths' Hall the following Tuesday. This was the day of the annual Barentyn Feast provided for the brotherhood in the will of Sir Drue Barentyn more than a century before on the understanding that we would gather every 9 August to pray for his soul and dine sumptuously in his memory. Our obligation to prayer had ceased, by order of parliament, at the beginning of the present reign. Somerset, with the backing of most of the bishops, had exiled such papistical practices as masses for the dead and the funds provided for it had been diverted to the provision of education for poor boys of Aldersgate Ward. Not a few of the members resented this break with tradition but none felt sufficiently strongly to absent themselves from the feast.

For three hours, the great arras depicting the life of St Dunstan gazed down on the long tables as mess after mess was brought to the hall from the kitchens and set before us. The rafters high above echoed to the sound of conversation and occasional laughter. Yet, there was something lacking in the conviviality that usually marked these celebrations. When the banquet was ended and most of us retired to the courtyard garden gathering in small groups, the talk was entirely of the instability of the country – and particularly of the cost of restoring order.

'I say the Protector dare not impose more taxes or debase the coinage still further. So what then?' The speaker was old Simon Leyland, ever one of our gloomier brethren. 'Why, the government looks to us for loans and who's to say whether we shall ever be repaid?'

There was a murmur of agreement from the five others standing, with me in the shade of our old mulberry tree, close by the window of the recently enlarged assay office. We were gathered around one of our feast guests, a major celebrity of the day. John Hooper was Chaplain to the Duke of Somerset and one of several preachers employed by the government in spreading the religious radicalism approved by the Protector.

'Be careful where you lay blame, Brother. We have a clear warning in Scripture,' the narrow-faced cleric asserted in a tone and volume I felt to be more suited to the pulpit. 'Do we not read in Ecclesiastes 10, "Woe to you, O land, when your king is a child and your princes feast in the morning"? His late majesty held back from fully purifying the church but he imposed order upon it and held in check the papistry and bishops and the mighty landowners who sought only to profit from change. Now, when our good Lord Protector is bringing to completion the work of reform, they think to oppose him. 'Tis rumoured that Princess Mary will flee abroad and return at the head of an imperial army. They impose their own will in their localities and scheme against the duke in court and parliament. 'Tis they who provoke the commons; they who turn tenant against landlord; they who foment civil disorder. Grudge not, Brother, to expend your gold for the restoration of peace and the establishment of true religion.'

107

I took advantage of the silence that followed to draw aside my old friend, Will Fitzralph. 'What do you know about Brother Dannery?' I asked quietly.

'Stephen Dannery? We do not see much of him. His premises are outside the City.'

'At Holborn?'

'Aye, hard by Lincoln Place. He seeks his business more at Whitehall. Rather a court hanger-on, by all accounts.'

'But an honourable member of our fellowship?' I asked.

Will shrugged and looked at me with a mischievous smile. 'More honourable than some; less honourable than others. I seem to recall he was up before the Wardens' Court a couple of years back. There were complaints he had been spreading rumours about brother goldsmiths in hope to steal their business. He may have received a reprimand or a fine. I remember not the details. Why this interest, Tom?'

'I was hoping to have a quiet word with Brother Dannery. Do you see him anywhere?'

We both looked at the scattered members and guests.

'Over there, by the granary.' Will pointed across the courtyard to the far corner.

At that moment, Dannery looked in our direction. He muttered something to his companion and strode briskly across the grass towards the entrance gate.

Without a word to Will, I moved swiftly to the opposite range of buildings, passed through the passageway between hall and chapel and let myself out through the side gate into Guthrun's Lane. I turned to the right, ran along the east end of the chapel, and then along its southern side. I reached the corner of Foster Lane just as Dannery was passing.

I called his name.

He looked round, startled. 'No time, Brother; no time. I have to get back to the shop.'

'Then I will walk with you,' I said. 'It will help me digest our excellent meal.'

He hurried on, clearly agitated. 'Really, Treviot, I do not think ...'

'And I *do* think,' I interrupted. 'I think you should listen to what I have to say if you do not want to find yourself in trouble with the Wardens' Court – *again*.'

'I do not understand what ...'

I clutched his arm and forced him to a standstill. The street was quiet and I drew him into a doorway. 'Then, I will make myself as clear as I can. If the Wardens learn that you were responsible for a murderous attack on a Brother Goldsmith, you can expect more than a fine.'

'I know not what …'

'You deny that you set ruffians on me two weeks ago.'

'Absolutely.'

I stepped back a pace. 'Then we have nothing to discuss. I will simply set the evidence before our worshipful leaders and you can explain to them that I am mistaken. I thought you would prefer to settle the matter privately. I was obviously wrong. I bid you good day.' I turned back into the street.

'Wait!' His voice was quavering. 'What is this "evidence" you are talking about?'

'Simply that one of your cowardly knaves mentioned your name before I beat them off.'

''That is not possible,' Dannery blustered. 'They know …' He stopped abruptly.

'Yes? What do they know?'

He took a step closer. 'Look, Brother Treviot, I heard of the … incident … you were involved in and I was appalled. I assure you 'twas none of my doing.'

Until this moment I had kept my anger in check. Now I put out a hand and pushed Dannery up against the wall. 'Do not take me for a fool. At the Tower, you made a point of discovering who I was visiting. No-one else, outside a very close circle, knew that I had been sent to call on a prisoner by the name of William West. Someone else who has an interest in this man is the Earl of Southampton. Now, the Earl of Southampton is your principal patron. Why, you live almost on the doorstep of Lincoln Place, his town house. Within hours, you reported to his lordship and he instructed you to have me killed. Give me one reason why your murderous intent and divided loyalty should not be revealed to the Wardens.'

'But … but … no … you mistake! 'Twas not like that.' Sweat was now running freely down the large man's brow and cheeks. 'Yes, the earl is my very good Lord. I was at the Tower on an errand for him. When I reported back to him I happened to mention that you were visiting this West fellow on a warrant from the Archbishop of Canterbury.'

This was a detail I had not thought of. 'How much did it cost you to prize that information out of the porter?' I demanded.

Dannery rushed on without answering the question. 'When I reported back to his lordship I simply passed on to him what I had been told. I swear by holy Mary and all the saints 'twas my only part in this business. I did not know how my lord would use the information.'

'Say you so? Very well. As I see it, we both have important decisions to make. I must decide whether or not to believe you and you must calculate whether your best interests lie with your patron or with the Goldsmiths' Company. If you value your livelihood I know which I would choose.'

'You will say nothing to the Wardens, will you, Brother?'

I inclined my head. 'For the moment – and as long as you say nothing of this conversation to anyone.'

'You can rely on my discretion,' Dannery muttered eagerly.

'As to that, I still need convincing.' I turned and walked back to Goldsmiths' Hall.

That evening Ned and I were once more seated alone in the parlour. When I had described my exchange with Dannery my friend smiled a grim smile. 'That was well done. It has provided the confirmation we needed.'

''Tis you I have to thank for pointing the finger of suspicion at Southampton.'

'He was foiled by his own reputation. Not for nothing do people call him the cruellest man in England. The more I thought about West's account of his interrogation, the less sense it made. Did he seem to you the sort of man who could keep his silence under any kind of torture?'

'No, no more than I could.'

'Exactly. So how could he have resisted the extreme pain inflicted by England's master of pain?'

'We saw the marks on West's wrists.'

'Oh, he had suffered the *strapado*, no doubt, and very unpleasant it is to be dangled by the wrists for several hours, but if his interrogators had really wanted West to reveal the name of Robert Allen they could certainly have done so.'

'Which is why you concluded that his interrogation was only intended to frighten West.'

'Or to impress other interested parties that the poor man had, indeed, been tortured to the limits of endurance. That led me to question why Southampton was involved at all. It was strangely considerate of him to offer his expertise to Lord Chancellor Rich, the man who had ousted him from office. I could only see one answer: Southampton's involvement in West's interrogation was not to force the prisoner to tell what he knew, but to ensure that he did *not* tell what he knew.'

'How devious can a man be? Since he was stripped of his office at the beginning of the reign he has given every appearance of bearing no grudge. He has supported the Protector and worked his way back onto the council. Cranmer, who thinks well of everyone, believes the earl to be a penitent and reformed character. He will hear no word said against him, which is why I could not speak out last Friday.'

'Could you not go to the archbishop now, with the confession you have forced out of Dannery?'

'He would not be convinced without very clear proof.'

'By the way,' Ned asked, 'how did you persuade Dannery to tell you that Southampton organised the attack on you?'

'Oh,' I replied nonchalantly, 'threats and lies. I warned him that I would expose him to the senior officers of our Company. And I told him that one of my attackers had blurted out his name.'

Ned stared at me across the table in mock reproach. 'You are spending too much time with politicians,' he said.

It was at that moment that Adie slipped into the room.

'This has just been brought by a man in fine livery.' She handed me a letter.

I stared at the seal. 'A bear and ragged staff.'

'You know the emblem?' Ned asked.

'Oh yes,' I replied. 'this letter is from the Earl of Warwick.'

Chapter 11

'NOW, REMEMBER, YOU stay here in the stable yard with the horses. Talk with the servants by all means but do not venture into the house. Make me not regret bringing you.'

Ever since I had received Warwick's summons Raffy had pestered me to allow him to accompany me to Ely Place. His interest in the warrior-earl had developed into hero worship, so that the possibility of finding himself under the same roof was something he could not ignore. Eventually, I had given way to his entreaties but I had made it clear that there was no question of my introducing him to Warwick. It was this condition that I repeated as we rode through the impressive arched gateway on the morning of 11 August.

Ely Place, widely recognised as the finest episcopal residence in the capital, was currently leased to Warwick and served to enhance his prestige, though he spent little time there. Having left Raffy and the horses with the grooms, I was led through the cloisters and the great hall and up a narrow staircase to a solar which obviously served as a secretarial office. Clerks were busy at three tables copying, dry-stamping and sealing piles of letters and documents. I was shown to a bench running along one wall. During the next hour or so various servants and officials came and went through the door facing me which led to the earl's business chamber. At last, it opened to allow a group of booted and jerkined military officers to emerge. They were talking animatedly among themselves but one paused when he saw me.

'Thomas Treviot,' John Cantrill said as he crossed to where I sat. 'You do show up in the most surprising places.'

'I suppose you have been making plans for his lordship's expedition to Norwich,' I said as we shook hands.

'Yes. Much to be done. We will have a larger force this time – and properly led. We'll not be made fools of again. Is your business here also to do with the rebellion?'

'Aye, though I know not what help I can be. I am no soldier.'

'You will find his lordship is very thorough. He does not neglect any source of information.'

'Master Treviot!' The man who now appeared in the doorway was rather above average height and in his mid-forties. His frame was loosely swathed in a brocaded floor-length gown.'

'My Lord.' I bowed.

'Come, we will walk in the garden. I am stifled in here.' He turned to one of the secretaries. 'You, too, Richard. I may want to make notes.'

Cantrill and the others stood aside as Warwick led the way down the staircase.

Three men were scything the wide lawn as we emerged from the house. A welcome breeze was blowing down the slope of Saffron Hill. Warwick took several deep breaths. 'The air here is a rare physic. I could almost imagine myself back in the Welsh Marches. Sometimes I wish ... But enough of that. I want to hear your assessment of the situation in Norwich. Any good general knows that a battle is won before 'tis fought. All lies in the planning and preparation. Good intelligence is beyond price. So, tell me, how reliable are the citizens.'

'Reliable, My Lord?'

'Yes, are they loyal to his majesty at all costs or would some of them willingly throw in their lot with the rebels?'

'I think that depends on how much they have to lose. The wealthy merchants and tradesmen will support you in hope to protect their property but some of the commoners, being poor men, would welcome violent change.'

'And a chance to join in the looting, no doubt. Richard, have you noted that?'

The secretary was following us, writing on his portable desk. 'Yes, My Lord, but if you could walk a little slower…'

'Very well.' Warwick pointed to a stone arbour at the edge of the lawn. 'We will sit over there. That will make it easier for you.'

We steered our way between the piles of mown grass being raked up by a row of young boys.

'I gather you spent some time in the rebels' camp. What was your impression of this Kett? Does he inspire loyalty or devotion?' Warwick asked.

I had to think hard before answering. 'I did not hear anyone speak of him with adoration. No-one seemed to be in awe of him. There were others there who certainly did have that kind of power.'

'Really? Who were they?'

We had reached the arbour and seated ourselves on a stone bench.

'Preachers and magicians,' I replied. 'One in particular, who calls himself Parafaustus. He stirs the simple people up with false prophecies and bogus visions. He is one of the most dangerous men I have ever met. If I may suggest it, My Lord, it would be very much worth your while to seek him out.'

'Tell me more about him.'

I gave a brief account of my pursuit of the magus (being careful not to mention my suspicions about his connection with the Earl of Southampton). 'So, unfortunately, he has escaped us. I have had a likeness of him made and his grace of Canterbury is arranging for it to be printed. You will be able to have copies to take to Norwich. Pray God he has not moved on.'

'You think he might have deserted Kett?'

'I doubt he ever saw himself as a disciple of Kett. He has other, more powerful masters. His only reason for being at Mousehold Heath was to stir up hatred and cause dissension. He is very slippery. If he has the slightest suspicion that we are on his trail, he will disappear.'

'Who are these "powerful masters" you speak of?'

'I know not, My Lord. That is why I think it important to find him and interrogate him.'

Warwick had several more searching questions to which I tried to give well-considered answers while Richard's pen scratched details down for him lordship's later consideration. Warwick was particularly interested in the topography of the area Kett had chosen for his camp.

'Mousehold Heath lies atop rising ground offering a good view of the city.'

'And beyond it?'

'The heath gives way to a broad expanse of marsh. There seems ...'

I broke off suddenly. A figure was running towards us from the house. Raffy! I jumped to my feet as my son came to a halt before us and made a low bow to his lordship. 'What is the meaning of this, Boy? I gave you strict instructions ...'

'I am sorry, Father,' he panted, speaking to me but looking at Warwick. 'There has come a message from home. 'Tis Adie, your wife, taken sudden sick.'

'Sick? What sick? She was in good health when we left, not two hours since.'

'Well, I think ...' he faltered. 'Perhaps 'twas an accident. Anyway, 'twas thought you should be informed without any delay. Forgive the intrusion, My Lord. Captain Cantrill said I might find you here.' He bowed again.

'How dare you be so familiar!' I cried. 'If you must speak, speak to me. You will return home immediately. If my dear wife is unwell, Master Longbourne is on hand to minister to her. Go now and say that I will be there as soon as Lord Warwick gives me leave to follow.'

With another bow, Raffy turned and went towards the house with less speed than he had left it.

Deeply embarrassed, I made my apologies to Warwick. 'My Lord, please forgive this unpardonable behaviour. My son shames me.'

But Warwick was smiling. 'How many boys have you?'

'But the one of my body. Two others I have taken as my own.'

'Treasure them, Master Treviot. They are your future.'

'I will treasure that lad's backside as soon as I reach home. How dare he burst in here with such a tale.'

'You do not believe him?'

'That I do not, My Lord. 'Twas but a pretence to meet Your Lordship. He admires you greatly.'

Warwick laughed. 'And I, him. It took courage to disobey you.'

'More like impetuosity,' I grumbled.

'Not always easy to tell the one from the other. Is he your prentice?'

'No, he is not apt for business or interested in it. His head is full of grander ideas. A while back he thought to be a scholar. Then he fancied himself a courtier. His latest ambition is for military adventure. Sometimes I despair …'

'You should not. The boy has spirit and that is to be valued. I have been blessed with five sons. The eldest died fighting with me at Boulogne. But I have hopes of the others. Two of them are around the same age as your boy. He might make a good companion for them. Would it please you to place him in my household for a spell?'

I was stunned by this unexpected suggestion. 'My Lord, I am speechless. It is more than Raffy deserves.'

'I can assure you he would learn discipline. I employ the best tutors. Talk with him. If you both like the idea bring him back to see me. But be quick. In two days I leave for Cambridge to muster my forces.'

There was, of course, no doubt about Raffy's reaction to this offer. Adie was scarcely less excited. Her over-heated imagination mapped out a glittering career for her stepson. He would rise rapidly in the earl's service, become a bosom companion of the young king, have honours and offices showered upon him and become a Great Man. As soon as arrangements were made with his lordship, the whole household at the Sign of the Swan was a-bustle with tailors, milliners and provisioners of all kinds furnishing Raffy for his new life. I hired two sturdy and seemingly level-headed young men as body servants and, within a week, the three of them departed for Dudley Castle, Warwick's principal residence.

In truth, I had little time to involve myself in these preparations. My obligations, as a member of the Company, and of the Bread Street Wardmote, the body responsible for maintaining law and order in my neighbourhood, increased almost daily in those crisis weeks of high summer. As fear of a general rebellion mounted in the wake of Kett's success in Norwich, the City's Common Council bombarded us with instructions. We were to enforce a strict curfew, double the watch which guarded our streets at night. Then we were required to organise watch patrols by day also. We were earnestly enjoined to make search for arms and gunpowder. We were to order all householders to lay in a month's provisions so that the ward could withstand a siege. We were to contribute guards to augment the force manning the walls and gates as well as labourers to clear the ditch and make repairs to the City's defences. We were to be vigilant at all times to detect and report troublemakers, rumour-mongers, and distributors of subversive material.

Of this latter there was plenty.

'Henry A. to all true Englishmen:

Be loyal and not deceived by crafty traitors who aim at one target and shoot at others. They have murdered the King's subjects and now, hearing that the Lord Protector would have redressed things in parliament to the ease of the commons, have conspired his death. That done, they will murder the King because of their ambition to restore popery. As for London, Merlin says that twenty-three of its aldermen will lose their heads in one day, which God grant be shortly.'

Lizzie read the handbill, then dropped it on the table. ''Twas thrown in at the door at half-light,' she said.

It was the afternoon of the day Raffy had ridden off. Bart and I had brought Ned back to the Miller's house in Milk Street. The old man's head had mended and though he was still less than steady on his feet, he had insisted on returning to his lodging. and the bench where he concocted his herbal remedies. 'People depend on me for their simples and salves,' he said. 'I must not disappoint them.'

Now we sat round the table drinking ale that Bart poured for us and stared at the crudely-printed sheet.

'There is that in me that says "Amen" to this,' Lizzie muttered.

Ned frowned. 'You would see heads roll?'

'No, not that,' she replied, 'but I feel for the Protector. Sure it is he would see right and justice done for poor men. 'Tis shame that the lords of the Council and their friends conspire to bring him down.'

Bart scowled. 'Hush, Dearling! Women know nought of these things. Somerset is but a counterfeit friend of the people. He talks of his concern for cottagers turned off their land but you have seen the great palace he is building for himself on the Strand.'

Pointedly ignoring her husband's demand for silence. Lizzie turned to me with a sigh. 'Thomas, what will be the end of all this commotion? Is anyone safe?'

'Safer here, I think, than in many parts of the realm,' I said. 'Weeks back I had purposed to take us all to my estate in Kent but the news from Hemmings is of numerous disturbances and mounting unrest in the area. 'Tis a similar story in many places.'

Bart pointed to the broadside. 'What of this plot to kill the Protector. I have no love for him but surely only chaos would follow if he were brought down.'

Ned shook his head. When he spoke it was with an uncharacteristic, slow solemnity. 'Mayhap we must all go through chaos to reach truth and peace. The late king led England into the slough of heresy when he turned against the pope and now the Protector would see us yet more deeply mired in sin and error. I fear the only way back will be a bloody one.'

I stared at my old friend in disbelief. 'Then you would favour Somerset's overthrow?'

'No, I pray for him and I entreat Mary and St Zackary, the patron of peace, that we may be restored without violence to the true church.'

'Well,' I said, 'as to that, we stand on different ground. I know only that we must do all we can to frustrate the schemes of those who would overthrow the government. Our present course is to find Robert Allen and make him talk.'

Ned sighed and I had never seen him look more unhappy. ''Tis my fault you are embroiled in this, Thomas, and I repent me of it. Had I known when we interviewed Master West where 'twould lead …'

I interrupted him. 'Well, 'tis too late for regrets. We are probably the only people who can unmask this Parafaustus.'

'Sadly, I agree,' the old man responded, 'though for a different reason.'

'What reason?'

'Your safety. Has it not occurred to you that while you are seeking out this foul dabbler in forbidden arts, he may seek out you? And his task is the easier. He knows exactly where to find you.'

'Oh, I think his paymasters will think more than twice before they sanction another attack on me.'

Ned stared mournfully across the table. 'Do you suppose he will wait for sanction? Please, take care, my friend. Take very great care.'

◊

It was all very well for Ned to advise me to take care but what, exactly, did that mean? As well as running my business I had the extra responsibilities forced upon me by the current crisis. This meant that I had to be out and about more than usual, aware all the time that danger had many shadowed passages and darkened doorways from which to attack unwary travellers. During those days, I thought often of my dear friend, Robert Packington, shot dead a dozen or more years ago on those very streets*. I went everywhere with my little escort and I made sure always to be well armed but there were no other precautions I could take. My mind would only be eased by news that Robert Allen had been captured. But a week passed and no such news came.

Reports a-plenty circulated in the City's inns and marketplaces. There were rumours and there were facts solemnly vouched for by eye-witnesses but which was which it was difficult to tell. In Middlesex, villages men were flocking to the standard of 'Captain Red Cap'. In Berkshire, magistrates were rounding up people circulating 'rude prophecies'. In Chichester, some of the local gentry had signed a petition calling on the council to depose Somerset and install Princess Mary as Protector. Bystanders on Tower Wharf reported seeing a bargeload of chained prisoners brought upriver from Kent 'to be examined for insurrection'. London was awash with worrying anecdotes but good, solid, reliable, well-authenticated information was in short supply. That was why I was particularly glad when Ralph Morice arrived at my house in the forenoon of 23 August.

'Have you any news of Parafaustus?' It was the first question I put to him as we sat in the parlour sampling a cask of sack I had recently had delivered.'

'I was about to ask you the same question,' Morice replied. 'The churl's picture has been given to our most trusted agents. We have men watching the main roads out of Norwich and we have even sent observers to the east coast ports, in case he tries to ship out of the country.'

'And no sightings?'

'Oh, aye. We've had a couple of men sent up to the council because they share the name of "Allen" and search was even made of a woman at Harwich who covered her face with a shawl.'

'Disguise?'

---

* See *The First Horseman*

119

Morice grimaced. 'I gather the investigation was very thorough. It seems she was trying to escape from an enforced marriage.'

'I had not thought that such a fellow who hawks his spells and nostrums abroad would be so hard to track down.'

'Many who walk the narrow edge between lawfulness and felony have well-honed their instinct for self-preservation. They make sure to have friends amongst the criminal dregs as also protectors in high places. I should tell you, Thomas, that we have discovered someone else on the trail of Parafaustus. You may come across him. His name is Edward Underhill and he is one of the Gentlemen Pensioners.'

'The royal bodyguard?'

'Yes, an upright man of good family, but ...'

'But?'

'He is ... well ... what I suppose you would call a zealot. He is much marked among the fashionable cynics. They call him the 'Hot Gospeller'. His story – which he tells to any who will listen – is that in order to furnish his expensive life at court he took to gambling and was on the brink of ruin when, Lord be praised, he had a dramatic conversion. Now he spends much of his time preaching, particularly in the gaming dens of the City and Southwark.'

'What has that to do with Parafaustus?'

'The magus is one of those drawn to the dicing and card houses like flies to meat. His victims are the credulous gulls who believe that his magic can assure them good fortune.'

'Then this will make him the easier to find.'

'Not so. You know how secretive these gamesters are. They run their iniquitous and illegal business in hovels, cellars, and allies, and seldom twice in the same place. They are at pains to protect themselves from the constables and, sad to say, some of them are the very magistrates who should be closing down these noisome assemblies.'

'Then, let us hope that Master Underhill will sniff out the scent of our man.'

'I do not hold out much hope of that. I fear he is more like to end up stabbed in a back alley than providing us with good information. I only mention him in case you come across him. We have no reason to believe that Allen is in London. Our hopes are pinned on finding him I or near Norwich. According to our latest information, my lord of Warwick will reach the city today.'

'I know.'

'You *know*?' Morice's eyes widened in surprise.

'The earl has taken my son into his household. I had thought by now that the boy would be safely lodged in Dudley Castle, well away from danger but this morning I received this. It was sent by one of the men I have hired to attend Raffy and report to me regularly on his progress.' I handed Morice the letter I had been brooding over ever since it arrived. It read:

> 'My humble commendations to your Honour. This is to inform you Master Raphael is commanded to leave here this forenoon and ride to Norwich. The command is from my lord Warwick who would have your son at his side for that he has knowledge of the rebels and their camp. I beg your honour to be of easy mind over this. Your servants will continue to keep close guard over your son.
>
> Sent in haste from Dudley Castle this 21st day of August.'

Morice handed back the letter. 'I assume his lordship will keep your boy well away from harm.'

'I hope so.'

'You should not worry about this. Warwick is a master precision. Whether on campaign or in the council chamber he carefully gathers all the information he can before making a decision. That is why he is our best commander in the field. It is wholly in keeping with his nature that he should want at his side someone who was but recently in Kett's camp.'

'I realise that but what worries me is the effect this will have on Raffy. He saw terrible things in Norwich. I would not for all the world have him return to that accursed place. Oh, God in heaven!' I cried. 'When will this nightmare be over?'

After a long silence, Morice said, 'I cannot speak for God but all my senses tell me that the critical moment is almost upon us. The cord is straining ever tighter and must soon snap. If only the Lord Protector would hear wise counsel.'

'Why cannot he take command of the situation?'

'He will not change his policy, or confide in anyone or listen to advice. So, inevitably, his support is seeping away by the day.'

'But not among the common people.'

'Perhaps not but, in the final reckoning, they count for little. 'Tis the men of property whose backing he needs – whose backing any government needs.'

I pushed aside my goblet, the dry wine suddenly seeming unpalatably bitter. 'But if Somerset is overthrown, what then?'

Morice sniffed his drink and wrinkled his nose. 'That is what we are all asking ourselves. You should see them all around the council table,' he said with a cynical laugh. 'They debate policy matters like reasonable men but all the time they eye each other, trying to guess their hidden thoughts and intentions. The only question is not "Will anyone challenge Somerset?" but "Who will be the first to do so?"' He looked up as rain began to drive heavily on the window. 'A welcome break in the weather,' he said.

I gazed at the rivulets appearing on the dusty panes. 'There is something I must tell you. Perhaps I should have done so 'ere this but I wanted to be sure before I made any accusation. I know who is behind all this business with West and Parafaustus. I think he must be the most dangerous man in the country.'

Morice raised his eyebrows. 'Truly? Then, in God's name, tell me.'

'I am speaking of the Earl of Southampton.'

Morice's reaction was not at all what I had expected. He laughed. 'Thomas Wriothesley? Oh no! If there is one man we may be most sure of – his grace of Canterbury alone excepted – that man is Wriothesley. What can have led you to suspect him?'

Though discouraged by this response, I laid out the sequence of events that had led me to suspect the ex-Chancellor. 'Granted, we cannot fit the capstone to the arch of evidence until we can force the truth out of Allen,' I said, 'but do not other factors point to his guilt?'

'Such as?' Morice asked.

'Southampton is well known to favour the old way in religion.'

'That is true but I doubt he would ever let that stand in the way of his ambition.'

'Then there is the fact that the Protector stripped him of his office and removed him from the Council two years ago,' I argued.

'Indeed, and how has he spent the last two years? Not thirsting for revenge and plotting rebellion, but working his way back into the Lord Protector's good graces, unlike the Earl of Arundel, who was also demoted by Somerset and mutters his discontent to any who will listen. If ever there was a whisper of suspicion against Southampton – the merest suggestion of disloyalty – he would be completely finished, once and for all and this he knows only too well.'

I was still reluctant to see my carefully-constructed case against Southampton demolished. 'By your account, Ralph, things at court are finely balanced. So who do you see as those who could be behind this labyrinthine plot to use West and Allen and De la Warr to disgrace the Protector and his inner circle?'

Morice frowned. 'Thomas, you must not press me to name names. There are rumours enough abroad and I must not be seen to be adding to them. What I will tell you is those who are above suspicion. If you wish to speculate beyond that ...' He shrugged his shoulders.

'Very well. Who is beyond reproach?'

'The archbishop, of course. Also my lord Warwick. He and Somerset are old comrades in arms and much of a mind in religious matters. Paget, for all his impatience with the Protector, is reliable. Beyond that, I must say nothing in public – not even to friends.'

A little later, having escorted my visitor to the door, I went in search of my wife. I found her in the kitchen and she was in a mood of high indignation.

'How can we help people who are so ungrateful?' she demanded, brandishing what seemed to be a grey woollen cloak.

'Whatever is the matter?' I asked.

'Yesterday afternoon, not twenty-four hours since, there comes a beggar in at the yard, asking for old clothes. He was a poor wretch, in tatters, his bare arms covered in sores. I felt pity for him – more fool I.'

'Why say you so?'

'Because of this.' She waved the garment at me. I went to the press in our chamber and found this old riding cloak of yours. It is shabby and I have often asked you to throw it out. Now, since there was someone whose need was greater than yours I knew you would not mind if I gave it to the beggar.'

'That was well done, Poppet.'

'So I thought, and very grateful the wretch seemed. He put it on and went away happy. Then, this afternoon, Meg, the kitchen maid, found it in the alley behind the house – thrown away – and deliberately ruined.' She held out the garment to reveal a large, square hole cut in the back. 'If ever I see that lewd ingrate, I'll ...'

'The Master knows him.' It was Henry Holbein who spoke. The boy was sitting at the table and, as usual, scribbling on a sheet of paper with a piece of charcoal.

'*I* know him, Henry? What do you mean?' I asked.

Without looking up, the little artist said, 'He was the man whose face you asked me to draw.'

Chapter 12

'ARE YOU SURE?' I stared at the boy, who was bent over his drawing with a frown of concentration.

'Oh yes,' Henry replied casually.

'How do you know? Many people look alike.'

'No. Everyone is different.'

I realised from the boy's simple certainty that he was declaring what, to him, was a self-evident truth. 'But did you get a really good look at the man?' I persisted.

Now Henry at last laid down his charcoal and condescended to look up. 'Yes. His hood was pulled over his forehead. Funny that, it was so hot. He had smeared grime over his face. But his straggly beard was as you described. And his drawn-in cheeks. When he put the cloak on, his hood got lifted and I saw he had drawn wrinkles around his eyes. That was a funny thing to do, wasn't it?'

'Not if he was disguising himself,' I thought.

Adie drew me aside and there was fear in her eyes as she whispered, 'Thomas, is it the necromancer you have been looking for? Has he been here in our house? Has he put a curse on us all? And what means this?' She pointed to the torn cloak.

'Mere malice,' I replied. 'If your beggar is Robert Allen, he has come to give me a crude warning. 'Tis all he can do.' I was thinking hard as I spoke, trying to dispel Adie's anxiety. 'He thinks to frighten me into abandoning my search.' I held up the cloth to show the hole. 'He is saying, "I will do the same to you if you try to catch me." But I am well guarded. He and his ruffians will not get near me.'

What I knew but did not say was that there was more to Allen's bizarre behaviour. I doubted whether he had intended us to find the torn cloak. There was, I suspected, an altogether different reason why he had cut out a square of cloth.

This was confirmed later that afternoon by Ned. 'The Law of Contact, without a doubt,' he said.

I had sent a message for him to meet me and Bart at Gerard's Hall. This spacious, not to say cavernous, hostelry, in Basing Lane was scarcely a stone's throw from Goldsmiths' Row and was a favourite meeting place of ours, largely because it had the best of the few London brewhouses where customers could buy the increasingly popular beer as well as ale. But that was not why I had chosen the tavern today: I wanted to be able to discuss the latest developments away from the house so as not to alarm Adie and the servants any further.

'Law of Contact, Ned?' Bart asked. 'Explain it in a way a simple man like me can understand.'

Ned sat back on the bench, resting his head against the panelled wainscot. ''Tis basically a simple idea. Everything is connected – everything in heaven and earth. God moves the planets and by this means affects the flow of humours in the human body. God endows plants whose virtues also correspond to the four humours and can, therefore, cure ailments by restoring the balance.'

Bart scowled into his wooden tankard. 'Yes, well I leave all that sort of thing to the physicians and the apothecaries. What has it to do with the hole in Master Thomas's old cloak?'

Ned suppressed an impatient sigh. 'Simply that there are those who believe that there is contact between people and the things they touch, carry, wear.'

'Well that is pretty obvious,' Bart scoffed. 'How can you touch, carry or wear something without being in contact with it?'

Ned tried again. 'The Law of Contact suggests that some kind of association between man and object continues even after the object has been discarded.'

'Like Master Thomas and his cloak?'

'Exactly.'

126

'Stupid!' Bart thumped his tankard down on the table and drew the back of his hand across his lips.

'Stupid or not, 'tis a belief the church has encouraged for centuries,' Ned observed. 'How many fragments of the true cross or spikes from our Saviour's crown of thorns have been preserved and venerated in shrines throughout Christendom?'

'Do you support the worship of holy relics, Ned?' I asked.

The old man's lips creased in a rueful smile. 'It was much open to abuse. All I will say is that King Henry's abolition of shrines and pilgrimages was one of the few changes I least regret.'

Bart was not to be silenced. 'Master Thomas's cloak is not a relic of some long-dead saint. I still do not see …'

I tried to help with the explanation. 'The church taught that something of the saints lived in the objects they left behind. Magicians believe that that is true of everyone. So there remains a connection between me and my old cloak.'

'Which may or may not be true,' Ned resumed, 'but what the unholy dabblers in black arts believe is that through things they can reach the owners of those things – and so have power over them. This vile Parafaustus creature thinks to do harm to Thomas by using the fragment from his cloak in his spells and incantations.'

Bart sniggered. 'Who is taken in by such folly?'

Ned shrugged. 'Enough people for Parafaustus and his ilk to make a living by promising desperate maids that they can make men fall in love with them and householders that they can rid them of vexatious neighbours.'

'So your Law of Contact is about making foolish connections to explain things.' Bart pointed upwards to the high rafters above. ''Tis like the old legend people tell of this place. Because 'tis so tall they say it was built for Gerard the Giant.'

'All this is not to the point,' I protested. 'We now know that Allen is in London. The question is how are we to find him?'

Bart shook his head. 'The City's a warren. There's thousands of places a man can hide and the constables none the wiser. It might be possible to flush out this scelerous lorrel but only if we could send out enough searchers.'

'That would only warn him, and then he would disappear again.' I protested. 'The one advantage we have at the moment is that Allen does not know he has been recognised.'

Ned looked thoughtful. 'I wonder what I would do in his position. Sometimes 'tis useful to ask that question. We know that Allen was very popular among the Norfolk rebels. He must have made a deal of money out of those gullible folk. I gather from what you say, Thomas, that he assured Kett's people that the spirits had told him they would be victorious. If he believed that, why did he not stay to share their triumph?'

'Because he is not stupid enough to believe his own lies.'

'Yes, Bart,' Ned continued, 'I think you are right. Norwich is no longer safe for him. If he is not captured by Warwick's men he might well be lynched by Kett's followers. So where could he go to find safety?'

'To his patron?' I suggested.

''Tis a good guess,' Ned agreed, 'in which case we should probably keep watch on Lord Southampton's house.'

'I fear some doubt has been cast on our ideas about his lordship,' I said. 'Cranmer believes Southampton is completely trustworthy – or so his secretary says – and we certainly have no proof to the contrary.'

'Oh, good.' Bart's face wore a cynical smile. 'We need Allen to lead us to his paymaster but now we need to identify his paymaster to lead us to Allen. We are like a dog chasing its tail.'

'More like a blind wrestler at the mercy of his adversary,' Ned observed solemnly. 'We are threatened by evils we cannot see. Even if we set no store by Allen's conjuring of demons we know he is a dabbler in poisons and that his master is not above hiring ruffians.'

I was deflected from these depressing thoughts by a light tug at my sleeve. It turned to see Carl Holbein standing behind me.

'Your pardon, Master,' the boy said. 'There has come a fine gentleman to see you. Mistress Adie told him you were from home but he said his business could not wait. So I was sent to fetch him here. He stood aside and a tall man in yellow and scarlet royal livery stepped forward.

The newcomer inclined his head, just sufficient to show respect. 'Edward Underhill, servant to our Saviour, Jesus Christ, and to his majesty King Edward,' he said.

Bart drew up a stool for the guardsman who seated himself and surveyed us all with quick, darting eyes of an intense blue.

I made the introductions. 'You are most welcome. It was only a few hours ago that Ralph Morice mentioned your name to me.'

'Then I expect you know why I have sought you out, Master Treviot.'

'It is to do with Robert Allen.'

'Aye, that limb of Satan. Like Simon Magus, we read of in the Acts of the Apostles, he seeks to use the power of God for his own ends.'

'He must be found and stopped,' I agreed. 'Do you know where he is to be found?'

Those heaven-blue eyes scrutinised me again. 'First, I pray, tell me of your dealings with the man.'

While Bart fetched another tankard and had our pitcher refilled by one of the servers I gave Underhill an abbreviated version of our quest for Parafaustus. When I concluded by telling him about the torn cloak he frowned and muttered under his breath some words I did not catch.

Then, he stood abruptly, raised one hand in the air and declaimed in a loud voice, 'Almighty God, Master of all things in heaven and earth, we beseech you for your servant, Thomas. Send your angels to guard him and his family. Keep at bay the minions of Satan and they who do his bidding on earth. Crush the evil one under his feet and visit with your wrath the man who has bargained away his soul for powers not granted to humankind. Amen! Let it be so!'

He resumed his seat, oblivious or careless of all the heads turned in his direction.

I stuttered a few words of thanks which I hoped were appropriate.

'You will be safe, now,' Underhill announced confidently. '"The prayer of a righteous man avails much if it be fervent"; Epistle of James chapter five.'

'So,' I prompted, 'Can we work together to find this ... limb of Satan?'

Underhill leaned forward and beckoned us to do the same. Our heads were close together across the table as he spoke softly and confidentially. 'My friends, until you told of your encounter with him I knew not for certain that Allen was back in town, though I suspected it. London draws his sort like iron to lodestone. This city is like Sodom and Gomorrah. There are many haunts of iniquity where men carry out unspeakable evils. I know it to be so because once, to my shame, I frequented such hell holes.'

I recalled Morice's comment that this earnest convert loved to tell his own story to any who would listen. I determined to head him off. 'And Allen is addicted to such company?'

'Aye. As a dog returns to its vomit, so he is ever to be found in places of ill repute.'

'And lodges in one of them?'

'Nay, he is a vagrant, ever on the move, ever on the lookout for fresh dupes and ever wary of the constables.'

'So you cannot tell us where to look for him?'

For the first time, the guardsman's assertiveness faltered. 'I could as soon tell where the pestilence will break out next, though for sure 'twill break out somewhere.'

Bart stood abruptly. 'In that case, Master Underhill, we thank you for your concern ...'

'Be not so hasty!' The response flashed back with the sharpness of a man well accustomed to giving orders.

As Bart resumed his seat, Underhill continued. 'I cannot tell where you will find Allen at this moment but I have studied his movements. I know something of his habits and the places he frequents. There are established gaming rooms at taverns like the Bull in Southwark and the Cardinal's Hat in Cornhill that are protected by corrupt magistrates. He finds ready welcome there among the dicers and card-sharpers.'

'Why so?' Ned's interest had been captured by the speaker.

'Because he brings in dupes – loggerheaded lads up from the country. He tricks 'em into buying spells certain to give them success at the tables. I was once gulled by just such a knave ...'

I hastened to steer him away from personal reminiscences. 'So much for gambling dens. Where else might we look for Master Allen?'

'Oh, I could tell you how he mingles in St Paul's with the crowds come to gawp and gossip rather than pray, and of the marketplaces where he offers love potions to maidens and widows but all this takes us not forward. Why think you I have chosen this particular day to enlist your help?'

The three of us exchanged puzzled glances.

Underhill sighed. 'This is St Bartholomew's Eve. For the next three days, everyone from the City and miles around will be flocking to Smithfield for the fair.'

'And you believe Allen will be there?'

'I believe he would find it difficult to stay away.'

I thought hard about what Underhill was suggesting. Was this the change of fortune we had been hoping for? ''Twill be mightily crowded. If he is there, how will we find him? And if we find him how will we arrest him?'

We spent the next half hour or so discussing these questions. We agreed that we would meet the next day, that Underhill and I would bring trusted servants, and that we would all make our way to Smithfield, suitably but discreetly armed. Underhill would bring some of the pictures of Allen that Morice had had printed so that all our people would know who they were looking for. By the time I returned home that evening I actually allowed myself, to hope, for the first time in a month, that we might be bringing this business to a conclusion and that I might be able to resume my life as a simple London merchant.

◊

'There must be more people here than last year,' I said as we approached. From where we stood at Pie Corner there seemed to be nothing but a shifting sea of people lapping up against the bastion of St Bartholomew the Great.

'It seems that way because of the new buildings between Hosier Lane and the sheep pens,' Lizzie said. 'More fine houses for rich men instead of tenements where honest workers and their families might live.'

We had decided to patrol the crowd in pairs so that, if Allen was spotted, one could keep him in view while the other went for help. I had brought six apprentices and craftsmen from Goldsmiths' Row and Underhill had recruited a like number of his own men. Everyone had memorised the face of the villain we were looking for. I had had to endure Adie's wrath by refusing to bring her on this expedition but, as I explained, since she was concerned for my safety, it was right and proper that I should be concerned for hers.

Lizzie and I arrived at the fair a little after noon and weaved our way, arm-in-arm, between the tradesmen's stalls and the little stages where jugglers and actors held their audiences spellbound.

'Quite like old times,' Lizzie jested. 'Remember how you used to visit me in the Southwark stews? Some of my gossips used to think you would set me up as your private strumpet.'

'Well, thank the Lord, Bart rescued me from any such folly.'

Lizzie wrinkled her nose. 'I would not have had you for a lover, anyway. You were far too priggish and affected.'

'And you were the shrewest whore in Southwark, I am glad Bart has tamed you.'

'That he has not,' she protested, and grimaced.

We laughed together but did not let our vigilance falter. Two or three times we manoeuvred ourselves close to someone who resembled our quarry but, as the crowds thinned towards evening we called off our search, hoping for better fortune on the morrow.

Sunday's dawn was ushered in to the drumming of thunder. When I threw the casements open I peered through streams of rainwater rushing from the eaves.

'This will keep many people from the fair,' Adie said as she came to stand beside me.

'I fear you may be right. If Allen decides there is not enough profit to be made in Smithfield this day, we shall have to start our hunt all over again.'

It was with no great confidence that I met up with Underhill for another day of patrolling the fairground. The rain was intermittent and heavy. Hundreds of trampling feet turned the grassy field into a surface of clinging, slippery mud. Despite the weather, Smithfield was filled with determined revellers. The ale booths did a particularly flourishing business and, during the course of the morning, we witnessed a couple of drunken brawls. But of the magus, there was no trace. Until shortly after noon.

By the time the unmusical clock-bell of St Bartholomew the Great clunked twelve I was growing very tired and was about to suggest to Underhill that we should call off our search when he nudged me and pointed to a small circle of people gathered close by the corner of Long Lane. The performer holding their attention was Robert Allen.

'Try to get closer,' Underhill muttered. 'I will find some of the others.'

I edged out to the periphery of the crowd, moved around until I was in a line with Allen and behind him. Then I nudged my way forward until there were only three people between us. Now, I could hear his performance.

'Citizens, rest your eyes upon this parchment.' I caught a glimpse of the object he brandished, which bore lines of writing in various garish colours. ''Twas given me by Cardinal Forrante when last I was in Rome. A knavish servant was filching from his treasury but his eminence could not discover the man. I offered him this spell – a revelation spell. I bade his eminence inscribe upon clean paper these sacred words, "Agios, Agios, Agios, Crux, Crux, Crux, Spiritus, Spiritus, Spiritus be with this servant of God", with certain holy numbers to complete the charm. Then I charged him to place it upon his pillow at night.

Now, that cardinal was sceptical. He mocked me, "How may your magic work when the prayers of all my chapel priests do not?" he said. "Because to me has been given wisdom more ancient even than the stones of holy Rome," I replied. "Let your eminence but try the spell and you will discover the truth." That very night he secretly employed my charm. And what happened, think you?'

Allen stared round at his audience. 'As that mighty prince of the church slept he had a dream. And in that dream what did he see? Why, he perceived his most senior chaplain going to the treasury with a counterfeit key and unlocking his coffers.'

Allen paused to allow a murmur from his audience before hurrying on. 'Now, good citizens, you will ask yourselves, "Since this great magician is well known in the courts of princes, why does he come among us to share his wisdom with ordinary folk?" It is a good question; an honest question; a fair question. The answer is that the true magus is careless of fame and wealth. I am the humble guardian of sacred wisdom and I am charged by God and the holy messengers he sends me to make the benefits of ancient truth available to all. Now, who among you needs wisdom, needs revelation, needs knowledge that can only come from the heavenly realm? Would you see into the secret thoughts of your lover?'

Another pause, this time for ribald remarks.

'Would you know who seeks to do you mischief? Would you peer into the future? Come forward now. In my scrip here I have spells of all kinds. Spells that are nothing less than ladders, aye ladders reaching right into heaven itself.'

I felt a tap on my shoulder. Underhill whispered, 'There are six of us now, all set to encircle him. Are you ready?'

I nodded.

'Then, let us go.' He drew his heavy rapier and barged forward through the throng of Allen's admirers. 'Robert Allen!' He gripped the man's arm. The magician whipped around like a startled ferret. He drew a long blade from beneath his cloak and lashed out with it. Underhill fell sprawling in the mud, clutching his arm. His weapon fell from his hand. Allen jumped over him. He cleared a path by brandishing his knife.

'After him! Take my sword!' Underhill struggled to get to his feet.

I picked up the rapier and sped in pursuit. 'Stop that man!' I shouted and other took up the hue and cry.

With a dozen people in pursuit, escape was impossible for the fugitive and his long, image-spangled robe hindered his flight. It was my man, Dickon, who brought him down. He threw himself at the magus and sent him sprawling in the muddy ruts some fifty yards up Long Lane.

He was being hauled to his feet as I ran up. 'Master Treviot,' he snarled, and I had never seen such a look of hatred on anyone's face. 'Your days are numbered!'

'All our days are numbered,' I said, 'but the only day that interests me now is this one.' I held the swordpoint to his chest. 'You will take us to your lodging where we will conduct a search for evidence of your treasons and felonies.'

A sneer of defiance twisted his grime-spattered face. 'I will do no such thing.'

'Then we must persuade you.' Underhill had joined us. He was clutching his upper right arm and his sleeve was well stained with blood.'

'We must tend that wound,' I said.

'In time. 'Tis not deep. First, we must deal with this fellow.' Underhill called to his men. 'Bind the villain's hands!'

'You do not frighten me, Master Underhill,' Allen taunted, as his arms were pinned behind his back.

'No, Master Allen? In that case, I must try harder.' Underhill looked around and pointed to a narrow gap between two houses. 'That should serve our purpose. Take the devil's spawn down there and see if you cannot bring about a change of mind.'

As the necromancer was dragged away, Underhill turned to me with a smile. 'Thank you, Master Treviot. I have waited long for this day.'

'I, too, am much relieved to have caught this fellow at last. I have many questions to put to him. Now, let us look to this wound.'

Bart and I helped Underhill out of his tabard, emblazoned with the royal insignia, and rolled up his shirt sleeve.

There came a sudden shrill scream from the alley where our prisoner was being 'examined'.

'I hope your colleagues are not too enthusiastic. I need information from him.'

'Have no fear, Master Treviot. My friends and I are guardians of the king's person. We know how to interrogate men who pose a threat to his majesty. A dead informant is no use to anyone.'

Allen's stiletto had penetrated flesh and muscle as far as the bone of the guardsman's upper arm and blood was still oozing from the cut. I tore strips from his silken shirt and bound the wound tightly. 'Bart will take you to my friend, Ned Longbourne' I said. 'He is no surgeon but there is not a man in London with a better knowledge of salves and healing herbs.'

'Not until we have this hellhound safely under lock and key,' Underhill insisted.

Moments later Allen emerged from the alleyway, half-walking and half-dragged by two guardsmen. He had, with his captors' aid, 'remembered' where he lived. He indicated that it was near at hand and that he would lead us there.

The place he took us to was a stinking hovel at the back of Aldersgate Street just outside the city wall. The tiny ground floor room was furnished with little more than a table, a stool and a pile of woollen cloths that, presumably, served as a bed.

'You dissembling puttock!' Underhill cried. 'You have learned well from your satanic master. He was ever the father of lies. This is not where you lure simpletons to impress them with your tricks and gull them out of their coin.'

'You wrong me,' Allen whined, still refusing to give in. 'I am but a poor scholar using my humble skill for the betterment of all and no thought of personal gain.'

'Really, scholar is it?' Bart could not resist mocking our prisoner. 'And where did you study?'

The reply was prompt, well-rehearsed. 'Heidelburg and Padua. They know more of the astronomical science there than all the so-called doctors in Oxford and Cambridge.'

'This is time-wasting!' Underhill stepped forward. Coming behind Allen he hooked his good arm around the man's throat. 'Take us to your base straightway or I will have my men exert more persuasion.'

'This is torture!' Allen croaked. ''Tis not just or fair.'

'I never heard yet that the devil is just or fair. I merely repay him in his own coin.' Underhill tightened his grip till the magician's face turned red and rasping noises came from his mouth.

The treatment worked. The magician's prevarication ceased. Within half an hour we were all in the fashionable district around the Guildhall where Allen rented a chamber from a respectable lawyer – proof that his disciples were not only drawn from the ranks of the simple and scantily-educated.

Allen's London base was equipped with all the things he needed to practise the black arts – or, at least, to impress clients that he was accomplished in the black arts. Star charts were pinned to every available wall space. A large, open chest was filled with books and with scraps of parchment bearing what appeared to be archaic script. A long shelf carried the jars and distilling equipment necessary for the work of an apothecary.

'We will need to sift through all this very carefully,' Underhill said. ''Twill be a job for tomorrow. I will leave a man on guard here to make sure that nothing is tampered with. What is to be done with this fellow, meanwhile?' He prodded our prisoner.

'I will see him lodged in the Bread Street gaol, the Compter. 'Tis in my jurisdiction. He can stay there while we obtain an order for his removal to the Tower.'

'Which I will obtain from the council as soon as I return to court.'

'Very well, but first we must let Ned see to your wound.'

That was how we left matters on Sunday evening. Everything was tidily arranged. We would reconvene on the morrow, have Allen conveyed to the Tower where Cranmer could take up, for himself, the unravelling of the William West affair and my involvement in it would be at an end.

Not for the first time, I had grossly underestimated the enemy.

Chapter 13

IT WAS THE next day, Monday 26 August, that I began to realise the forces we were up against. Underhill arrived at my house in the middle of the morning. He appeared very subdued and not, I soon realised, because of the sling holding his right arm.

'How is your wound?' I asked as we sat in the parlour with a hot posset.

''Twill mend,' he grunted. ''Tis bothersome having it bound like this but your friend assured me it will speed the healing. I have had worse, far worse.'

'Yet, you seem somewhat distracted.'

'I fear our business does not run smoothly.'

'Why say you so? What is the problem?'

Underhill shook his head and sighed. 'I had hoped to be here this morning with a warrant to convey our necromancer straight to the Tower. I have spent hours at Whitehall last night and this morning. I saw Master Secretary Paget. He told me that the matter must be considered by the whole council. When I eventually found Ralph Morice, he said that his grace could not take the responsibility upon himself – that there are "circumstances" which must be thought on. He is content for us to search Allen's chamber, but as to incarceration in the Tower ... Pah! Politics!'

I was puzzled. ''Twas the archbishop who set me upon this business at the start. He wanted Parafaustus unmasked. He seemed delighted when I had identified him. So now, when we have this magic-dabbler in our power, why does he suddenly retreat into caution?'

'Satan has disciples at court. Some of them belong to the gambling dens where Allen is well known.'

'Such places are illegal,' I said.

'Aye, there is the nub of it. Illegal they are and the Protector is hot against them. So they must continue in secret. The Saviour said, "Men prefer darkness to light because their deeds are evil."'

'So Allen's friends at court mean to protect him from interrogation because it might expose them.'

Underhill nodded sombrely. 'The enemies of righteousness ...'

'Yet it goes deeper.' I hurried on to avoid a sermon. 'Now I begin to see things more clearly.'

'What things?'

'Cranmer and Paget were overjoyed when I revealed Parafaustus as involved in a certain matter they wanted investigated secretly. They said they had suspected him but lacked proof. I thought they wanted to silence rumours against the Protector's allies. Now I think they were being much more active – not defending their friends but attacking their enemies.'

'Then why ...?'

'Why should they now be blowing hot and cold? Indeed. You would think ... Something must have changed ...' I cudgelled my brains for some kind of answer. 'Has anything unusual happened at court these last days – anything that would change the balance of forces?'

Underhill shook his head. 'Everyone has been too concerned with affairs in Norwich ...'

'Then, perhaps, that is it!'

'I do not ...'

'Fear, Edward, fear! We are all worried about this rebellion. What if Kett and his peasant rabble defeat a second royal army? 'Tis the question on everyone's lips. London is in a frenzy as we try to make ourselves secure against attack. People are frightened and when they are frightened they look for someone to blame. Many here are turning against the Protector. They say, if he had been firmer with the malcontents from the start, matters would not have reached this point. Are our leaders not thinking the same at court?'

'Yes, support is draining away from Somerset, quite steadily.'

'Who do people want to replace him?'

Underhill gave a cynical laugh. 'Oh, 'tis far easier to complain about bad government than shoulder responsibility for producing better government.'

I recalled what Morice had said about council members all eyeing each other to see who would make the first move. 'Then this explains the paralysis among our leaders. England is like a drifting ship. The captain stays in his cabin and no-one on deck is ready to put a hand to the whipstaff.'

Underhill sighed. 'This is all very well but we cannot change anything. We have to deal with Allen. Keep him off the streets. Bring him to trial. That is all I know.'

I rose from the table. 'You are right. Let us see what evidence we can gather at Allen's lodging.'

But in the house at Aldermanbury Street, we encountered another obstacle. Outside the door of Allen's chamber, an argument was in full flood. Or rather, half an argument was in full flood. A short, balding man in a lawyer's robe was shouting at the guardsman who had been left on duty. The latter was maintaining an unruffled silence.

At our approach, the declaimer turned his attention upon us. 'At last, someone who can explain this unlawful outrage.'

'Unlawful?' I questioned.

'Aye, unlawful! It matters not that the intruders are of his majesty's own guard, they are, none the less, intruders. A citizen's home is shielded from violation by the law. I am a lawyer, Sir, and an alderman. I know my legal rights.' He advanced to within a pace and thrust his rage-reddened face close to mine. Then he stepped back. 'Do I not recognise you? You are of the Goldsmiths' Company I think.'

I introduced myself and Underhill.

The little man nodded. 'Ah, yes. I thought we had met. I am Christopher Gaston. I must say, Master Treviot, I am astonished to see a man of your standing in the City embroiled in this scandalous invasion of privacy.'

'We come in execution of a warrant from his grace of Canterbury,' I explained. 'You will doubtless wish to peruse our warrant.'

Underhill handed over the authorisation he had obtained from Cranmer.

Gaston held it close to his eyes, frowning as he read short-sightedly. 'What is this all about? Master Allen is a tenant. He has been for the last two years. He has never given any trouble.'

'The man is a necromancer.' Underhill said.

'And, so?' Gaston shrugged. 'Nothing illegal in that. In 1541, parliament made it an offence in the Act against Conjuration. Six years later that statute was repealed by our own more enlightened government. Anyway, it was always a nonsense. In all the time that it was on the book how many prosecutions were brought – eh, eh!' The lawyer glared truculently. 'One! Just one! So what do you mean by hounding Master Allen as a magician?'

'We are not investigating him for dealing in the black arts,' I replied calmly. 'He is under examination on suspicion of foretelling the death of the king, which, as you know is treason, and also of being an accomplice in an attempted murder.'

'And you have proof of all this?' Gaston's bluster was subsiding.

'We are here in quest of such proof,' I said. 'Our instructions come from the Lord Protector and the council. I feel confident, Master Gaston, that you would not want to be seen as hindering our investigation.'

The lawyer opened his mouth to reply, thought better of it, turned abruptly and went into another room, slamming the door behind him.

My companions and I spent more than three hours going through the contents of Allen's sanctum. We had brought sacks with us and into them, we carefully packed the magus's books and star charts. Amidst the arcane paraphernalia in Allen's coffer, there were several letters which I took to a corner and read cursorily while the others were examining the rest of the contents.

At one point, Underhill cried out triumphantly, 'Aha! Fullams!' He handed me a pair of dice fashioned from bone.

'What is special about them?' I asked.

'Subtly weighted with lead. They look not suspicious but a skilled thrower can cast them in such a way that they show a high value when he wishes them to do so. Is there anything useful among those letters?'

'Yes,' I said, 'names.'

'What names?'

'People at court men with whom Allen had had dealings on various matters. I think this is what he relies on for his security. This is why he can be so confident, so cock-sure of avoiding conviction. If he is arrested he can point the finger at others. You must keep these separate and ensure that you only give them to Cranmer. It is of the utmost importance and that no-one but his grace sees them. Otherwise, they could cause all manner of mischief.'

What I did not tell Underhill was that I had taken one document and thrust it inside my doublet.

Having seen Underhill and his companions on their way back to court with their bundles of evidence, I returned home and immediately penned a long report to Cranmer. Evening was setting in as I despatched a servant to take it across to Lambeth.

'Praise God that is all over.' Adie stood beside me as we watched my messenger ride out of the yard.

'I pray heartily that you are right.'

'No doubt about it. That horrid black magician is in prison and you have found enough evidence to make sure he stays there for a very long time.' Despite my wife's certainty there was a tinge of anxiety to her voice.

'I shall not be fully at ease till Master West is released from the Tower.'

'Surely, that is only a matter of time. When the council know of all Allen's villainies they will set West at liberty.'

'I hope so. I certainly hope so.' I put an arm around Adie's shoulder. 'Let us indoors. The air grows chill.'

◊

I shall never forget the twenty-eighth day of August 1549. The excitement on the streets, the ringing of church bells, the relief in my own household and the black foreboding that cloaked my soul by day's end.

That Wednesday morning began quietly enough. I was sat at table with my family – Adie, the Holbein boys, Carl and Henry, and little Meg with her nurse. We were enjoying a simple breakfast when there came a buzz of excited voices from the kitchen. Moments later, Raffy strode in, casting aside his rain-soaked cloak as he did so. I

141

stared at the boy in amazement. Until that moment I had not realised that someone could change so much in only a few days. For, in truth, my son was a 'boy' no longer. His swagger was not now the anxious self-assertiveness of a half-child but that of a half-man confident of his place in the world. After a cursory greeting, he slumped into a chair and reached for some bread.

'I am hungry. We have ridden non-stop with only one change of horses.'

'It is so good to see you,' I said. 'We have worried ever since we heard you were ordered back to Norwich. But why are you home again so soon? Not sent away in disgrace by his lordship, I trust.'

Raffy laughed. 'Not at all. He is quite pleased with me. At least, I hope so.' He fumbled in his purse. 'Here, this should explain everything.' He handed me a letter with Warwick's bear-and-ragged staff imprinted in the wax. I opened it hurriedly and read its brief message.

Master Treviot, I greet you well.

Your boy has made a good start in my household and is companionable to my own sons. I have had him with me in Norwich these last days and his knowledge of the rebels' camp has been useful. Now that our main business here is concluded satisfactorily and I am despatching a report to the Lord Protector I thought to send Raphael with my messenger to await my return to London in a few days. You are well placed to spread the news of the royal victory God has granted us here and Raphael will provide you with more details than I have time to set down in writing.

In haste from Norwich this 27 November, 1549.

'The rebellion is truly over?' God be praised!'

'Aye,' Raffy replied, through a mouthful of cheese, 'God and the Earl of Warwick. He is a great man.'

Carl stared wide-eyed at his step-brother. 'Tell us about the battle, Raffy! Was it exciting?'

'Oh, yes!' Raffy, enjoying the attention, became voluble. 'It was an inspiration. He is an inspiration. The first thing he did was win over the mayor and aldermen. They were scared. They thought "If the rebels win, Warwick will turn tail and run as Northampton did. Then we will be at the mercy of Kett and his cutthroats." So what did my lord do? He gathered them all in the marketplace. He had all his captains kiss one another's swords and swear a solemn oath. "We will never desert Norwich" He shouted. "We will defend this city with our life blood."'

'Then what happened?' Henry urged the speaker on.

'My lord called on the rebels to lay down their arms. Promised them a pardon. But they were stubborn and stupid. They were urged on by some sort of wizard who had given out written prophecies that they could not be beaten. I have one such here.' He pulled a crumpled scrap of paper from his purse and handed it to me.

This what I read:

'The country churls, Hob, Dick and Hick,
With clubs and hob-nailed shoon,*
Shall fill the vale of Dussindale
With slaughtered bodies soon.'

'Were these put about by the man who calls himself Parafaustus?' I asked.

'Aye, that was him. Many of the sluggards swore by him but I heard tell he was nowhere to be seen when the fighting started.'

'No,' I said, 'he was well away by then.'

'What does "Dustingale" mean?' Henry wanted to know.

'Not "Dustingale", Harry. The word is "Dussindale",' Raffy said.

'Henry, who did not like being called "Harry", frowned. 'Well, anyway what is it?'

'That was where the battle was – an area of level ground near the city wall. My lord made them fight there. He was brilliant.'

Adie looked puzzled. 'But if it was the place prophesied for the battle how can you say that Lord Warwick chose it?'

Raffy responded eagerly. 'Because he heard the prophecy he knew that Kett would move his men to Dussindale if they were forced out of the Mousehold camp. So, while his infantry defended Warwick and prevented the rebels getting back in, his cavalry harassed Kett's

---

* 'shoes'

143

camp, cutting off his supply lines and forcing him out. The enemy had to move hurriedly to defend Dussindale. They dug ditches and built fences but they were completely disorganised – men and wagons going to and fro, getting in each other's way. I rode out with his lordship to watch them.'

'Not getting too close, I hope?'

'No, Father, we were careful. Anyway, the empty-headed churls were too busy to think of firing at us. They were like cattle in the shambles, shuffling about, waiting to be slaughtered.'

Raffy was now warming to his tale and enjoying an eager audience. 'Before the battle, Lord Warwick drew up his troops in lines and urged them to fight fearlessly against men who had shown themselves to be no better than brute beasts. It was a thrilling sight – especially the German mercenaries in their colourful uniforms and plumes. It was the Germans – *landsknechts*, as they are called – who truly won the day. The order was given – "Charge!" – and they crashed through the rebels flimsy barriers like standing corn. Kett's men stood no chance. They were cut down as they fled.'

Adie said, 'I think I would have felt pity for them.'

'Pity? Pity?' There was an almost savage glint in my son's eyes. 'Not I, Mistress. Not after what they did to Walt.'

'You have had your revenge in full measure,' I observed quietly.

'Aye, and glad I am of it,' Raffy responded.

When I left the table Raffy was still answering an eager flow of questions from Carl and Henry. I penned brief messages passing on the good news from Norwich to the mayor, the prime warden of the Goldsmiths' Company and the officials of neighbouring wards.

Good news? Yes, of course, a massive relief to know that the rebellion had been stopped before it had any chance to spread further. Why, then, could I not share in the euphoria that, within half an hour, was setting church bells ringing and bringing citizens out on the streets in excited chattering groups? The answer was not difficult to see. It declared itself in that look of hate and vengeance on my son's face. He took pleasure in the destruction of some of our fellow countrymen. So did the exultant citizens who, later, lit bonfires in many parts of the City. They made me ask myself, 'What now?' One military victory had not banished the misery, discontent and confusion that had sent men to arms in several parts of the country. England was fractured; split from top to bottom into rival groups. Some called for harsh measures to prevent further popular unrest. Some demanded conciliation and a move towards a reformed 'commonwealth'. Some harked back to a Catholic past and wanted the government's religious policy reversed. Many questioned the Lord Protector's competence and hoped to see another at the helm of national affairs. Some were openly calling for the victor of Dussindale to be appointed the new regent. Others championed the cause of Mary, the king's half-sister, who would restore the old religion and the stability of the 'good old days'. Whichever way I looked, I could see only further strife – probably bloody strife – ahead.

And then there was that letter I had taken from Allen's coffer. What was I to make of that? Did it suggest that matters were even more complex than I had feared? I had thought that once Allen was in the Tower,the truth would be wrung from him and West would be released. But could I be sure even of that now?

Allen's confiscated correspondence confirmed what Underhill had told me: there were those at court who had personal reasons for wanting Allen's mouth to remain shut. So who would interrogate the magician? Would that person be a disinterested party, concerned only to unravel the plot against West and whatever political manoeuvrings lay behind it or would he be more concerned about his own dealings with the magus being exposed? Well, Cranmer would have to deal with that matter. None of the letters, as far as I knew, where from major political players. Except … I took from my purse the brief note I had brought from Aldermanbury Street and read the few brief words:

My master Sir William Paget thanks you for the potion which he finds efficacious.

The note, signed by one of the Secretary's scribes, was harmless enough in itself but it was a link between the magician and a member of the royal council who had always denied any knowledge of him. For several minutes I stared at the narrow strip of paper. Then I rose abruptly, went to the kitchen and threw the message into the fire. It was consumed in an instant. Not so my anger. I did not relish being made a keeper of other men's secrets.

When a further twenty-four hours had passed with no sign of a warrant for Allen's removal to the Tower I decided to call upon the archbishop in person.

First, I crossed the river to Lambeth Palace, only to be told that his grace was on council business at Whitehall. There I had to wait for hours in Cranmer's quarters among a score of other suitors. I might have wasted yet more time had I not caught a glimpse from the anteroom window of Ralph Morice crossing the courtyard outside. I hurried down the stairs and reached the secretary before he disappeared through a door on the far side of the courtyard. He did not look overjoyed to see me.

'Thomas, what brings you here?'

'His grace's business,' I replied sharply. 'The matter of Master West that I was set to investigate.'

'This is not the best time, Thomas. His grace is very busy. Things are … difficult here.' He reached out a hand for the door latch.

I grabbed his arm firmly and dragged him away. 'No, Ralph, I will not be put off! These last days I have suffered too much, seen things I never thought to see, done things I certainly never thought to do. All of it was to find your magician. Well, I found him. With Master Underhill's help, I got him safely under lock and key. We sent word that we were waiting his grace's pleasure for a warrant to convey Allen to the Tower. What do we receive for all this? Nothing. No thanks. No communication of any kind. It seems his grace has forgotten about us – and about poor Master West, still languishing in the Tower. In God's name, Ralph, what is going on?'

His tone in reply was quiet but urgent. 'Thomas, I can see things have been difficult for you but your problems are, quite frankly, insignificant compared with what is happening here. The plain fact is England has two governments – one at Hampton with the Protector and the other here, the council. Messengers are constantly travelling up and down the Thames. Getting decisions takes hours, sometimes days. 'Tis a miracle any business is done at all.'

'Are you saying that this business of West and Allen is no longer important? We can just leave them in their cells till the day of doom?'

Morice shook his head wearily. 'No, we would dearly love to know the truth of that matter but it is more complicated than we thought.' He dropped his voice to a whisper. 'There are people here who would not want to have Allen questioned.'

'Then, surely, the sooner we see him securely locked in a Tower cell, the better.'

'True, but ...' Morice wavered. 'Look, wait here and I will see if I can get a warrant signed for you to convey the prisoner. Will that satisfy you?'

'I suppose ...'

'You will have to provide your own escort. If I give you a troop of his grace's guards it will attract attention.'

'I like not this secrecy,' I protested.

'You must accept my word that it is necessary. And you will have to accept responsibility for Allen's safe delivery. Otherwise, matters must stay as they are until ... well, until the situation here is clearer.'

It was more than an hour before Morice returned. In that time, I must have asked myself a dozen times whether I was doing the right thing. This was not, after all, my problem. I had done what I had been asked to do. I did not need to do any more – did I? But the fact that I was asking the question meant that I knew the answer.

'His grace cannot be disturbed but I managed to find Lord Southampton and he has signed this.' Morice handed me the sealed warrant. 'You were best to do this by night – and, in God's name, take care, Thomas.'

I needed no urging on that score. I had learned by painful experience that Allen had powerful allies and I felt some anxiety that the Earl of Southampton was privy to my mission. Despite Morice's assurances, I still had my suspicions about his lordship. As soon as I reached home I chose my six strongest men to act as an escort. I instructed the keeper at Bread Street counter to have his prisoner ready. And, after nightfall, I assembled my little band in the stable yard.

'At least 'tis a bright night,' Bart observed. He had insisted on being a member of the party.

I glanced up at the half-moon flitting between fast-moving clouds. ''Tis as well. We've to ride right through the city.' I gave my instructions to the group. 'We will keep to the wider streets – Cheapside, Lombard Street, then, by way of Gracechurch Street, to Tower Street We keep a steady trot. Our prisoner will be lashed to his horse and I will have it on a lead rein. Dickon and Ben, you go before. Bart and Simon, you will be on the flanks. Harry and Rob will bring up the rear. Keep your eyes and ears open and your weapons handy.'

At the jail we were kept waiting by the keeper, one Pastelar, a churlish fellow, who resented having his sleep disturbed. He took his time fetching Allen, who struggled and screamed a stream of invective at us until we pinioned his arms and closed his mouth with a tightly-tied cloth. We hoisted the prisoner onto his mount and lashed his ankles together with rope under the horse's belly. Then we set out on our journey.

The streets were very quiet because the curfew was still strictly in force. Twice we were stopped by a ward watch and had to explain our business before being allowed to proceed. Otherwise, our journey along West Cheap, Poultry and Lombard Street was uninterrupted. Gracechurch Street, usually thronged with traffic passing to and from the bridge was eerily quiet. Our noses told us when we entered the fishmongers' district. We turned into Little East Cheap and though it was darker in this narrow thoroughfare, I began to relax. There were only a few hundred yards to our destination.

Someone ahead was waving a lamp. I assumed it was the Billingsgate Ward watch. Then I heard my name called.

'Master Treviot?'

'Yes.'

'Tell your men to stay where you are and bring your prisoner to us.'

Chapter 14

I PEERED INTO the darkness and could just make out three horsemen. 'Stand aside!' I shouted, with as much authority as I could muster. 'We are on the king's business.'

'No matter to us,' came back the reply. 'You are surrounded. Some of my men are behind you and we all carry guns. Release your prisoner and none of you will be harmed.'

'The sound of gunfire will bring the watch,' I countered. 'Then 'tis you who will be surrounded.'

'You are wasting time, Master Treviot.'

That was exactly what I was doing – that and calculating my options. If the threat of firearms was a bluff I could risk a hand-to-hand fight. If it was not I was putting all our lives in danger. 'Shoot at will,' I called out, 'and pray you do not kill the man you have come to rescue.'

There was a silence. Perhaps I had given our enemies something to think about. I drove home my advantage. 'We, too, are armed.'

The words were greeted with a harsh laugh. 'With sticks and staves, Master Treviot?'

'Show him, Dickon,' I muttered. 'The lamp if you can.'

The young man raised the ready-primed crossbow he had concealed beneath his cloak.

There was a twang as Dickon released his bolt, followed instantly by a cry from the group ahead. Their lantern fell to the ground with a clatter and went out.

We had to take advantage of the confusion. 'Now!' I shouted, spurring my horse.

We surged forward, crossing the empty ground between us and our enemy. I was vaguely aware that the horsemen behind us were following. Then all became noisy confusion. We and our assailants hit out at each other with clubs and knives. But in the gloom, it was difficult to be sure who was friend and who was foe. Shouts, screams and the stamping of hooves filled the air as the two forces became a congealed, squirming, struggling mass. Needing both hands to ward off blows, I thrust the leading rein at Bart. 'Hold this fast!' I ordered. Lights appeared in neighbouring windows. A trumpet call told of the approach of the ward watchmen. The appearance of the authorities seemed to scare our opponents for I was suddenly aware of hoofbeats retreating in the direction of Tower Street.

'What's afoot here?' The man who now approached, lantern in one hand and sword in the other was the ward constable.

With the help of this fresh light, I looked around at my little party. Three men were sprawled on the ground close to my horse's front hooves. Bart lay across the legs of one of our attackers and Rob had the squirming figure pinned down by his arms.

'What's to do? I say – who is responsible for this affray?'

I introduced myself and produced my warrant. 'We are conveying a prisoner to the Tower,' I explained. 'We have just been ambushed by some of the varlet's friends.'

The official did not look altogether convinced. 'This your captive?' He pointed to the man Bart and Rob were hauling to his feet.

'No, that is one of the attackers. This is our pr...'

I peered around with mounting panic. Of Robert Allen, there was no trace.

'Gone! The slippery rakehell! Quick man, after him! Raise the hue and cry!'

The constable – a bulbous fellow, whose jerkin stretched tight across his frame – laughed. 'Tell that story in Bedlam, Master Treviot, or whatever your name is. The loonies there might believe you.'

By this time, doors were opening and a crowd had begun to gather.

The constable raised his voice. 'All's well, friends. Just some gentlemen with too much strong beer inside 'em having a fight.'

I was not listening to him. All I could think was that Allen was not going to escape me again. 'Ben, Harry, quick, after them!' I ordered. 'See if you can find out where they are headed.'

The two men spurred away down the street, ignoring the cries of the constable to stop.

'Sorry, Master Thomas, 'tis my fault. This lout grappled me and we both fell to the ground. I had to let go the leading rein.'

'Fret not, Bart. We will catch him. If we have to track him to the ends of the earth we will bring him back. See what you can get out of this fellow.' I pointed to the man struggling to free himself from Rob and Bart's clutches. 'And be not gentle about it.'

As they dragged their prisoner away to a gap between two buildings the constable bustled up and stood in front of my horse. 'I am in charge here,' he bellowed. 'Now, Sirrah, dismount and come with me or it will go ill with you.'

'You – Sirrah,' I responded angrily, 'are in deep trouble for aiding the escape of a dangerous enemy to the king. If this rogue remains at liberty I will see you suffer for it. Master Goodrich is alderman for this ward, is he not?'

'Aye, but…'

'I know him well. I offer you two choices, Master Constable. We can go, straightway, to rouse Master Goodrich and explain this fracas, or you can disperse these people, go about your business and let me go about his majesty's business.'

With that, I turned my horse and walked a few paces along Little East Cheap. I hoped that my bluff had worked. Yet, I also felt a strange indifference. My anger was so consuming that I really did not care what the constable decided. What I had said to Bart about going to the ends of the earth in pursuit of Allen had been unpremeditated. It came from somewhere deep inside me. I knew that my destiny was bound up with the magician's and that I would stop at nothing to bring to justice this deceiver, this manipulator, this stirrer of hatred, this liar who preyed on people's gullibility and who was a willing player in the sinister political game that was tearing England apart.

When I glanced behind me I saw that the constable and his watch companions were urging the onlookers back indoors. I ambled across to where our captive was being interrogated. Bart had his single arm tight around the man's throat and Rob was freely wielding both fists.

'Is he talking yet?' I asked.

Rob shook his head. 'Says he speaks no English but he knows well enough to insist that he is servant to the Emperor's ambassador and that we must not molest him.'

'Well, carry on,' I said. 'If he will not tell us where Allen is being taken, kill him and dump his body there in the corner.' I wheeled away again.

Of course, I did not have murder in mind and I knew my men would not go too far but their victim could not be sure of that. Already we had learned something important. Our captive was a member of the imperial ambassador's household. It came as no surprise. Francis van der Delft controlled the traffic between Europe's Catholic powers and Catholic sympathisers in England. The ambassador was known to have cultivated good relations with the Earl of Southampton. Who was it who had authorised the warrant for Allen's transfer to the Tower? Southampton. Who knew that the magician would be conducted across London under cover of darkness? Southampton. My original suspicions were confirmed. What I had to do now was persuade Cranmer, against his will, to regard the ex-Chancellor as a dissembling foe.

I heard my name called. Turning, I saw Bart and Rob dragging their prisoner between them, his heels scraping the ground. I was momentarily alarmed.

' You haven't …'

Bart laughed. 'No, Master Thomas; he is only unconscious.'

'Did you get anything useful from him?'

'Oh yes. They are taking our man to Lion Quay. The ambassador keeps a ship there for carrying messages across the Channel.'

'Yes, of course. They mean to get Allen out of the country. Well, somehow we must stop them.'

'What about this fellow?' Rob asked.

'Throw him over one of the horses with his wrists and ankles lashed beneath. One of you can walk him. 'Tis not far now.'

Lion Quay lies hard by the bridge on the seaward side. This bustling waterfront sleeps scarce two hours in twenty-four. Vessels come and go on the tide and since captains always want their cargoes stowed or unstowed quickly crews and dock hands are busy most of the time. Lion Inn, a small hostelry between two warehouses, caters for the needs of those who work on the wharf and it was there that we established ourselves to see out the rest of the night. Having tethered the horses I appointed two men by rote to stay with them and also to keep an eye on our prisoner. There were some twenty workers in the main room. Most were sleeping slumped over the tables, though in one corner a dice game was in progress.

I wandered casually among the tables looking for someone who might help to identify the ship I was looking for. The first man I spoke to was a Netherlander with little English but I fared better with the next. He was a sailor seeking work and much in need of cash, At first, he was suspicious of a landsman asking questions but once silver had changed hands he proved both helpful and knowledgeable. Yes, he knew the craft I was looking for – the *Peregrine*, a pinnace of about forty tons. 'Sleek and fleet', he said approvingly. No, he did not know the master and crew. They were all foreigners. Judging by the activity on board, he thought the ship was getting ready to leave on the morning tide.

I decided to take the seaman – who introduced himself as Willy Stub – into my confidence.

'We have reason to believe that this ship is being used to smuggle the king's enemies out of the country,' I said quietly. 'Would you be able to check that?'

'Nothing easier,' he replied, his palm open upwards on the table.

When it had been furnished to his satisfaction, he went on, 'I will go aboard and ask if they are in need of an extra hand. They'll not take me on – being English and Protestant – but I should be able to have a nose around.'

'Excellent. Be careful not to ask too many questions. We must not raise their suspicions.'

'You can trust me, Master,' he said, pulling his seaman's cap down over his forehead. 'I like not these papists – too secretive by far. If they are hiding something, I will smell it.' He stood up. 'Best be about it.' With that, he strode to the door.

It must have been about half an hour before he returned. He was chuckling as he resumed his seat opposite me. 'Well, Master, you have done me a right favour. It seems that they are short-handed. One of their crewmen has gone missing and they cannot wait for him. They are taking me on to replace him.'

'Where are they bound – the Netherlands, Spain?'

'No, 'tis but a short, coastal voyage they make, as far as Worden*
in Sussex.

'Strange,' I muttered.

'They said something about delivering a package,' Willy Stub
commented, with a shrug.

'And they are about to sail now?'

'Aye. I must be back aboard. Tide's on the turn even as we speak.'

'Devil take it, then! I cannot stop them.'

'You could follow,' the seaman suggested, 'if your gold is as good
as your silver.'

'What mean you?'

'Go down to the wharf. Ask for Johnny Morian of the *Mary and
Joseph*. Do not worry about his colour. His father was a Moor but
he knows the coastal waters better than many of our own captains.
There's some merchants as like not to do business with him. That is
why his ship lies idle today. He will gladly take your money for a
voyage along the coast and back.'

I sat for some minutes after Stub had left working out how I
could use his information to advantage. As soon as I had the vestige of
a plan I gathered my group in the yard where we had left the horses.
Quickly I gave my orders.

'Dickon and Rob, you will stay with me. Bart, you and the others
go first to the Tower. Take the spare horses and set this fellow on one
of them. We should deliver him in reasonable shape.' I handed him
the warrant. 'This authorises you to hand over a prisoner. It does not
mention his name, so they will not question you when you present
our friend here. Then go home. Talk to Adie and Lizzie. Tell them
enough to set their minds at rest and say that we shall be back in a
few days. After that make all the speed you can to Worden, a small
harbour on the south coast, near Shoreham. Keep watch on all
incoming vessels.'

Bart looked worried. 'Where will you be, Master Thomas? I must
tell our people something.'

'I am loth to let Allen out of my sight so I am in hopes to hire a
ship, in order to follow the *Peregrine*. But if I cannot find transport we
too will make our way overland to Worden.'

'What do we hope to find when we get there?' someone asked.

---

*   Worthing

'I know not, for sure, though I suspect Allen is being taken somewhere he will find sanctuary.'

We were about to disperse when another thought struck me. 'Bart, when you are at Goldsmiths' Row, send to Master Underhill at Hampton with a note of what has passed. If he could gain leave to join us in Sussex with others of the royal guard his support would be a great help.'

As soon as Bart had ridden away with his party I returned to the wharf with the others. I noticed with alarm that the *Peregrine* was already unmoored and standing out into the tideway. We picked our way around bales and barrels in search of the *Mary and Joseph*, finding her, at last, at the far end of the line of moored vessels. I called out to the watchman that I was looking for Johnny Morian. After scrutinising us carefully, he beckoned us aboard.

The man who came out on deck to greet us was tall and dark skinned. He moved with a slow casual gait. The brown eyes in his long face scanned us gravely. 'Welcome to my humble home, Master. How may I be of service?'

I stepped across to the rail. 'I should like you to follow that ship,' I said, pointing to the *Peregrine* which was now in mid-channel and turning into the wind.

'And why would I do that?'

'Because I will pay you well.'

His demeanour changed on the instant. His eyes blazed and a hand clutched the curved dagger at his waist. 'Do you take me for a pirate, because I am not of your colour?' He called to a crew member. 'Hugh, set these fellows ashore.'

I responded quickly and quietly. 'I am sure you are no pirate. Neither am I and I intend no harm to that vessel or any aboard her. I simply wish to know where she goes. As soon as she makes landfall you may put my men and me ashore.'

Morian's frown faded. 'This is strange business. You will have to tell me more of it.'

On the *Peregrine,* sailors were aloft unfurling the mainsail. Obviously, the ship was manoeuvring to gain whatever help the wind had to offer. I watched her slow progress as I replied. 'That, as I am sure you know, is an imperial vessel manned by a Spanish crew. Aboard it is an English traitor trying to escape justice.'

The captain showed no sign of believing my story. 'And you wish me to chase his imperial majesty's ship across the Bay of Biscay and capture this fugitive, without committing an act of piracy? That would be an amazing trick. I am sorry, Master, even if I wanted to help you I could not. I am not victualled for such a voyage.'

'No, that is not my meaning. We believe the *Peregrine* intends to make landfall on our own south coast, perhaps to transfer the traitor to another ship. We hope to apprehend him as soon as he sets foot ashore.'

'I see.' He took a few paces along the deck. He turned. 'If I help you, how valuable will my service be to his majesty and to the Good Duke?'

I mentioned a figure. 'But we must start immediately if we are not to lose our quarry.'

The tall man shook his head. 'My crew are spread around the local taverns and brothels. I could not have them here fit and sober enough to take us out on this ebb.'

My heart sank. 'Then I am sorry we cannot do business.' I turned away, calling to my companions. 'Come, lads. We've no help here.'

Just as we reached the gangplank I heard a peal of deep-throated laughter behind us. 'Twice the sum you offer and we will be ready in one hour,' the half-caste roared.

'An hour? We will have lost them by then.'

'Lost them?' Again the hearty laugh. ''Tis not for nothing men call Johnny Morian the fastest ship's master on the tideway.'

Not without some misgivings, I agreed to the captain's terms.

For the second time, the man's languid demeanour changed rapidly. He shouted a string of orders to the few crewmen standing around the deck. They, too, leapt into action, as though stung by invisible wasps. Clearly, Morian was an effective disciplinarian. Three men ran down the gangplank and disappeared among the wharf buildings. Others scurried about the decks, responding briskly to the master's shouted orders. Morian, himself, strode about, brandishing a curious, carved staff with a heavy knop at one end. The returning mariners, as they shuffled aboard, received 'taps' from this implement to hurry them about their duties. It was within the promised hour that Morian's ship slipped away from the quay.

The *Mary and Joseph* was a three-masted broad-bellied craft that did not seem built for speed but once we were in midstream, propelled by a bank of oars protruding from her lower deck, she made good progress. Manoeuvring through the crowded waterway past the Tower and beyond demanded great skill. Morian prowled the afterdeck watching the way ahead and calling instructions to the steersman at the whipstaff.

My men and I found a corner where we could lie down without getting in the way of the crew. After a sleepless night, it did not take long for the gentle movement of the ship to make me drowsy and I would have slept there on the deck if Morian had not offered his passengers the use of his cabin. The captain's berth was narrow and hard but scarcely had I crawled into it than I fell into a deep sleep. Rob and Dickon, as they told me later, also slept soundly in a corner of the cabin.

When I awoke and went on deck the sun was low in the sky astern and the *Mary and Joseph* was making good speed with her main canvas catching a west wind. I joined Rob and Dickon at the midships' rail. 'Where are we now?' I asked.

'Somewhere east of Gravesend,' Dickon said. 'We anchored there when the tide turned and have just got underway again on the next ebb. The captain means to make the most of the daylight and talks of mooring at Sheerness for the night.'

'Any sign of the *Peregrine* yet?'

Rob shook his head. 'No, Master Thomas. The blackamoor reckons she's still in front of us.'

'Yet, he plans to spend the night at anchor? I must have a word with him.'

I found Morian leaning on the aft-deck rail watching the Kent coast slip by. 'I trust you are well rested, Master Treviot. You must be hungry. Please join me for a meal.'

'You are very hospitable but I am more concerned with the successful conclusion of our mission. Is it true that you propose to spend the whole night at anchor?'

Without looking at me, the captain replied in his deep, musical voice. 'Your men tell me you are a goldsmith.'

'That is correct.'

'One of the best in London.'

'I value my reputation.'

'If I said I could tell you how to make a jewelled necklace fit for a queen would you take my advice?'

'I meant no impertinence.'

'This is one of the most difficult estuaries in Europe. It is crowded. The tides run fast. There are hidden shallows. And the wind can veer in the blink of an eye. Even were this not so, how, think you, we should find the *Peregrine* in the dark?'

'Will she also have to moor overnight?'

'Unless her master is a fool.' He chuckled. 'Most Spaniards are, but not all.' He turned away from the rail. 'It grows chill. Let us eat.'

Back in the cabin, the chart table had been cleared to make space for trenchers of cheese and salt beef and beakers of ale.

'I gather you have no love of Spaniards,' I said.

'And with reason.' He cut into the meat with movements that were surprisingly delicate. 'My family is from Spain – many generations, all mariners, sailing the Mediterranean and beyond. We had a fleet of ships and a fine estate in Granada. Then, one day the Inquisition came to call. They offered my grandfather a choice: become Catholic or get out and lose everything. He was a proud man, my grandfather. He defied them. And so they burned him and took everything he had. Or almost everything. My father – a young man at the time – was at sea with two of our ships. He and his crews escaped and came to England where he married and settled.'

'That is a terrible story. I understand how you must feel.'

'I doubt you do. It was hard. A new homeland. New trading contacts to make. New sea routes to explore. We lost two of our ships in the treacherous waters around your coast. But what was worse was the inner anger we had to cope with. The hatred. Have you ever hated anyone, Master Treviot?'

I sat back to consider the question.

But Morian continued. 'If you have to think about it, the answer is "No". You do not know what it is to long, with every fibre of your being, for someone else's destruction.'

'You feel that for all Spaniards?'

'For Spaniards? No. For Catholics. For the power of their system. For their wealth, their corruption, their god.' He took a long draft of ale. 'And for our own god, too. Where was Allah, I asked, in all the suffering inflicted on his people? I know not how many nights I stood on deck, gazing up at the stars and asking, "Where are you? Who are you?" Then, one day, I heard about a man who was asking the same questions – and actually putting forward some answers. His name was

Martin Luther. As a young man I spent many hours talking with his followers – in secret, of course, for they were then persecuted in this country. For that very reason, I could understand them. For I knew what persecution was.'

'You became a Lutheran?'

A wide smile stretched across his face. 'I care not much for labels. Let us just say that in Luther's book, the Bible, I found answers. I began to make sense of life. I crawled out of the darkness – the lunatic darkness – of hatred.'

A long silence followed this confession. I could think of no suitable response.

Then the man's changeable mood once again veered wildly. His laughter filled the cabin. 'Enough solemnity! Tell me about yourself. How does a respectable merchant come to be chasing traitors out to sea?'

Morian was an intriguing and agreeable companion and we talked until well into the afternoon.

A few more hours sailing on the morrow took the *Mary and Joseph* out of the estuary and into the open channel. I was very relieved that we could take up the pursuit in earnest, sailing by night as well as day. Yet still we had not sighted the *Peregrine*. This was not for any want of seamanship on the part of our captain and crew. Morian expertly used sails and oars to obtain the maximum speed. I peered anxiously at every vessel we sighted but our quarry was not among them. I was by now wondering whether I had been wrong to trust Willy Stub, a man who would do anything for money. Supposing he had been paid by the Spaniards to feed me wrong information. By now the *Peregrine* could be heading across the North Sea with Allen and his rescuers laughing at my expense. But it was too late for second thoughts. I was committed to my present course.

'Now we have a choice,' Morian said.

It was late morning and we were standing on the aft-deck. The ship was making good way before a breeze off the land.

'Choice?'

'Aye. As we run south we can sail in mid-channel, closer to the French coast or we can keep inshore in what is called The Downs. Between the two routes lie the Goodwin Sands, a treacherous, long sandbank which has been the death of many a good ship.'

'Which is the better route?'

159

'The Downs is quicker if you know how to navigate it, as I do. The other is safer.'

'Which way do you think the *Peregrine* will go?'

'My guess is that the Spaniards would take the easier route. They are not familiar with our inshore waters. Also, with wind coming from the West they will want to avoid any risk of being driven onto the Goodwins.'

'So, if we go via The Downs and the *Peregrine* goes the other way, we might gain some time over them.'

'That is very possible.'

'Then let us do that.'

For the next hour or so we sailed, close to the coast between Ramsgate and Deal. The sea was quite calm, as the force of the waves on our port side were broken by the sandbank, which we glimpsed from time to time as a still flat, brown-grey carpet, unnaturally spread upon the water. The sight of it made me shudder. It was easy to imagine the fear and panic of any crew whose craft was thrown upon that sinister ledge.

We did not have to rely on imagination much longer.

'Starboard bow! Ship on sands!' The cry came from the lookout at the main top.

We hurried to the rail and strained our eyes in the direction he was pointing. I could just make out the bare masts of a vessel, motionless on the sandbank.

'Poor devils,' Morian muttered. 'Caught on the nether end of the Goodwins. We must go to their aid.'

'Will they not float off when the tide rises?' I asked.

'Depends how fast she is held,' the captain said, grimly. 'More likely wind and waves will break her before they free her.'

'So we must lose more time trying to help?'

''Tis what I would expect her crew to do for us if we were in like peril. 'Tis the mariners' lore. 'Twill be difficult. I must ask you and your men to keep out of our way while we do what we can.'

With Rob and Dickon, I found a place well clear of the open deck.

Dickon sat down in a corner, scowling. 'Here's an end to our chance of catching the *Peregrine*,' he said.

'I fear so,' I replied. 'But the captain is right. We cannot leave those sailors to their fate.'

'Pray God, we do not end up sharing that fate,' Rob said. 'I hate these sandbanks. To be caught there, watching the sea coming in and in and in – Horrible!'

Morian had all sail taken in and the oars manned. His men rowed the *Mary and Joseph* in the direction of the stricken vessel. The captain himself climbed nimbly to the maintop to assess the situation personally. From there he bellowed his orders. When he judged he'd come as close as was safe the rowers stopped and anchors were thrown out fore and aft to hold the ship's position.

Morian returned to the deck and strode across to us. 'Well,' he said, 'we have found your *Peregrine.*'

Chapter 15

'YOU ARE SURE?' I peered at the craft, still some distance away across the water. I could make out figures scurrying about her decks but lacked a seaman's skill at identifying ships.

'Oh, aye. 'Tis the imperial pinnace. Were I not an honourable man I would leave all those accursed Spaniards to their fate, and I suppose you would be happy to see your traitor perish.'

'His death would be no loss to the world,' I replied. 'Unfortunately, we need to interrogate him. If you can rescue that crew, well and good, but I pray you, do not put your own men to unnecessary risk.'

'We will do our best. 'Tis as I thought, they have come to grief by ignorance of these shifting sands. Their bow is towards us, which means they were moving inshore from deeper water. No doubt they thought to come around the southern end of the bank but they know not how it moves. It can spread half a mile in a day in stormy weather and retreat again just as quickly.'

'What can we do?'

'The only way she will come off is the way she went on. We must come around behind her, get a line aboard and try to tow her off. 'Twill be difficult. Perhaps impossible.'

My companions and I watched, enthralled and apprehensive as the *Mary and Joseph* attempted the rescue. She was brought by the oarsmen round the southern tip of the Goodwins, a linesman calling out the depth of the water every couple of minutes. Aboard the *Peregrine* men were waving frantically at us but we were giving the sands a wide berth and were not within hailing distance. Out in the main channel and lying astern of the other vessel we came to anchor again. Morian ordered the ship's boat to be launched and four men rowed it cautiously over the shallow water, carrying a coiled line to the *Peregrine*. Everyone aboard the *Mary and Joseph* watched breathlessly. Was there enough depth of water or would the boat also become stranded on the sands? It was with relief that we saw the line thrown aboard the pinnace. Our end of the line was attached to a rope, which the Spaniards now hastily pulled in and made fast to their stern.

'How fast held is she?' Morian asked as his boatmen climbed back on deck.

'I'd say she went on fairly hard,' one of the men replied. 'She may be holed. With the tide coming in they will soon know.'

'We will wait awhile for the water to rise. Man the oars in readiness.'

Morian stood on the aft castle, his eyes fixed on the other ship and ready to respond. After some minutes, he gave the order to his oarsmen to start rowing. I watched as much of the rope came clear of the water. I felt the deck beneath my feet shuddering with the strain. The distance between us and the *Peregrine* lessened.

'Stop!' Morian shouted. He turned, glaring his frustration. 'They are not moving. We are in danger of being pulled in.' He glanced up at the ship's pennant. 'Wind is freshening. Still offshore, thank God.' He sent some men aloft with the order to be ready to loosen mainsail. Then he returned to his position at the aft rail. Watching him closely, I saw his lips moving in silent prayer.

Water was now creeping rapidly over the sandbank. The *Peregrine's* masts swayed slightly.

'Loosen mainsail! Ply oars!' Morian bellowed.

Once again the rope tightened. The wind bellying the sail and the oars straining against the water stopped us being dragged backwards. But were they strong enough to shift the *Peregrine*?

A chorus of shouts and whoops from the other ship answered my question. With a grinding sound, the *Peregrine* was moving. Sluggishly – it seemed reluctantly – the *Mary and Joseph* bowed and bobbed over the incoming waves. After several minutes, she leaped forward so suddenly that I was almost thrown off balance. Looking up, I immediately saw the reason. The other ship had released the tow rope. She was floating free.

Some half-hour later when the two ships rode at anchor a short distance from each other, a boat was launched from the pinnace and rowed across to the *Mary and Joseph*. The man who clambered up the netting to be greeted by Morian on the main deck was short, thin, almost frail, but his well-cut, pointed beard, the silk shirt under his seaman's jerkin and the emerald ring worn on his right hand suggested a person of style and substance. A flicker of surprise passed across his face on seeing our half-caste captain but he recovered instantly and made a low bow as he introduced himself.

'Luis de Mandora, servant to his imperial majesty Charles V,' he announced. 'I am deeply indebted to you, Sir, for your prompt and merciful action. My master shall be told of your bravery and your seamanship but I know that I can speak for him in declaring his profound thanks for preserving the lives of myself and my crew.'

'I am glad my men and I were in a position to help. These are difficult waters. Better captains than you, Luis de Mandora, have come to grief here. Where are you bound?'

'A small port farther along the coast – Worden. Do you know it?'

'I have been there once or twice. It is a place of little importance. What can it have of interest to his imperial majesty?'

'That I am not at liberty to say – 'tis a diplomatic matter.'

Morian shrugged. 'Of course. And afterwards, you return to London?'

'Yes, I have to keep my ship in readiness for the ambassador at all times.'

'Well, your ambassador is very lucky that he still has a ship and a captain and a crew to do his bidding.'

The Spaniard nodded sombrely. 'I shall not fail to acquaint him with all the details of today's events. If there is any service he or I can render to express our gratitude please do not hesitate to name it.'

A smile spread over Morian's face and he glanced sideways at me. 'There is one thing you could do which would recompense me for putting my own vessel at risk on your behalf.'

'Tell me,' de Mandora replied. 'Your request is granted before you speak it.'

'Then,' said Morian, slowly and deliberately, 'please be so good as to hand over into my keeping Master Robert Allen.'

I have never seen anyone more shocked than the Spanish captain was at that moment. He stared up at Morian, mouth open, eyes wide and, for several moments speechless. When he replied it was with a weak attempt at a bluff. 'Allen? Allen? Who is this Allen? I do not ...'

I stepped forward and spoke sharply. 'Robert Allen is a renegade subject of his majesty King Edward. He is a political activist in the pay of his imperial majesty and his continued treasons can only sow discord between our two nations.'

'Ridiculous!' The captain responded with a great show of indignation. 'His majesty has nothing to do with Master Allen ...' He closed his mouth quickly, but too late.

'Then you do know the man.'

De Mandora blustered. 'These are matters of state. I cannot discuss them.

Morian took a step forward, glaring down at the diminutive Spaniard. 'We have just saved the lives of you and your crew. Yet you refuse our courteous request?'

De Mandora backed away. 'What you ask... It is not possible. It is beyond my power ... I am under orders ...'

Watching our captain, I saw his fists clench. I sensed that he was about to flare up, perhaps releasing all his loathing of Spaniards against the master of the *Peregrine*. I intervened quickly. 'What we ask, Senõr, goes deeper than "matters of state". We are speaking of honour, of Christian duty, of human decency. You have incurred a debt – a very considerable debt. An hour ago you and your crew were facing a certain and horrible death as a result of your own incompetence. We have saved not only your lives, but also your reputation.'

'Yes, yes, what you say is true.' The little man was trembling and almost in tears. 'But you do not understand what will become of me if I fail ...'

'I understand full well the loyalty you owe to your master, but I am sure you can think up a story to explain how you lost your passenger. Perhaps your ship was attacked by pirates...'

At that, there was a growl from Morian.

I hurried on. 'Or perhaps Master Allen simply fell overboard.'

'I do not know!' The captain covered his face with his hands. 'I am confused. I must return to my ship and think.'

He turned towards the rail but, at a gesture from Morian, two sailors blocked his path.

He spun round, trying to regain some dignity. 'Do you think to hold me prisoner?'

Morian shook his head. 'No, I think to offer you hospitality – temporary hospitality, until we have resolved this little matter.'

There was a long pause before the Spaniard spoke again. 'Look, there is another matter. This Allen is a strange man. He has "powers". He is popular with my crew. They will not readily relinquish him.'

'Are you saying you lack control of your own men?' Morian growled.

'You do not know this man,' de Mandora protested.

'Oh, we know him very well,' I said. 'He is a fraud, a trickster. He would have you think he is a scholar of magic. Truth is he is a schemer, a troublemaker, an exploiter of simple-minded people. He mixes with criminals. His conscience is in his purse and he recognises loyalty to no-one but himself. Do not for one moment suppose that he is a faithful servant of the emperor. He will betray him as readily as he has betrayed anyone who has ever placed trust in him.'

'And who are you? What is your business with him, Master …?'

'Treviot,' I replied, 'currently employed by the Lord Protector and the royal council to apprehend Robert Allen and present him for trial on several counts.' I enumerated briefly some of Allen's recent misdemeanours. 'Believe me, Senör,' I concluded, 'if you assist the course of justice you will be doing your master a favour. As long as this man remains at liberty he is a menace, an enemy to God and men.'

De Mandora took a few paces back and forth across the deck. At last, he came up to us, a picture of abject misery, a man who seemed to have withered inside. He sighed a long sigh. 'Very well, gentlemen. I will have him sent across to you….' He shouted an order to his boatmen and they set out to return to the *Peregrine*.

'A wise decision,' I said.

'I hope the ambassador can be persuaded of that,' de Mandora replied gloomily. 'He is not very tolerant of failure. Would you help me to explain…'

He was interrupted by a shout from one of the sailors. 'Captain, look! The *Peregrine*.'

We ran to the rail to stare at the other ship. Its decks and rigging were a frenzy of activity. Sails were being loosed and trimmed. She

166

was getting under way. Gathering speed, she moved across our bow. As she passed we all saw a figure on the aft deck, waving at us. Robert Allen!

Morian sprang into action, calling for the anchors to be raised and sails lowered. All this took several minutes, by which time there was half a mile of clear water between us and the *Peregrine*. The work of the mariners was made no easier by the Spanish captain who was pacing back and forth screaming imprecations at his mutinous crew.

Morian clapped a hand on my shoulder. 'In Jesu's name take him to the cabin and cool him down,' he said.

That was easier said than done. Seated in the cabin the Spaniard hammered the table with his fists and let fly a stream of oaths in his own tongue whose meaning I could only guess at.

'I am sorry you had to learn the truth about Robert Allen from personal experience,' I said.

'And I am sorry I ever listened to him. He is, as you have said, tricky and persuasive. The dog has destroyed me.'

'We must see if we can get your ship back.'

De Mandera threw up his hands in a gesture of despair. 'Hopeless. The *Peregrine* is fast. She can outrun you.'

'Only in the hands of a good captain. Who will be in command now?'

'I suppose Miguel Borges, my second officer. He was much impressed by Allen.'

'Where do you think he will head for now?'

'Saints alone know. He dare not go to Spain or the Netherlands. When news of his treachery reaches the ambassador he will be a marked man throughout the emperor's dominions.'

'That will not worry Master Allen. As soon as your crew have served his purpose he will abandon them. Know you what that purpose is? Why did he want to go to Worden?'

De Mandora shrugged. 'My orders from the ambassador were simply to take Allen there and row him upriver to a ford where he would be met and taken to a place of safety.'

'You know not who was meeting him?'

The captain shook his head.

I thought carefully. 'Then I suppose Allen will keep to his original plan. If the *Peregrine* can stay well ahead of us he will persuade Borges to land him at Worden. He will not care what happens to the ship and its crew as long as he is safe.'

Back on deck, the light was fading. The *Mary and Joseph* was now wearing full sail and making good speed. But not good enough for the captain.

'The Peregrine is a good sea mile ahead now,' he muttered.

'Will we lose her overnight?' I asked.

'Our only hope is a slackening of the wind. If I can put men to the oars we can close the gap.'

'Can you tell yet what course the *Peregrine* is taking?'

'She is keeping well inshore at the moment.'

'From what I hear from de Mandora, Allen seems to have mesmerised the crew and taken effective control. My guess is that he will keep to the original plan. He is expecting to be met at Worden and taken into hiding. There is nothing for him on the other side of the Channel. How long is it likely to take us to reach Worden?'

'If the wind continues on our starboard quarter, twelve hours, perhaps fifteen. Sometime tomorrow morning.'

'If you will be good enough to land us there you will have done all that I could expect and more.'

'You will find it difficult to pursue him on foot.'

'I am in hopes to have some of my own men there in readiness. Between us, we may catch him. We *must* catch him.'

Morian nodded vigorously. 'Yes, I see that now. Seldom have I come across anyone so dangerous.'

Looking down to the main deck, I saw de Mandora emerge from the cabin beneath us. 'What will you do with him?' I asked.

Morian frowned. 'I never yet felt pity for a Spaniard, but for a captain to lose his ship to mutiny – it is the ultimate disgrace. I suppose all he can do is return to London and throw himself on the ambassador's mercy.'

There was a flapping sound from the canvas above.

'Ah,' Morian exclaimed, 'the wind slackens. Let us see what a turn at the oars will do for us.'

That night, the motion of the ship soon lulled me to sleep. When I awoke the sun was already shining on the eastern edge of the sea on our port side. To starboard, we had a clear view of the Sussex hills and the occasional small settlements along the coast. Morian was on the foredeck, standing with the Spaniard when I joined him. Silently, he pointed ahead. I strained my eyes to peer at the horizon and, after some moments, made out a solitary speck in the distance.'

'How far?' I asked.

'Perhaps five miles.'

'And Worden?'

'Perhaps eight.'

'Then we shall not catch her in time.'

'We may have a chance. The captain here tells me his men do not know the coastline. There are several inlets and small fishing villages all the way along. To find Worden they must needs take in sail, slow down, move farther inshore and identify the landmarks marked on their charts. That will give us a chance to close the gap.'

De Mandora turned to me. 'I have prayed all night to St Mary and Saint Nicholas that you will catch this villain. When you do I beg you will allow me to slit his throat.'

'Nothing would give me greater pleasure than to watch that,' I replied, 'but I have to take him as my prisoner to London.'

'Anyway,' Morian said to the Spaniard, 'you and I will be busy retaking your ship.'

The Spaniard gave a weary sigh. 'How think you to do that?'

'At this moment, I know not.' The dark face wore a broad grin. 'Mayhap I will think of something.'

'Do you know our exact position?' I asked.

'I was looking at the chart while you slept. That church tower on the hillside yonder is at Brightelmstore.* Yonder, lies Shoreham, largely closed by shingle banks. Beyond that again is Worden. It too suffers from barriers of silt and shifting shorelines. No vessels of any size can find shelter there now, which is why it is scantily habited. There is not much of a living to be had there.'

'An ideal place to land a fugitive,' I observed.

'If you can find it,' Morian said, his eyes fixed on the *Peregrine*. 'Your crew should be steering closer inshore if they know where they are going.'

'Aye, and taking in sail,' de Mandora agreed. 'This lively breeze with make them overshoot.'

We watched our quarry carefully but were not close enough to be sure of its movements. It was several minutes before we heard a call from the masthead. '*Peregrine* going about!'

---

*   Brighton

'She has left it late,' Morian said with a smile. 'She will have to beat back against the wind. Now we can close on her.'

He ran back to the aft deck to set a course with the helmsman that would take us directly to Worden. De Mandora and I watched as the two ships converged.

'Devil take them!'" The Spaniard shouted his frustration. 'Those hell's spawn rogues will still be there before us!'

He was right. The *Peregrine* reached the mouth of Worden's river and dropped anchor. We were now close enough to make out the movements of the crew. As soon as the ship had come to a halt they launched the boat and two men rowed it into the estuary.

Morian now had the oars manned. The *Mary and Joseph* surged across the water towards the other vessel.

'Mother of God, does he mean to ram her?' de Mandora cried in alarm.

It soon became apparent that that was not our captain's intention. He was endeavouring to put our ship between the *Peregrine* and the shore. We heard the linesmen calling out the depth as our ship crossed shallower water. When we were a hundred yards from the river mouth, he slowed the ship and had the boat launched.

'Master Treviot,' he called out, 'you and your men can man the boat now.'

I ran across to the midship rail with Rob and Dickon and we scrambled down the netting into the boat. Immediately our oarsmen dug deep at the waves and headed for the shore.

Staring ahead, my vision interrupted by the rise and fall of the boat as she rode the waves, I made out the other craft, now well inside the narrow estuary and heading upriver.

'Where are they going, Master?' Dickon asked.

'To some point where they will be met by horsemen ready to hurry Allen to his hiding place. That, at least, is my guess.'

'Will they be armed?' Dickon hugged his crossbow lovingly.

'Probably, but I doubt there will be a fight. We are too far behind. If Allen's rendezvous has been well organised he will be gone before we can catch him. The best we can hope for is to be able to scour the area and try to find clues to his sanctuary.'

'Why has he come to this place?' He gazed around at the sprinkle of cottages that was Worden and the meadows around them, sparsely populated with sheep.

'Because there is someone powerful round here who can offer effective protection?'

'Who is that, Master?'

'I wish I knew.'

Rob said suddenly, 'Look, the blackamoor is picking a fight.'

I turned to look back at the ships. The *Mary and Joseph* had closed the distance. We could not see clearly what was happening but it seemed that Rob might be right. If Morian tried to board the *Peregrine* the Spanish crew would be facing a real dilemma. They could stay and defend their ship or hoist sail and abandon their colleagues in the boat.

'They will be rueing the day they ever set eyes on Robert Allen,' Rob said.

'Yes,' I agreed. 'Most people do.'

''Tis getting shallower.' Dickon was gazing over the side of the boat.

The river was wide and running between overgrown banks and reed beds. Beneath our keel, the mud and shingle of the bottom was clearly visible.

'It narrows again ahead,' I said, pointing to where a derelict watermill stood beside the water. ''Twill deepen again there. The other boat is making steady progress.

The rowers stopped so that one of them could disentangle weed from his oar. I took the opportunity to stand up in order to gain a better view. Between us and the ridge ahead lay a wide expanse of marshy ground extending on both sides of the river. Clearly there could be no meeting point in this desolate lowland plain. But the hill ahead, topped with sparse woodland would be an excellent place for Allen's rescuers to keep watch for his approach.

'Keep your eyes on the rising ground,' I said. 'Say if you see any movement.'

It was, perhaps, ten minutes later that we heard it – a single trumpet note. From the slope on the right-hand side of the river, three horsemen emerged walking slowly downhill and leading a riderless horse. They halted at the water's edge and the riders dismounted. Allen's boat reached them moments later. One of the riders helped him ashore. I saw him gesticulate, pointing towards us. 'Quickly,' I urged the rowers. 'We must not lose them now.'

The oarsmen strained their muscles but the gap between us and the ford closed agonisingly slowly. Allen climbed into the saddle of one of the horses and we were still fifty yards from the landing place.

'Stop rowing!' Dickon shouted. 'I can get him!'

He stood, winding his crossbow, as our boat stopped rocking. He took aim. He waited for several seconds. Then he loosed the bolt. The next moment Allen's horse whinnied and reared, throwing its rider to the ground. Now the sound of confused shouts carried across the water. Allen was being dragged to his feet but was hanging limply between his helpers. Now they were struggling to hoist him onto another mount. Sailors from the *Peregrine* were jumping ashore, trying to help but only adding to the confusion. Somehow they got Allen astride a horse, in front of one of the riders. They turned uphill, riding or running, rushing for the cover of the trees.

At last, our boat nosed into the bank. We all leapt ashore and gave chase.

But it was a hopeless pursuit. Allen and his group were too far ahead.

Then I heard shouts from the other side of the river. Down the slope came six horsemen, cantering to the ford. Friends or foes? I could not immediately tell. Then I saw a flash of scarlet and gold. Royal uniforms!

The king's guards splashed across the river and charged across the flank of the hill, brandishing their swords. Allen's rescuers scattered in confusion. The riders spurred their horses violently. Those on foot ran in all directions. Allen fell to the ground a second time but no one stopped to help him. The three horsemen disappeared among the trees. The guardsmen declined to give chase.

By the time I had run, panting, up the slope to where Allen lay, I found Edward Underhill already bending over him.

'Is he dead?' I asked anxiously.

'Unfortunately, no,' came the reply, 'but his evil mischief making is over. Thank God we were here in time. If he had reached Broadwater I think his powerful friends would have made sure we never found him.'

'Broadwater? Where is that?'

'Just over the hill. Most of this land belongs to its lord.'

'Who is that?' I asked.

'Baron De La Warr,' Underhill replied.

Chapter 16

IFELT AS though I was being whirled around in a circle like someone in a country dance. I had become involved in this business because De La Warr claimed that Robert Allen and his own nephew were conspiring to murder him. Now, it seemed that this same De La Warr was going to considerable trouble to help Robert Allen escape from justice.

'Are you sure?' I asked.

Underhill nodded emphatically. 'When your man, Bart Miller, told me that Allen was being brought to this part of the coast I suspected his lordship would be involved. He is the principal landowner hereabouts. He is a covert papist. And he is very close to my lords Southampton and Arundel and others of that ilk.'

We watched as our prisoner's arms were securely trussed by two of Underhill's colleagues.

'We should move,' I suggested, 'in case he sends men to recapture Allen.'

'Oh, I doubt he will risk a skirmish with the king's own guard. Yet, we would be wise to be on the road before his lordship has decided what action to take. I have commandeered a stout wagon. 'Tis beyond the trees yonder with Bart and two of your own men. It will carry Allen and your people. If all is well we should reach London not long beyond nightfall.'

'I am right glad that Bart reached you,' I said as we walked through the thicket.

'No more glad than I. It grieved me greatly that Allen had escaped you.'

'He will not do so again. That I swear.'

'Where will you take him?'

'To the archbishop and we will have the truth out of him.'

'Cranmer is certainly the wisest member of the council. He opposes the papists and also the extremist commonwealth men. But he is vulnerable. He is like a man crossing a river on stepping stones: any false move will cast him into the water on one side or the other.'

'Yet he has powerful friends,' I suggested.

'Pah! Politicians!' Underhill scoffed. 'They pretend their support for the Gospel but they will not let that stand in the way of their own ambition.'

We emerged onto the grassy hilltop where Bart, Simon and Henry were waiting with the wagon and the rest of the horses. It was a relief to see my own men and a pleasure to be able to commend them for carrying out their part of a plan that had been so hastily and inadequately put together.

Allen, who was now conscious and complaining noisily, was bound hand and foot and thrown unceremoniously into the wagon with a burly guardsman to watch him closely.

"Twas not easy,' Bart said, as we mounted and began our journey northwards. 'Master Underhill needed to obtain permission to go in search of the traitor. That took a long time. It was only when he gained an audience with the Protector himself that our mission was sanctioned. There was little time left. We had to ride through the night. How did you manage to catch up with Allen, Master?'

As we travelled I recounted my shipboard adventures. Afterwards, we rode mostly in silence. I tried to think out what I would say to Cranmer. Yet I was quite unprepared for the greeting I received that night when I arrived at Lambeth Palace.

'Thomas, have you any idea the annoyance and embarrassment you have caused?' The archbishop was seated in his study above the cloisters, light from flaring torches reflected in the surface of the table before him. He did not invite me to sit.

'I realise, Your Grace, that what I did was unorthodox but I had to make quick decisions.'

'Unorthodox! Reckless would be a better word. You had one of van der Delft's men locked up in the Tower. The ambassador was furious. He protested to the Earl of Southampton, whose name was on the arrest warrant. His lordship was ... Well, I have never seen him angrier. As a seasoned diplomat, he prides himself on his good relations with the Emperor. He claims you have besmirched his reputation.'

'Did the ambassador think to mention that he had sent some of his men to attack me and take my prisoner from me?'

Cranmer scarcely listened. 'His lordship, of course, blamed me for setting you on this irresponsible course. As if that was not bad enough, a rumour is now going about that you have hired some Moorish pirate to attack van der Delft's personal ship. Tell me that that, at least, is not true.'

'Your Grace, I am truly sorry for any distress I have caused but if I might explain what happened I believe you will see matters in a different light.'

Cranmer sat back in his armed chair and waved a hand. 'Very well.'

I described the sequence of events from my receipt of the warrant to the recapture of the magician.

The archbishop seemed little mollified. 'And what has become of the *Peregrine*?'

'I have reason to believe or hope that Morian may have recovered it from the mutineers and returned it to van der Delft's captain.'

'Doubtless for a large fee,' Cranmer muttered.

'I found Morian to be an honourable man, Your Grace.'

'Well, Thomas, your judgement is not something in which I repose a great deal of confidence at this moment. However, if your friend has rescued the *Peregrine* from mutineers that will save the ambassador having to make an embarrassing report to his imperial master.'

'Perhaps it will also suggest to him the need to be more cautious about the friends he chooses at court. The only person who could have told the ambassador how to rescue Allen on his way to the Tower was my lord of Southampton.'

'Impossible!' Cranmer scowled. 'In Jesu's name, why would he do such a thing?'

'For the same reason that he involved himself in William West's interrogation and ensured that nothing was said which would lead to Parafaustus. I am sure that Southampton is Allen's protector.'

The archbishop shook his head vigorously, his wispy beard dancing across his chest. 'No, I do not believe it. Someone else must have overheard the arrangements for Allen's delivery to the Tower.'

There was a long pause. When Cranmer spoke again it was in a quieter, more reflective tone. 'Thomas, these are difficult times. The very survival of sound government is at stake. Rivalries and suspicions are rife and we must not add to them. I will not accuse any of his majesty's councillors of deceitful practices and, similarly, you must not spread such rumours. Do I have your word that you will not broadcast these suspicions, which, I am sure, are groundless?'

'Certainly, Your Grace. I would only point out …'

'Good. Oh, and do sit down.'

Thankfully I sank onto a chair on the opposite side of the table. 'I hope Your Grace will forgive me if I remind you that you asked me to seek out the truth of the accusations against poor William West. I have done my inadequate best to meet Your Grace's wishes. It is only in doing so that I have reached certain conclusions. Now that we have apprehended Robert Allen we can test those conclusions.'

'Ah, yes, indeed. Where is Allen?'

'In the outer courtyard, Your Grace.'

'Here?' Cranmer seemed surprised.

'I assumed Your Grace would want to examine his personally.'

'Well, in that, at least, your instinct was correct. I am currently authorising a purge of all such diabolical practices as fortune telling and necromancy. Parliament has also just enacted a statute against false prophecy.'

'I can certainly give evidence against Allen on all those counts.'

'I am sure you can. I will have him taken to my prison. Meanwhile, please put in writing your testimony and give it to Master Morice.' He stood up. 'Now the hour is late and you must be tired after your recent ordeal. I would not keep you longer from your home and your bed.' He held out his hand for me to kiss the ring.

I hesitated.

'Something still worries you, Thomas?' Cranmer asked.

'It is just …'

'Yes?'

'Only this Your Grace: I have learned – and learned the hard way – not to underestimate Robert Allen. You mentioned diabolical practices. This man not only does evil things; he *is* evil; the very personification of evil. He will lie and scheme and use his influence with powerful patrons. He really does possess power – Satanic power. I know not how to describe it but he has ways of getting inside people's head. He can twist their thoughts, make black seem white, and bad appear as good. I always look for the best in my fellow men. With Allen, such an attitude is a profound error. There is no 'best' in him. He even chooses to call himself 'Parafaustus', after the proud scholar who sold his soul to the devil.'

'And you think I will be fooled by him?' Cranmer asked, probing me with searching eyes.

I considered my answer carefully, anxious – almost desperate – to convey a strong warning without giving offence. 'I had good reason to know and thank God for Your Grace's qualities of kindness and gentleness. I beg you to lay these virtues aside in your dealings with Robert Allen.'

For the first time that night the archbishop smiled. 'I take not your advice amiss, Thomas, and I will certainly heed it.'

With that assurance, I had to be content but I was far from easy in my mind as I continued my journey home. Cranmer offered the use of his barge to cross the river and I gratefully accepted it while Underhill and the others travelled by way of the bridge and the wagoner, given money for a night's lodging, was released from his enforced service. I took Bart with me in order to deliver him to Lizzie and the children as soon as possible. As we reclined in the unaccustomed cushioned comfort of the barge I described my interview with the archbishop.

'Well,' Bart said, stifling a yawn, 'you have done all you can – and that is more than most men would have done. Now it is all up to our political masters.'

'That was what his grace said.'

'Then, why ...'

'Because I hate unanswered questions, Bart. Who is this Baron De La Warr? Why is he involved with a devious, unprincipled churl like Robert Allen? Who is he connected with at court?'

'Well, I can tell you he is not well loved locally,' Bart said. 'Some men were talking about him in an alehouse where we stopped on Saturday. They say the devil has his tongue.'

'What mean they by that? 'Tis not an expression I have come across.'

'Nor I. I think it must be a way of speaking they have in Sussex. From what I can tell it means double-tongued. His lordship cannot say his words properly. He stutters. Yet I think that is not all folk mean when they call his speech cursed. They reckon his words cannot be trusted. He says one thing and does another.'

'How so?'

'Well, he swears he will have none of the new religion. Yet when some commonwealth men were stirring the local commons he was slow to take action and accused the other magistrates of being overzealous.'

'Mayhap he is beside his wits.'

'That may be so. He is old. Men say he held sway hereabouts in their grandfathers' days.'

'Did you hear anything about his connections at court?' I asked eagerly.

'No, though someone did say he was close-bosomed in the last king's reign with the old Duke of Norfolk who is now in the Tower for treason and hankering after the pope's religion.'

The barge rocked slightly as it nudged Queenhythe stairs. Bart stood up. 'I will be glad to find my bed this night, Master Thomas, and gladder still to have all this politics behind us. 'Tis sore wearying for simple folk like me.' He was too respectful to add 'and you' but I knew well enough that that gentle warning was what he had in mind.

And he was right. Allen and West and De La Warr and Southampton and all those caught up in the web of their lives were no concern of mine. I was free of them. What if William West was condemned by parliamentary attainder for the attempted murder of his uncle? What if Parafaustus worked his 'magic' on the Primate of All England and spirited himself out of prison? What if Southampton picked up the loose ends of his plot and tied them back together? I had neither the right nor the power to stop them. At least, that was what I told myself at least a dozen times daily.

Five days later, on Saturday 7 September, the Earl of Warwick returned. He rode through the City at the head of a company of *landsknechts,* and the entire population – or so it seemed – turned out to welcome the hero of Norwich. The streets were lined with cheering crowds. Raffy was determined that our household should enjoy a prominent position. He was out early, stationing servants in front of our house in Goldsmiths' Row to keep a space for us.

But the rejoicing was far from universal. London had more than its fair share of 'commonwealthers' who regarded the overthrow of Kett and his 'freedom fighters' as a disaster. There was a knot of them standing behind us as we waited for the earl to approach along Cheapside. We could not help overhearing their conversation.

'They say he slaughtered ten thousand poor souls.'

'Aye, he and his foreign butchers.'

'And burned down their houses.'

'He only serves the rich.'

'Aye, and the papists. He would make us all slaves of Rome again.'

'Would that the Good Duke had gone to Norwich. Then we had seen a better outcome.'

I could sense Raffy tensing beside me. At last, he could not restrain himself. He spun round. 'Close your traitorous mouths, you ungrateful dogs!'

His hand went to the hilt of the small sword he now wore and he would have drawn it had I not grabbed his wrist. But I could not stop him shouting his anger.

'Ignorant curs! You defame a great man – and a merciful one. I was there. Three times Lord Warwick offered the rebels a pardon. Three times! And when the stubborn clay-brained gulls would have none of it, know you what he did? He wept!'

At that moment, the cavalcade approached. A stern-faced Warwick raised a gauntleted hand to acknowledge the cheers and passed by, leading his troops towards Newgate Street. By the time the mercenaries had passed, the grumbling commonwealthers had moved away. But Raffy's indignation had not cooled. As we walked back indoors, he continued his defence of his hero.

'He *did* weep, Father. After the battle he walked among the bodies at Dussindale, shouting his anger.'

'With the rebels.'

'No, with those who had lured them into such folly. Men like Parafaustus.'

'Then, he will be glad to know that that false prophet is now captured at last.'

'Pray God he is made to suffer like the poor wretches cut down at Norwich!' Raffy said bitterly. 'What will happen to him now?'

179

'He will be questioned by members of the royal council. If they decide he has charges to answer...'

'IF?' Raffy exclaimed. 'How can there be any doubt? You and I both know how much blood that lying enchanter has on his hands!'

'That is very true.'

'Then, is there nothing you can do to make sure he pays for his crimes?'

'The archbishop knows what I think. What more can I do?'

We walked through to the workshop where the craftsmen were returning to their benches. I went along the two rows, checking the progress of those who were cutting, shaping and filing gold and silver or matching gemstones to be set into pendants and brooches.

Raffy was still in an excitable mood. 'Father, how can you spend your time with jewellery while all these terrible things are happening?'

I replied calmly. 'If I did not, who would pay for all these fine court clothes you keep asking for?'

That silenced him. He had nothing more to say until we exchanged the clamour of the workshop for the panelled and tapestried calm of the parlour. Then he stood in the doorway, eyes downcast. 'I am sorry. I was being foolish and ungrateful.'

It was the first time in many years that I had heard him apologise and it greatly warmed my heart. 'You are simply being an impatient young man and, believe or not, I can remember how that feels. Come in and have a glass of canary. Ned always prescribes it to balance the humours.'

As I poured the wine, Raffy said. 'There is something I could do.'

'What is that?'

'Talk to his lordship. Tell him what has been happening here while he has been in Norfolk.'

'I am sure he is kept well informed by all his servants and agents.'

'Yes, he spends several hours every day reading and writing letters. But that is my point; he listens to people; considers what they tell him.'

I laughed. 'I fear you flatter yourself to think his policy would be swayed by anything a junior page says.'

'But he might be swayed by what you say,' the boy replied. 'I rejoin my lord's household at Ely Place this afternoon. Let me take a letter to him. You can explain how you struggled with Parafaustus like a slippery, wet fish until you finally had him in the net.'

I laughed again. 'How very poetic. Perhaps you do have the makings of a courtier. Soon you will be writing sonnets to one of Lady Warwick's attendants.'

'Do not mock, Father. I am serious. No-one else can tell the tale of the sorcerer's treachery and how you chased him down the Channel and finally caught him. My lord needs to know these things.' He drained his goblet at a gulp. 'And where's the harm in a respectful letter.'

In truth, I took little persuading and when, three hours later, Raffy rode off to Holborn it was with a letter from me in his purse.

It was to be the first of three important letters I handled that day. The second arrived within minutes of my son's departure. It was written on crumpled paper in a scrawled, untidy hand.

Master Treviot, it is seven weeks since you visited me in this fearsome place and promised to ease my suffering. Since then I have been attainted by the lords in parliament on the false charge of attempting my uncle's murder. Praise be God, the Commons house rejected the bill. Yet the upper house mean to raise the matter again. So still I languish here and know not what is to become of me. I pray you, keep your word and aid me how you can. I cannot endure much longer here.

I supplicate you from the gates of Hell

William West

It was as the shop's shutters were being closed that a messenger in green livery arrived and handed in the third letter. I did not recognise the griffin's head seal and set the message aside. Only after supper, when I was relaxing with Adie in our chamber did I open it and read it by lamplight.

Master Treviot, I am not a little surprised to learn that you have been meddling in my affairs. That a mere merchant should presume to interfere in the private and family dealings of his betters is not to be endured. You will call upon me tomorrow morning at my house in the White Friars in Fleet Street to give an account of yourself.

Thomas, Baron De La Warr

Chapter 17

THESE LETTERS MADE it plain that I was up to my neck in this affair whether I liked it or not. Cranmer might think that I had become an embarrassment and should now retire quietly but I could not reject West's appeal and I certainly could not ignore De La Warr's summons.

My first problem was how to prepare myself for my meeting with his lordship. Thinking about that filled my wakeful mind throughout most of the hours of darkness. De La Warr was a man of consequence with friends at the centre of power. I would have to mollify him if I could. But this was also my opportunity to get much closer to the heart of the matter. Could I discover something about his relationship with Robert Allen? Would it be possible, without arousing suspicion, to learn what De La Warr's connection was with Lord Southampton?

When I left Goldsmiths' Row the following morning I was accompanied by three of my men. It seemed a wise precaution to take when visiting a man who did not hesitate to resort to extreme measures, though I could not help reflecting that travelling with a 'bodyguard' even in the City and its confine was becoming an unwelcome habit.

The old headquarters of the Capuchin or White Friars covered several acres between Fleet Street and the river. For several years since the departure of the religious, this area had been an untidy building site as the conventual buildings were levelled or converted into private housing for wealthy citizens or courtiers. On enquiring for Lord De La Warr's residence, we were directed to a substantial, three-storey building fronting its own courtyard, flanked by stable and coach house block. We were shown into a smallish parlour and told to wait.

Wait we did – for more than an hour. I had little doubt that this was a deliberate attempt by his lordship to keep a 'mere merchant' in his place. Eventually, I was escorted to the first floor and ushered into a long room, something between a chamber and a gallery. On each side, placed at regular intervals, were three green-liveried servants. At the far end of this 'corridor', I was faced by a high-backed chair in which sat the figure of Thomas West, Baron De La Warr. I restrained the impulse to smile at this display of intimidation, reached the 'throne' and made a slight bow.

The man before me was thin to the point of gauntness. His dress and beard were of the fashion of thirty years earlier. For several silent moments he peered at me with grey, watery eyes. Eventually, he spoke.

'M-m, master m-m-m-merchant, you are here to m-make an ex-p-planation of your c-conduct.'

'What conduct, My Lord?'

His scowl deepened and his anger made his speech impediment even worse. 'In-vading m-my p-p-property with a bunch of rogues and ab-d-ducting my g-guest.'

I met his hectoring with a calm that possessed its own defiance. 'I am very much afraid that Your Lordship must have been misinformed. The men who apprehended Robert Allen were members of his majesty's personal guard, executing a warrant issued by his majesty's council against someone under investigation for criminal activities.'

De La Warr leaned forward. 'What c-c-criminal activities?'

'Inciting rebellion, publishing false prophecies, which, as Your Lordship knows, has recently been declared a statutory offence by parliament, facilitating illicit gambling, piracy…'

'P-p-piracy?' He seemed genuinely surprised by that.

'Yes, My Lord. In order to reach your Lordship's house in Sussex, this man Allen commandeered a ship belonging to his imperial majesty Charles V, Holy Roman Emperor and a valued ally of his majesty King Edward.'

'Imp-p-p-possible. The amb-bassador assured me …' He stopped suddenly, stood up and took several paces back and forth. I realised at that moment that his bluster covered deep anxiety, perhaps even fear. He clapped his hands and his six attendants filed out, leaving us alone in the large chamber.

I grasped my opportunity. 'Unlike you and I, My Lord, this Allen has no regard for truth and honesty. He holds in contempt anyone who distinguishes between right and wrong. He is deceitful and diabolically clever. He makes a fool of anyone who trusts in him.'

De La Warr stopped in front of me and peered with a gaze of suspicion and uncertainty. 'M-master m-m-merchant, how know you of this m-m-man?'

I gave a brief account of my visit to Norwich and my subsequent search for the magus, being careful not to mention William West. 'Once we had Allen under lock and key,' I concluded Lord Southampton signed a warrant to have him removed to the Tower.' I watched carefully to see how De La Warr responded to the mention of the earl.

He flinched but made no comment. He moved to a window overlooking the broken walls that were the only remains of the White Friars' church. After several moments, he spoke without turning round. 'You have been to m-much t-t-trouble, M-Master m-m-merchant but you have been m-misinformed about M-Master Allen.'

'I wish that were true, My Lord,' I replied, trying to find a way to turn the conversation, 'but I have seen with my own eyes the lives he has ruined. He is a traitor to his majesty and to the Lord Protector. We must thank God that he is now in prison where he will be interrogated and made to reveal his plans and accomplices.'

I allowed the implication of those words to sink in before I continued. 'I am surprised that Your Lordship thinks well of him. Has he performed some valuable service for you? I suppose even such a rogue as Allen is sometimes capable of good deeds.' I offered the bait in a casual tone of voice. Would he take it?

He shrugged, still gazing out of the window. 'A f-family m-matter,' he muttered. A young relative g-g-getting into b-bad c-c-company. Allen helped s-sort him out. I s-scarcely knew the m-man.' There was another pause before De La Warr turned. 'To b-be interrogated by the c-c-council, you say?'

'Certainly. In these troubled times, we must look to them to uncover any plots that could lead to fresh disturbances. I am sure Allen's entire seditious network will soon be completely exposed.'

'Who is s-suspected of involvement in his p-p-plots?'

'Oh, My Lord, I said, 'I am a mere merchant. Such matters are well above me.'

The old man either missed or did not choose to recognise my sarcasm. 'Indeed, indeed. P-pity it is others do not k-keep to their p-proper s-station. England has ever been r-ruled by our ancient f-families – till now. The De La Warrs have shared c-control of S-Sussex, K-Kent and Hampshire for centuries. We are l-l-linked with f-families equally ancient – M-Mortimer, FitzAlan, Copley, G-Guildford, P-Percy, Bonville. Who knows this l-land and p-people better?' He resumed his striding back and forth, his speech impediment overborne by his enthusiasm. 'Certainly not Boleyns and Seymours and other upstarts. Why are our ancient f-faith and c-customs under attack? Why is there rebellion everywhere? Why all this n-nonsense talk of c-commonwealth? Because m-men no longer keep to their p-proper s-station!'

I did not point out that denouncing the Seymours and, by implication, the Lord Protector was tantamount to treason and I doubt whether De La Warr grasped the significance of his angry oratory.

He turned and pointed an accusing finger. 'Master merchant, stick to your m-merchanting and leave the running of the c-country to your b-betters. You may go!'

Thus dismissed, I made my way home, turning over in my mind what I had learned from the confused and confusing ramblings of this angry old man. I certainly had some leads I was anxious to follow up with his nephew. I decided that my visit to William West in the Tower could not be delayed any longer.

The following afternoon I went back to the ancient royal fortress. I took Ned with me again. He had obviously impressed West at our first meeting and I hoped that my old friend's presence would encourage the prisoner to reveal to us things he had not mentioned before. On this occasion, I could show no written authority but the warders recognised me and money opened the necessary doors.

West was seated in the same place as he had been the last time we had seen him. It was almost as though he had not moved in the intervening weeks, except that his face was more haggard, his hair and clothes even more unkempt. When he rose slowly to his feet, resting a hand on the table to do so, his movements were those of an old man.

'Master Treviot, Master Longbourne, thank God you are here,' he said. 'I had despaired of ever seeing you again. Do you bring news? Is there any hope for me?'

'Well, Master West,' I replied, 'much has happened these last weeks and we now know that your plight is part of something much larger. Do you receive any news here of what is happening in the country?'

'I know there have been many rebellions. Some government prisoners here, such as the Duke of Norfolk and Bishop Gardiner, are in hopes to see Protector Somerset overthrown and Catholicism restored. But I take little interest in these things and they have nothing to do with my fate.'

'There you are much mistaken, Master West,' Ned said. 'Pray be seated. We bring you important news but you must take care not to be over-excited.'

West slumped back onto his stool. 'Any news must be good, for nothing you can tell me could possibly make my situation worse.'

'Then know that your tormentor has been located,' Ned continued. 'The originator of all your woes – the man who calls himself "Parafaustus" has been found, thanks in large measure to the tireless activity of Master Treviot. His real name is Robert Allen and we can assure you that he is in no position to do you any further harm.'

West looked at us warily. 'How can you be certain that his powers have been broken?'

'For two reasons,' Ned replied. 'The first is that he has and never has had any powers. The man whose scheming has brought you to this place is a fraudulent magus; a peddler of potions and horoscopes: a scheming trickster; a garrulous flibber-gibber whose spells and incantations are empty words to gull the simple-minded. He is no serious scholar of magic, either black or white. The second reason is that he is in prison.'

'And there,' I added, 'he will be closely questioned. We will find out from him exactly how he interfered between you and your uncle.'

If I expected to see the prisoner's face light up with relief and joy I was disappointed. West shook his head despondently. 'It is good that this fellow should be exposed. But it will avail me little if my uncle continues to trust him. His lordship is a man very set in his ways. Once he has an idea in his head it is very difficult to dislodge it.'

'When last we came,' I said, 'you told us that your relationship with your uncle was good and that you were astonished that he charged you with attempted murder. Surely, there must have been something behind his action – some argument or disagreement, perhaps?'

West gave a long sigh. 'It was nothing – or so I thought at the time. My uncle had no children and, seven years ago, he nominated me as his heir.'

'You were his favourite?' Ned asked.

'His least un-favourite,' West replied with a cynical laugh. He cares little for any of his relatives but there needed someone to carry on the barony. He trained me well – showed me all the houses, farms, pastures and woodlands. He had his steward introduce me to all the accounts, deeds and documents. He satisfied himself that I would continue to run the estate properly.'

'In other words, you were to do things as they had always been done,' I suggested.

'Oh, yes. He is a thorough traditionalist. I soon learned not to suggest any ideas of my own. But I did not mind. I knew that once the estate passed to me I could modernise it. Of course, he knew what I was thinking. Sometimes he would say "You are only waiting till I die so that you can ruin everything". But mostly we were on good terms and I did not take his grumbling seriously.'

'But I suppose his attitude changed when he realised you were ready to take over,' Ned said. 'That is quite common in these situations. The old lion begins to fear the young one.'

'I was not aware of any real change. 'Tis only as I have had time to think about it, sitting here day after day, that I have realised two things happened which affected him more deeply than I realised at the time. About three years ago my uncle took ill with a tertian fever. The physician told him that the malady was not fatal but he convinced himself that he was going to die and he spent time closeted with priests. He had scarcely recovered when King Henry died. That troubled the old man greatly.'

'Why so?' I asked.

'Because he thought the country would go to ruin. Friends like Bishop Gardiner and the Duke of Norfolk were removed from the council and power fell to new men – Edward Seymour – now become Duke of Somerset – and those my uncle called "Seymour's heretical copesmates".'

'But you were in favour of the change,' Ned suggested.

'Yes, I am for the new men and the new learning. I never argued about such things with my uncle. I did not want to upset him. But he knew what I believed. It obviously worried him much more than I realised at the time.'

'He must have begun to see you as a threat,' Ned observed. 'His whole life was built on ancient, Catholic tradition and he realised you would not preserve that tradition.'

'The poor man must have been easy prey for Robert Allen,' I said. 'Do you know how your uncle met him?'

'No, I never saw him. I believe he was recommended by one of Uncle's friends at the royal court as someone skilled in horoscopes.'

'Meddlesome churl!' Ned's face grew red with anger. 'Typical of these fraudulent "magic men" who sink their claws into vulnerable people. 'Twas a truly diabolical plan he tricked Lord De La Warr into playing on you. I never thought to say this of anyone but I pray God grant me length of days to see Robert Allen swinging at a rope's end.'

'Now that he is exposed,' I said, 'I hope his lordship will make haste to distance himself from the rogue.' I gave West an account of my quest for Allen and the catalogue of offences of which he was guilty. 'All this I have explained to your uncle,' I concluded. 'Surely, he will now set matters right with you.'

West sighed deeply. 'My friends, you have been very kind and I know not how I can ever repay you but 'twill take more than facts to sway my uncle. His prejudices are unshakeable. He shunned my Aunt Eleanor Guildford's family for years until very recently and he bears other grudges that he will probably carry to the grave.'

'And he is still pressing his bill of attainder against you?'

'Yes, the Commons house rejected it but he is determined to see me condemned and has persuaded his friends in the upper house to put it forward again.'

'I fancy he will make little progress once his dealings with Allen become common knowledge,' Ned said. 'Pray do not despair. However black things appear now, night will give place to day and you are not without friends.'

That was all the comfort we were able to offer West at that time. As Ned and I made our way back through the busy streets I felt dejected. I had hoped for much from my meetings with De La Warr and his rejected heir but I had achieved nothing. And yet, it seemed to me that some things had been said that were important if only I could recognise them. Like a water-stained letter, the reason for West's troubles had been set before me but the words were too smudged to read.

'Do you not think this may be all about families?' I asked, as we pulled to the side of the road to allow an overloaded hay wagon to pass down Poultry.

'You mean noble clans forming alliances with and against each other in their constant competition for power?'

'Yes, I could not have put it better myself. Old De La Warr is obsessed with his ancestry and his connections with the FitzAlans, Guildfords, Mortimers and their like – the guardians of the old order. He resents new kindred groups like the Seymours intruding into their private world.'

'Well, he has much to complain about. The new men in power have enriched themselves with lands and ennobled themselves with titles since the old king's death. Edward Seymour becomes Duke of Somerset; Thomas Wriothesley is made Earl of Southampton; John Dudley is now Earl of Warwick. They and the other new men are certainly thrusting the ancient nobility aside. Were I in De La Warr's shoes I would certainly be worried.'

'Would you fight back or accept the inevitable and make friends with the hated upstarts?'

Ned reined his horse in as the contents of a bucket poured from an open window splashed onto the road a few paces ahead. 'Ah well, now, that would depend on the strength of my faith.'

'What mean you?'

'That it may be too simple to think that De La Warr is motivated solely by dynastic pride. Master West tells us that his uncle is a devout Catholic. He might regard it as his duty to stop this country's headlong rush into the religious chaos that calls itself church reform.'

'But how would blackening his own nephew's name serve the cause of the old religion?'

Ned shook his head. 'That I do not know. Perhaps he hopes to detach West from the Protector's party; bring him back into the Catholic fold. None of West's court friends have come to his aid. They will be keen to avoid the taint of murder and necromancy.'

We rode in silence for a few minutes and had passed the Great Conduit before Ned spoke again. 'Of course, De La Warr might also seek new alliances. Lord Southampton is known to favour the old religion.'

'Yes,' I agreed. 'Everything keeps pointing to him. Cranmer is immovable in his conviction that his lordship is reconciled to the new regime and a faithful supporter of the Protector.'

'Which is precisely the impression he would try to give if he was secretly plotting against Somerset.'

'Very true … and yet …'

'You are beginning to doubt that Southampton is Allen's patron and the man behind all the mischief we have seen in this business?'

'No. But I am sure we are missing something. 'Tis like trying to mend a broken pot – no use until you have all the pieces. There is at least one piece we have not found.'

We had reached Milk Street. As Ned turned in the direction of his lodging, he said. 'Then the best advice I can give you is "Stop looking". If this potsherd is hiding somewhere in your head it will probably jump out when you least expect.'

For once Ned's wise advice failed to bear fruit. I still had more questions than answers but, busy as I was with the shop and my ward responsibilities, after a week or so I stopped worrying away at the questions. I was still concerned about the prisoner in the Tower but I suppose I was influenced by the change of mood in the City. There was a feeling of profound relief that the crisis was over. Lord Warwick's mercenaries were encamped just beyond the northern walls. We all felt safe and were concentrating on getting our lives back to normal.

Then, the problem of Robert Allen once more demanded my attention.

To my good friend Master Thomas Treviot my hearty commendations. His grace has commanded me to request your assistance in the investigation of Robert Allen. The prisoner has a proud stomach and hotly denies some of the allegations against him. His grace believes that your evidence will help effectively counter Allen's lies and prevarications and enable us to establish the truth without further delay. I will come to escort you to Lambeth tomorrow forenoon and will then open matters to you in more detail.

Ever your friend

Ralph Morice

Thus ran the letter I received on Wednesday 19 September and, the following forenoon I found myself once more crossing the river in the archbishop's barge. Morice, usually so reticent about telling me any more than he thought I needed to know was, on this occasion, a gushing fountain of information. He bustled me down Bread Street to Queenhythe, talking all the time.

'We have to convince the council of this villain's guilt. Then we can commit him to the Tower to await trial.'

'Surely there is no lack of evidence,' I suggested.

'No, nor lack of pressure from certain parties who wish to see the prisoner set at liberty.'

'Lord Southampton?'

Morice allowed himself a wry smile. 'You persist, then, in believing that he is our villain's principal patron? No, several people have been persuaded to vouch for the churl's good character.'

'I assumed that once Allen was in custody pressure would be exerted to draw valuable information and even a confession from him.'

'Not in the archbishop's house,' Morice replied ruefully. 'His grace will not countenance the kind of "pressure" you refer to. He will have the preliminary investigation carried out in an orderly fashion by a magistrate in front of witnesses so that Allen cannot claim to have been bullied into submission. That is why we must remove him to the Tower quickly. We shall not have all the truth from him till then. Unfortunately, time is not on our side.'

'Why the hurry?' I asked.

We had reached the quay and Morice did not reply until we were settled in the stern cushions, the curtains tight closed around us.

'The moment of crisis we have all dreaded is almost upon us,' he said solemnly. 'His grace and the other heads on the Council have tried to preserve unity between the Protector and the other advisers appointed by his late majesty to govern the realm but Somerset is determined to go his own way and constantly snubs his colleagues. A man could be forgiven for thinking that the Protector enjoys making enemies. He has even put a strain on the relationship with his old friend and comrade-in-arms the Earl of Warwick. It is no exaggeration to say that England is heading for chaos, with two governments; one at Hampton, where the duke keeps his majesty close by him, and one at Westminster, where the council meets daily. If we are to avoid this we need to expose those who have been plotting against the Protector.'

'Catholics like De La Warr, who want a return to the old ways?'

'Yes.'

'And if we can show that Allen is a traitor in the pay of the Protector's enemies this will put a stop to their intrigues?'

'I am sure it will.'

'But, on the other hand, if Allen is exonerated and walks free West will appear to be a liar and a man prepared to murder his own kin. The stain of scandal might well spread to taint West's friends in Somerset's entourage.'

'That is what Allen's backers will hope and they will be vigilant in spreading rumours.'

'Who are their targets?'

'William West did a few terms at Cambridge. It was there that he accepted the teaching of Luther and his mentor was one of the university's brightest scholars, John Cheke. This Cheke is now the brains of the Protector's court. He is tutor to his majesty and very close to the king and his uncle. They are as inseparable as the three points of a triangle. If Somerset's enemies could unseat Cheke they would have struck a major blow.'

The barge nudged Lambeth Stains and we went ashore.

The room Morice took me to was bare save for two rows of stools and facing them, a table and two chairs in which the president, a grey-haired local justice and his secretary, were seated. Four paces away and flanked by two members of the archbishop's guard stood Robert Allen. He wore a grubby white smock. He was hatless and his greasy black hair draped loosely onto his shoulders. His hands were tied in front of him. Deprived of his 'magic' garb he appeared extremely ordinary. He might have been a farm labourer, dragged away from his plough to answer a bewildering set of questions from strangers. There were seven other people in the room among whom I recognised Edward Underhill and Gaston, Allen's landlord. The interrogation was already in progress. Gaston was on his feet and speaking volubly.

'Master Allen is a reader of horoscopes and, to my certain knowledge, nothing more. 'Tis true he advised people of auspicious times to try their fortune at the dice or the cards. I never heard there was any law passed against this. As to illicit gaming rooms, I never heard that Master Allen was associated with such.'

'Yet we have had evidence presented of false dice and other deceits found among the accused possessions ...' The president paused as Morice stepped forward to whisper in his ear.

Thank you, Master Gaston,' he continued. 'Pray be seated. We will return to this later. Now we have been joined by someone who is come to give evidence of more important matters. Master Treviot, be so good as to stand and tell us why you accuse the prisoner of incitement to treason.'

Allen fixed me with a glare of intense hatred as I began my evidence. I explained my visit to the rebels' camp at Mousehold and described how the self-styled magician deliberately stirred his hearers to rebellion, promising them success and assistance from the spirits of the dead. Three times I was interrupted by Allen, who shrieked 'Lies!' 'Perjury!' 'This man is in the pay of the king's enemies!' But he fell silent when I produced an item I had found in the Aldermanbury lodging - one of the bills Allen had distributed among the crowds in Kett's camp.

The president turned to Allen. 'Now you have your opportunity to answer these serious allegations. Were you present at the Norwich rebellion?'

'Yes, I, ...'

'And were you there of your own free will?'

'I was present as a loyal subject of his majesty,' Allen blustered.

'To what intent?'

'To restrain the poor people the deceiver Kett was leading in rebellion.'

The president held up Allen's broadside. 'Then what say you to this inflammatory document?'

''Tis a damnable forgery!' Allen shouted. He raised both hands to point at me. 'That man is a traitor and a ruffian. More than once he and his copesmates have assaulted me most violently.' He took a step forward but was immediately restrained by the guards. But he continued to shout, his voice growing steadily more shrill. 'Your Honour, listen not to this tradesman! I am known to great scholars, and noblemen and members of his majesty's household. I have done them many services. They will speak for me'

'Silence!' The magistrate rose to his feet. 'You will answer my questions when I bid you and only when I bid you.' He turned to me. 'Master Treviot, we are grateful to you for your time and need detain you no longer.'

Morice left the room with me. 'Excellently done, Thomas. Your evidence was all we needed to have him detained in the Tower.' He shook my hand. 'I must stay to the end of the hearing but his grace's barge is at your command.'

'Send me word of what happens. With Allen discredited we must surely see poor West released.'

I walked down to the quay. A few steps from the archbishop's barge I heard my name called. Turning I saw a tall man expensively dressed in black court clothes. He had been present at the interrogation.

'You return to the City?' he asked.

'Yes.'

'Then please allow me to convey you in my boat.'

'That is good of you but his grace has been kind enough to …'

I suddenly felt something sharp pressing against my lower ribs. Looking down I saw that the stranger was holding a long-bladed stiletto.'

'I am afraid I must insist,' he said.

Chapter 18

MY FIRST REACTION was to turn and run back to the palace.
Then I saw that the man in black had two companions, rough-
looking fellows in riding boots and leather jerkins. All I could do was
bluster a useless protest. 'What is the meaning of this?'

In fact, the meaning seemed quite clear: these were friends of
Allen, intent on exacting revenge for my part in his arrest and
ensuring that I would never be able to repeat my testimony.

My captor nudged me forward. 'My boat is at the end of the
quay. Pray, Master Treviot, be not alarmed. I simply want to have a
conversation with you. A private conversation.'

The craft I was handed down into was a broad-beamed wherry,
somewhat larger than those used by Thames watermen. It occurred
to me to leap over the side, swim a few yards and call for help but
there was no-one in view at the landing stage and my abductor sat
beside me with a hand firmly clamped to my arm. His accomplices
manned the oars and steered the boat out onto the river. London's
main thoroughfare was, as usual, busy with traffic. Were these men, I
wondered desperate enough or foolish enough to slit my throat and
dump my body overboard in front of so many witnesses?

'Please do not think of calling out,' the man beside me said
quietly. 'I assure you there is no need. We only wish to talk with you.

After that, we will deliver you to Queenhythe. Alive,' he added with a light laugh.

Moments later, he called out an order. 'This will do.'

His companions stopped rowing and used their oars to hold the wherry's position against the current. We were in mid-steam on the broad bend half way between Whitehall and the Bridge. We could see clearly the site, alive with workmen, where Somerset House, the duke's large, new residence was being built.

'You are a remarkable man, Master Treviot,' said the man in black. 'On the surface a successful, highly respected London merchant, a confidant of some of the greatest in the land. I confess I was curious to meet you and – I admit it – something sceptical. "Could this staid citizen," I asked myself, "really be a trusted agent of his majesty's council, a daring adventurer who relishes danger, a thinker of brilliant intellect, adept at solving puzzles and unravelling secrets." But when I heard you describing your encounter with Master Allen, all my doubts dissolved like morning mist.'

'You have not committed this outrage in order to flatter me,' I protested.

'Indeed not and I regret the dramatic means I employed to engineer this interview. However, I doubt very much whether you would have responded positively to a simple request.'

'That would depend on the nature of the request. I would be obliged if we could get to the point of this meeting.'

'There you are, you see, that proves the accuracy of my judgement. You go straight to the heart of the matter. You sit here in this apparently precarious situation but you banish fear and, with a cool head, you tell yourself, "I must find out what this fellow wants." Very well, Master Treviot, the point is this: we wish to employ you.'

'And who are "we"?'

Again the light laugh. 'You are too intelligent to expect a straight answer to that question. We have observed that various attempts – some rather crude – have been made to discourage you from dabbling in what might, rather grandly, be called "affairs of state". They have all been unsuccessful. You are not a man who gives up once he had undertaken a task.'

'If the task is honourable and just.'

He ignored the caveat. 'You obviously cannot be removed from the business of Master West and the obnoxious creature who calls himself "Parafaustus". Moreover, it would be a waste of considerable talent simply to murder you here and slip you into the Thames.'

'And also very risky,' I pointed out.

'That is why we have decided to make use of your considerable talents. We want you to work for us.'

'Oh, really!' I tried to manage a scornful laugh. 'If this is your usual way of conducting business I want nothing to do with you.'

'You have not yet heard what we are asking of you.'

'Whatever it is, I am not interested.'

He continued as if Ii had not spoken. 'Your son has a position in the Earl of Warwick's household. Doubtless, he hears much about his lordship's plans. He observes some of the people who call upon his lordship. He hears servant gossip. He enjoys the company of his lordship's sons. Now, we would very much like to be recipients of such information.'

'What?' The monstrous demand caught me off guard. It was some moments before I could frame a reply. 'Out of the question! I am no man's spy and I certainly will not force my son to become one!'

My abductor continued in the same quiet infuriatingly self-confident tone. 'We were confident that this would be your immediate reaction – that you would need some persuasion. We have, therefore, prepared very carefully for this eventuality. Two weeks ago you received a box of jewels from an old customer, a noble lady of impeccable pedigree. She sent the casket with a note asking you to buy these trinkets. This you were happy to do, knowing that you would have little difficulty disposing of the items to other members of your clientele. You would either sell them on as they were or have them re-fashioned in your workshop.'

'You are damnably well informed but I have no reason to deny what you say.'

'What you would certainly want to deny is that four of those gewgaws were stolen and that you have already resold two of them.'

'Nonsense! The lady in question …'

'Knows nothing of this and will truthfully deny ever having the items in her possession. They were added to the consignment after they left her and before they reached you. This means that you have become a dealer in stolen merchandise – a crime which would probably bring you before the courts but would certainly lead to your expulsion from the honourable Goldsmiths' Company.'

I gasped. 'No! They would never believe it of me. They would know I was being accused on the basis of false evidence.'

'Is that not what Master Allen is also claiming – that you have presented a forged document in order to condemn him for treason?'

'That is not the same! I have an excellent reputation!'

'Undoubtedly, but how many reputations have been destroyed by suspicion? Suspicion will likely bring Allen to Tyburn and may just as well see you locked up in King's Bench prison.'

'So all this is about revenge for my part in Allen's conviction.'

'Oh, no!' The black-clad courtier replied with a laugh. 'We care not a farthing for that tricksy peddler of spells and potions. There are much more important matters at stake.' He called out to his companions. 'Pull away, lads!' Then to me, he continued. 'Take a few minutes to reflect on what I have said.'

We were passing Paul's Wharf and had almost reached journey's end before he spoke again. 'One of other of my friends here will be at your yard gate at noon each day. You will pass him a note of anything noteworthy in my Lord Warwick's behaviour. Fail us or attempt to identify us and an anonymous note will find its way to the prime warden of your company.'

◊

Anger, frustration, self-pity – those were just some of the emotions that clashed and clanged in my head like men-at-arms in a violent skirmish over the next couple of days. I conceived – and discarded – various courses of action: report the threatening behaviour to Cranmer and let the devil decide the consequence? Check my ledgers in order to locate and recover the stolen items unwillingly sold? Follow the man in black's emissary when he called for his daily report? None of these was without risk.

It was Adie who set my thinking on a different course and one which was to have unforeseen consequences.

'I have an idea,' she said brightly as we dressed the following morning. 'Because Raffy has been from home we have missed his birthday. Why do we not have a dinner here for him and some of his new friends?'

Black though my mood was, I could not avoid a smile. 'This has nothing to do with ingratiating ourselves with his lordship's family, I suppose?'

'Not al all!' She bridled. 'Come and tie my sleeves for me. I think it would please Raffy and show his lordship's people that, though we are not noble, we do keep a good table. Anyway, have you not always told me that family alliances are good for business?'

It was agreed that we would invite my son to bring some of his new companions to dinner on the following Saturday – the 2 September. But some of Adie's words stuck in my head and evoked an echo – 'family alliances are good for business'. Where had I heard something similar? It was, of course, the hubristic Lord De La Warr who had boasted of his family connections. His nephew had also made comments that now took on the vivid hues of enhanced significance. What if the business in which I had unwittingly become embroiled was not at root about magic, or murder plots, or treason or even government policy but about alliances, shifting associations of self-interested men, determined in these chaotic times to gain or maintain power for themselves and their kin.

When Raffy came in person from Ely Place to accept our invitation I had a question for him. 'You tell us your have become firm friends with one of his lordship's sons.'

'Gilly?'

'Yes, that is his pet name. He is really called "Guildford" is he not?'

'That's right.'

'Know you how he came by that name?'

''Tis a family name. His mother is one of the Sussex Guildfords.'

'Has he ever spoken of an Aunt Eleanor?'

'No, why do you ask?'

'Mere curiosity. Someone mentioned her to me recently and I wondered if there was a connection. I hope we shall have the pleasure of getting to know Gilly on Saturday.'

When the day came Adie had everyone working at full stretch from first light in order to impress our guests. I kept well clear of the kitchen where my wife fussed and fumed and fretted and flurried over our own cooks and scullions as well as others borrowed from neighbours and of the parlour where Bart oversaw the setting out of our best silver on the table and ensured that there were sufficient flagons of claret and canary for our small party set upon the buffet. I had arranged for Bart to be in charge of the servers and had taken him partly into my confidence. 'Listen carefully to all talk around the table,' I instructed. 'I want to know anything of interest about Lord Warwick and his family.' Up to this point, I had had no information to pass on to the unwelcome noontide visitors who appeared, as had been threatened, at my yard gate but I had countered their importunity with promises of hoped-for revelations following our celebration dinner.

On the day, Raffy rode into the yard with Guildford, his younger brother, Henry, and two of their household companions, Simon de Vere and Robert Mortmain. They were a spirited group and fell upon the venison, capons, jellies, tarts and other delicacies with an enthusiasm that much delighted Adie. I had seated Guildford between me and Raffy. I made polite enquiry after the young man's father.

Guildford, slim with a touch of fair hair, replied in the nonchalant manner typical of a lad of his age.

'He is well. Glad to be away from Norwich.'

'Dealing with the rebellion must have been very unpleasant.'

Guildford skewered a morsel of beef on his knife and dipped it in the pepper sauce. 'He hated it. He would rather be fighting the Scots or the Frenchies. I think he felt sorry for the rebels. Not me. I would have shown the rabble how to respect their betters. But you were there, were you not, Master Treviot? Raffy tells me how you fought a gang of the churls, single-handed. That must have been thrilling.'

I laughed. 'Oh, I am no hero. Soldiering is not for me. I found that Norwich business sad, tragic.'

'Interesting. 'Tis what my father said also; too much unnecessary killing. This venison pastie is great.'

Conversation ambled around several subjects and it was not until I steered it onto the young man's ancestry that I confirmed something I had already guessed – and also had a surprise revelation.

'I assume you are named "Guildford" after your mother's family,' I said. 'Do you see much of them?'

He shook his head and muttered through a mouthful of custard tart, 'No, my grandfather died before I was born.' He took a long draft of hippocras. 'My mother was his only child, so we have most of the Guildford land now. The best part is the park in Sussex. Great hunting. You and Raffy must come down sometime.'

'Thank you. We would much like that. Where is the estate?'

'On the coast, near Worden. I will speak to my father and see if it may be arranged. I think he will not come. He is very busy since his return.'

'Visitors throng Ely Place every day,' Raffy added.

'No doubt his responsibilities for the German troop take up much of his time,' I suggested.

'Especially as he has to pay for them,' Guildford muttered.

'Surely that is a charge on the government,' I said.

'Not according to the Protector.' My young guest sat back and patted his stomach. 'Ooh! My ship is overloaded. That was a great dinner.' He raised his goblet to my wife, sitting opposite. 'My thanks to you, Mistress Treviot.'

The other guests all murmured their approval.

Everyone seemed ready to leave the table but I did not want to abandon the conversational lead which has just emerged.

'Are you saying that the Protector refuses to pay the mercenaries their wages?'

'Well, not enough. At least 'tis what my father says.'

'They were superb,' Raffy enthused. 'You should have seen them charge at Dussindale. Magnificent!'

I sat back, scarcely listening while the young men aired their enthusiasm for and slender knowledge of matters military.

◊

'We have been on the wrong scent. 'Tis as master West said – all about alliances.'

It was several hours later. The company had dispersed and I sat in the lamp-lit parlour with Ned.

'We have to think everything through from the beginning. That is why I asked you to come.'

'What has happened to change your mind?' the old man asked.

I described my encounter with the men in black. 'You may imagine how worried I was by his threats,' I said, 'but had it not been for his pressure I would not have thought to probe Lord Warwick's affairs.'

'So, what have you learned?'

'That there are things we must unlearn. We assumed – on reasonable grounds – that the Earl of Southampton was the driving force behind a bizarre and complex plot to discredit William West and his pro-Somerset associates at court. It seemed reasonable to assume that Lord De La Warr was the earl's accomplice. They both have grievances and desire a return to the old ways. Yet Cranmer would not countenance our suspicions. He has an unshakeable faith in Southampton's loyalty.'

'Archbishops are not infallible,' Ned observed wryly.

'Agreed. But this one is no fool. We could not – I could not – challenge his convictions because I could not produce an alternative suspect. It would certainly never have occurred to me to connect my Lord Warwick with Parafaustus, let alone with William West, but now ... alliances! 'Tis all about alliances!' I pointed to a sheet of paper on the table between us. 'I have sketched out the family connections as far as I can. Now, as I understand it, Baron De La Warr's father was twice married. The present baron was the sole issue of his first marriage. By his second wife, he had a son who was the father of William West, and who, as we know, was designated as the baron's heir.

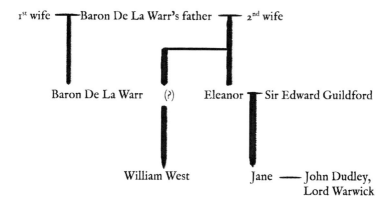

'BUT by his second wife he also had a daughter, Eleanor, who married Sir Edward Guildford and they had a daughter who is none other than the wife of the Earl of Warwick.'

'So the hero of Dussindale is Lord De La Warr's nephew by marriage? Interesting,' Ned mused. 'The monastery at Farnfield where I spent many happy years was surrounded by Guildford land. Hardly surprising; much of Sussex and Kent was owned and ruled by the

Guildfords. But now? Their empire is broken up, dispersed to distant relatives and eager land-buyers. *Sic transit gloria mundi.*'

'And one result is that my lords Warwick and De La Ware are not only related, they are close neighbours in Sussex.'

Ned clenched his eyes and nodded. 'Ah, yes, now I think on't there was a John Dudley who was a ward of Sir Edward Guildford. He must have married the daughter. It is, as you say, Thomas, all about alliances.'

'That means that when we captured Robert Allen in Sussex, he believed he was heading for a very safe haven, where he would be protected by two powerful lords.'

'True,' Ned replied, 'but let us not jump from one hasty conclusion to another. Why would Warwick want to use De La Warr's nephew and heir in a vicious plot?'

'Remember that William West is also his nephew (or, to be strictly accurate, his wife's nephew). Perhaps both lords planned it together. You recall what West, himself, told us: De La Warr and his Guildford relatives had been estranged *until recently*. Might they not have found common cause, in their plot?'

'Perhaps,' Ned persisted, 'but I come back to my question – "Why?" We know the baron and his heir were at odds over religion. I quite understand the uncle not wanting to see a new head of the family encouraging heretical preachers, replacing parish clergy with men of the new faith and removing ancient objects of devotion from churches on the grounds that they were 'superstitious'. But Warwick is a man of the new faith. He would have no reason to see West disgraced, disinherited and, in all likelihood, executed for attempted murder.'

'The underlying motive must remain the same,' I insisted. 'An attempt – albeit bizarre and ill-conceived – to discredit the Protector and his friends.'

'Friends – exactly!' Ned nodded enthusiastically. 'That, surely, is where your theory fails. Warwick and Somerset *are* friends – have been for many years.'

'Yes,' I agreed, 'and that is why it would never have occurred to me to suspect Warwick – until today. His lordship's son told me that his father and the Protector had fallen out. I did not want to press the lad too far but what seems to have happened is this: Warwick had to go and sort out the mess at Norwich and it was a job he hated. He was put in the position of slaughtering fellow Englishmen. Now, those men were not ordinary rebels, as I have good cause to know. They were not enemies of the king. Indeed, they claimed to be acting in support of his majesty's (or, rather, the Protector's) declared policies. They believed themselves to be in revolt against grasping landlords; enemies of the common people. Other members of the council blame Somerset for the recent disturbances. They claim that his "commonwealth" policies encourage social unrest and that matters have got out of hand because he did not deal firmly with discontent. I believe Warwick has come round to their way of thinking.'

'Why are you so sure of that?' Ned asked.

'Because I know what he saw and heard and smelled at Norwich – the blood, the dead bodies with only billhooks in their hands, the moans of the wounded, the wailing widows. His lordship may be a seasoned general but I doubt he will ever forget those sights, any more than I can.'

'And you believe he blames all this on Somerset?'

'I think he must feel like the cat in the old story who pulled the chestnuts from the fire. The monkey ate them and all the cat had for his pains were singed paws. But there was worse. When the victor came back from Norwich seeking adequate reward for his troops, the Protector refused him money.'

Ned's eyes opened wide. 'That was unkindly done,' He frowned thoughtfully. 'And yet such grievance is recent. The plot against West was hatched in midsummer.'

I admitted that this did not fit easily with my version of events. 'And yet disenchantment must have been building for months. Resentment is a slow-growing plant. Perhaps ...' I searched for arguments to support my new theory. 'Perhaps the arrest of West was just an early attempt to detach Somerset from his closest advisers; to make him listen to other points of view. But this is all in the past. Whether I am right or wrong, I have a decision to make now.'

'What decision?'

'One that may destroy me and all I have if I get it wrong.' I told Ned about my meeting with the man in black.

Ned was aghast. 'My dear friend, this is terrible. Who is this man?'

'I have been racking my brains for an answer to that question. Obviously, he represents a group who want to know what Warwick is thinking; how he feels about the present situation. Probably courtiers or councillors trying to decide which way to jump if there is a conflict.'

'A challenge to the Protector?'

'Yes.'

'Pray God it will not come to that.'

'I thought you were no friend of Somerset and his policies.'

'Nor am I but I am for a peaceful life The thought of England slipping into another spate of baronial wars … That is a nightmare.'

'So what should I report when the courier comes tomorrow? I have promised some interesting information following my meeting with young Guildford.'

'Oh, Thomas, Thomas, Thomas.' Ned shook his head mournfully. 'You have often asked my advice and I have always tried to play the wise counsellor, but this time I know not what to suggest. If you say truth – the Lord Warwick might be open to an approach from the Protector's enemies, you may promote that very crisis we would all want to avoid. But if you colour your report; suggest that his lordship's support for Somerset holds firm, your deception will, at some point, be detected, and then …'

He had no need to finish the sentence.

I sat up late in my chamber, working by the light of a single candle. Several times I began a draft report of what I had learned from Lord Warwick's son and, as many times, I tore it up and threw it into the embers of the fire. By the time I had concocted something which was as non-committal as I dared make it, Adie had been long asleep. I slipped into bed beside her hoping against hope to follow her into unconsciousness.

◊

When light filtered through the gap in the bed's curtains I awoke, surprised to discover that I had slept. The morning passed slowly. The congregations at St Matthew's still struggled with Cranmer's new, all-English prayer book and the vicar followed the liturgy with a long sermon. Neither held my attention and, though I was not looking forward to my encounter with the courier, it was a relief to emerge into the balmy autumn breeze that wafted down Friday Street. As

Paul's clock chimed twelve I crossed the yard of my house to the outer gate. One of the man in black's servants was already loitering by the entrance. I joined him. Slipped the letter from my hand to his and turned back towards the house. Nothing was said or needed to be said. This was the simple ritual we had established over the last couple of days.

I had scarcely entered the kitchen when there was a commotion behind me. Shouts and the noise of a cantering horse came from the alley which ran at the back of Goldsmiths' Road, between Friday Street and Bread Street. I ran back to the gate to discover the cause of the disturbance.

A few paces away two of my neighbour's servants were bent over a figure sprawled in the dusty lane Striding across, I found myself looking down at the courier. He lay on his back, eyes staring with a trickle of blood dribbling from his mouth.

Chapter 19

I TORE MY eyes away from the murdered man. 'Did anyone see what happened?' I asked as a small crowd gathered.

It was one of the scullions from next door who tried to answer though she was trembling and tongue-tied. 'Horrible. Oh, horrible … I was here throwing out the vegetable parings and I see …' She sobbed and lifted her apron to dab the tears from her cheeks. 'I see this man coming away from your gate, Master Treviot.' She fell silent, her eyes fixed on the body.

I took her hand and drew her aside. 'Don't look. Come over here. Just tell me simply what you saw.'

'Well,' she mumbled. 'There was this horseman come down from Cheap. I see he had his sword drawn. He called out to that man. He looked up. Then …' The rest of her words were lost as she sobbed into her apron.

I called over an older woman. 'Look after her,' I ordered. 'Try to calm her. What she has to tell us may be very important. Dickon was among my own servants who had now gathered in my gateway. I sent him to fetch the constable. Then I turned my attention to the dead man. I realised now that he was not one of the pair who had rowed the boat when I was abducted, though there was, I thought, something vaguely familiar about him. I knelt and unfastened his purse, hoping to find in it some clue to the poor fellow's identity. It contained a few coins, some scraps of paper and – I was relieved to see – the letter I had given him only a few minutes before. I stuffed the purse inside my doublet. Then I returned to the girl who had witnessed the crime and who now seemed slightly recovered.

'What is your name?' I asked gently.

'Mary, Master,' she replied.

'Well, Mary,' I said, 'I know all this has been a terrible shock for you. You will want to try to blot it out of your mind. That is very natural. But you must not do that. You may be the only person who can identify the man who did this terrible thing. The constable and the magistrate will question you and you must tell them every detail you can remember. Do you understand?'

She nodded.

'Good. The best thing you can do is to make a start by telling me everything you saw while it is fresh in your mind. Will you do that, Mary?'

Again the inclining of the head which now dislodged a ringlet of dark hair from her cap.

'Describe the rider to me. What was he wearing?'

'He wore a brown cloak.'

'Good. And a hat?'

'A flat cap – black I think.'

'Excellent, Mary. You are a bright girl. Was there anything on the cap – any jewel or feather?'

She clenched her eyes and answered slowly. 'Not as I noticed, Master Treviot.'

'Was he bearded?' I asked.

'Oh yes,' came the prompt reply.

'Did you note the cut of his beard – pointed, square, forked?'

'Definitely pointed.'

'He was, perhaps, handsome. The sort of man you might turn to look at in the street.'

The suggestion obviously shocked her. 'I'm not the sort of girl as ogles young gentlemen.'

'So he was young, then?'

'Aye. I'd say so. A fair and proper looking man. Only, of course, he was not so, was he?'

'No, Mary, he was a murderous villain and we must make sure he pays for his crime. I have just one more question. Then you may go indoors and rest. Did this rider say anything?'

Again the girl creased her face in an effort of memory. Hesitantly she said, 'Aye, Master, I do remember me, he called out something, not as I made any sense of it. I thought he called this poor man, a snake.'

'Snake?'

'No, Master.' The girl was becoming flustered.

'"Snake". 'Tis not quite right. It was rather, "Adder". Aye, that was it, "Adder"... I think. I must ha' misheard.'

I thanked the girl, told her she had been really helpful, and enjoined her to give her evidence just as clearly to the authorities who would also want to question her. I had more questions for the bystanders but learned only that one of them, an apprentice come to visit friends, had given chase to the horseman, and seen his spur his mount into Cheapside and ride eastwards towards the heart of the City.

Back in my chamber, I examined the dead man's meagre possessions. My letter I swiftly consigned to the glowing sea coals in the hearth. The other scraps of paper I could make nothing of. They might have been lists but they were badly scrawled or possibly in some code or foreign language. Nevertheless, I set them aside before closing the purse, which I handed to the constable when he called an hour or so later.

Hardly had he departed when Ned arrived, eager for details of the murder.

'You have heard already then,' I said.

'Bad news rides a fleet horse,' the old man replied. 'Do you know who the poor fellow was?'

I shook my head. 'Only that he was the courier sent to get my report for the man in black.'

He nodded. 'Ah, I did wonder as to that.'

'Why did you think so?' I asked. 'It could have been anyone. Heaven knows, there are enough killings in back alleys every week in our fair city.'

'Aye, but mysteries usually come not in pairs. When they do... well, I tend to look for connections. Someone knew about this attempt to spy on Lord Warwick and did not approve. Who could that be?'

'I have, of course, been asking myself the same question. The most obvious answer is my lord himself.'

'Which would mean that he knew that you were being used against him. Let us hope, for your son's sake, that that is not so.'

'I say a hearty Amen to that. If Warwick turned against me that would be bad enough but if Raffy thought … Well, I doubt he would ever forgive me. 'Tis why I am trying to persuade myself there is another reason for this assassination. Perhaps it was some private vendetta, unconnected with the man in black.'

'Perhaps,' Ned echoed in a tone that totally lacked conviction. 'All my senses tell me there must be a link.' He rubbed a finger along the bridge of his nose. 'Mary and all the saints, was ever a business more complicated! 'Tis like playing hide-and-go-seek in a dark wood. There are so many people involved. Everywhere we turn we glimpse figures flitting among the trees. We go in pursuit but before we can reach them they have vanished.'

'Worse than that,' I remarked. 'They all seem to be pursuing each other.'

Ned moved over to the fireplace and held out his hands to the glowing coals. 'Winter comes early to my old bones. Now, since we must start somewhere, what do we know about the assassin?'

'Little enough.' I relayed the scanty information I had gathered from witnesses.

'He made for the City, you say,' Ned remarked, turning away from the fire. 'That is good.'

'Why so?'

'If he is in Warwick's employ he would surely have made haste to reach the safety of Ely Place. But he turned the other way.'

'That might be significant,' I admitted grudgingly.

'Let us work on that assumption. If the murderer was not Warwick's man, he was someone who knew of the scheme to obtain information about Warwick.'

'And wanted to put a stop to it? But why?'

Ned shrugged. 'This track only leads deeper into the wood. Oh, for a lamp! Is there nothing else that might shed some light?'

'There are these,' I muttered, indicating the scraps of paper from the dead man's purse. See if you can make anything of them. They mean nothing to me.'

Ned took the notes over to the window to scrutinise them closely. 'Well,' he said, after a few moments, ''tis an illiterate hand but I think I can decipher a couple of items – and they are not English. In the monastery, we had a brother from our Spanish house. He was in charge of the kitchen and I picked up a few words from him.' He brought the papers back to the table. 'This word looks like 'carne'. That's Spanish for "meat". And this could be a bad attempt to write "pimiento" which means 'pepper'. The poor fellow might have been a cook or a kitchen worker.'

'But Spanish you say?'

'I think so.'

A cloud in my mind dissolved and I suddenly saw something clearly. A dark street, then fighting. Light from a window slanting across the mêlée. 'Yes!' I cried. 'I thought I had seen him before. He was one of the ruffians who attacked us in *Little East Cheap* when we were taking Allen to the Tower.'

'They were the imperial ambassador's men, were they not?'

'I am sure of it.'

'And their ambush was planned with the aid of the Earl of Southampton?'

'It was he who signed the warrant. I can think of no-one else who could have alerted the ambassador in time.'

'Then we can rule out both the earl and the ambassador. They would not murder one of their own agents.'

'Oh,' I groaned. 'this is hopeless. We have argued ourselves into a corner. If this murder was not planned by Lord Warwick or by Lord Southampton or Ambassador van der Delft, who is left? We have been wasting our time. This must have been the work of someone who has no liking of foreigners.'

Ned nodded. 'Well, there are many of them to choose from. Yet there is one other interested party we have not considered – my Lord Protector.'

'No, no!' I objected. 'That will not serve. The duke is the one man above all others who would love to know what Lord Warwick may be planning. I have wondered whether he might not be the man in black's patron. He would certainly not want to stop a valuable flow of information coming from Ely Place.'

When Ned left, we were neither of us any the wiser. What he had said was very true; we were stumbling about in a dark wood. When Monday and Tuesday noontide passed without any messenger appearing at my gate awaiting information I decided that I could safely make a report of recent events to the archbishop. Having learned that he had returned to the Protector's court I set out for Hampton on Tuesday afternoon, with my now customary escort.

As soon as I disembarked I was aware of a changed atmosphere about the palace. It was uncharacteristically quiet. There seemed to be fewer people about and those who were there were going about their business with sombre faces and unhurried tread. There were few suitors in Cranmer's outer chamber but even so I had to wait a long time for him to see me. At last, it was Morice who emerged from his office and came to find me.

'Let us walk by the river,' he said, shaking my hand, 'I need fresh air. Everything is getting horn-mad in this place.'

I had never seen the archbishop's secretary so disconsolate. 'What is the problem?' I asked.

We were away from the buildings and walking along the bank before he replied. 'The problem is the same only worse. Not only will the Protector no longer listen to anyone; he will no longer speak to anyone. He issues instructions from his own rooms and expects them to be acted on without question – however ill-conceived they may be. Most councillors have left. Southampton, Arundel, Rich – they have all discovered urgent business which demands their presence at Westminster. The duke is surrounded only by sycophants – and their number grows smaller by the day. His grace is here most of the time, though, I think, more for the young king's sake than for any love he bears the duke. Sir William Paget remains loyal, though he grumbles more than ever. However,' he managed a smile, ''tis good to see you, old friend. I suppose there is no chance that you bear good news.'

'I bear bewildering news.' I told Morice about the man in black and his accomplices. 'Know you this fellow who abducted me on the archbishop's very doorstep?' I asked.

'I do not recall such a man at Robert Allen's examination but I was paying very close attention to the rogue's answers. There are several people he could have been working for. The biggest question everyone is asking is, "What will Lord Warwick do?".'

'Why so? As you say, there are other malcontents.'

'He is the only one with an army. Will he use it and, if so, to what end?'

We stopped to watch a group of swans and cygnets gliding past.

'Some people in London are speculating about the outbreak of another barons' war,' I said. 'Surely that could not happen.'

''Tis scarcely half a century since England had another child-king on the throne. That led to regicide and the clash of rival armies. Think you that men and their ambitions have changed since those bloody days?'

We turned back towards the palace.

'What is happening to Robert Allen?' I asked.

'Confined to the Tower.'

'And under interrogation?'

'I fear all the council are too preoccupied to spare time for our little magician.'

'Jesu!' I exclaimed. 'How much longer must poor West wait for truth and justice?'

'Regrettably, a little longer. But no-one can harm him now – certainly not Parafaustus, with all his boasts of supernatural power. He remains unrepentant, by the way. He rants and rails against those he calls his persecutors. He threatens to bring down all his enemies.' Morice laughed. 'He has a special fate in store for you and your family – nothing less than all the plagues of Egypt.'

'What are they?'

'Frogs, boils, locusts, hail … Read the Book of Exodus if you want all the gruesome details. But I should not worry. If Allen can organise such an array of curses from his cell in the Tower, why, even I might start to believe in his magic powers.'

Cranmer was ready to receive me by the time we reached the palace but, before I could make my report, his grace had something to say.

'It has started,' he muttered, shaking his head. He was bent over his desk, one hand supporting his forehead. He looked up and handed Morice a sheet of paper. 'He has ordered all the scribes to work through the night to make as many copies as possible for general distribution tomorrow.'

Morice read aloud the brief message:

'By order of his Most Sacred Majesty Edward VI by the grace of Almighty God King of England, France and Lord of Ireland. All loyal and able male subjects between the ages of 15 and 50 are hereby ordered to come immediately to our royal palace at Hampton armed and ready to defend our royal person against a most contumacious and satanic conspiracy.'

◊

It took two or three days for the rumours to start spreading through the City but when they did start they were many, varied and frightening. Some spoke of a new band of rebels making for Hampton Court to present demands to the Protector. Others said that disaffected councillors were seeking to depose Somerset and offer the regency to Princess Mary. According to other 'informed sources,' approaches had been made to the Emperor to invade England, taking advantage of the political divisions. Preachers harangued their congregations, urging them to defend the religious status quo or join the ranks of those who opposed the Protector's 'heretical' regime.

The duke's printed summons was in circulation and small bands of 'commonwealthers' had left the City en route to the royal court. The majority of the Council, ensconced in Whitehall, were not slow to issue their own handbills. Citizens were instructed to remain calm, not to concern themselves with matters of state and to put their trust in the king's loyal body of advisers and in their own leaders, the Mayor and Common Council of London. Such injunctions made little impression on the more radical inhabitants of the City, who denounced both the Whitehall clique and their own civic leaders and backed their inflammatory sentiments with reference to ancient prophecies. 'Note how they be come up late from the dunghill, more meet to keep swine than to hold the offices which they do occupy.' So read one bill thrown in at my door. It continued:

Give no hasty credit unto their doings and sayings, but stick fast unto your most godly and Christian king, for though they traitorously call themselves the body of the Council, yet they lack the head and such a body is nothing without a head. The Lord shall destroy such a body at his pleasure. And as for London, Merlin foretold 'twenty-three aldermen shall lose their heads in one day, which God grant be soon. Amen!

Such over-simplified rhetoric obscured more than it revealed. London was not divided between rulers and ruled, rich and poor, respectable citizenry and servants. Arguments broke out everywhere, from the meanest hovel to the finest mansion. It was widely known that our Commons Council was faction-ridden. In the hope of discovering more about that I invited Simon Minchin to dinner. Simon, a level-headed cordwainer, was our ward alderman and representative on the Common Council. To assert my authority I called all my household together and warned them not to pay heed to street-corner rabble-rousers or to read fiery manifestoes. I reminded them how Raffy had been taken in by hotheads with disastrous consequences. Alas for my good intentions. The very next morning I was awoken with the news that two of my stable hands had decamped during the night to go to Hampton Court and taken two horses with them.

Nor was that the only unpleasant incident experienced at the sign of the Swan. Early on the day I had arranged to entertain Simon Minchin there was a hubbub in the kitchen. Adie burst into the parlour where Bart and I were working on the accounts.

'Oh, loathsome creatures!' She was wiping her hands on her apron and her face was a creased mask of revulsion. 'They're everywhere. Must be a dozen. Must have come up from the river. How can they have got here?'

I looked up from the table. 'Dearest, what are you talking about?'

'Frogs!'

'Frogs?'

'Yes, frogs. Come and see for yourself.'

I followed her to the kitchen. It was in a state of uproar. Stools were overturned. Servants were everywhere, some on hands and knees, others probing dark corners and under tables with brooms and sticks. The cook was wielding a ladle like a battle axe.

'In mercy's name, shut the door!' Adie shouted as a large, green amphibian hopped between us. She stood in the midst of the chaos, arms akimbo. 'We have killed seven already but there must be as many again in here.'

I made a grab for the frog on the floor before me but it made a long leap into the gap between two cauldrons.

'Shall I send in some of the men from the workshop?' I asked.

'No,' Adie replied, with a weary sigh. 'We will manage. What I want to know is how they got here.'

I asked myself the same question.

Order was restored in time to prepare dinner and we were able to sit down calmly with our guest to enjoy the meal. I had asked Ned and Bart to join my wife and I in welcoming Simon to our board. We all knew him well as a near neighbour with an affable nature and a ready smile. The smile was not much in evidence today.

We had hardly started to eat when he said. 'I suppose you want to know what is happening in the Common Council.'

''Tis always a pleasure to welcome you, Simon, but, yes, we would like to hear the truth from someone like yourself,' I admitted. 'There are too many rumours around.'

'We have, of course, been under pressure from the Protector and from the Earl of Warwick,' he said.

'Warwick? Then he is personally challenging Somerset?' I asked.

'I will come to that in a moment. Things are not so simple. As everyone knows, he who holds the capital holds England. No government could last long without our financial support. So our decision was vital.'

'You had to decide where your loyalty lay,' Ned suggested.

'Exactly, Ned. As always, you strike the hot metal in the right place. There was much argument about that word "loyalty". It went on for three days. We were quite evenly divided. But eventually we saw things clearly – or, most of us did. We realised that our greatest responsibility is, and always must be to no individual, except the king.'

'So you will support the Protector, then?' Bart asked.

Simon shook his head. 'We could not satisfy ourselves that he truly represents his majesty.' He sighed. 'Oh, everything would be so much easier if our sovereign lord was not so young. Somerset and Warwick both claim to speak for him. As I say, we could not put our weight behind either individual. Therefore, we can only be swayed by what we believe to be best for our citizens. What will ensure their peace? We have to be practical, realistic.'

'Bart snorted. 'Realistic! 'Tis the excuse politicians always give for ignoring principles.'

'Well, friend,' Simon replied, 'put yourself in our place. What it all comes down to is this: do we open our gates to Warwick's band of disciplined professional troops or to Somerset's horde of scythe-waving commonwealthers?'

Images of Norwich's burning, corpse-strewn streets came into my mind. 'You had no other choice,' I said.

Adie added, 'Well, I would certainly trust my lord Warwick. Our son is of his household and knows him to be a man of honour.'

'What happens next?' Ned enquired.

'At first light tomorrow a detachment of Lord Warwick's mercenaries will take control of the Tower and others will station themselves at the City gates.'

Bart was not convinced. 'You say the aldermen's loyalty is not to individuals but you are making the Earl of Warwick master of London – and England.'

Simon frowned. 'Not so. What we have agreed – and I hope all responsible citizens will support us in this – is that the Protector step down and his authority will be shared by all the royal council. Such was always his late majesty's intention for the governance of the realm during his son's minority.'

'Fine words,' Ned muttered, 'but from all I have read and heard tyranny – cold, hard tyranny – is like ice; it always rises to the top.'

'And from all I have read and heard,' Simon retorted with uncharacteristic waspishness, 'criticism is all too often hurled from the ramparts of ignorance. Be thankful, Ned, that you are not called on to make decisions of life and death.'

I hastened to calm the atmosphere before the argument could become heated. 'What communication have you had with my lord Southampton and other members of the council in Whitehall?'

'Messages come with the combined authority of all the councillors, though I gather Warwick and Southampton are recognised as the leaders. Most meetings, as I understand it, actually take place in one or other of their Holborn houses.'

'And do they work well together?' I asked.

'I believe they are the best of friends.'

I thought to myself, 'They were once the Protector's "best of friends".'

After dinner, I retired to my chamber. I had something else on my mind. Of course, I did not take Allen's threats seriously and the appearance of frogs in my kitchen was, undoubtedly, a coincidence. But, well, there could be no harm in familiarising myself with the story of the plagues of Egypt. I took down my Bible and found the information I was looking for in chapters seven to twelve of the Book of Exodus. It was certainly a frightening story. Moses and Aaron had demanded that Pharaoh should set free all his Israelite slaves but Pharaoh consistently refused. Therefore, God inflicted a series of punishments to bring the ruler to a better frame of mind. The plagues were: water turned to blood, infestations of frogs, lice, flies and locusts, a disease fatal to all animals, universal boils, severe hail storms and the darkening of the sun. Morice was right: there was no way the magician locked up in the Tower could replicate all these terrifying events. However, it would not have been difficult for one of his friends to collect a basket of frogs and tip them in at door or window when no-one was about. It was really a rather pathetic demonstration of Allen's 'power'. Even if he had an army of accomplices to perform tricks at his behest, they would be unable to make a convincing demonstration of his revenge.

It was when I read the account of the last plague that my heart missed a beat: 'At midnight the Lord smote all the firstborn sons of the land of Egypt'.

Chapter 20

BY NOW I knew Robert Allen too well. No longer could I assume that the incident of the frogs was a coincidence. It was a warning that he could carry out his threat to be revenged on me. He was demonstrating that stone walls and firmly locked doors were no barrier for one possessed of his powers. He would have me believe that those were occult powers and there were certainly times – usually, when I awoke, sweating, in the middle of the night – when I wondered whether the amphibians had, indeed, been delivered by some supernatural agency. Dismissing such a notion brought no comfort. Quite the reverse. If the frog infestation was just another example of 'Parafaustian' trickery it meant that Allen had associates at large in London, able and willing to do his bidding. Was there among them an assassin? The very thought drove icicles into my heart. I had, somehow, to banish such emotions and think clearly about my situation. I could not ask advice or talk over Allen's throat with anyone, for that would simply spread panic to Adie and the household.

I studied once more the relevant chapters of the Bible. The story was horrifying but simple. God demanded that Pharaoh should set free the people of Israel. He refused and was visited with the sequence of divine punishments that culminated in the death of his son and the eldest sons of all the Egyptian people. Allen's message? He wanted his freedom. I was in a position to secure that freedom – or so he thought. If I did not oblige he would avenge himself in the way that would cause me maximum anguish.

What could I do? Nothing I could say now would open to Allen the gates of the Tower. Nor could I secure extra protection for Raffy. As a member of Lord Warwick's household, he was beyond his father's authority. At this time of political crisis when all the nation's leaders were trapped in a personal conflict that might explode into civil war, I could not approach his lordship with my problem – a problem I could not substantiate with any proof. I was left with only one option – and one that appeared difficult to the point of impossibility. Somehow I must uncover Allen's network of agents and destroy it.

One problem was eased the following morning. To my intense relief, Raffy returned home. The note he brought from Lord Warwick was typically brief and businesslike. In the current crisis, it explained, his lordship was temporarily reducing the size of his household and leaving Ely Place.

'Where is my lord going?' I asked.

'I really do need new ones.' Raffy was seated in the parlour and easing off his riding boots.

I repeated the question.

'Oh, he plans to lodge in the City with one of his supporters, in Walbrook. Sheriff Yorke, I think. All the Councillors are going to do the same.'

I gasped. 'Then they mean to make a fortified encampment of London?'

Raffy nodded. 'Aye, fortified and well defended. All the troops are to be stationed strategically. I heard his lordship say, "He may gather together an armed rabble but, by God, he shall not make another Norwich of London."'

'Well,' I said, changing the subject, ''tis good to have you home again for a few days.'

'I should be out there if there is more fighting to be done.'

'Think not to avoid danger by being within the walls. There are enemies inside the City as well as outside.'

'What mean you by that, Father?'

Before I could find some way to mention the peril I feared Raffy was facing, Adie bustled in and began fussing over the boy. He happily accepted her embrace and the cakes and ale she set before him. It was good to see their relationship improving. I only hoped they would be granted several years to enjoy that relationship.

I began to formulate a plan of action. It was rudimentary in the extreme, but I had to start somewhere. I was sure that the lawyer, Gaston, must be one of Allen's active agents, so I arranged to have him watched. I sent Bart with a small team to take turns at observing the comings and goings at the house in Aldermanbury. They were able to make their base at the Millers' home in nearby Milk Street where Lizzie saw them well supplied with bread and ale. Meanwhile, I made my way to the Tower where, once a little silver had changed hands, I gained some useful information from one of the senior warders. He was a garrulous fellow and only too ready to explain the particular precautions being taken over Robert Allen.

'I knew he'd be trouble so soon as I set eyes on 'im,' the corpulent official said. 'Talk, talk, talk! We could na stop 'im. An I like not the way he looks at you all the while he's talking. Seems to be peering inside your head, if you take my meanin. I made sure to lodge him on the top floor of the Salt Tower, as far as possible from other prisoners. He could talk his head off there an' no one to hear. I only let my most trusted men near him. Even so, I had to remove one of them because he'd a-got funny ideas from the prisoner.'

'Funny?'

'Aye. Horoscopes and the like devilry. 'Tis the sort of thing as turns men's heads inside out.'

'Does he have many visitors?'

The man wagged a podgy finger. 'Ah, now there's a funny thing. For such a slack brained lewdster he has visitors what are men of quality. Two of 'em. Been three or four times each. One's a city lawyer. T'other has a pass signed by one of the king's councillors.'

'Can you describe him?'

'Very well spoken. Very smart looking gentleman.'

'Tall? Black doublet and hose?'

'Aye. That fits him. You know him?'

'We have met.'

My informant could tell me little more of value but I felt reasonably satisfied with my visit, which had, at least, confirmed my own suspicions. As I strode across Tower Green around noon to collect my horse from the tethering place I made a mental catalogue of what I now knew. The man in black was obviously a link between

Allen and a member of the council. But who? It could not be Lord Warwick; the scoundrel had been spying on him. Must I, then, revive my earlier suspicions of the Earl of Southampton? Of was there some other councillor among the conspirators – someone careful to keep his identity a close secret? Whoever it was was also in league with the imperial ambassador. The man in black's henchmen were Spanish and at least one of them had been in the mob that ambushed my party when we had tried to deliver Allen here to the Tower five weeks earlier.

But what did these meetings in the Salt Tower mean? Allen's highly-placed friends had gone to considerable lengths to protect Allen in the past. Now that the self-styled magician was under lock and key it might have been diplomatic for them to distance themselves from the prisoner. Yet, here they were, planning something with Allen – something so important and, perhaps, complex that their emissary had to pay repeated calls to the prison. Were the conspirators organising a raid on my house or devising some other means to lay their hands on Raffy? Whatever was afoot did not augur well for Robert Allen's enemies. And my name probably headed his hate list.

I had just mounted my horse and turned him towards the twin towers guarding access to the causeway when I found my path blocked by a party of mounted troops. There was nothing unusual about the sight of soldiers in the fortress and I held my gelding in check for the armed men to pass. But they did not pass. At a shouted command they halted and the captain approached.

'Who are you and what is your business here?' he demanded.

What could I say; that I was conducting a private investigation and had just bribed one of the royal officials into providing information which had implications for affairs of state? Clearly not. I thought quickly.

'My name is Thomas Treviot, goldsmith,' I said. 'I have routine business here at the mint.' I tried to look relaxed and hold in check my anxiety. It would have been extremely easy for the captain to check my story and discover my lie.

'Proof of identity,' he ordered sharply.

I fumbled in my purse. The only letter there bearing my name and address was the one I had received from Ralph Morice summoning me to give evidence against Allen – scarcely the communication of a simple merchant not involved in politics. I handed it over.

The captain scanned the name and address and grunted.

I prayed fervently that he would not open it.

He opened it.

There was a clattering of hooves from the direction of the causeway. Orders were shouted. The troopers moved aside to make room for another group of six armed men. They were escorting someone I recognised by sight as Sir John Markham, Lieutenant of the Tower. He looked pale and stern-faced as he passed on.

The captain returned my letter with a curt, 'Be on your way Master Treviot.'

'Is there some trouble?' I enquired meekly.

'Only for those as supports the Duke of Somerset,' he replied. 'You may tell your friends that his writ no longer runs in London. He made a plot to seize the Tower and overawe the city but all is discovered and we are here to secure it for the king and his loyal councillors.' He heeled his horse and led his men onward.

Instead of riding straight home I called in at Goldsmiths' Hall. Whenever there was important news to be shared my colleagues customarily gathered there to discuss it. Today was no exception. A steady rain had set in, and the clusters of brethren, who had come for the same purpose as I, were to be found in the hall and the parlour. It was in the hall that I joined Will Fitzralph and Simon Leyland. The old man was, as usual, taking the blackest view of forthcoming events. 'There will be fighting in the streets,' he solemnly prophesied.

Will disagreed. 'Any hotheads ready to challenge Warwick's mercenaries would do well to learn the lesson of Norwich.'

'The earl and his friends now hold the Tower and its armoury,' I said. 'I have just come from there.' I described what I had seen. 'Sir John Markham is either reluctantly won over or taken prisoner.'

'Then all is up with the duke.' Will sighed. 'And I am sorry for it.'

At that moment, Stephen Dannery sidled past us, deliberately not looking in my direction.

I plucked him by the sleeve. 'Brother Dannery, pray join us a moment. We are trying to understand what is happening between our lords and masters. Doubtless you are better informed, being so close to the Earl of Southampton.'

'Close? No, no certainly not.'

'Oh, come, you are too modest,' I persisted. 'What is the latest news from Holborn?'

Dannery scowled. 'The latest news from Holborn is that there is no news from Holborn. My lord Southampton, like other councillors, now lodges in the City.'

'Aye,' Leyland scoffed, 'looking to us to protect him.'

'At least, he has stopped dissembling,' Will observed. 'He always had a secret hatred of the Protector. Now he has come into the open and thrown in his lot with Warwick.'

That comment stung Dannery. 'Not so! My lord is an honourable man. He dislikes some of the Protector's policies and has remained at his side in hope to dissuade him from extremism. Now that persuasion has failed, he has come to support Lord Warwick.'

Leyland sneered. 'Southampton and Warwick – strange bedfellows.'

'Perhaps they have long been secret allies, plotting the duke's downfall,' I suggested.

'There are some as think they mean to restore the old religion' Will observed. ''Twas ever close to Southampton's heart.'

'But not, I think, to Warwick's,' I said.

Leyland responded with another cynical offering. 'These politicians are all the same. Power is their only religion.'

'So, my brothers, what comes next, I wonder. We stand here supported by foreign troops. The Protector lies at Hampton with a few thousand ill-armed rustics…'

'What, Brother Treviot?' For the first time, Dannery smiled his superior smile. 'Have you not heard? Somerset is no longer at Hampton. Last night he took the king and rabble army and made a dash for Windsor. He now holds the castle there and defies anyone to assail it.'

Dannery's words were still echoing in my head when I arrived home. My first concern was to learn what Bart and his colleagues had gleaned from their vigil in Aldermanbury. Their news was not encouraging. Casual conversations with some of Gaston's neighbours had established the fact that the lawyer was not much liked. He numbered several unsavoury characters among his clients and the good wives of Aldermanbury were careful to keep their children and servant away from the thieves, cutpurses, highway robbers, forgers, and bawdy baskets* who called upon Gaston's professional services.

---

*   bawdy basket = a female hawker of trinkets and obscene ballads; often the companion of an 'upright man' or criminal gang leader

As one disgruntled neighbour observed, 'You may see a rogue in the pillory one day and knocking on Gaston's door the next'.

It was no revelation to me that the man who provided lodging for Allen was working both sides of the law and almost certainly hand-in-glove with the leaders of London's criminal fraternity. But this did not help me to discover what Gaston was doing on behalf of his client in the Tower. If they were hatching a plot against me, which of the nefarious visitors to the lawyer's house were involved in it and what was being discussed behind its closed door?

It was this not knowing that was so disturbing. A clear threat I could deal with but the hint of a threat, the possibility of a threat – this held me taut with fearful expectation. I felt like a sheet of cloth stretched on tenterhooks. My most difficult task was keeping Raffy safe without telling him or anyone else what I was keeping him safe from. When I insisted that he should not leave the house without two servants for company, he was indignant.

'Why?' he demanded when I went to his chamber to discuss the situation with him the morning after my visit to the Tower. 'I only want to meet John and Jacob Vance at Gerrard's Inn. 'Tis but a step along the road.' He sat on the edge of the bed, pulling on his hose and did not look at me as he spoke.

I sensed a return of the old truculence and tried to dampen it. 'All this inconvenience is wretched. I hate having to be close guarded where I go but you need not me to point out the dangers of the time we live in.'

'You are a wealthy merchant and worth robbing.' He turned to me with a smile. 'The contents of my purse would be scarcely worth a thief's trouble to take.'

'But you are of Lord Warwick's household and he has enemies.'

He paused in the tying of his points. 'I think we are no better than the captive animals in the Tower menagerie, unable to leave our cage.'

''Tis a just image. The whole city is become a cage and Lord Warwick's men are our keepers. 'Twas bad enough when Norwich fell and we all wondered whether London would be next but now everyone is even more on edge. We have doubled the watch again and are enforcing the curfew yet more strictly.'

'Even though we have my lord's *landsknechts* to guard us?'

'Aye, and even though most members of the Council are shut in here with us.

Raffy stood up and hung round his neck the gold pomander I had given him for his birthday. 'What will happen next, Father?'

'Who is to say? Nothing like this has happened before. The duke is summoning all able-bodied men to go to Windsor to protect him and the king from the traitorous lords of the council, as he calls them. He has taken up a defensive position and is defying his rivals to do their worst.'

Raffy scowled. 'Then Lord Warwick must face them again.'

'No, my Son, there will be no second Dussindale. Windsor is impregnable. Worse than that, the mood of the country is uncertain. If Lord Warwick were to lay siege to the castle he might find himself having to face bands of rebels converging on Windsor, believing they were come to rescue their young king from traitors.'

'My lord is no traitor!' Raffy declared hotly.

'No, indeed, but, then, who is? Of a truth, I think that "traitor" is a word that has lost all meaning.'

Raffy replied quickly. 'A traitor is someone not loyal to the king.' But then he stopped, suddenly thoughtful. After some moments he went on, 'Lord Warwick says the Protector keeps the king almost as a prisoner in order to maintain his own power. I suppose that makes him a traitor.'

'Yes,' I said, 'and the Protector claims he is keeping his majesty safe from his rivals on the council who would like to control him themselves. He claims that Warwick, Southampton and the rest are the real traitors.'

'And what think you, Father?'

'I think that if I were to say to you, "Raffy, London is a dangerous place and I forbid you to leave the house", I would be a kind of traitor to you, taking away your freedom to discover the world for yourself. But if I believed you were at risk on the streets and did nothing to protect you would that also not label me a traitor?'

He looked puzzled. 'And am I at risk – more than any other man in this divided city?'

I thought very hard about my reply. 'Yes, Raffy, you may be. I did not come in here this morning to say this but now I see that I must. That self-styled magus you saw in Norwich...'

'Parafaustus?'

'Aye, so he calls himself. Well, he is an extremely dangerous and evil villain.'

'But, thanks to you, he is now safely locked up in the Tower.'

'Yes, but he has many accomplices – men who for various reasons are under his sway.'

Raffy nodded. 'I know what you mean. I saw in Norwich how he gained influence over people. It was uncanny.'

'He has agents at liberty in London who are under his spell – how many I know not. What I do know is that he will use all his wiles to regain his freedom.'

Raffy grinned. 'That would take some doing. No-one has ever escaped from the Tower.'

'There is one other thing he is set on…'

'Go on, Father.'

'He believes I am responsible for his downfall.'

'Well, he is right in that. The way you have pursued him and…'

I interrupted him. 'It seemed the right thing to do but now I am not so sure.'

'Why not? What you did was great. I boast about it to my friends.'

'Allen has vowed he will pay me back. I can deal with that threat for myself but I have no right to endanger others.' I explained Allen's allusion to the plagues of Egypt and the business of the frogs. 'From his cell, he was able to organise accomplices to collect a barrelful of creatures from some pond or other and let them loose here.'

Raffy giggled. 'I wish I had seen it. It must have been a merry dance.'

'This is no prentice prank,' I said sharply. 'If he can arrange that, he can have his copesmates track you and … Well, I nearly lost you once. I do not want…'

I was interrupted by the door opening after a cursory knock. Lizzie hurried in. 'Ah, Thomas, Adie said you were here. I have something to tell you… something about you-know-what.' She glanced at Raffy.

''Tis all right, Lizzie,' I said, 'you may speak in front of my son. I have been telling him about this business.' To Raffy I said, 'Bart and some of our men have been watching Allen's lodging in the lawyers' house, to see who comes and goes there.'

'Much use they are!' Lizzie said scornfully, seating herself on the bed. 'They know not the London underworld as I do. 'Tis years since

I worked in the Southwark stews but I still recognise faces. More's to the point, I can smell 'em. The stink of that place seeps into a man's clothes – into his very skin. It takes more than a scrubbing with scented Castile soap to get rid of it.'

'So you came across one of your old acquaintances?' I prompted.

'Bart and the others were getting so crabbed with standing in draughty alleys with nothing to show for it that I was weary listening to their grumbling. "Sit you here, then," I said, "and let a woman show you how 'tis done." So I wandered up and down Aldermanbury, talking with some of the goodwives and their children – there's much to be learned from children if you know the right questions to ask. I had not been there an hour when I saw Beefy go into Gaston's house.'

'Beefy?'

'Aye, Beefy Boyes They call him so for his bull-like frame. I have known him since he was a lad. He was evil then – cold, cruel; someone who inflicted pain just for the pleasure of it. He was an errand boy for the notorious John Doggett, who you had some dealings with years ago.* He was marked, then, either for the gallows or for the leadership of his own band of pitiless hell hounds. Well, he has 'scaped the hangman so far, despite his crimes. If you want a house burned down or a throat cut Beefy is your man. There's many as know of his doings but none dares speak.'

'What has Gaston to do with the likes of Boyes, I wonder?'

'Whatever 'tis, Thomas, 'tis important,' Lizzie replied. 'According to a bright six-year-old across the street, he visits there most days.'

'Do you think this churl and his mob will come looking for me?' Raffy asked, seeming more curious than afraid.

'We must assume so, whether 'tis true or not. Lizzie, you say this fellow has his base in Southwark?'

'Aye, close by the bear garden.'

'Then we should keep a watch there,' I said.

'As well as in Aldermanbury?' Lizzie gave her familiar mocking laugh. 'And who is to look after your home and your business while we are chasing lorrels all over London?'

'There are problems, certainly.' I agreed, 'but what are we to do else? Wait for Boyes to make his murderous attack?'

'If we know not what Allen and his curs are planning we cannot arrange proper protection,' Lizzie said in a tone that allowed of no

---

* See *The First Horseman.*

229

contradiction. "Tis as simple as that. We would need an army to guard against all chances.'

'This is foolishness!' Raffy burst out. 'I need no army to protect me!'

Lizzie looked puzzled at this and I explained why I was expecting an attack on my son.

While she absorbed this new information I thought fast. 'An army? No. But… I just wonder. Raffy, do you recall John Cantrill?'

'Of course.'

'Know you where he is billeted?'

'No, but sure it cannot be far from here. Think you he would help us?'

'I am willing to ask. How may I get a message to him?'

'Some senior officers are at Ely Place. His lordship set up a command post there to watch the western approach to the city. If Captain Cantrill is not there someone will know where he is.'

'Good. I will write to him directly. If he would allow a few of his troopers to be lodged here that should deter any attack.

◊

It was two days before I received a reply from Cantrill but then he came in person with four of his troopers assigned to us for our protection.

'They are good men,' he said, as he mounted his horse in the yard. 'Some of my best. But I pray you will not need them. Messages are flying daily between here and Windsor. I believe the two parties will reach a settlement without the need for force.'

'If you are right, that is the best news we have had in months.'

'When things are settled, our new masters – whoever they might be – will be able to deal with many matters that have been neglected of late, including Master Parafaustus.'

'I hope so. You have no idea how much I long to put these last months behind us.'

'You are not alone in that,' the captain replied as he gathered his reins. 'There are things I, too, long to see safely dead and buried.'

I reiterated my thanks as Cantrill walked his horse out of the yard.

His prophecy proved true. Within days, it was widely known that Edward Seymour, Duke of Somerset had resigned as Lord Protector and that he and the young king would be brought to the safety of the Tower, where some kind of political settlement could be reached. The sense of relief throughout the City was almost tangible. It was as if a communal sigh ascended to heaven from the streets. Only diehard 'commonwealthers' were unable to share in the general rejoicing. When the duke was led through the City under heavy guard on Friday 14 October the mood of the crowds who turned out to watch was quiet and restrained. Two days later most citizens attended their churches to give thanks for a crisis passed.

It was as I was assembling the household for our short walk down to All Hallows Church that Sunday morning that Bart came to me with a letter in his hand. 'Sorry, Master,' he said. 'This arrived yesterday and I was sore busy it went clean from my mind.'

I opened the letter and hurriedly read the few lines. ''Tis from Captain Cantrill,' I said, 'asking for the release of his men. I will attend to it after service.'

Minutes later I took my place, with my family, in the front pew of the church. The vicar appeared and began the simplified Matins to which we had by now become accustomed. Scarcely had he begun the Lord's Prayer when a crash from the back of the church made us all turn round. The west door had been thrown open. Four masked men ran down the aisle waving swords. One of them, a big, thick-set fellow, stood at the chancel step brandishing a pistol. He shouted out. 'Stay still, all of you. Anyone who moves will be shot. We are only here for one person. Then we will be gone.' He pointed his weapon at Raffy.

Chapter 21

ONE OF THE attackers stepped forward and grabbed Raffy's sleeve. I tried to grapple with him. I immediately felt cold metal pressed against my neck.

The leader's eyes glared through the holes in his mask. He forced the muzzle of his wheellock pistol harder against my flesh. 'Please give me an excuse to pull the trigger, Master Treviot,' he snarled.

'If you want a hostage, take me,' I said.

'No!' Raffy stood up. 'Do not dare to hurt my father. I will come with you.'

He allowed himself to be pushed roughly down the aisle. Then, while one of the gang stood in the doorway waving his rapier, we heard the others running away down the street. Less than a minute passed in frozen silence. Then, he, too, turned away, slamming the door behind him.

'After them!' I shouted and four of my men stumbled to the back of the church.

As I turned to follow I came face-to-face with Lizzie. 'Was that ...'

'Beefy Boyes? Aye, I am sure of it.'

'Then we know where Raffy is being taken.'

'Very likely.'

'Then, go back to the house and tell Cantrill's men. Ask them to get there as fast as they can.'

'Where are you going?'

'After the hell-rats,' I said, striding to the door.

I knew the villains must be heading for the river and would have a boat waiting for them at Queenhythe, less than four hundred yards away down Bread Street Hill. Never had I run so fast as I did in the next few minutes. I arrived at the quay to find my men staring across the water at a craft already some fifty yards from the shore. Boyes, standing in the bow, waved as two of his underlings plied the oars and another stood pointing his weapon at something lying in the bottom of the boat. I was in no doubt what that 'something' was.

'We must after them!' I shouted, looking around at the craft moored alongside the staging. Among the river barges, there were three wherries. Their owners were standing together, watching the drama being played out before them.

I ran up to them. 'We must follow that boat!' I shouted.

The watermen looked at each other. 'Them has guns,' one said. 'Aye, and ready to use 'em, I'll wager,' another agreed.

'No time to argue the matter,' I said. 'Those are wanted villains. We have to stop them getting away.' Thinking quickly, I added. 'There will be a reward for their capture.'

'And coffins for us if we fail to catch 'em,' one of the boatmen replied, as he and his friends went into a huddle.

'I'll not waste time arguing,' I said. I turned to Dickon. 'We will take that one.' I pointed to the nearest craft. 'You and Matt work the oars.'

As they stepped into the boat and prepared to cast off, the owner took a step forward. He and his friends were obviously ready for a fight.

I loosened my purse and threw it at him. 'You will find more than enough in there for a whole day's hire.'

I climbed aboard as the watermen peered into the purse to check my claim.

We pushed off and my oarsmen dug deep into the river to get us moving quickly. I kept my eyes on the other craft and called instructions to the rowers. I had no plan beyond remaining in contact with my son and his abductors. It was obvious we would not catch up with them in open water but if we could land on the south bank not far behind them we would give them plenty to think about. They would be hampered by a prisoner who, knowing Raffy as I did, I was sure would make progress as difficult as he could for them.

The Thames itself was creating problems in its own way. A strong current was running and the oarsmen had to work hard to avoid being swept towards the bridge.

'Bring the prow round to the right,' I called. 'They will have to make for Falcon Stairs, farther upriver.' I surveyed the row of tenements on the opposite shore built close to the water's edge. There was a narrow strand before them but mud and shingle made it no easy place to land for men in a hurry with an uncooperative prisoner.

By the time we were in midstream I gauged that we had gained perhaps ten or twenty yards on our quarry. Suddenly, the boat ahead stopped. I saw Boyes, steady himself with his legs apart and point his gun in our direction. In the same instant, I heard the crack as he discharged it. I saw no sign of the ball, which must have passed well wide of us. Under such conditions, he would have been very lucky to have scored a hit.

'What was that?' Matt looked up.

'An attempt to scare us off,' I said. 'Mayhap the cowardly villains are getting worried.'

The incident had cost Boyes another twenty yards of his lead and now his men fell to their oars with redoubled effort. As the south bank drew closer I urged on Matt and Dickon, thinking all the time of Raffy, lying in that other boat, frightened and anxious about what fate his captors had in mind for him.

I need not have been quite so worried. Suddenly, there was a commotion from Boyes' boat, which came to another halt. There were shouts and moving figures. Raffy was obviously being troublesome. He would be powerless against three armed men but he could slow their progress and that is exactly what he was doing. We closed rapidly on the other vessel.

Now I could see clearly what was happening. Boyes bent down and yanked Raffy to his feet. At the same time, one of his henchmen was leaning over the side. At first, I could not see what he was doing. Then, I realised that he had lost an oar in the struggle and was desperately trying to recover it. I saw it drifting on the current several inches beyond the rower's grasp. Boyes was trying to control his struggling captive and, at the same time, shout instructions to his crew. Desperately, they manoeuvred their craft towards the floating oar. So did we.

For several minutes, the confused race continued. Both boats converged. I knelt down, one arm gripping the seat, the other reaching out over the water. Boyes' ruffian did the same. We were now parallel, the long wooden blade between us. The other man got a hold first. His fingers closed on the flat end. But I was able to grasp the handle. I turned it sharply. My opponent swore as the oar twisted out of his grasp. I held fast to my trophy as Matt and Dickon widened the gap between the two craft.

As we stowed the captured oar in our vessel I was aware that Boyes was shouting. Raffy, had his arms pinioned to his sides with rope. Boyes was firmly holding him with one hand and pointing a pistol to his head with the other.

'Return that oar or the boy dies!' the villain shouted.

'Harm him and we will ram you and send you all to the bottom of the Thames!' I replied.

Boyes' response was a series of oaths.

My mind was rapidly turning over the possible outcome of the situation. If we left the abductors floundering on the river they would eventually be able to make landfall. Would Cantrill's men, riding around via the bridge, be able to reach Boyes' headquarters before the gang leader? Unlikely. Anyway, my first priority was rescuing my son. I tried another ploy.

'Perhaps I will not let you drown, Boyes. I could leave you to the mercy of your masters. They will not be happy about your failure. If you kill my son, be sure that I will redouble my efforts to see that Robert Allen swings and that his backers are exposed.'

He swore again. I guessed he was angry at having been recognised.

'Then I must shoot you, too.' He pointed the gun at me. 'That will solve all our problems.'

'Not so,' I called out. 'For one thing, Allen needs me to withdraw my accusations. For another, I think you have not had time to reload your pistol.'

One of Boyes' men muttered something I could not hear. His leader cursed him roundly but failed to silence him. All three churls fell into a murmured argument. The only words I made out were the leader's rasping, 'My way! My way!'

The quarrel gave me time to manoeuvre our craft. Boyes' vessel was now sideways on to the flow. I had my oarsmen bring our boat round with its prow pointing at the side of the other craft. This relative position could only be held for a few seconds. 'Go!' I whispered. Matt and Dickon strained at the oars and our wherry leapt forward.

In ramming Boyes' boat, I had no clearly formulated plan. I was just using my only weapon to best advantage.

Boyes swung his pistol around to point at me.

Then, everything happened at once.

The boats collided.

There was a pistol shot. I had been wrong!

Boyes fell as he was firing.

Raffy jumped into the water.

I watched anxiously for him to surface and reached out to clutch his clothing as he did so.

But other hands were grabbing our boat. Boyes tried to pull us alongside his craft and Raffy was between us.

Raffy sank again as the two craft met.

I just managed to hold on to him.

'Come on!' Boyes shouted to his men. 'Get in while I hold...' His words ended in a yelp. Dickon smashed the spare oar down on his hands. He let go and the boats drifted apart.

With all my strength I pulled my son up again, gasping and spluttering. I clung on while my rowers put more distance between ourselves and the villains. Then Matt helped me to haul him inboard.

While we pulled back towards the north bank, I untied Raffy's bonds, pulled off his sodden doublet and shirt and wrapped him in my own dry doublet. He lay on the bottom boards, pale and shivering. But, by the time we regained Queenhythe he was sitting up.

'What happened to those whoreson churls?' He asked.

Matt pointed across the water. 'Still trying to make land with one oar.'

'We sent troopers round by the bridge,' I explained. 'I hope they catch up with the villains.'

It was hours later that we heard the end of the story. We were sitting in Raffy's chamber before a vigorous fire Adie had insisted on laying in. Raffy was well wrapped in blankets – also at his stepmother's insistence. We were all sipping a sweet cordial prescribed by Ned for its soothing qualities while Raffy insisted – not for the first time –

that he was perfectly recovered from his ordeal and needed no fretting over. Lizzie entered and, with a long sigh, completed our semicircle by sinking onto the only empty stool.

'Ah, good it is to rest my limbs. That young bay gelding of yours takes some holding, or else I have lost my saddle skill these last few years.'

'We heard, when we arrived back, that you had ridden with the troopers,' I said.

''Twas the only way. They would have taken hours else to find Boyes' place.' She grinned. 'You should a' seen the looks to their faces when I mounted man-style. I'll warrant they had never seen a woman riding astride before.'

'You did reach his lair, then. What happened?' Raffy urged.

'We were there just as Beefy and his churls were coming up from the river. They were in a right flurry – shouting and cursing each other. I was glad they had not Master Raffy with them but a-feared lest something should have happened to him on the river. As soon as we challenged them, they scattered. That was a merry chase!' She thankfully drank from the beaker Adie handed her.

'Did you catch them?' Raffy asked.

'Two of 'em. 'Tis hard to pursue anyone in all those twisting alleys.'

'Boyes?' I asked.

'Alas, no, though Cantrill's men made a thorough search of the villain's lair. We took our two prisoners to the Clink – one with a bad sword cut to his right arm. We questioned them briefly but they said little. So we left them there to await your pleasure, Thomas. Tell me, now, what passed on the river?'

Between us, Raffy and I related the morning's events.

'So I pushed Boyes and his gun went off, pointing in the air and I jumped into the water and Father pulled me out and we all came home,' Raffy concluded.

'You were very brave,' Lizzie said.

'I suppose I was,' he agreed.

I was glad to see that the day's near-tragedy had already become, for my son, an adventure to be recounted – doubtless with embellishments – so I did not mind his immodesty.

Lizzie turned to me. 'So, what happens now?'

'First of all, I must go and thank Cantrill's men,' I said. 'Are they in the kitchen?'

'Aye, and eating a hearty supper, I'll be bound.'

They were, indeed, seated around the table, hungrily devouring a capon, a cheese and some pasties. Bart was there, too.

''Tis well that you forgot to deliver Captain Cantrill's message,' I said to him, 'else would our friends here have departed and we should not have some of Boyes' gang in prison.'

'Nay, Master Thomas,' Bart replied. ''Twas false.'

'False?'

'Aye,' one of the soldiers – a young fellow with a reddish beard – replied. 'Bart has shown us the letter. 'Twas never writ by our captain.'

One of his colleagues agreed. ''Tis not his writing or his style. Our orders were to stay here just as long you needed us. He would not have recalled us – certainly not without discussing it with you, Master Treviot.'

'Saints in heaven!' I exclaimed. 'Is there no end to these men's guile? Boyes' paymasters knew you were here. They knew the name of your officer. And they knew how to get you out of the way in readiness for Boyes' attack. You see what devilry we are up against.'

'Well, at least we foiled their plans,' the bearded trooper said.

'But they could have succeeded, had I not been too busy to set about my master's business,' Bart said mournfully.

'This time, you are more than forgiven,' I said. 'Thank you for your poor memory. And thank you all for capturing Boyes' men. We will have them questioned and, I hope, pick up the trail of their ringleader.'

Back in Raffy's chamber, I reported what I had just been told. 'All the time, Allen and his circle seem to be well informed. They know what we are doing – even before we know ourselves, or so it seems,' I grumbled.

'Perhaps Allen really does converse with spirits,' Adie suggested.

'He would love us to think so,' I said. 'But, no, what we are up against is a wide web of spies and informers. It links the stinking middens of Southwark with the perfumed chambers of the king's noble councillors. Its strands include lawyers like Gaston and the likes of Dannery, one of my own brother goldsmiths.'

'Then, 'tis good that you have broken the web,' Adie said. 'Now that that fat lewdster is on the run he is no more use to his masters.

Lizzie shook her head. 'We must not be so sure. Boyes was never the kind of man to leave the ring after one fall. He will be set on revenge for today's humiliation. You must not drop your shield.'

'I fear you are right,' I said. ''Tis not just revenge he will be set on. He must redeem himself in the eyes of his clients. His reputation depends on it.'

Later, as I lay in bed, I was still thinking about Lizzie's warning.

Adie nestled up to me. 'I think I have never been so frightened in all my life. Those horrible villains bursting into the church like that. Then you and Raffy fighting with them on the river. I went down to the quay for a while to watch, but I could not make out what was happening. I had to come back. I could not bear it. I stayed here, in our chamber, praying.'

I held her close. 'This must stop,' I said firmly. 'I will not have those I love threatened and terrified any longer.'

'But what can you do, my Sweet. For sure, you have done enough already to stop this Allen and his allies and still he reaches out to us – even from inside the Tower.'

'All because you performed a service for the archbishop. Oh, I feel so guilty about that.'

'Why, Dearest?'

'It was I who urged you on. In my vanity, I wanted to see you and Raffy ride high in his grace's favour.'

I stroked her hair. 'Think no such thoughts. I accepted Cranmer's commission of my own free will. But you are right – it all began with the archbishop. Now, it must end with the archbishop.'

'What do you mean?'

'It all began with a favour for the archbishop. And what happened? I have been, as it were, driven out, hither and yon. Hampton, Norwich, Worden, Lambeth, Ely Place. I have been sent to sea. I have been set down in a bouncing Thames wherry. 'Tis time I stopped being pushed and did some pulling of my own. The archbishop began it. Sure I am that he must end it.'

'I still do not understand.'

I kissed her gently. 'Nor do I, Dearling. Nor do I. I only know that if it is to end, I must end it.'

We fell to love making, seeking in it an urgent healing.

◊

In the days that followed, the City was calm. Somerset's arrest had not put an end to the divisions between those who had widely differing opinions about England's future but the threat of civil strife had been removed. Foreign troops no longer stood guard over our gates. The councillors had returned to their various mansions. They met, usually, in the Holborn residences of Warwick or Southampton, where the shape of England's new government was decided behind closed doors.

Of course, there were rumours. Everyone knew that the two earls were the leading members of the council and the most popular theory was that they had agreed to set aside the Protector's radical policies, return the country to Catholicism and make peace with France.

While such weighty matters were being discussed I had no hope of being able to approach Cranmer to discover what was happening about Robert Allen and William West. Though I was wary of the magician and his addiction to trouble-making, it was poor West who most occupied my thoughts. I had promised to discover the truth about the affair in which he had become entangled and to secure his release. Yet he was as much a prisoner as ever and, although the fog in my mind was beginning to clear, I still could not understand who was behind all the mischief that was being deliberately created and why West's continued incarceration was important to them.

My first move, I decided, must be to seek another interview with Lord De La Warr. This would, undoubtedly, mean risking a snub, but if I could persuade his lordship to withdraw his accusations against his nephew, West could be released and able to add his testimony to the evidence piling up against Allen. I sent a letter to the house in White Friars but my messenger was back within the hour with the news that Baron De La Warr had gone to the country. So it was that on Thursday 20 October, I set out to ride into Sussex. After a night at an indifferent inn, I arrived the following morning at Offington Hall, Broadwater.

My first impression was of an extremely well cared for estate. The woodland was in good order. Old timber had been felled and replacement planting was well in hand. Nearer the house the grass was recently scythed and hedges tidily trimmed. Once through the gatehouse the mansion that came into view was of middling size, though there had obviously been an amount of new building. Staff ran to tend the horses of myself and my attendants and a liveried servant opened the arched front door as soon as I knocked. He admitted me to the main hall and took my name and bade me wait. I stepped across to the fireplace where lazy smoke drifted up from smouldering logs and warmed myself there while looking up at the carved and painted De La Warr arms above. Recalling my previous encounter with his lordship, I wondered whether I should expect a curt dismissal or whether he would even trouble himself to see me at all.

However, it was only a few minutes before Baron De La Warr appeared from an inner door, booted and spurred and with a large hound padding at his side.

He pointed to the heraldic device. 'Gules, c-crusilly and a l-lion rampant argent,' he declared. 'Arms g-granted to my f-family by Richard II.'

'Impressive,' I replied, for want of anything better to say.

'How old is your b-b-business, Master T-Treviot?'

'Founded by my grandfather.'

'You m-must be p-proud to keep it g-going. T-Tradition matters, d-do you not agree? D-D-De La Warr's were here before the N-Normans c-crossed the Channel.'

For some seconds, we stared at the proof of the baron's ancestry. Then he said, 'Have you c-come all the way f-f-from London?'

'I have.'

'For what p-purpose?'

'I come in the hope that Your Lordship might agree to continue our previous conversation.'

'Still w-worrying your head about M-Master Allen? I thought you were g-g-going to leave that m-matter.'

'It is difficult to abandon interest in a man when he send godless villains to abduct my son.'

He looked round sharply. 'N-n-nonsense. Allen is a m-magician not a violent l-l-l-lawbreaker.'

'If Your Lordship will grant me a little of your time, I hope to prove that your confidence in this fellow is misplaced.'

'I have b-business on the estate. It d-does not run itself.' He moved away and took a few steps towards the outer door. Then he turned. 'If you want to t-talk, you may accompany me.'

241

Minutes later we were riding away from the house. I complimented him on the appearance of his patrimony.

'B-Building on the f-foundations of my f-forefathers. Every g-generation must do that.'

I allowed the silence to extend itself, hoping De La Warr would make the first move. The tactic worked.

'This abduction of your s-son,' he said. 'What d-did you mean?'

I described Boyes' raid on the church and the chase that followed.

'Why do you th-think Allen was involved?' the baron demanded.

'Because Boyes has had several meetings with a corrupt lawyer by the name of Gaston, who frequently visits Allen for instructions.'

We were walking the horses along a broad woodland path. De La Warr looked straight ahead frowning. At length, he turned to me. 'I am s-surprised that you are s-so intent on blackening Allen's name.'

'And I, My Lord, am surprised by your determination to whiten it.'

An angry scowl appeared on the baron's face.

Before he could denounce my 'impudence', I hurried on. 'If this necromancer, this peddler of potions provided the poison that endangered Your Lordship's life, why were you prepared to grant him safe haven here?'

De La Warr urged his mare into a trot. 'Your questions are t-tiresome, Master T-Treviot.'

'Then, I pray you forgive the rough manners of a mere merchant, My Lord, I suppose my questions are irrelevant. When the Council completes their interrogation of Allen, the truth will become plain.'

'You think s-so?'

'I am sure of it.'

We came upon a well-worn rutted track. De La Warr turned to the right. Within minutes, we came to a cluster of houses.

'Broadwater,' he announced.

Outside the church, he dismounted and tethered his horse. 'Come. I want t-to sh-show you something.'

We entered by the north porch and walked down the nave. At the chancel step, my guide halted and crossed himself before proceeding beyond the screen. He pointed to an elaborate canopied tomb, richly carved with armorials and other decorative motifs.

'My f-f-father's memorial,' he said. 'I b-built it five years since. You s-s-see what is m-missing?'

I looked at the empty slab. 'There is no effigy.'

'Exactly. I ordered one from the c-country's f-finest mason. But since that d-devil S-Seymour came to p-power I durst not b-bring it here.'

'For fear it will be defaced.'

'T-terrible things have been d-done in other ch-churches hereabouts. Mobs s-smashing windows, b-breaking s-s-statues. I had to organise t-teams to g-guard St M-Mary's here! 'Tis t-terrible to s-see the marks of centuries of d-devotion destroyed by God-hating churls.'

I began to understand what might have passed between De La Warr and his nephew. 'It must have been hard to see your heir siding with the new men.'

'F-Foolish boy! Grovelling to the P-Protector and his friends.'

'So, you devised a plan to teach him a lesson?'

'I? N-No.' He paused awkwardly, either wondering how to explain or debating how much he should confide in this stranger. 'William is not a b-bad man but he l-lacks a feel for t-t-tradition and that is vital for s-someone in the p-position he was to inherit.'

'So sending him to the magus to buy a counterfeit poison was to teach him a lesson? 'Twas a very elaborate plot.'

'N…Not mine. I was complaining about William one d…day and s..someone suggested this p.plan.'

'Who was this someone, My Lord? Whoever it was did you a grievous wrong.'

'No m…matter.' The old man turned abruptly and strode back down the aisle. ''Tis too late now and n…nothing to be done. William has s….signed a c…confession. Nothing can s…save him now.'

Chapter 22

'A CONFESSION?' I exclaimed. The door creaked as I closed it behind us. 'Then, for sure it must have been tortured from him.'

The old man said nothing until he was once more in the saddle. As he looked down, I detected, for the first time in his gaunt features, a suggestion of concern for his nephew. 'It sh-should not have happened.'

'What do you mean?' I asked as I mounted. But De La Warr was already clattering along the lane.

When we were once more riding side by side, he said, 'Can you n-not see, M-Master Treviot, I had to m-m-make him understand his responsibilities – the p-past as well as the f-f-future?'

'Believe me, my Lord, I see that very well indeed. I am the third generation Treviot as a member of the Honourable Company of Goldsmiths. I would dearly love my son to be the fourth generation. Alas, he has no taste for the business. It would be wrong of me to force him to become my apprentice.'

''Tis his d-duty,' De La Warr protested.

'To take charge of a business for which he has neither love nor skill? Nay, 'twould ruin all, I think. Treviots would, like as not, fail within a few years.'

'A s-strange philosophy. M-Mayhap it will work for m-m-m…'

'Mere merchants, my Lord?' I prompted.

The old man turned to me and the smallest ghost of a smile flitting across his features. 'I b-believe I may have m-misjudged you, M-Master Treviot.'

I decided to press home my advantage. 'Whose idea was it to lay false charges against William? His grace suspected that William – and you, my Lord – were being used by unscrupulous schemers, whose only interest was to undermine the Protector and his friends.'

'But how?' The question was almost a wail. 'I c-c-can see no c-c-connection.'

'I understand your bewilderment, My Lord. It has taken me many days to sort out what was afoot and I have no reached the bottom of the well yet. As I see it, there was no carefully-constructed plot. The conspirators, like yourself, longed to see a return to the old, Catholic, order. Unlike yourself, they would use any means to achieve their ends. Rumours, rebellions, murders, abductions – nothing was rejected that might be used to shake Somerset's hold on power.'

'But William…'

'Is on close terms with Sir John Cheke and others of the Protector's intimates. I believe the duke's enemies hoped, by implicating William in black magic and poison plots, to cast suspicion on his friends.'

We seemed to be retracing our steps to the manor house, his lordship's 'estate business' apparently forgotten. De La Warr listened attentively to my theory.

'I l-liked not the P-P-Protector, but I was not p-part of any p-plot against him.'

'I am sure of it, my Lord. You were duped. The conspirators played on your ancestral pride and your desire to have William continue your traditional ways in this fine estate. As a result, your heir faces execution and then your patrimony will be passed to distant relatives – perhaps even broken up. You may be sure that the men behind this plot will not lose a moment's sleep over that prospect.'

'Mary and all the s-saints!' the old man cried aloud, stirring a pair of pigeons from their branches. 'If you are right, they will p-p-pay for their villainy. I will be revenged, though I s-swing for it!'

'Pray God, it comes not to that, my Lord. We may yet see justice done – and save William. I made a promise to your nephew and I intend to keep it.'

◊

As I rode back to London the next day I had several hours to reflect on the assurance that I had given the distraught De La Warr. One voice in my head told me that I had been foolishly rash to offer the old man any hope. But another voice was quick to reply. 'The conspirators have achieved their objective,' it said. 'The Protector has been plucked down. So they have no need to continue their persecution of William West or their threats against you.' 'Ah, that is all very well,' Voice Number One protested, 'but Robert Allen and his friends are still bent on revenge. You and those you love are not yet safe.' To that, there was no answer.

The more I considered how I had been lured, seduced, cajoled into treacherous, fast-moving waters that threatened to overwhelm me and my family, the angrier I became. Southampton, Warwick, the archbishop and all their creatures on the Council were used to the rapids and whirlpools of politics. Well, let them jostle for power! Let them squabble over the Protector's replacement! But why should innocent citizens like William West and Raphael Treviot be destroyed by their ambitious stratagems? It was no easy matter to push such splenetic resentment to one side and force myself to think clearly but, while my companions chattered among themselves, I used the journey to go over everything that had happened since that day more than three months earlier when I had been commissioned by the archbishop to undertake a 'simple' task which, I was assured, had no political implications. I tried to piece together every event and every conversation. I analysed things said and things not said, comments seemingly unimportant at the time but now significant. I made myself remember details – the look askance that accompanied a lie, the tight-lipped silence prompted by fear, the hatred smouldering in a man's eyes.

By the time we made our last brief stop at an alehouse in Kingston I had constructed from all these fragments a story which, though complex, was the only one that made sense. It allowed all the little schemes and plots to find their place within an overall plan and it identified the minds in which this plan had been conceived.

Knowing all this was one thing. Proving it was, of course, another. Even that would not be as difficult as persuading the men in power to act on the evidence I had assembled. Yet, unless I could achieve that, I had achieved nothing. It was time to make a plan of my own; to take a lesson in cunning and deviousness from those more accomplished than I in manipulating men and events. Although the hour was late when we reached London I lost no time in contacting those I intended to enlist in my conspiracy. I rode straight to Milk Street and presented my scheme to Ned and Bart.

As we sat around the fire in their main room, my friends listened in silence to my proposal.

'I have considered every other option I can think of,' I concluded, 'but I am sure this is the only way to be free of the threat hanging over us.'

The others stared at me in wide-eyed silence.

'You seriously intend to confront the most powerful men in the land?' Ned demanded, at last.

'''Tis more a matter of getting them to confront each other,' I said.

Bart gave a cynical half-laugh. 'Hah! You think they will listen to you? Even if they are rivals for power, they will support each other against your accusations. That sort always stick together.'

'I believe the archbishop will stand by me,' I replied, 'and old De La Warr, for all his haughtiness, trusts me, I think.'

Bart was unconvinced. '"Believe"? "Think"? I would want more certainty before I put my trust in great lords.'

'So your recommendation is to do nothing!' I snapped. 'We must just wait for Allen to organise fresh outrages from his cell in the Tower! Well, I doubt we shall have to wait long.'

Ned stretched out a foot to turn a log in the fire. 'It seems we are sailing between the Scylla of frustration and the Charybdis of fear. You look to starboard, Thomas, and see the perilous shallows of inaction and Bart's eyes are fixed on the rocks of hostile reaction that lie to port! Pray God, there is a channel deep enough for our purpose but it will take some finding.'

'Fine words, Ned,' I said, 'but they take us no further forward.'

He nodded. 'Fairly said. Yet, forgive me if I press the nautical analogy a stage further. The only guiding star we dare follow is truth. You would have to present an account of the facts so clear and so precise that there can be no gainsaying them. Allen and his accomplices and his masters will wriggle and squirm. We may expect nothing from them save plain denials and counter-accusations. We must be prepared for that. Bart is right. These great men will only act if the plain truth leaves them no other alternative.'

''Twill not be easy,' I admitted, 'and, more than ever before, I will need the support of my friends. I know I am asking much of you. Are you content to do what we have discussed?'

Both men nodded unsmiling – an acquiescence which was more than I had a right to ask.

◊

I spent most of the next two days arranging hurried meetings with John Cantrill and Edward Underhill. My proposal amazed them but, being young men of spirit, they took little persuading. My next task was to visit Cranmer. I rode down to Whitehall early on Monday 24 October. Never had I seen the archbishop's antechamber so full or so frenzied. Two of the archiepiscopal guards had been posted at the door to the inner chamber and they were kept busy turning away importunate supplicants and arguing with suitors who tried to assert some right of entry. When I asked one of these sentinels to convey a message I was met with the curt reply, 'His grace is very busy.' Hours passed. It seemed that my plan was doomed to fail before it had begun. Then I saw Ralph Morice emerge from the inner room and make his way through the throng with hurried steps.

'Thomas!' He looked genuinely pleased to see me but too distracted to stop and talk. 'If you have come to call on his grace, you have chosen a bad day… Not that there is a good day at present. 'Tis like Bedlam here,' he added grimly.

'Why all this commotion?' I asked.

'Change at the top of the ladder means change all the way down. Somerset and his closest supporters are out. So all ambitious men in the kingdom are ajostle to take their places. I am on my way to the Lord Chamberlain's office with a list of his grace's recommendations of new men for the privy chamber.'

I fell into step beside him and we made our way along the passageways that formed the thoroughfares of the little city that was Whitehall Palace.

'Ralph, it really is vital that I have a few words with his grace,' I said.

'Is this still about the West affair?'

'Yes and no.'

'I am afraid that is rather a long way down his grace's agenda now. I do not exaggerate when I say that he is fighting to save all that has been achieved since old King Harry freed us from the tyranny of Rome. Amidst all the confusion, Southampton and Arundel hope to take over the government. You know what that would mean: Princess Mary to become regent and under the influence of her cousin, the Emperor; England meekly submitting to Rome and the Catholic heresy restored. Our main hope is the Earl of Warwick but even he is wavering. The situation is absolutely critical.'

'Exactly! And that is why I must speak with the archbishop.'

Ralph halted abruptly. 'You have new information? You have stumbled across something important?'

'I know exactly what is afoot – what has been in the planning these last months, and who is behind it.'

'Truly? Then tell me!' He stared at me eagerly.

''Tis only for his grace's ears. But you may trust me. I would not intrude upon him at such a time were I not the bearer of vital information.'

Ralph nodded. 'His grace trusts you, and not without reason. Pray God your news is as important as you say. We are desperate to turn the tide on the papists. Come!' He turned and led the way back to Cranmer's quarters.

The archbishop listened in complete silence to what I had come to say. His face betrayed no emotion. When I had finished I did not know whether he would dismiss me for my presumption or congratulate me for my diligence. He did neither.

He rose from his chair. 'This demands prayer,' he said, and left through the door leading to his private oratory.

Half an hour or more passed before he returned and took his place behind the table. He looked up at me with careworn eyes. 'I believe you have discovered the truth, Thomas, and you have done so at great cost. What you ask of me is presumptuous. Yet, it would be presumptuous of me to deny you, after all you have suffered. It would be even more presumptuous of me to turn my back on the truth. I will make the necessary arrangements for Friday. I would urge you to spend the intervening days in much prayer.'

It was with mingled relief and anxiety that I made my way home. Within the week, I reflected, either there would be an end of all our woes or I would probably be joining William West as a prisoner in the Tower. At my house, I was met by a scene of anguish.

'Oh, Thomas, Thomas, it has happened again!' Adie threw herself into my arms. 'They have taken Raffy.'

Lizzie, standing behind her, said, 'I feared Boyes would not take defeat so easy.'

'What happened?' I demanded.

'Better let Captain Cantrill tell you,' Adie said. 'He is come in person to explain.'

Cantrill was seated in the parlour, a flagon of ale before him. He jumped to his feet when I entered. 'Thomas, I am so sorry. My men have failed you. I should have doubled the guard on your son but I did not reckon these wretches would strike again. I ignored one of the basic military rules – never underestimate your enemy.' He described how Raffy had been abducted a second time.

In truth, there was little to tell. Raffy and his guard had set out in mid-morning to return to Ely House at the Earl of Warwick's behest. They were clear of the City and had crossed Holborn Bridge. Halfway up Holborn Hill they were confronted by a dozen or more masked horsemen. Cantrill's men had put up a good fight but the odds were against them. One of the villains grabbed Raffy's reins and set off down Shoe Lane with some of his copesmates while the others prevented the troopers from following. ''Tis my belief they were making for Bridewell Dock. I have already sent men across to Southwark to watch Boyes' base there.'

'A good move, John, though I doubt they would be so foolish as to return there.'

Adie collapsed into a chair. 'For sure they will kill him this time,' she wailed.

'No, Sweetheart, fret you not. Raffy is worth more to them alive than dead. They will try to bargain with him.'

'So what are we to do?'

'First, we will post notices all over town offering a reward for any information.' I turned to Bart. 'Will you see to that? Oh, and while you are out attend to that other matter. The archbishop has fixed the meeting for Friday and, now, it is more important than ever.'

Cantrill said, 'I will send patrols out and bring in some of the City's worse villains for questioning. News travels fast in their community. If anyone knows aught of your son, by all the saints, we will have it out of them.'

'Good,' I said. 'Then there is no more to be done but wait for news and pray.'

In fact, there was much to be done. Over the next few days, our shop was visited by a succession of visitors, all claiming to have seen Raffy and hoping to share in the reward. We took details of these supposed sightings and I had men follow up the few – the very few – that seemed genuine.

What occupied most of my time was the precise planning for the Friday meeting in Cranmer's Whitehall lodging. There were several intricate details to be arranged, all of which had to come together in the right sequence. By Thursday morning, all the pieces seemed to be in place, except one. Despite Bart's vigilance, he had failed to locate the one person who was vital to my reconstruction of events. Each evening Bart returned to Goldsmiths' Row with mournful countenance. 'Still no sign,' he reported at the end of Wednesday vigil. 'Are you sure you are right about the address?'

'I must be,' I said. ''Tis the only one that fits the facts.' But I was not as confident as I sounded. Again and again, I questioned my interpretation of events. If I was wrong about this one then I would be like the man in the Bible story who built his house on sand. I would have no case to present to the archbishop and the sceptical audience he was assembling to hear my story.

After dinner on Thursday, I was in the workshop, trying to distract myself overseeing the execution of some jewellery designs. The door from the shop flew open and Bart strode in. 'Yes!' he shouted, unable to contain his excitement. 'You found him?'

'Aye. He was where you said. I followed him to a fair house in Sydon Lane. Expensive. When I asked a pair of urchins in the street who lodged there, they gave the name "Stanley".'

'Stanley! Henry Stanley! Good!'

'You already suspected him?'

'Suspected? No, but I am not surprised. I recall hearing something about him from Sir William Paget. This is the missing fragment torn from the picture. Now all fits together. You have sent word to Cantrill?'

'Immediately.'

'Then tomorrow cannot come soon enough.'

◊

On Friday 28 October I arrived at Whitehall shortly before noon. I was met in Cranmer's quarters by a visibly nervous Ralph Morice.

'Much hangs on this, Thomas,' he said, firmly grasping my hand. You will need all your powers of persuasion.'

'If the leading council members are here all I can do is present them with the truth.'

'They are expected for dinner in an hour or so. His grace has sent a pressing invitation, urging them to set faction aside and form a united government. After the meal, he will present you to them as an important suitor. I will come and fetch you to the chamber. Meanwhile, I have had some vacant offices across the courtyard made ready for you and those who are giving testimony.'

'Thank you, Ralph. It is vitally important that all my witnesses are kept apart and know not that the others are here.'

He gave a wry smile. 'You once accused me of playing politics. Are you now employing the arts of deviousness and concealment?'

'Perhaps I am,' I admitted ruefully. 'I suppose it is not possible to dip my hands in the mud without them becoming soiled.'

'Then, my prayer is that you can wash it off again. You have changed much in these last months, my old friend. I would gladly see a return to the old Thomas who always hoped to find others as open and uncomplicated as himself.'

'That man is long dead, Ralph – if he ever existed. But, now, I must away to oversee everything. 'Tis all like a game of the chess. I must move my pieces cunningly and to best advantage. I have wagered too much to lose the game.'

Chapter 23

TWO HOURS LATER I was in the archbishop's antechamber with John Cantrill, Edward Underhill and Bart Miller, my accomplices. We spoke little as we waited for the summons. We could hear the buzz of conversation within as Cranmer's guests enjoyed their dinner and we watched the to-and-fro procession of liveried servants with their laden trays.

'The sight of all this food is making me hungry,' Cantrill said at one point, to relieve the tension.

Eating was far from my mind and also, it seemed, from Underhill's. 'Our meat is to do the will of God,' he pronounced solemnly. 'Today that means bringing God's enemies to judgement.'

Gradually, the comings and goings slowed down. Still no summons came.

'Perhaps they have too much other business to discuss,' Bart suggested. 'We may have gone to all this trouble for nothing.'

But at that moment, the door opened. Ralph Morice emerged. 'His grace will receive you now, Thomas,' he said.

'Good luck, Thomas, 'Cantrill said, as I stepped forward.

Underhill added, 'The Lord grant you a clear head and a free tongue to speak his truth.'

With those sentiments echoing in my head I entered the chamber. A long trestle table had been set up – with a dozen or so councillors seated around it, it took up half of the long room. The space between it and the fireplace, where logs burned vigorously, was empty. Onto this large stage, I stepped. I bowed to Cranmer and his guests. 'Your Grace. My Lords. I thank you for hearing my plaints. I come before you as a humble subject of his gracious majesty and as a grieving father who has lost his only son – a son who was of my Lord Warwick's household and under his protection. I come seeking justice against those whose scheming and violent courses have deprived myself and my lord – and, I venture to say, also his majesty - of a young man who, had he lived, would have done his country good service.' I watched carefully for any reactions to my words. The Earl of Southampton stroked his square-cut beard and I fancy I saw the flicker of a frown on his brow.

'By your leave, My Lords, I will relate in order the events that have overwhelmed myself and my family during the last few months. Back in the summer – a terrible time of rebellions and riots in many parts – his grace was moved to compassion by the plight of Master William West, held in the Tower of London on suspicion of attempted murder. Being much occupied with high affairs of church and state, he commissioned me to talk with the prisoner to see if anything could be done on his behalf. Master West is here now and, with your permission, I will ask him to tell his story in person.'

Cranmer nodded to the guard at the door who went out and returned moments later with West. He had tried to smarten himself up for the occasion but his drawn cheeks and shabby clothes bore unmistakable witness to his sufferings. With a little prompting from me, he told the story of his brief consultation with Robert Allen and his subsequent arrest.

Lord Chancellor Rich scowled at the witness and cross-examined in his hectoring courtroom manner. 'Are you seriously suggesting that your noble uncle concocted an elaborate and vicious plot against his own flesh and blood?'

I intervened. 'My Lord, I share your scepticism. I, too, found it hard to believe this story. But subsequent events proved its truth, as I will show. In Baron De La Warr's defence, I must say that the plan was not his. It was proposed to him by someone who had his own reasons for making poor Master West suffer.'

Glances were exchanged around the table and Paget demanded, 'Who is this troublemaker? Speak plain, Master Treviot.'

'I beg you, hear me out, Sir William. It is for the council to judge. My desire is but to present evidence.'

'Very well,' he growled, 'but we do not have all day.'

'Then permit me to bring before your Lordships one of the most pernicious villains in the country; the man to whom Master West was directed to collect the supposed poison for his uncle; the evil necromancer who calls himself "Parafaustus".'

'Ah, yes.' Southampton muttered, 'one of these confounded "Commonwealth" doddypols.'

William West left the room as Robert Allen was brought in, manacled and standing between two guards. His face bore its usual superior smile and his demeanour was as truculent as ever. He seemed not a whit overawed as he gazed up and down the table. Was he merely enjoying his celebrity or was he confident that there were those in this room on whose protection he could still rely? I watched carefully to see how the various councillors reacted.

'My Lord Southampton is right. This creature is, indeed, one of the so-called Commonwealth Men, whose fanatical ravings and pretensions to magic revelations fired the poor wretches on Mousehold Heath to defy his majesty's armies.'

'I am only an orator,' Allen cried out. 'I declare what is pre-ordained, what is written in ..'

'Silence!' Cranmer shouted. 'You will only speak to answer questions.'

I continued. 'Your Grace has made a preliminary investigation of this fellow and, as a result, had him confined to the Tower. You have seen the evidence presented against him. For Your Lordships, I have made copies of various pernicious writings found among his papers.' I distributed several items to the councillors. 'You will see how this charlatan makes a living by gulling simple people. Worst of all is his claim to foretell the imminent death of our sovereign lord, the king.'

There was a murmur around the table. To forestall questions I hurried on. 'A Commonwealth Man, indeed – and yet, the more I probed his affairs, the less sense this simple label seemed to make. It was Allen who "prophesied" victory to the Norfolk rebels if they moved their camp to the low-lying ground of Dussindale, where they were, in fact, doomed to be crushed by my Lord Warwick's cavalry. So, did our black magician want the rebels to fail and, if so, why?'

Southampton spoke up. 'Doubtless, he had no deep plan. He is simply a mischief maker, stirring up trouble just because he can.'

'My Lord, I protest …' Allen shouted.

Once more the archbishop warned him to silence.

I continued. 'Again, I agree with my lord Southampton. Mere evil for its own sake seemed to be Allen's motivation. But I was learning not to underestimate him. Whatever else this villain is, he is no fool. He was playing his part in a plan devised by someone. The same someone who used him in his plot against Master West. What was the result of the defeat of the rebels? Did it strengthen the government? No, quite the reverse. We know how distressed my lord of Warwick was by his own victory. I doubt not you have all heard from his own lips his anger at the carnage of Dussindale. I suspect that for most of you seated around this table the defeat of Robert Kett – who always claimed to be acting in support of the Lord Protector's policies - was really a defeat of the Lord Protector and the final proof that he should be removed from power.'

Some of the councillors nodded. Others stared at me warily. I wondered how far I would be allowed to proceed before being stopped by angry protest. For that reason, I hurried on.

'And yet again, your Grace, my Lords, I was to learn that a plot against the Lord Protector was too simple an explanation. However, Master Allen's motives were not my concern. All I desired was justice for Master West. I was determined to bring this scelerous self-professed magus to account. By this time, he had disappeared, gone into hiding. For many days I hunted him.'

Briefly, I described how I had captured Allen, obtained a warrant to convey him to the Tower, been ambushed and pursued him by ship. 'Finally, I made sure of him on the coast of Sussex,' I explained, 'and brought him, under guard, before his grace at Lambeth. I had every reason to hope, then, that my work was done; that Allen would be put on trial, the truth would come out, Master West would be set at liberty and I could return to my life as a simple merchant. Unfortunately, I had not reckoned with the malice of this rogue and his paymasters.'

Again Allen blurted out. 'My Lords, do not listen to the rantings of this…'

'Silence!' This time, it was Warwick who reacted. 'You will listen to what is charged against you. If you cannot control your tongue you will be returned straightway to the Tower. Proceed, Master Treviot.'

'Thank you, My Lord. What I rapidly learned to my cost was that this necromancer was part of a secret movement whose members are drawn from all levels of society and pledged to nothing less than gaining control of government.'

'To what end?' Paget enquired.

'As your lordships know well there are many in the land who would long to see the restoration of papal authority in church and state - the reversal of everything achieved by his late majesty and continued by your lordships in the name of our godly prince, King Edward. I doubt not there are several such covens of which your lordships are aware and already investigating.'

At these words my audience became restive. There were several murmured conversations around the table. It was Southampton who spoke out. 'Such talk of conspiracy is fanciful. This merchant is floundering out of his depth in waters where he has no right to be.'

Some of the councillors nodded in agreement but Warwick responded with quiet authority. ''Tis no secret there are disloyal groups at work. I would hear Master Treviot further. If he can help us identify more papist traitors, we shall be in his debt.'

'I assure Your Lordships that I do not make these allegations lightly. If what I say is mere fancy I would not have become the target of violence. I have been attacked in the streets of London. I have been spied on by a member of my own merchant fraternity. My household has been invaded. One of my most faithful servants has been brutally slain. And now, my only son is abducted and, as I suspect, he, too, is murdered. I crave your patience, My Lords. I will not detain you much longer. I have two more witnesses, scarcely less villainous than Robert Allen, to call forth. The first is Henry Gaston, lawyer of Aldersgate.'

I gave a brief instruction to the guard on the door and, moments later, Gaston was led in by Edward Underhill.

He did not come quietly. 'My Lords, I protest at this outrage. This fellow and his men have dragged me from my home without a warrant.' But on sight of Allen, his blustering faltered.

'Master Gaston,' I said, indicating the magus, 'this man is, I think, well known to you. In fact, he lodges in your house.'

The lawyer gave a wary nod.

'And there he practices sorcery, necromancy, and other devilish arts.

Gaston shrugged. 'I know not what he does in the privacy of his chamber.'

'But you do join him there for illicit gambling, do you not?'

He shook his head. 'We...' He paused, looked hard at our prisoner and I could sense his quick lawyer's brain calculating his reply. 'He sometimes has friends in for dicing and carding but he assures me these are innocent games.'

'You are very trusting,' I said. Then, sharpening my tone, I added, 'For a respectable man of law you should be more careful of the company you keep. This rogue is under investigation for treason, incitement to murder and practice of black magic. Are you saying that you cannot help us discover the truth; that you know nothing of Master Allen's nefarious activities?'

Gaston hesitated, darting glances around the table, as though seeking someone who might support him.

I added, 'I need not remind you of the penalty for lying to his majesty's council.'

Gaston took a deep breath. 'I know nothing of any illegal practices with which the prisoner is charged.'

I smiled at him. 'Thank you for your help, Master Gaston. If you have no information about Allen's activities I need press you no further. It may be that their lordships will want to speak more with you so perhaps you would be kind enough to remain a little longer in the next room.'

The lawyer sighed with relief as Underhill led him towards an adjacent antechamber. When he was at the door I called out, 'One last matter, do you know Master Henry Stanley?'

'Stanley? ... Stanley?' The lawyer was caught off guard and thinking quickly. 'No, I think not.'

'Strange,' I said. 'He is a frequent caller at your house.'

'As are many men,' Gaston replied quickly. 'People come daily to me for professional advice and help. I cannot remember all their names.'

'Of course not. Nor, I suppose, are you acquainted with a villain named Boyes.'

The lawyer shook his head and hurried out.

I called in my last witness and when Henry Stanley entered dressed in his usual black and guarded by John Cantrill, there was a stir around the table. Several muttered the young man's name. Lord Arundel called out, 'What is this, Master Treviot? Are you charging members of his majesty's chamber with murder?'

'Aye, have a care,' Southampton seconded.

I well knew that the next few seconds were crucial. I would either be allowed to proceed to the central issue or be dismissed. I chose my words and my tone with great care.

'Your Grace, My Lords, this gentleman is, of course, known to all of you as one of his majesty's closest attendants; a man of honourable family and well trusted. My intention in asking him to present himself is so that I might explain how I made his acquaintance.' I turned quickly to Stanley. 'Do you recall how you and I first met?'

He smiled nonchalantly.

'Aye, 'twas at his grace's palace at Lambeth, where your prisoner here was under examination.'

'What happened after that event?'

'I offered you a lift and had the pleasure of your company as we were rowed back across the river.'

'And what did we discuss?'

He shrugged. 'Polite trifles. I recall not the details.'

It was the reply I had expected. Stanley knew that I could not prove his threats and his attempts to have me spy on Lord Warwick.

'My recollection is somewhat different,' I said, 'but let us leave that aside. Their lordships will, I think, be more interested to hear what you know about the prisoner, Robert Allen. You are, I believe, acquainted with him and have occasionally visited him at his lodgings in Aldersgate ward. What think you of him?'

'Well, he is a rogue,' the courtier said, with a light laugh, 'but he is an engaging rogue.'

'So you took part in his necromantic orgies?'

'No, no, nothing like that.'

'Perhaps you and others resorted to him to play at dice and cards.'

He adopted a mock-sheepish tone. 'Well, yes, a man must have some pleasures.'

'Even though there are laws against illicit gambling?'

'Oh, 'twas scarcely gambling. The stakes were never high.'

'These harmless gatherings were presided over by Master Gaston, I believe.'

'Aye, an upright lawyer. He would not condone reckless gambling.' He surveyed his audience with a conspiratorial smile. 'My Lords, if all games of chance are to be prohibited I fear you will need to examine several of our mutual friends at his majesty's court.'

The response drew a few laughs from the hearers around the table. I hurried on. 'These must have been very convivial occasions.'

'Indeed.'

'And Master Gaston a gracious host?'

'He is very attentive.'

'Strange, then,' I said, 'that not a few moments since, Master Gaston assured my lords that he had no knowledge of you.'

Stanley waved a dismissive hand but his self-assurance faltered as I press on. 'When you visited Robert Allen, your carding and dicing partner, in the Tower I assume your purpose was not for playing games.'

Stanley now put on a show of outraged honour. 'Have you been spying on me?'

'Aye, spying is the word. 'Tis a pastime you are well acquainted with.'

'This is an outrage!' the young man protested and I could see one or two of the hearers nodding in agreement. Now was the time to strike and strike hard.

'Enough of your bluster!' I snapped. 'You were often seen making journeys between Gaston's house, the imperial ambassador's and Allen's cell in the Tower. You are a courier between the three. You are the connection between those who planned the death of my son.'

I steeled myself to face the uproar I knew the accusations would provoke. But the sudden loud noises that now filled the air did not come from the councillors. A peculiar babble of shrieked sounds issued from the prisoner. Allen stood, his manacled arms outstretched towards Stanley, his eyes staring in his head which rocked from side to side. What poured from his lips was a rhythmic incantation in a deep growl, quite unlike his normal voice. For several moments, we were all spellbound by this crazed display.

Then the archbishop was on his feet. Firmly, clearly he called out, louder than the prisoner, 'In the name of the Father, the Son, and the Holy Ghost, be silent!' He pointed a long finger at Allen. I had never felt an atmosphere as strange as the one that now pervaded that room. It was as though some invisible joust was in progress; two unseen forces galloping towards each other. The confrontation seemed endless but can only have been seconds. Then a long, gurgling gasp emerged from Allen's lips. He slumped forwards and would have collapsed to the floor if his guards had not held onto him.

'Enough of this devilry! Take him away,' Cranmer ordered. Half-dragged, half-stumbling, the magus was removed from the room.

When I had recovered my composure, I turned to Stanley. 'That demented but dangerous creature is the one you and your confederates have been protecting. I beg you to stop while you can. He will hang but you need not. Break free of Robert Allen's evil coils and tell their lordships the plain truth.'

In the shocked silence, the man in black looked appealingly along the row of faces staring at him. 'My Lords... Your Grace... must I...?'

'The truth, Master Stanley,' Cranmer said solemnly.

Stanley's braggadocio had evaporated. 'As you say, Master Treviot, I was a mere courier.'

'Yet you were present when the decision was made to hire a villain called Boyes to murder my son. This Boyes,' I explained to the council, 'is one of the most notorious rake-hells in the City – a thief and a murderer. He leads a band of knaves guilty of all manner of villainy.'

'That was Gaston's idea,' Stanley said quickly.

'To have this rogue kill my son?'

'No, no, not that.' Beads of sweat were now glistening on the courtier's brow. ''Twas but to warn you to pursue Master Allen no further.'

'I wonder if Master Gaston's recollection is the same.' I signalled for the lawyer to be recalled.

I would trade a chest of new-minted sovereigns to be able to relive the next few moments. Gaston halted suddenly in the doorway. He and Stanley exchanged glances of shock and dismay. At that moment, they knew that all was lost.

Gaston was the first to recover. 'What lies has this knave been telling you?'

'Master Stanley, a knave? I thought you did not know him.'

'Would that I knew not him or his master!'

'And just who is his master?' It was the Earl of Warwick who asked the question, leaning across the table. 'He is, presumably, the moving spirit behind all these complex plots.'

'Indeed so, My Lord,' I explained – and I now had everyone listening attentively to my words. 'This moving spirit, or, rather, these moving spirits and their guileful schemes are at the root of Robert Allen's treasons, William West's sufferings, the attacks on me and the hiring of Boyes to murder my son. The strange truth is – and for long it has puzzled me – these schemers were ignorant of each other and, indeed, were working against each other.'

'What riddle is this?' Southampton protested.

Before I could respond, Gaston called out, 'Your son is not murdered! He was rescued from Boyes.'

'How know you this?' I asked. 'By your own admission, you are not acquainted with this arch villain.'

The lawyer waved a hand impatiently. 'Do not play the cat and the mouse with me, Master Treviot. You yourself freed your son from his abductors.'

'Aye, and now they have taken him again.' I raised my voice to an angry shout. 'By all the saints, if my son is dead, as I greatly fear, I will find this Boyes, though it may take a lifetime and when he hangs you will hang with him.'

'Boyes does not have your lad!' Gaston matched my tone. 'He came to me when he saw the notices you have posted around the City. He knows nothing of your loss. Nor do I.'

'Nor I,' Stanley echoed.

'This takes us no further forward, Master Treviot.' It was Warwick who intervened again. 'You were going to identify for us the instigator of all these troubles.'

'Yes, My Lord. I had my suspicions for some time. It was only as I put together scraps of information and rumour…'

'Thank you, Master Treviot.' Southampton rose to his feet. 'We are much indebted to you for your help but you may now leave everything to us. We will have all these fellows confined and examined to plumb the depths of all their intrigues.'

Warwick responded with quiet authority. 'And yet, I would hear what our merchant friend has concluded after all his investigations. I think I speak for others around this board.'

There were nods and murmurs of assent.

'Your Grace, My Lords,' I said, 'I can only tell the story as I have been able to piece it together. Doubtless, I have misjudged some of the details, though they do all seem to fit. I leave it to Your Lordships to decide how close I am to the truth.

'Our land has been torn by divisions and factions and our enemies have not been slow to take advantage of the fact. The imperial ambassador, as you all know, has his network of agents busily working among those who would like to see England return to the papal fold. One of his plots was the one that has ensnared poor Master West – an ill-conceived stratagem to connect West with necromancy and attempted murder and bring into disrepute West's friends at court. One of van der Delft's biggest mistakes was including Allen in his plans. He is uncontrollable, unpredictable. When they discovered this it was too late. The more he drew attention to himself the more they had to protect him, hide him.'

Cranmer said, 'And you believe that when he was captured they had to bring pressure on you to make you withdraw your evidence against him.'

'Yes, they were prepared to do anything, including abduction and murder to ensure my silence.'

'This is nonsense,' Stanley blurted out. 'I had nothing to do with capturing your son.'

'Yet, you were working for the ambassador,' I countered. 'Your family are strong supporters of the old faith. I have had the privilege of doing business with the Earl of Derby, your father. He makes no secret of his beliefs.'

'My religion does not make me a murderer!' Stanley was trembling. 'I had no part in these plots. I was a pretended participant. I was sent to infiltrate this fellow's group,' he pointed at Gaston, 'to discover their treasons.'

'Sent?' Cranmer enquired.

'Aye, Your Grace. Sent by the Lord Protector.'

'False, lying knave!' Gaston shouted.

'No,' I said. 'Now he is speaking the truth. I have reason to know that Master Stanley was a spy for the duke.'

'His lordship was surrounded by enemies. He needed people he could trust,' Stanley cried.

'Which is why he had you keep a close watch on his majesty to discover who had access to him,' I said. 'But what the Lord Protector did not know was that you were already selling information gleaned at court to the imperial ambassador. You think yourself a very clever young man, do you not? A master intriguer skilled at inspiring trust – and just as skilled at betraying it. To my cost, I have seen you at work. Will you tell their lordships how you tried to recruit me to spy upon Lord Warwick, or shall I?'

Stanley made no reply.

I explained the attempt that was made to force me into gathering information through my son. Warwick thumped the table with his fist and swore loudly.

I said, 'Fortunately no harm was done, My Lord. Master Stanley, confident in his own talent as a spymaster, used some of the imperial ambassador's men as his own agents. One of them tried to emulate his employer, serving both sides at once. He offered to sell information to your Lordship.'

All eyes turned towards Warwick, who nodded. 'A man did come to Ely Place with some story of a plot. Of course, I had him turned away. He never came back.'

'He could not, My Lord. His double-dealing was discovered and he was murdered, by one of the ambassador's officers – or so I believe.'

'How do you know all this?' Cranmer asked.

I explained how Stanley's messenger was cut down outside my gate. 'It was a local serving girl who provided a clue to the assassin's identity. She told me that the horseman who cut the wretch down shouted something as he did so. She said the word sounded like "adder", which made no sense neither to her nor to me. But, My Lords, I have been some few times to Antwerp on business and I have a little of the language. There is a Flemish word for "traitor". It is "verrader". The assassin, carrying out his master's vengeance on a disloyal servant, came from the Spanish Netherlands. Whether the order was issued by the ambassador or Master Stanley, I know not.'

''Twas van der Delft!' the young courtier shouted. 'I swear I had nothing to do with any killings – not of disobedient servants, nor of Master Treviot's son!'

'Well, perhaps so.' I looked along the row of faces. 'Perhaps the real villain in all this is not the person we suspect, but suspicion itself.' I paused. 'And that, My Lords, concludes what I came here to report. May God give you wisdom as you decide what use to make of my words.'

For several moments, the room was abuzz with many conversations. Then Cranmer stood up and called for order. 'My Lords, I am sure that we all agree that we owe Master Treviot a considerable debt for unmasking this strange tangle of pernicious conspiracies. On behalf of the council, I would like to express our gratitude to him. As to the tragedy of his son I assure him, not only of my prayers but of our concerted efforts to discover what has happened to him.'

'Your Grace is very kind,' I replied. 'But I must now confess to a deception.' I crossed to the outer door, went through and, moments later, returned with Raffy. 'My Lords, I beg to present Master Raphael Treviot, my son. Regard this, if you will, as my own piece of magic. It was I who planned his second apparent abduction – not to deceive your Lordships, but to sow confusion among these rogues.'

Cranmer laughed. 'Well, Master Treviot, you are readily forgiven. I rejoice that this young man is safe. Having heard something of his involvement in your adventures, I believe he may grow into a man as remarkable as his father.'

'Thank you, Your Grace.' I bowed and turned to leave.

'A moment, if you please, Master Treviot.' It was Warwick who spoke. 'You have given us much to think of. There are some things I am not clear on. For example, when you apprehended Allen, who provided the warrant for him to be taken to the Tower?'

'My lord of Southampton.'

'And no-one else knew of this business?'

'I think not, My Lord.'

'And yet, within hours, you were waylaid by the ambassador's men and your prisoner removed from your charge. Who, think you, organised that?'

'In very truth, My Lord, I know not.'

I turned and, with one hand on Raffy's shoulder, I left the room. As the door closed behind us we heard the sound of voices raised in angry argument.

Epilogue

WITHIN WEEKS OF the conclusion of this fictional tale, a dramatic real-life meeting occurred at Ely Place. The council had gathered to consider the fate of the late Protector. But there was a subtext to the agenda, as everyone present knew. There had been vigorous canvassing by the supporters of the Earl of Southampton who led the party of reaction and the Earl of Warwick, who was pledged to steady Protestant advance.

Southampton took the initiative. An eye witness set down a summary of his speech. 'The Lord Protector is worthy to die for his many high treasons,' he asserted and he hoped to carry the majority with him. But, 'the Earl of Warwick with a warlike visage and a long sword by his side, laid his hand thereon and said, "My Lord, you seek his blood and he that seeks his blood would have mine also".' Warwick exposed the plotting of his rival and made it clear that he would fight to prevent a return to pro-imperial, Catholic policies.

Southampton never recovered from the rebuff. He watched, powerless, as Somerset was restored to the council and some of his own supporters removed. In January, he, too, was ordered to absent himself from meetings and remain in his London home under virtual house arrest. Within months he was dead – some said that he was broken by failed ambition. It was even suggested that he took poison rather than continue to live under the heel of his political enemies.

John Dudley, Earl of Warwick, became Duke of Northumberland and *de facto* ruler of England. He did not assume the title of Lord Protector.

Francis van der Delft was relieved of his post. He was allowed to plead ill-health as the reason for his departure. He was not replaced until 1552.

Lord De La Warr and his nephew were reconciled. West was released from the Tower and, when the old man died, he acceded to the family estates. However, his attainder prevented him from taking the barony. This was set to rights early in the reign of Elizabeth I when the title was bestowed afresh on West who became 'Baron De La Warr of the new creation'.

And Robert Allen, alias Parafaustus? Our only knowledge of his fate comes from a lament in the brief autobiography of Edward Underhill:

'He was in the Tower about the space of a year and then by friends delivered. In such ways the wicked always escape and those God ordains not to live defy him, so that I think me that I see the ruin of London and this whole realm to be even at hand, for God will not be mocked.'

And finally ...

Some readers like to know where fact ends and fiction begins and may find the following character checklist helpful. The following people really existed:

Thomas Cranmer, Archbishop of Canterbury
Ralph Morice, his secretary
John Dudley, Earl of Warwick
Thomas Wriothesley, Earl of Southampton
Sir William Paget, Secretary to the Council
Richard Rich, Lord Chancellor
Thomas West, Baron De La Warr
William West, his nephew
Henry Stanley, later Earl of Derby
Edward Underhill, a member of the royal guard
Francis van der Delft, imperial ambassador
Robert Allen, a self-styled magus
Gaston, a lawyer

The last two are very shadowy characters of whom little is known. All the rest are inventions.

Meet D. K. Wilson

Derek ('D.K.') Wilson scarcely needs introduction to lovers of history, whether fact or fiction. In a writing and media career spanning almost 50 years he has delighted and stimulated readers with such detailed and well-crafted studies as "Uncrowned Kings of England", "Hans Holbein - Portrait of an Unknown Man" and "Henry VIII Reformer and Tyrant." The Devil's Chalice is the third in a ground-breaking series of Tudor crime stories based on real-life unsolved mysteries, novels that rank alongside the works of C.J. Sansom and Bernard Cornwell for fact-paced narrative and attention to period detail.

Other books by Derek Wilson

The First Horseman
The Traitor's Mark
The Devil's Chalice

Discover more about Derek Wilson on his website:
http://www.DerekWilson.com/

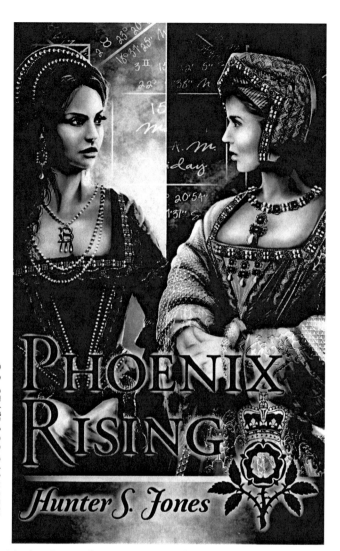

ISBN: 978-84-943721-4-8

The last hour of Anne Boleyn's life...

Court intrigue, revenge and all the secrets of the last hour are revealed as one queen falls and another rises to take her place on destiny's stage.

A young Anne Boleyn arrives at the court of King Henry VIII. She is to be presented at the Shrovetide pageant, le Château Vert. The young and ambitious Anne has no idea that a chance encounter before the pageant will lead to her capturing the heart of the king. What begins as a distraction becomes his obsession and leads to her destruction.

A NOVEL OF ANNE BOLEYN

Between Two Kings

OLIVIA LONGUEVILLE

ISBN: 978-84-944574-9-4

Anne Boleyn is accused of adultery and imprisoned in the Tower. The very next day she is due to be executed at the hand of a swordsman. Nothing can change the tragic outcome. England will have a new queen before the month is out. And yet...

What if events conspired against Henry VIII and his plans to take a new wife? What if there were things that even Thomas Cromwell couldn't control, things which would make it impossible for history to go to plan?

TONI MOUNT

A
Sebastian Foxley
Medieval
Murder Mystery

THE

COLOUR

OF

POISON

ISBN: 978-84-944893-3-4

The narrow, stinking streets of medieval London can sometimes be a dark place. Burglary, arson, kidnapping and murder are every-day events. The streets even echo with rumours of the mysterious art of alchemy being used to make gold for the King.

Join Seb, a talented but crippled artist, as he is drawn into a web of lies to save his handsome brother from the hangman's rope. Will he find an inner strength in these, the darkest of times, or will events outside his control overwhelm him?

If Seb can't save his brother, nobody can.

PLEASE LEAVE A REVIEW

If you enjoyed this book, *please* leave a review at the book
seller where you purchased it. There is no better way to thank
the author and it really does make a huge difference!
Thank you in advance.

CPSIA information can be obtained at www.ICGtesting.com
Printed in the USA
LVOW07s1530210916

505617LV00001B/213/P